First to Last Picking

Legas
Sicilian Studies
Volume XXI
Series Editor: Gaetano Cipolla

Sebastiano Santostefano

First to Last Picking

Sicilians in America:
Yesterday, Today, and Tomorrow

LEGAS

Library of Congress Cataloging-in-Publication Data

Santostefano, Sebastiano, 1929-
  First to last picking : Sicilians in America : yesterday, today, and tomorrow / Sebastiano Santostefano.
       p. cm. -- (Sicilian studies ; v. 21)
  Includes bibliographical references and index.
  ISBN 1-881901-80-7 (pbk. : alk. paper) 1. Santostefano, Sebastiano, 1929- 2. Physicians--Massachusetts--Biography. 3.   Italian Americans--Massachusetts--Biography. I. Title.
  R154.S248A3 2011
  610.92--dc23
  [B]
                                        2011029202

We are grateful to Arba Sicula for its generous grant that in part made this publication possible.

Although drawing upon the author's experiences, including growing up in an immigrant Sicilian family and working on a tobacco farm during the summer, this novel is a work of fiction. Except for details about the history of Italy, Sicily, Middletown, Connecticut, and the harvesting of tobacco in Connecticut, the names of characters, businesses and locations involved in the events described are a product of the author's imagination. Any resemblance to actual persons and places is coincidental. The history of Italy, Sicily and Middletown Connecticut, and some details about the experiences of Sicilian immigrants when entering the United States, are derived from the sources listed in the acknowledgments.

For information and for orders, write to:

Legas

P.O. Box 149   3 Wood Aster Bay
Mineola, New York   Ottawa, Ontario
11501, USA   K2R 1D3 Canada
                    legaspublishing.com

Dedication

To my mother, Giuseppina, and my father, Sebastiano, who taught me and my sisters and brothers how to keep Sicilian customs in our lungs as we breathe in customs from other cultures of the United States.

To my wife, Susan, who has been an excellent center for the famiglia we have been fortunate to create which, in spite of occasional storms that have surrounded us, continues to grow within as tightly knit leaves of an artichoke: Damon Natalie, Stephanie, Jessica, Cristiano, Isabella and Olivia. Also, although our Sebbie's brilliant flight in life was tragically interrupted by cancer, he continues to be an everlasting part of the family

Bibliography

Vincenzo Ancona. *Malidittu la lingua/Damned Language.* Mineola, NY: Legas, New York, 1990.

Gaetano Cipolla, *What Makes a Sicilian?* Mineola, New York: Legas, 1996.

M. I. Finley. *Ancient Sicily to the Arab Conquest.* New York: The Viking Press, Inc. 1968.

Richard Gambino. *Blood of My Blood: The Dilemma of the Italian-American.* Garden City, New York: Doubleday and Company, Inc. 1974.

Norman Lewis. *The Honoured Society.* Collins, London: St. James Place, 1964.

Jerre Mangione and Ben Morreale. La Storia: *Five Centuries of the Italian-American Experience.* New York: Harper Perennial Division of Harper Collins Publishers. 1992.

Stephen Puleo. *The Boston Italians.* Boston: Beacon Press, 2007.

Allon Schoener. *The Italian Americans.* New York: MacMillan Publishing Company. 1987.

Denis Mack Smith. *Medieval Sicily: 800-1713.* New York: The Viking Press, Inc. 1968.

Denis Mack Smith. *Modern Sicily: After 1713.* New York: The Viking Press, Inc. 1968.

Elizabeth A. Warner. *A Pictorial History of Middletown.* Norfolk, Virginia: The Donning Company Publishers. 1990.

Table of Contents

First Picking

Without Attachments to Family Members and Rules
You Are Like an Empty Sack,
A Nothing Mixed With Nothing

Just before sunrise, thick fog slowly rolled over the Connecticut River and crawled through bushes that cluttered the riverbank. It was a Monday early in June, 1943. I was standing by the edge of the river staring into the fog with my foot propped up on a boulder which I frequently liked to do. Dozens of boys, ranging in age from nine to about fifteen years, milled about in an open area under the bridge that spanned the river where it separated the cities of Middletown and Portland. I could hear the commotion they were making, but my mind turned it down so that it sounded as if everyone was a mile away. We were all waiting to learn if we would be hired to work on the Goodrich Farm where shade tobacco plants were grown and leaves harvested to be used as outside wrappers in manufacturing cigars. The farm was one of several located in the Connecticut River Valley which had become known as Tobacco Valley, because this area was a major producer of cigar leaf tobacco.

Just like the past few summers, since I was first hired as a picker when I was nine years old, everyone had arranged themselves in two separate communities. About twenty boys were clustered under the bridge at the upper end of this open area. Many of them had blond hair, blue eyes and light complexions. Their shirts, trousers and shoes were new, or in good condition, and each carried a lunchbox. For the most part, they stood relatively still while talking quietly in small groups.

Several yards away, another cluster of boys stood near me along the river's edge. All of them had dark brown or black hair, dark eyes and a darker skin complexion. Their shirts and pants, although somewhat worn, had obviously been laundered, because it was important to arrive for work dressed as neatly and clean as possible. Instead of a belt, their trousers were held tight around the waist by a piece of rope. Each wore a hat shaped like

9

a baseball cap but, instead of displaying the name of a team, each cap carried the name of a store that sold construction supplies. And each one of these boys held a black, metal, lunch pail, typically used by construction workers, on which was scratched his nickname. Unlike the group standing at the top of the slope, the boys near me constantly stepped back and forth, vigorously gestured, and pushed their arms forwards and backwards, up and down, as they talked and joked.

I turned away from the river for a moment and spotted a couple of the boys at the top of the slope staring at us. One of them pointed to his belt and grinned. Melo, who was not too far from me, happened to notice him too and mumbled, "Look at that jerk up there. I'm sure he's making fun of us because we don't have belts."

Suddenly Dan O'Neil, a boy I got to know during this past year in eighth grade, took a few quick steps forward and yelled, his blonde hair flapping in the breeze, "Hey you guys down there! I got a question for you! When you drop a pizza on the floor what sound does it make?"

His friend, Jack Kane, whom I also knew very well, joined in. "I'll bet you don't know the answer! Well, I'll help you. The answer is wop!" All of their friends roared with laughter.

Bart, who had been talking with Melo, turned away from him and shouted back with a grin, "Very funny, Jack! You Harp! I mean you mashed potato!"

"Oh, yeah! After the trucks arrive, you're gonna see that you guys can't get on. Let's see how your day goes, you Dagoes!" yelled Dan O'Neil, laughing and waving his arm from the very top of the ramp.

One of my buddies, Ancio, suddenly became angry and started to step up the incline with fists clenched to his side. "Hey, Dan, what sound are you going to make when I whack you?"

At that moment, my brother Tony, who was only eighteen months older than I was, turned away from the river, jumped toward Ancio, grabbed him by the shoulders, and pulled him to a stop. "Come on, Ancio. They're just joking." Then he looked up at the crowd and shouted, "I got a question for you, Dan! What

sound do you make when I stuff a four leaf clover in your nose?"
Now everybody clapped their hands laughing.

Turned on by what Tony just said, Louie jumped in front of
him and called out. "Hey, Dan! You know what! Your day won't
go unless we Dagos mash your potatoes."

Right then I noticed Bongi, who was much shorter and
heavier than all of us, grabbing Bart's arm and yanking the rope
around his large stomach with an edge of anger. I wasn't sure
what was going on. He scowled, leaned toward Bart, and slowly
slid his index finger across his thick neck, as if he were slicing it
with a knife. "Do you hear me? I'm telling you I don't know why
I'm here. I know I'm not going to be hired." I tapped Tony's arm
with my elbow to make sure he kept an eye on Bongi.

Bart was the tallest of my friends. More than that, his broad
chest and shoulders stretched the jersey he was wearing. His
muscular arms were already showing sprinkles of black hair that
matched the curly black hair covering his head. He took a deep
breath, stretched out his fingers, and pushed them into Bongi's
large belly. "If I hear you say that once more, you're gonna limp
all the way home. I'm telling you for the last time, you're gonna
be hired. If you don't get hired, we'll all go home."

Tony quickly walked over and pulled Bart's arm back, yanking his fingers away from Bongi's belly. He looked at Bart, rolled
his eyes, and whispered, "Come on, Bart, knock it off. That shit
isn't helping at this time."

"Sorry, I guess I got carried away."

"Thanks. Just help Bongi hang on."

While the shouting and joking continued between the two
groups, Tony approached me. I turned to face the river, stared
into the fog, and again propped up my foot on a boulder. Tony
whispered, "Isn't that something the way Brian's gang and our
gang still go at it. They really love to bug each other."

I glanced at Tony. "I know it. All that joking about pizza
making a wop sound, and about mashed potatoes, got me thinking about all of what happened here in Middletown before our
parents and *paisani* (neighbors) got here, and what happened
when they got here."

Tony grinned. "You really love that history stuff, don't you?"

"I sure do. You know, like I told you before, half the time while I'm walking around in what's happening today, I find myself walking around in what happened years ago."

"You are always lost in history half the time, *sonnambulu* (dreamer)."

I stared into Tony's eyes, turned again to gaze into the fog, continued talking, but didn't realize I was mumbling.

"Santo, I can't hear you so good."

"What I was saying was that all the Irish, and other people in Middletown, couldn't believe it when a lot of Melilli, Sicily showed up a few years ago. The history of this place and what happened is really interesting."

Tony was right that I always loved to get lost in history. But I also tried to figure out how what happened yesterday has something to do with what is happening today, and what might happen tomorrow. As I continued scanning the river, the following details, which I had gathered over the past couple of years, swept through my mind again.

In 1651 the Massachusetts Bay Colony established a settlement at a bend in the Connecticut River to facilitate shipping goods between what would become New England and Long Island Sound. Because the location of this settlement was in the center of the territory that eventually defined Connecticut, it was named Middletown. There, Yankee settlers established ship building facilities, salmon fisheries, textile mills and brownstone quarries. As one example of the active industries that emerged in this settlement, barges shipped brownstone from these quarries down the Connecticut River to Long Island where the stone was used to build Manhattan. By 1790 Middletown become the largest city in Connecticut populated primarily by descendents of early settlers from Great Britain.

Beginning in 1800 Irish immigrants were the first non-English settlers to arrive. They were welcomed with enthusiasm because of the need for cheap labor, in sharp contrast to the negative reception Irish immigrants experienced in Boston, New York City and Philadelphia. When the famine in Ireland reached its peak in 1847, thousands more arrived in Middletown, enlarging their community much of which was located on streets leading from the center of town to the Connecticut River. A number of the descendants of these first arrivals from Ireland eventually became very prosperous, establishing pharmacies, plumbing and heating companies, and clothing stores.

From 1870 to 1900 four smaller groups of other, non-English speaking immigrants arrived in Middletown. Immigrants from Poland purchased small farms that had been abandoned by Yankee farmers, located in the outskirts of the city. Another group from Sweden initially worked in the brownstone quarries and then shifted to working in building trades. Germans from urban environments invested in small businesses, and Jews from Austria-Hungary either established businesses or were hired by the many textile mills that sprung up in the area. In spite of this influx of ethnic groups, the Irish population remained the largest in Middletown. This was illustrated, for example, by the fact that in 1900 the chief of police, and all of the officers and patrolmen of the police department, were of Irish descent.

Then, during the early 1900's, a new wave of non-English speaking immigrants arrived who were among the more than four million Italians who entered the United States at this time, nearly eighty percent of whom were from villages located in southern Italy. But these new arrivals who settled in Middletown created a unique situation because most of them were Sicilians from the same village, Melilli, located in a mountainous area of Eastern Sicily. As was the case at the time in Boston and New York City, inhabitants of Middletown experienced the arrival of these Southern Italians as a threat to their economic and personal welfare and viewed them as inferior to northern Italians because they were of darker complexion, illiterate and refused to speak, or had difficulty speaking, the English language. More than that, Sicilians were not welcomed because they were "foreign looking." The townspeople of Middletown, as was the case in other cities, did everything possible to encourage these immigrants to stay in their place. But these Sicilians were searching for ways to end the abuse they and their ancestors had endured and, therefore, persisted in their efforts to locate jobs. As a result, for example, by 1939 they became the major ethnic group employed by textile mills.

One example of the prejudice experienced by these Sicilians occurred at the Catholic Church that had been built by the Irish more than a half century ago. Before 1935, when Sicilians began to build their own church, some of them and their children attended Sunday mass at the Irish church, but were not allowed to sit in pews. Instead, they were required to remain standing in the back of the church. Occasionally, this expression of quiet prejudice resulted in episodes of open aggression. One Sunday, for example, when the priest and altar boys entered and Sunday Mass started, an eighteen year old Sicilian boy marched down to the front of church, pushed his way into a pew and knelt down. Several Irish men stood up, grabbed him, and dragged him to the back of the church, while the other Sicilians stood still watching. Of course, after the mass was over, a few Sicilian and Irish adolescents met in a nearby street and got into a gang fight.

What complicated matters even more, however, was the fact that these Sicilians located themselves near or in tenement houses along the Connecticut River in the area that had been home for many of the Irish. As a result, after the first Sicilian immigrants arrived, the Irish population gradually relocated in other sections of the city. Eventually the streets in Middletown's North End, which stretched from Main Street to the Connecticut River, served as the geography in which these Sicilian immigrants formed a tightly knit community where they relocated their village and were able to keep their ancient customs alive. But forming this enclave also had disadvantages. These Sicilians and their children delayed, for example, learning to speak and read English and becoming familiar with American customs. In addition, and of equal importance, by remaining clustered in the North End, Sicilians prevented the Irish and other ethnic groups from becoming familiar with them and the possible value of their customs.

Another issue that illustrated how Sicilians in Middletown were viewed related to the prejudice against Blacks that dominated in the United States for centuries. A small group of Blacks were clustered in tenement houses located along the river in Middletown's South End which abutted the North End. Similar to other cities, like Boston and Philadelphia where Blacks and Southern Italians lived near each other and developed friendships, a number of Sicilians and Blacks in Middletown worked together performing the same kinds of physical labor such as digging ditches in which water pipes were set, sweeping Main Street, and shoveling sand from a truck onto roads after a snowstorm. And so the two groups were viewed as similar.

Actually something happened in Tallulah, Louisiana around 1900, illustrating in a dramatic way that Sicilians and Blacks treated each other as equals and, at the same time, were victims of the same prejudice. Three Sicilian immigrants who were working in shops allowed Blacks to enter and gave them the same rights and attention whites received. As a result they were arrested. But a vigilante mob dragged them out of their jail cells, captured two other Sicilian immigrants, and hung all five of them because of their "offense." It's interesting that a description of this incident was printed on posters and distributed throughout Southern Italy and Sicily because the middle class was trying to discourage peasants from immigrating to the United States, leaving Italy without manual laborers. Of course, this incident became a frequent topic of discussion among Sicilian immigrants. My parents, and others in our neighborhood, often talked about what happened in Louisiana whenever they needed to emphasize the prejudice they were experiencing.

In addition to incidents that occurred like the one in Louisiana, people did not realize that the United States Bureau of Immigration also contributed to this negative viewpoint because Italian immigrants were classified as two different races, either Northern or Southern. Southern Italians were considered a different race because of a number of reasons, some relating to the Arabs, Greeks and Africans who had settled in Southern Italy during ancient times, others relating to, for example, the attitude that dominated in the United States about skin color which included Southern Italians who tended to be of darker complexion.

When both of my parents passed through Ellis Island to enter the United States, each of them was listed as "Southern Italian" in the race column of their entry papers.

The educational system that was developed in Middletown Connecticut, to serve the increasing number of Sicilian immigrants arriving in the 1920's, also contributed to the tension that developed between Sicilians and descendants of the English and Irish founders of the city. Sicilian children attended Green Street School, a very small building located in the heart of the Sicilian district. When some of these children reached their teens, they attended the city's middle and high schools which were located on the other side of town in what Sicilians considered the "American district." For the first time, therefore, these teenagers found themselves among classmates who were descendants of other ethnic groups who rejected Sicilians. Accordingly, Sicilian teenagers tended to establish friendships with African American students who were also rejected.

The prejudice against Sicilians in Middletown increased three years ago in the summer of 1940, when Benito Mussolini, the leader of Italy, announced his decision to join Adolf Hitler's German forces which, a few months before, had invaded Poland, conquering it within days, followed by Norway, Holland and Belgium. Just hours after Mussolini announced his decision, a comment made by Franklin D. Roosevelt, President of the United States, during his commencement address at the University of Virginia, magnified discrimination against Sicilians in Middletown as well as Boston, Chicago, New York, Philadelphia, New Orleans and San Francisco. Referring to Mussolini's decision to turn against England and the United States and join Hitler, Roosevelt proclaimed, "On this 10th day of June, the hand that held the dagger has stuck it into the back of his neighbor." This remark was highlighted in all major newspapers across the United States. Italians, especially Southern Italians, were discouraged that the President used a popular stereotype of an Italian, especially of a Sicilian, viewed as a person who always bore a stiletto. Italian American newspapers argued that the "stab-in-the-back" statement by the President served to fan the flames of anti-Italian, especially anti-Sicilian prejudice.

During the past couple of years, then, because of this increased wave of prejudice, gang fights occurred occasionally outside of the high school between first generation Sicilian Americans and descendants of the English and Irish founders of Middletown. More than that, once in a while, older guys from my neighborhood would arrange a fight with someone from the British or Irish districts, or someone from my neighborhood would be invited to step into a fight with someone from the British or Irish districts. These organized battles took place in remote areas. Anyone could come and watch, so crowds usually gathered at each event, cheering the gladiators. In one sense, these events were organized street fights. Several months ago, Joe Salemi from my neighborhood eagerly agreed to take on Bill Donovan. Joe was defeated. A week later when he received notice that he was drafted into the military and arrived at the recruiting center, he was sent home because he had a broken nose.

―――――――――

All of this history flashed through my mind in seconds when Tony reminded me that I love history and called me *sonnambulu*. And the picture of Joe Salemi's broken nose froze in my mind when Tony yelled at Dan, asking him what he would do if Tony stuffed a four leaf clover in his nose. When I snapped back to the present and compared what happened yesterday with what is happening today, I noticed that although the boys standing at the higher end of the ramp were third and fourth generation sons of Irish immigrants, and all of us milling about by the river were first generation sons of Sicilian immigrants, the exchanges between these two groups included a heavy dose of humor reflecting, at the same time, the prejudice whirling about in Middletown and other cities. More than that, a number of us were acquainted and even friends.

As soon as Tony screamed at Dan, Jack Kane screamed back, "Hey Bart! Where are you? You didn't answer the question! I told you what sound pizza makes when it hits the floor." Grinning, he added, "What happened, did you slip away on your grease, you grease ball?"

Bart shouted back, laughing. "But Dan didn't tell us the sound he'll make when Tony sticks a four leaf clover in his nose!"

I still tried to ignore the bantering that was going on, while standing by the river's edge staring into the fog. Tony moved closer to my side, and our gang milled around us. I glanced at each of them, and then another moment from the past flashed into my mind. A year ago when Bart, Melo and I arrived at Central School in the American District for eighth grade, our classmates told us that some of the names of the guys in our gang sounded weird.

Once in a while, Sicilians refer to a person by his or her actual first name. This was the case with Angelo, Filippo and Vito. And, sometimes, they assign a nickname that represents an abbreviation of the person's first or last name. This was the case with Bart, whose first name was Bartholomeo, with Tony whose first name was Antonio, with Louie whose first name was Luigi, with Dom whose first name was Dominic, and with Bongi whose last name was *Bongiornu*, which in Sicilian means "good day." But frequently, however, Sicilians assign a person a nickname based upon something the person did or liked.

"Why are those Irish guys giving us shit?" Sal asked. Sal's nickname came from his habit of sprinkling a lot *sale* (salt) on everything he ate.

"Ignore them," Melo responded. "They're just kidding." Another member of my gang was "*Melo*" who loved to climb apple trees and eat apples at the Baldwin orchards outside of town. (*Melo* is the Italian word for apple tree).

"Sal, I think Dan O'Neil is a pretty nice guy," Suggi commented. "He helped me once when some kids were picking on me." Suggi's nickname got started when he was very young, because he enjoyed sucking on his thumb. (Suck in Sicilian dialect is "*suggi*").

"Yeah, Sal. When you get to know those guys you'll see they're just kidding," Pesci added. Pesci was given this nickname because he was obsessed with eating fish (*pesci*).

Another gang member's nickname was Ancio because he loved to eat *anciovi* (anchovies), and Musca always loved to play a game in the summer that involved swatting flies (fly in Sicilian dialect is *musca*).

"I know Jim Murphy over there," Baggi joined in. "He was in my class, and he's really a nice guy." Baggi loved to roll around in piles of straw whenever possible. (Straw in Sicilian dialect is *"pagghia"*). As a matter of fact, his nickname stemmed from a neighborhood joke that involved his father, and was passed on to his son. In the village from which they immigrated, some of the peasants slept on straw with their goats and sheep nearby. Baggi's father was frequently observed stepping out of the small stone hut in which he slept with straw sticking out of his buttocks. Hence his nickname became *"Pagghia nculu,"* Sicilian dialect for "straw in the ass."

Although my first name was Sebastiano, as was my father's, I was assigned my nickname years ago by childhood friends who teased me because I frequently seemed to be lost in deep thought. When that happened they laughed and yelled, "Hey, are you a *Santo* in heaven?"

Melo turned away from the Irish crowd, faced all of us, and anxiously commented that the trucks from the Goodrich Tobacco Farm should arrive soon. He pushed his arms forward and exclaimed, "Yes, I think we're going to be in the big forty," expressing hope that all of us would be hired again. Typically each summer this farm selected about forty boys from Middletown's North End to harvest tobacco leaves and work in the sheds.

My friends began to cluster closer together and ignore the gang standing yards away. "Guess what guys?" It was obvious that Bart was very excited. "Yesterday we got a letter from my brother." Bart's older brother, Carlo, had been drafted into the Army several months ago. "He said he's leaving for the Pacific because he's all done with training at Fort Dix."

Tony was turned on by Bart's news. "Well, you know, Bart, my cousin, Lucky, is already there. He left two months after Pearl Harbor. I hope they get to meet." Lucky was the son of Gaetano, our father's older brother.

"Wow, that would be great wouldn't it!" Bart sighed.

With his fists clenched Louie barked, "This war is really getting to me. I hope it's over soon."

"Are you kidding? Did you hear the news on the radio last

night?" Tony jabbed a finger at Louie. "That battle in North Africa is still going on. And some news guy said they might invade Sicily from there. What the hell will our relatives do?"

I heard what Melo, Bart, Louie and Tony were saying and, as usual, became lost in my private thoughts.

Melo turned, glanced at the others, and pushed his arms out with palms turned upward. "OK, guys. Santo is gone again. But we know he'll come back, right?"

At that moment Bongi walked over to me and grabbed each of my shoulders. "Those jerks are not going to choose me. I think I'm fatter than last year!" Bongi was referring to the fact that if a picker was too large and heavy, he usually was not hired because he could bruise tobacco leaves as he crawled on his knees between rows of plants, while harvesting those designated for that particular picking.

Taking Bongi's concern as an invitation, Pesci's face looked very worried. "I'm not going to be chosen either. I'm still slower than you guys."

Bart joined the chorus. "Oh, yeah! What about me? I'll bet they don't hire me because of the fight I got in last summer with that ass hole from Wethersfield. And don't forget that jerk, the big foreman, Mr. George, docked me one full day."

Suddenly a boy, standing several yards away, yelled, interrupting the conversations. "Hey, you Dagos! You think you're gonna be hired? Forget it!"

"Shut your mouth, Jack!" Bart shouted back, "That's enough of your joking. Do you want me to whack you?"

"Oh, yeah! Come over here, grease ball, and try it."

"Here I come, green horn!"

As Bart leaned forward, Tony grabbed him by the arm and held him still. "Come on, Bart. You know he's kidding."

It was especially Bart's outburst that helped me snap out of my trance, face my gang, and try to help them not be so nervous. I stretched my arms out, turned my palms upward, and grinned in confidence, repeating an ancient Sicilian saying each of them had heard many times from their parents. "Hey! *Semu da stissa cacocciula.*" ("Hey! We are from the same artichoke.") Since the tightly knit leaves of an artichoke all stem from and share one center, for Sicilians the artichoke represents the connected and mutually committed members of a family, or gang, or neighborhood.

I had been floating in and out of fantasy since I was a young kid. Because I frequently did this, my parents jokingly call me *"Sonnambulu,"* which means sleepwalker or dreamer. For example, this morning, while Tony and I were getting our lunches ready before leaving, our mother asked me to get chicken cutlets from the icebox, and Tony to get oranges from the pantry. Tony immediately picked up the oranges, but, at that moment, I was lost in my own thoughts and did not respond. Our father yelled out in a playful tone, mixed with some irritation, "Hey! *Sonnambulu, unni si?*" ("Hey dreamer, where are you?"). I snapped back, quickly went to the icebox and took out the cutlets. So I proved once again that, although I had been lost in fantasy, I had heard what mamma said.

So this morning there I was, standing at the river's edge, staring into the thick fog, feeling it roll around me, touching my face, and drifting over my wavy, dark brown hair. I heard Melo's concern about whether we would be hired. I heard Bart's excitement over his brother's letter, and I heard the jokes and wise cracks the gangs threw at each other. At the same time, as usual, I experienced sensations that were very familiar to me. During these moments, I frequently recalled some event I heard my parents and relatives discuss many times. Sometimes I reflected on how that event relates to the present moment. Sometimes, though, I did not think about how the memory that sweeps through my mind has something to do with what is going on today. Actually, I tried to describe this experience I have from time to time when my eighth grade teacher gave the class an assignment as the school year was coming to a close.

———————

Each student was asked to write about a topic related to discussions the class had concerning aspects of history and social science. In my essay I tried to discuss my understanding of an idea, proposed by a person named James, that had found its way into the field of psychology. I apologized for not remembering the person's first name. From the way the teacher pronounced it, I wrote that the first name was something like "Gugliamo" or "Williamo".

The day after I submitted my essay, Miss Press, dismissed the class when the school day was over. As kids walked out, she yelled, "Santo, please come here for a moment!" Even though she used the word 'please,' the tone of her voice made clear there was some kind of problem. When I approached her desk, I was certain something was wrong because of the glare in her eyes. "Yes, Miss Press."

She pushed my essay toward me. "Please, could you tell me what you said in your essay?"

I felt a whirl of confusion spin around in my head. "Well, I put in there what you told us, Miss Press."

"What did I tell the class?"

The way she pushed my essay across the desk, plus the tone of her voice, now said to me that she was irritated or even angry. I glanced up at the ceiling, took a deep breath, and tried to gain a feeling of confidence, since history was my favorite subject. "Well, you talked about how in that book, this guy James wrote in 1890, he said a person's personality starts to take shape during the first years of life. And he said this first sense of who a person is comes from different experiences he has with other people he's close to, like how he was fed, and how his parents and aunts and uncles talked to him, played with him, hugged him, and scolded him." I took another deep breath, noticed that Miss Press' eyes were still filled with anger, but tried to keep going. "So Miss Press, you said what us kids make of what is going on around us comes from these different experiences we stored when we were little."

She tapped the palm of her hand on the top of the desk. "Yes, Santo, we did discuss those ideas in class. But you added some things."

Now I was more confused. I looked down at my feet for a second and collected the thoughts that came to me when I was trying to shape my essay. "I wrote that these experiences we have when we're kids could include stories parents tell their kids about things that happened to them. You know what, Miss Press?" I began talking one hundred miles an hour. "My parents, aunts and uncles tell us stories all the time. While I'm listening to these stories, sometimes I feel I'm there with them. Like my father tells stories about when his father had to live in caves and ..."

This time Miss Press slapped her hand on the desk top. "Santo, you added that and something else!"

My mind screeched to a stop. I took another deep breath, and again glanced up at the ceiling. "Miss Press, I think you mean I said that what we talked about in class made me realize that those stories parents tell a kid could make the kid feel like he's there, having the same experience. So what a guy thinks is happening today could include certain memories that belong to his parents or relatives. When that happens, a guy is standing in today and in a long time ago at the same time. Then he could take a look ahead and notice what he could expect tomorrow and..."

Miss Press interrupted me again. Even though I tried to explain to her what I thought she was asking about, she still wasn't satisfied. "That's right, Santo. You did say all of that, and then you talked about theaters and actors in a person's mind."

I wondered why she was so upset with my idea about theaters and actors in a person's mind. Maybe I wasn't clear enough. I held my hands together and made up my mind that I would keep trying to make sure she understood, because my essay was about ideas that I had thought a lot about all year. "Well, Miss Press, I asked how could a guy be walking around today and, at the same time, be walking around a long time ago, and then looking at tomorrow. So in my paper I said this could happen if we think that a guy has three stages in his head and a lot of actors." Miss Press was staring at me and listening, so I continued, taking one slow step at a time. "If something is happening, actors come out on one stage and show what the person is thinking about as he watches what's going on in front of him. At the same time, actors come out on the other stage and act out a story that went on a long time ago that has something to do with what is going on now. And then actors could come out on the other stage and show what might happen tomorrow from what is happening

23

today and from what happened years ago. So a kid is watching three plays at the same time while something is going on. You know, Miss Press, like when I listen to stories on the radio, like 'Jack Armstrong' or 'The Shadow,' I see what is going on in the story, and, at the same time ..."

Before I finished, she pushed my essay toward me, now almost shoving it off the desk. "Santo, where did you get these ideas?" Before I could respond, she exclaimed with an accusatory tone, "Didn't you copy these ideas from some magazine or newspaper?"

Now my head felt like a storm was whirling around in it. I thought to myself, 'Why the hell would she get such an idea?' I looked down at my hands, and my last words slipped out in a whisper. "No, Miss Press, I didn't copy anything. I've been thinking about what I wrote for you all year."

She slapped the palm of her hand against my paper. "Santo, you better tell the truth!" She leaned forward, reached toward me, but then suddenly flopped back into her chair.

At this moment, I noticed fear in her eyes, and was sure an incident that occurred several years ago, that involved my father, flashed into her mind. It had to do with what happened one day when a group of seven and eight-year-old children, who were huddled in a classroom of the small school that had been set up in our Sicilian neighborhood, anxiously stared at their teacher, Miss Mutt. The incident became a legend in the school and our neighborhood, and at that moment tumbled on that stage in my mind reserved for yesterday.

Because our parents were immigrant Sicilian peasants who had never attended school, we all spoke the Sicilian dialect and broken English at home. At the time, schools ignored and depreciated the language we spoke at home and, in the view of most teachers, the Sicilian dialect interfered with our educational progress. Miss Mutt had been assigned the task of teaching us English vocabulary. We frequently joked about her way of teaching. She swaggered and marched around the classroom, holding a long wooden pointer across her shoulder. Then she suddenly stopped, whipped the pointer forward, and aimed it at some

24

object, like a lamp or eraser, while calling out a student's name. That student's job was to yell the English name of the object that she had pointed out. Miss Mutt believed that requiring children to be called upon unexpectedly to verbalize a word in English would strengthen their English vocabulary as well as cultivate their ease in speaking English. But over the years, her pompous manner and swagger, which all of the children playfully imitated, had become the target of much joking in the neighborhood.

One day, after strutting about for a minute, while we anxiously waited to see who would be called upon next, Miss Mutt abruptly stopped near a window, thrust the pointer at the window shade and shouted, "Santo!" I usually drifted into some fantasy whenever she swaggered about the classroom. When she called my name, I quickly looked up and yelled, "*Tendina!*" which in Italian, as well as in dialect, is the word for curtain or window blind. All of the children understood what the word I blurted out meant, and exploded in a burst of laughter. But because of what Miss Mutt had learned from a neighborhood teenager, she came to a different conclusion On occasion, when pupils walked by her in the hallway, they muttered some Sicilian word. Since several of the words were repeated, she remembered their sounds. One day, pretending she was interested in learning the Sicilian dialect, she asked a teenager what they meant. Miss Mutt was stunned to learn that, when walking by her, children frequently whispered, "testadura" (hardhead), "maladitta" (damn), "fessa" (fool), "pazza" (crazy), and "schifusa" (lousy, filthy one).

Because of these past experiences, Miss Mutt apparently assumed that, when I blurted our *tendina*, I had expressed some insult. She quickly walked toward me and hit me a number of times on my back and chest with her wooden pointer, as I struggled to deflect the blows by squirming about in my chair and raising my arms. Then she immediately dismissed the class. Everyone ran out of the classroom into the streets, and what happened quickly spread throughout the neighborhood like wild fire.

Although I was very confused, I did not mention the incident when I arrived home. My mother noticed bloodstains on my shirt and asked me "*Ch'è successu?*" ("What happened?").

I mumbled, "*Niente* (Nothing). We were playing by the river and I fell on some rocks."

When my sisters came home, though, they frantically described to our mother what had happened. A short while later my father arrived at dinnertime and my mother took him to one end of the kitchen. For a number of minutes they engaged in a quiet discussion, but I did not overhear what they were talking about. The incident did not come up during dinner.

The next day at the Green Street School we were again sitting still in Miss Mutt's class, anxiously watching her and waiting to be called upon to speak some English word. Suddenly, the door to the classroom pushed open. Miss Mutt's head, as well as the heads of all of the kids, quickly turned toward the doorway. There stood my father, wearing a dark suit, necktie and hat. My mouth opened wide, and I mumbled to myself, 'Wow! When he's dressed up like that he really means business.' As he scanned the room, slight grins crept across the faces of all the kids since they knew who he was. Miss Mutt, however, had never seen him before and stiffened her posture, preparing to deal with this intruder and order him to get out. Before she said a word, my father slowly walked forward and stopped in front of her. He turned his head in my direction, stretched his arm out, and pointed at me. Then he turned his head back and looked directly into Miss Mutt's face which was inches away. In a quiet, raspy voice, he said, "You touch-a my boy, I kill-a you," and slowly strolled out of the classroom.

After a long moment, during which Miss Mutt remained motionless and some of us snickered, she gulped and said, "We'll continue tomorrow. Class is dismissed."

We scrambled into the streets. During the weeks that followed, the children who witnessed the event, as well as others in the neighborhood, invented and played the game of a parent-teacher conference which they called, "Touch-a my boy, I kill-a you." With this game they relished visiting many times a scene in which the teacher, who had caused them so much fear and tension, finally got what she deserved.

Like I said, when Miss Press leaned toward me and reached

out, I was sure she must have recalled this incident which, although several years old, was still echoing throughout the neighborhood and school. I was sure because of the way she quickly lowered her arm and flopped back in her chair. She took a deep breath, and with a less intense tone remarked, "Santo, maybe you got help for your ideas from something you read. Do you remember anything you read? I would be very interested to see it myself."

"No, Miss Press. Like I said, what I wrote came out of me thinking about what you talked about in class."

"Okay, I give you a passing grade. You may go now."

While I was standing at the river's edge waiting for the trucks to arrive, I realized that these surges of memories I experience, with actors performing on the different stages in my mind, had been occurring more often during the past few months. I looked up, scanned the bridge overhead, and imagined that because I would be turning fourteen during the summer, I was crossing a bridge over a river that separates being a kid from the beginning of being a grownup. Soon I would be leaving one part of life that seemed easier, and approaching another part of life that looked much more complicated and tougher. From where I stood, I could see one thing on the grown-up side of the river of life that was going to take a lot of work to handle, while I tried to keep growing up. When a guy lives on that other side, he has to figure out how to handle the people who are in charge, like the bosses on the tobacco farm, teachers in high school, and even parents. I had to figure out when should I follow orders and do my best, and when should I try to be on my own and do what makes sense to me.

In the next moment, I remembered how this morning I caught a glimpse of Carina walking toward Rapello Avenue where girls who worked on the farm were picked up. With the image in my mind of Carina ambling along, I experienced a tingling feeling all over my body and focused on something else that I could see on the other side of the river that would also take a lot of work.

A guy has to deal with all those feelings he gets when he sees a girl he likes. I wrote a poem a couple of months ago that my older friends liked a lot, especially one line. "Then one day to my surprise I found that from a tiny stream I had grown into a river great, splashing, dashing, down the hill." What does a guy do with all that water in that big river, and which way should he make the river flow?

Bart suddenly yelled, "What time is it anyway?" I snapped back and looked around. The Irish boys, as well as all of us from the North End, were now becoming fidgety.

"It's gotta be almost seven o'clock," Melo replied. "See, the sun is starting to break through the fog."

Suddenly Tony threw his arm out toward the ramp and yelled, "Here come the trucks!"

Two trucks rattled off the bridge onto the ramp that led to the open area by the river's edge. The trucks were familiar to all of us because they have been used for several years to transport boys to the farm. They looked much like the trucks used to haul cattle in the 1930's. Large wooden slats, each separated by five or six inches, framed the sides. Except for the cabin, where the driver and passenger sat, the truck did not have a roof. Two long, wooden benches were set against the wooden slats on each side of the truck's platform. Two additional benches were placed side by side in the center of the truck's platform. With this seating arrangement, two rows of boys could sit face to face within inches of each other on one half of the truck's platform, and two rows of boys on the other. With this arrangement a truck carried about forty boys which gave rise to a saying exclaimed by those who were hired, "We made it in the forty!" and who also joked, "We are forty cows jammed together. Moo! Moo! "

After the trucks screeched to a halt, one of the drivers, who was familiar to most of us, opened his door and stepped down. He was wearing overalls, and his face was pocked, which we jokingly interpreted to mean that he was an accomplished drinker. He quickly walked to the other side of the cabin and opened the door. Mr. George, the senior foreman and timekeeper, hopped out. He was also familiar since, for several summers, he had harassed and intimidated us. As usual, he was wearing a neatly pressed shirt, trousers, and a broad brimmed hat over his long, dark-blond hair and sunglasses. He also carried a large leather-covered note pad in one hand, as if it were a sword.

When the superintendent of the farm slowly stepped down from the cabin of the other truck, some of us startled because he was not the person we had known over the past few summers. He was clean-shaven, wore a suit jacket and neatly pressed dark trousers, and held a leather-covered note pad in his right hand as if, I imagined, it was also the sword of a Duke. Moreover, his broad brimmed hat, rigid posture, elevated chin and facial expression conveyed, I thought, that this man felt he was nobility.

Chuckling, Bart ran over to me and whispered, "Will you look at that, they're both wearing *cappeddi*. I guess we're supposed to bow." *Cappeddi* were broad brimmed hats worn by wealthy owners of *latifondi* (large feudal estates) in Sicily, which were very different than the caps worn by peasants.

In sharp contrast to their animated joking before the trucks arrived, all of the boys glared at the superintendent and senior foreman, and closely knit groups were now scattered under the bridge. Several from the North End, including myself, stood squarely on both feet with legs spread slightly apart, hands resting on our hips, and elbows extended outward. The palms of our hands, however, were also turned outward from our hips. This posture was the opposite of a similar one some Americans assumed which involved placing the palms inward against the hips. In the body language of Sicily, the posture of hands turned outward, while resting on ones hips, stated for centuries, "Don't tread on me or my family and friends! See! My hands are ready for action." We Sicilian American boys inherited this body language from our parents who, during family gatherings, assumed this posture when they discussed how their ancestors endured hardships for centuries while living under foreign rulers who for us were represented, at this moment, by the new superintendent and senior foreman.

After the superintendent stepped down from the truck, he began a discussion with Mr. George, each poking a finger at a page of his leather-covered notepad, apparently engaged in a quiet disagreement. Mr. George pointed in my gang's direction and exclaimed, "I still don't think those wops can do it for us."

I had no idea why he made that comment, and while I continued to stare at Mr. George and the superintendent, Melo whispered franticly, "Come on! We've got to get closer or he won't choose us to be pickers."

I heard Melo's frantic plea but remained still with the palms of my hands turned outward on my hips. As I continued staring at the superintendent, who for me was the unknown, I argued with myself whether or not I should step forward and enter that unknown. At that moment, a story I heard my parents and relatives discuss swept on that stage in my mind reserved for yesterday. The story had to do with my grandfather struggling with whether or not he should step forward and enter the unknown, even though he had a good reason to do so. Because I've heard the story so many times, whenever it starts to take place on that stage in my mind I call 'yesterday,' I feel as if I'm there.

It all happened in 1899. My grandfather, Antonio, stood on the rocky slope of a hill leaning forward with his right foot set up on a boulder, while scanning the village below. A column of peasants, each walking along side of a mule, hobbled over a narrow, rocky road leading to open fields at the edge of the village where they grew vegetables and wheat. Today, as had been the case over the past three months during visits to this very location, Antonio felt a strong urge to slip down into the village to see his family.

Hoping to catch a glimpse of one of his six children, he especially studied those who were leaping out of the small stone houses, playfully running about the narrow streets. Maybe he would see his oldest daughter, Rosa, who tended to devour her morning fruit so she could spend time with her friends. Maybe he would spot Angela and Maria who loved to dance about outside. And maybe he might catch a glimpse of his sons, Gaetano and Aurelio. They loved to walk about outdoors after breakfast, carefully examining small rocks and selecting a few to add to their collection, which now formed a large heap on the side of their stone house. But Antonio wanted especially to hold, cuddle and kiss his youngest son, Sebastiano, my father, who was born just five days before Antonio had to escape into the mountains because he was being pursued by Italian troops. Antonio had been involved in a rebellion against the government which had its roots in developments that had occurred during the past decades.

In the 1800's, Italy was fragmented into eight separate entities. All but one of these was ruled by governments from other countries. The exception was the region of Piedmont in Northern Italy which was ruled by Italians. In an effort to oust foreign rulers, and establish a united Italian republic, a movement called the *Risorgimento* was launched. After several attempts failed, the movement achieved success in 1860 when Giuseppe Garibaldi led a volunteer army and liberated all the regions south of Rome. Many Sicilians had joined Garibaldi, contributing significantly to his success. Victor Emanuel II of Piedmont was proclaimed king of Italy in 1862 when Garibaldi handed him southern Italy. But the unification of Italy was not completed until eight years later, when the Papal State finally became part of the Italian republic.

The center of the national government of this new Italy was established in the city of Turin in the northern region of Piedmont. Sicilian peasants began to oppose this new government for several reasons. For example, Barons, whose families had owned and monopolized land in Sicily for centuries, established political connections with this new government and arranged to avoid giving peasants parcels of land Garibaldi promised they would receive as reward for their contribution to the revolution. As a matter of fact, several years after Italy became unified, almost three quarters of all the acreage in Sicily was still the property of absent landowners. In addition, this new Italian government imposed taxes on peasants that were higher than when the Spanish dynasty ruled Sicily. And what especially disturbed peasants was the new law that required all young men to serve in the military for seven years, robbing families of the help they needed. In response to these and other regulations peasants viewed as grossly unfair, the heads of many villages in Sicily formed a League to organize ways of opposing the government. With one strategy, this League encouraged peasants, who worked in the sulfur mines and on estate farms, to strike and not return to their jobs unless wages and work conditions were more appropriate. The task of suppressing this League and restoring order in Sicily was assigned to General Mara who dispatched forty thousand soldiers to Sicily, and set out to arrest the *Capo* or Chief of every village.

My grandfather, Antonio, was the *Capo* of his village and had been involved in this rebellion. To avoid being arrested he escaped into the mountains and hid in caves that dotted the rocky hills surrounding the village. He spent one or two days in each cave, following a sequence he and his brother, Gaetano, and close friends (*paisani*) of the village had outlined. When he arrived at any one of the caves, he found food and water that had been brought there by one of the villagers, all of whom were eager to help him escape because he was their *uomo rispettato* (man of respect).

An hour ago, when Antonio entered one of these caves, Vincenzo, the husband of one of his younger sisters, was sitting there waiting for him. Antonio immediately noticed that Vincenzo's head hung low, and his hands were twisting his hat. Greeting him, Antonio asked, "*Ch'è successu, figghiu miu? Picchì giri u cappeddu?*" ("What happened my son? Why are you twisting the hat?") The dialects of Southern regions of Italy, called *Mezzogiorno* because of the strength of the mid-day sun, but especially the dialect of Sicily, reflected for centuries the influence of the languages of the Greeks and Arabs. These languages stressed the "u" sound which Sicilians commonly substituted for vowels and sometimes for whole syllables. Thus Antonio said, "*figghiu*" for "figlio (son), and "*cappeddu*" for "*cappello*" (hat).

"I carry the burden of bad news."

"What is the bad news?" Antonio asked in his quite, raspy voice.

"Your brother, Gaetano (Antonio's oldest son was named after him), has been captured by *carabinieri* (government troops)."

Antonio fell to his knees and slowly made the sign of the cross.

Vincenzo continued, hurriedly reminding Antonio that before he had escaped into the mountains, members of the family, as well as Antonio himself, did not think the troops were attempting to locate Gaetano but were only after Antonio. Becoming more anxious, Vincenzo wondered whether the troops had mistaken Gaetano for Antonio, or if they were holding him as a hostage to be traded for Antonio. As Vincenzo went on trying to reassure Antonio and explain what could be the reason for the tragedy, Antonio said quietly, "*Basta è fattu.*" ("Enough, it's done.") "Someday we might have the privilege of collecting compensation for this insult so that my father is given the respect he deserves." Mentioning his father caused Antonio to drift for a moment from the present to his own early memories. He took a chunk of provolone cheese from the basket of food Vincenzo had brought, began eating, and spontaneously talked about details from the past.

Antonio was ten years old in 1860 when he waved good-bye to his father as he left the village, never to return. Antonio's father, along with hundreds of other Sicilians, joined Garibaldi's band of "Red Shirts" who defeated the Bourbon army in Sicily, and then invaded the Italian peninsula, eventually defeating the Austrian armies in southern Italy. Since Sicily had repeatedly revolted against Bourbon rule during the 1800's, Sicilian peasants joined Garibaldi with enthusiasm. Antonio's father was killed in combat outside of Naples.

When Antonio stopped chewing on cheese and recalled how his father lost his life, Vincenzo raised his voice to capture Antonio's attention, reporting with a tone of pleasure and a smile that he also had some good news. Government troops were preparing to leave the region. Then his eyes and face quickly shifted to an expression of concern as he went on to explain that, in spite of this, he was still worried because, several times over the past few weeks, he had observed Salvatore Alba talking to an officer of the federal troops in ways that seemed too familiar. While Antonio now munched on a piece of *schiacciata*, pizza stuffed with broccoli, Vincenzo reminded Antonio, who in fact did not need a reminder, that Alba had viewed himself as a *pezzo grosso* (big shot), and had openly disagreed with a number of decisions

Antonio made over the years when negotiating disagreements between Alba and villagers.

Salvatore Alba had been hired several years ago by the *latifundista* (rich land owner) from Austria who still owned large estates surrounding the village. These estates had been given to the Baron's father when, in 1814, the Congress of Vienna divided Italy into eight principalities under Austrian, Bourbon and Papal rule. Initially, Alba served as an assistant to the superintendent of these estates. Later, much to the surprise of the villagers, he was promoted to the position of *gabelloto* (superintendent). Everyone knew that, on a number of occasions, Alba had tried to intimidate sharecroppers into accepting contracts that were unfair. For example, he required them to give him a larger amount of their crops then originally agreed upon. In spite of the fact that he tried to exploit villagers, disagreements which Antonio had negotiated, Alba believed he should have become *Capo* of the village. This seemed ridiculous to all of the villagers because he had not accumulated the respect that had been invested in Antonio several years after his father, who had previously served as *Capo* with considerable success, was killed in battle when serving in Garibaldi's army.

Because Vincenzo believed that Alba could be up to no good, he urged Antonio to wait a few days before returning to the village. Antonio disagreed, making clear he wanted to see his family. After they argued for several minutes, Antonio paused, thanked Vincenzo for his advice, and in keeping with Sicilian custom, kissed each of his cheeks. Vincenzo also kissed Antonio on each cheek and began walking down to the village.

A few moments later Antonio stepped out of the cave and paused, recycling his argument with Vincenzo and experiencing intense turmoil. He understood why Vincenzo cautioned him to wait before visiting the village, but this collided with his wish to see his wife and children as well as his brothers and sisters. During their argument, Antonio had shared with Vincenzo that he imagined his brother, Gaetano, smiling and saying, *"curri a famigghia."* ("Run to your family.") But then the next moment he imagined Gaetano glaring and exclaiming, *"Chi fai, sì babbu?"*

("What are you stupid?") Antonio also told Vincenzo how the two images flashed back and forth in his mind, as he struggled to decide whether or not to enter the village and the unknown.

Some thirty yards ahead, Vincenzo turned, looked up, spotted Antonio walking down the hill, and shook his head, exclaiming, "No! No! Don't come down now." But Antonio continued, so Vincenzo raced into the village to make arrangements for Antonio's arrival which they had agreed upon, if he decided to return to the village. When Antonio approached the first cluster of olive trees, villagers who were working there spotted him and screamed, "Ciao, Antonio!" (Hello) He returned their greetings, but the villagers could tell he was very preoccupied.

I was called back to the crowd of boys under the bridge, from my fantasy of walking along side of my grandfather into the unknown, when the superintendent yelled, "Is there a Santo here?" I removed my right hand from my hip and slowly raised my arm. "Come here, boy!" As if I were still walking with my grandfather toward the village, I stepped forward and stood motionless several yards before the superintendent. "Santo, I am Mr. Williams the new superintendent. Our records show you picked tobacco for the past four years, and last year you were one of the best pickers in the Fast Gang. We need a straw boss for the Fast Gang this year. I decided that you can be the straw boss. Choose ten pickers to make five partners that you think should be in the fast gang, and choose five haulers." My friends grinned with victory, and Mr. George turned away with a look of disgust. The Fast Gang earned thirty cents an hour, while other pickers earned fifteen or twenty cents an hour. For children of Sicilian immigrant families, that was a very good wage.

I signaled to my gang. All nine ran forward and scrambled onto the truck. To complete my group of ten pickers, I pointed to Bongi's younger brother, Dominic. For haulers I picked my brother, Tony, and four other close friends from our neighborhood, who also hopped on the truck. At the same time, the superintendent appointed Brian Coleman straw boss of one of the

Regular Gangs. He pointed to Jack Kane, Dan O'Neil and other friends who climbed onto the truck in which my gang and I sat. The superintendent then called out the names of other boys who had worked on the farm before in the sheds where tobacco leaves were hung to dry. Once it was clear to the remaining boys that there was no more room on the trucks, they mumbled to each other and, with heads lowered, slowly walked away in clusters.

In minutes, the trucks rolled onto the ramp over the bridge. Brian Coleman's gang and my gang continued joking. "Hey, Santo!" Brian Coleman called out. "Do you know why you guys got picked for the Fast Gang? They know you're grease balls, and you can just slide along while you're picking."

I chuckled and flapped my hand at him. "Very funny. You're just jealous that you don't have any grease."

"I'll loan you some, Coleman," Suggi added. "But it's gonna cost you."

Jack Kane interrupted, "Hey guys! Do you remember that song we learned from those Jamaicans last year when they worked with us?"

Immediately everyone burst out in song, swaying back and forth with the rhythm.

"Going away forever to stay, heaven is not far away.
I will then say good-bye, to my sisters good-bye,
And then I will hear, will hear my savoir say,
Fly, up in the sky, fly,
Then I will, hey, skip away home on the wings of glory,
I am going home."

As I joined the singing, I felt another whirl throughout my body. Crossing the bridge over the Connecticut River again stirred up in my mind that, in a couple of weeks, I turn fourteen and face being in the world of grownups instead of being in the world of kids. But more than that, now I was going to be a straw boss, and I have to figure out how to show what I can do on my own, while taking orders from bosses, especially Mr. George.

After traveling several miles, the trucks turned off the highway, followed a dirt road, and came to a stop in the Central Lot. Here cabins served as offices for the superintendent and foremen. All of us hopped off the truck. Mr. George stood there with his arms folded, chatting with another foreman, Mr. Kelly. Tony, Bart and I, and other members of the gang, spontaneously waved to Mr. Kelly who smiled and waved back. We had become acquainted with him during the past two summers, and experienced him as a nice guy. As we were waving to Mr. Kelly, Mr. George glared at us. It was obvious to me, and my gang, that he resented the fact we had been selected to be one of the fast gangs.

All of the boys understood that Mr. George played a critical role in whether they would work for the entire summer. Although the superintendent selected the boys who could work that day, Mr. George was actually the one who decided whether a boy was hired for the entire summer. He came to his decision during the first days while the boys "suckered" the tobacco plants, and removed the leaves of First Picking.

At the start of the season, the tobacco plants were approximately four feet tall and eventually grew to the height of about seven feet. Each plant had a few leaves protruding perpendicular from its stalk. At the base of most of the plants, however, were one or two shoots, called "suckers". It was necessary to remove these suckers, without harming the leaves, because they were taking away, or sucking away, energy from the young plant.

During the first week, while boys removed suckers and the leaves of First Picking, their skill and style of working were observed by at least one foreman, in addition to Mr. George, who wandered through the fields. If they decided a boy had the necessary skills, Mr. George assigned an identification number to that boy, which meant he had been hired for the summer. But everyone knew from experience that, while other foremen expressed opinions about a boy's skills, they usually were not involved in who was selected. Traditionally, the ultimate decision was left to Mr. George who appeared to wallow in the sadistic joy he derived from the position he held.

When the time came to hire boys for the summer, Mr. George typically walked about with a regal-like stride, approached a boy, and declared with his usual, authoritative tone, "Your number is 319", for example. In this way he informed the boy that he had been formally hired. But if Mr. George did not give a number to a boy on that day, the boy understood he was denied a job and could not return for the rest of the summer. If a boy proved his worth and was hired, however, he still had to cope throughout the summer with Mr. George's harassments. Typically he strutted about, approached a boy, asked in his usual, derogatory tone, "What is your number?" and recorded it in his leather-covered book with a scribble that conveyed authority. But he was feared and hated by all of the boys for more than his daily condescending tone because of one particular, additional authority he held. While wandering about the fields throughout the summer, in addition to collecting numbers that identified each boy, he also scrutinized whether, in his judgment, the boy made an error. If Mr. George decided this to be the case, he had the authority to "dock" the boy's pay one or more hours, or one whole day, that is, to subtract an amount from the boy's wages.

———————

His arms still folded, Mr. George continued to glare at my gang and Brian Coleman's as we stood in the Central Lot waiting for assignments. We were keenly aware that during this week we had to prove ourselves. The superintendent leaned toward Mr. George, pointed to a page in his book and, for several minutes, they again seemed to be engaged in a disagreement. Suddenly Mr. Williams vigorously tapped his book, and Mr. George walked toward my gang with a stride all the boys enjoyed ridiculing. As he approached, I imagined him to be a good example of the *Gabelloti* I heard my father and uncles describe who managed the big estates owned by *latifundisti* (rich land owners) in Sicily and enjoyed the power they held over the peasants. I also thought to myself that the superintendent, Mr. Williams, seemed to be a living example of a rich, land owner. The way he dressed, walked, postured himself, talked, and pointed with his arm, all conveyed, I imagined, that he was from nobility.

When Mr. George approached me, he leaned forward, emphasizing he was looking down on something beneath his status, and with a sarcastic tone commented, "Santo, the superintendent still thinks you and your pals are one of the Fast Gangs. He still believes that you should be the straw boss." With a sneer he added, "Congratulations! I wish you and your guys the best of luck this week."

I understood Mr. George's message, slowly turned away and faced my gang. With a soft voice I reminded them of an often-quoted Sicilian proverb. "*Di dintra veni cu lu voscu tagghia.*" (From inside could come someone who cuts down your forest). In other words, keep an eye on a person who acts as if he's your friend, but also shows signs that he's intending to chop down your forest and cause you difficulty.

"What did you just mumble!" snapped Mr. George.

"Gee, I just told my friends you wished them the best for this week."

At this moment trucks transporting boys from the South End of Middletown, and from Wethersfield, pulled up in the Central Lot. Brian and I, and our gangs, recognized several of them because they attended the same school or had worked for the Goodrich Farm in past summers.

A Black boy waved vigorously and laughed. "Hey, Santo! How's my cousin doing?"

"Jimmy Lewis! How the hell have you been? Haven't seen you since school let out."

"Great, man, great! I hope you have some of that pizza for me. Why don't we set up a pizza stand in town to make money, instead of picking this stupid tobacco." Everyone laughed.

The laughter stopped when Mr. Kelly stepped out of the main cabin with instructions from the superintendent about which field we will work in on this first day. He approached me. "Your guys are going to work at Four Corners so hop on that truck over there. Hope things go okay." He walked toward Brian Coleman and gave the same order. Then he approached Jimmy and his group and the gang from Wethersfield. "You guys get on that truck over there. You're going to Four Corners too." All of us jumped on the trucks. After traveling a few miles, the trucks turned off the highway onto a dirt road and slowly rumbled past fields that were ready for suckering and First Picking.

Many fields along the Connecticut River Valley made up the Goodrich Tobacco farm. Some fields were 20 to 30 yards wide and 50 yards long; others were up to 50 yards wide and more than 100 yards long. To promote the growth of tobacco plants, the temperature and humidity surrounding the plants were kept at high levels by draping white gauze, or cheese-cloth nets, about 10 feet above the ground over the entire area of the field and along the sides, where the net draped to the ground. This was accomplished by setting rows of cedar posts, about 20 feet apart, across the width and length of a field and stringing a heavy wire over the tops of the posts, over which was draped the net. Given this feature, tobacco fields looked like seas of white, stretching for miles. The technique of draping nets over the fields was the reason why the crop harvested was called "shade tobacco." And because the net sagged slightly, forming bends from one row of posts to the next row of posts, this area with its tobacco plants was called "a bend." Accordingly, fields were referred to in terms of how many bends they contained. One of the fields in the Four Corners area, for example, was called a "Twenty Bender," but another, a "Forty Bender." Another feature was particularly relevant for pickers and haulers. Under these nets, the temperature could climb well above 100 degrees by midday. In one sense, then, standing in a field was like standing in a tropical forest.

There's one more thing that persons who had never visited a tobacco farm didn't realize. Although referred to as a "row," a picker actually harvested leaves from a column of plants on his left, and also from another on his right, while sliding along on his buttocks during First Picking. Accordingly, working in a field of twenty bends was approached with some relief. But all boys experienced the task of working in a field containing forty bends especially challenging because, once a boy started picking leaves, he could not stop until he had harvested all the leaves in his "row."

The leaves we picked were used as wrappers of cigars. They

were narrow where the stem of the leaf was attached to the stalk and much broader at the center, gradually becoming narrow again toward its tip. Early in the summer, during First Picking, the two or three leaves that qualified were about fifteen inches long and eight inches wide at the center. During the following weeks the stalks gradually grew to the height of about seven feet. Now the leaves designated for Second and Third Picking were almost two feet in length and protruded from the center of the stalk. The leaves designated for Fourth and Fifth (or last) Picking protruded from the top third of the stalk and tended to be slightly smaller.

Harvesting leaves was not at all a simple task. Most persons, unless they had worked on a tobacco farm, had no idea the skill that was required. Following the traditional method, a picker scanned the plant on his left to determine which leaves qualified for the picking in question. Then he carefully placed the thumb of his left hand at the top of the stem of the leaf, close to the stalk, and with his fingertips under the stem quickly snapped off the leaf with a downward motion, simultaneously doing the same with another leaf using the thumb and fingertips of his right hand. He again scanned the plant from which he had just picked the two leaves to determine if a third leaf qualified. If there were no other leaves to pick, he turned to the plant on his right and, moving quickly but very carefully, placed each leaf he had just picked under two other leaves that also qualified. With each of these second leaves resting on top of the other leaves he had just picked, he quickly and carefully pushed downward again, snapping off these two leaves while holding them over the others with his thumbs and fingertips. If there were other leaves that qualified for picking, he placed each pair of leaves he was holding under a third leaf, and picked these leaves by pushing his thumb down against his fingertips. In this way each hand simultaneously picked two or three leaves which were then stacked together forming what was called a "butt" of four to six leaves. The butt was placed on the ground between two plants, with the stems of the leaves pointing toward the row through which the hauler pulled his basket to gather the harvested leaves.

A good, fast picker was viewed as someone who was able to pick leaves with both hands simultaneously, gracefully and rapidly. Of particular importance, a picker had to be careful not to bruise the leaves as they were being picked, or set on the ground, since a leaf was unmarketable if it was bruised, and a picker could lose a part of his wage if it was discovered that he had carelessly bruised leaves. Also, pickers always worked in pairs and were seen as "partners," each pair, therefore, picked leaves from four columns of plants.

Another detail about harvesting tobacco leaves was not familiar to most people, but for pickers was a major issue. During First Picking, because the leaves to be removed are close to the ground, a picker sat on the ground with his legs stretched forward and knees slightly bent. After harvesting leaves from plants on his left and right, he dragged his buttocks forward to the next plants so that, by the end of the day, the back of his pants was caked with a thick layer of mud. With Second and Third Pickings, since the leaves to be harvested are higher up on the stalk, the picker was able to move along on his knees where mud also collected. Only weeks later, when it was time for Fourth Picking, were pickers able to stand and walk along as they harvested leaves, which was also the case with Last Picking.

A "hauler" walked along pulling a rectangular, canvas basket down the row between the partners he was assigned to serve, usually three or four yards behind them. He dragged the basket along the ground with a cane-like metal prong called a "hauler's hook," carefully picking up the butts on his left and right, placing them in the basket, and when the basket was full, pulling it with his hook out of the field onto the road. Then he retrieved an empty basket, returned to where his pickers were continuing to work, and gathered more butts. Soon, an open truck was driven slowly along the road that bordered the field, and a man lifted these baskets onto the truck's platform, while another carefully stacked the baskets. When the load the truck could carry was completed, the truck was driven to a shed where the leaves were hung to dry.

The truck in which my gang and Brian Coleman's gang were sitting, followed by the truck transporting Jimmy Lewis' gang and the Wethersfield gang, rumbled to a stop at Four Corners. This location was given the name Four Corners because two very long, straight roads intersected here, forming four right angles, each of which defined a corner of a tobacco field that spanned several acres. The two fields on the East Side were twenty benders. One field on the West Side was a thirty bender, and the other a forty bender. When these fields were covered with white net, the entire Four Corners area looked like an endless sea.

Everyone jumped off the trucks and waited to learn in which fields they were to begin working. As the trucks departed, Mr. Kelly instructed the boys to place their lunch pails in large baskets that were set along the side of the road and called for everyone's attention. "Okay, listen. Each gang is going to take on one of the fields." He turned toward me. "Because you guys are the Fast Gang, you get the Forty Bender."

I glanced at Mr. George who was standing a short distance away and noticed a sadistic grin on his face. Turning toward my gang, I whispered under my breath, "That lousy *cafuni* (Sicilian dialect: jerk) thinks he's going to get us. We'll show him we have *coraggio* (courage)."

Mr. Kelly continued, assigning Brian Coleman's gang to the Thirty Bender, Jimmy Lewis' gang and the Wethersfield gang each to one of the Twenty Benders. "Okay! You know what to do! Take off any suckers and the leaves that made it for First Picking. "

I faced my gang and felt all stirred up, like we were about to start a football game or a boxing match. "Today, Bongi and Suggi are partners, Bart and Melo, Ancio and Sal, and Mosca and Pesci. Baggi, I want you to be Dominic's partner. But I'll make sure Dom is in a row that's near his brother."

Bongi was obviously upset. "Santo. Why can't I be my kid brother's partner?"

"I don't think that's a good idea. Dom needs to get experience working with someone else in the gang. And Tony thinks he might get nervous being his brother's partner." I pointed to Baggi, "Stick by him," and turned to my brother. "I think it would be good if you haul for Baggi and Dominic. If they need help, you can pitch in." Then I assigned haulers to each of the other partners. "Let's go guys! Let's show them we can tackle this Forty Bender!"

We all walked toward the corner where the Forty Bender began. Bart and Melo waved to Brian Coleman's gang as they walked across the road to the corner where the Thirty Bender began. Bart always liked to joke when he worked. "See you later guys. Make sure you pick only four leaf clovers." I was glad to hear several members of Brian's gang chuckling.

"And you make sure you pick only garlic," shouted Jack Kane. Now everyone laughed.

Bart waved at Jimmy Lewis' gang. "Hey, you Blackies. If you do a good job, we'll save you some pizza." Everyone laughed again.

The part of the net that hung down to the ground had already been rolled up from the road to the top of the first row of posts. In this way the field was referred to as "open" and ready for picking. We stood at the edge of the field staring at what seemed like endless, straight rows of tobacco plants. I called out to Melo and Bart. "You guys take these first rows. And Vito keep your basket close to them. We know how fast they are, so we don't want the butts to stay on the ground too long." Then I assigned each of the other pair of partners to rows. Each picker immediately sat on the ground with his legs stretched forward and slightly arched, and began to harvest leaves and remove suckers. And each hauler immediately retrieved one of the many canvas baskets lined up on the road and pulled it into the row between the two pickers he was assigned to serve.

Everyone moved quickly and gracefully, back and forth, between the plants on his left and right, everyone that is except Bongi. Although he was eager to keep up with the gang, and had become skillful, he struggled because his belly, which had become much larger this past year, pressed against his thighs, as he pushed down on the heels of his shoes to drag himself forward to the next pair of plants. "God! The ground is really muddy this morning. I can hardly drag myself ahead."

His partner, Suggi, tried not to disrupt his own rhythm. "That's because there's a lot of dew this morning, Bongi. Just put your hands down and lift your ass up a little."

Their hauler, Filippo, also helped. "Come on, Bongi, pretend you're canoeing. Just keep swinging your arms back and forth. It'll help you drag your ass forward."

I watched Bongi from a couple of rows away wondering if I should step in, but decided to see how things developed, and let Suggi and Filippo work things out. I moved from row to row, encouraging each picker and scanning the plants that had already been picked. When I returned to Bongi's row, I noticed that, he was struggling to sway gracefully from left to right, and sometimes brushed against plants and yanked off leaves. I didn't want to hurt his feelings, but I had to step in. "Hey Bongi, you're not a *sceccu* (donkey). *Più gentile*." ("Be more pleasant.") I slowly passed the tip of a leaf along his forearm. "Doesn't that feel like the tip of a baby's finger? See, *sono bambini* (they're babies)."

"Okay Santo, I'll try to be more careful. I told you guys I was worried they wouldn't hire me, because I was too fat."

I placed my hand on his head. "Come on, look how big Primo Canneri is, and look how smooth he moves around the ring in a boxing match."

Bongi sighed. "I'll keep trying, Santo, I have to, or else that bastard Mr. George is going to dock me, or fire me, for bruising plants."

As everyone expected, Bongi's younger brother, Dominic, who did not have as much experience, also had trouble keeping up. He already was almost one bend behind the rest of the gang. Following the rules of the family, I immediately began to help him. I sat down just ahead of him, picking leaves and removing suckers from the plants on his right side, so that he had only the plants on the left side to harvest. A minute later Dominic looked up at me. I was already several yards ahead. "I can't do this, Santo. You shouldn't have to help me. I feel like a *sceccu*."

Tony heard what was going on and called out, as he dragged his basket forward. "Hey, Dom. Come on, that's what a family is for. If you keep practicing, you're going to get better and better."

"Okay, I'll keep trying."

Throughout the morning Melo and Bart finished their rows ahead of everyone. Without saying a word, one of them harvested leaves and removed suckers from Dominic's row, starting at the end of the row and working toward him, while the other helped Bongi. Each member of the gang, who happened to finish his row before the others, also helped anyone lagging behind.

By late morning I heard Melo complaining, "Hey Santo! Can you come over here?"

Hearing alarm in his tone, I rushed over and noticed that, although everyone was already sweating, Melo's shirt was drenched. "What's the matter?"

"I feel sick. I'm not myself. I don't know what the hell's the matter. My head is kind of dizzy."

"Melo, I'm guessing that the temperature is more than 100 degrees. Last year this happened to you when it got really hot and muggy. Remember? And why aren't you wearing your cap? You know sun rays go right through the net."

"I hope I don't screw things up for us."

"Don't worry Melo. Tomorrow, I think you should stuff a couple of oranges in your pockets. When it gets hot, eat one, and we'll see if that helps."

Throughout this first day I noticed Mr. George passing by frequently and looking over my gang's work. This didn't surprise me given that he had made clear from the start that he did not agree with Mr. Williams making us a fast gang. Near the end of the day he called me over to a particular row. When I arrived, his eyes said 'What I'm about to tell you is going to upset you.' Mr. George pointed and barked, "Look at this plant! Do you notice anything?"

"Oh, a sucker is here." I bent over, removed it and stared at him.

"Aren't you supposed to be checking the work your gang is doing?"

"Yeah, Mr. George, I do check my gang's work. I guess I missed this sucker."

"Don't let this happen again, Santo!"

At the end of this first day, as the truck rumbled toward Middletown, I asked Brian Coleman, "Did Mr. George give you any shit today?"

" No, not really. Why?"

"Did he say anything when he came by?"

"No, he just looked at some of our rows."

My anger spilled out. "Well, he seemed to be watching us like a hawk all day long. And, for God's sake, he showed me one sucker we missed out of a million plants. Can you believe that?"

"We know he's a jerk."

"For me he's more than a jerk. He's an asshole." At that moment I felt that I was a jerk for letting Mr. George get to me. I took a deep breath and lowered my head. "Well, let's forget it. We're almost to the bridge."

During the next day, everyone in my gang continued to help Dominic, Bongi tried to be more careful, and Melo ate several oranges and said that made him feel better. Of course, Mr. George came by often to check my gang's work. That afternoon he barked at me. "Look at this, boy!"

I carefully looked over the plant. "Oh, I guess this leaf could be picked."

The same thing happened the next day. But this time, when Mr. George yelled for me, I couldn't take it anymore. As I walked over, I mumbled to myself, "*Paci nun mi nni duna mai.* ("He never lets me have a moment of peace.") Now what the hell did he notice?"

He tilted his brimmed hat to one side. "Santo, your brother Tony tipped over a basket of leaves when he hauled it onto the road. You're lucky no leaves got bruised. Your gang is not doing so hot." With his teeth clenched together he growled, "Isn't it your job to make sure your gang's doing a good job?"

I clenched my fists by my hips, looked away, and struggled to remain calm. "Yeah, that's my job."

Of course, each morning and afternoon of the next two days, Mr. George found something to criticize. Either a leaf was not picked, a sucker was not removed, or a leaf was slightly bruised, as he saw it. On Friday afternoon, which marked the time when pickers will or will not be hired for the entire summer, Mr. George confronted me once again and pointed to a leaf that qualified for First Picking that one of my gang had missed. This time I did not bend over to pick the leaf. Instead, I just stared into his eyes.

Mr. George glared at me and snarled, "Did you hear me boy! Someone in your gang missed that leaf! Your gang is supposed to be really good, but I don't think so." Standing very erect, he tilted his shoulders and head way back.

That did it for me. His posture reminded me of the Dukes and Barons in Sicily that my relatives talked about who made the peasants bow when they went by in their carriages. During the past few days, I was able to keep silent or say very little. But now I suddenly lost it. "Mr. George, when you pick that leaf, stick it up your ass."

Mr. George grinned, scribbled in his book, and stormed off. Of course he had achieved the victory he was pushing to accomplish all week, and he will certainly report what just happened to the superintendent.

Later that afternoon, trucks transported us from Four Corners to the Central Lot. When we arrived, boys who had worked in other fields were also being dropped off. Today, instead of hopping on one of the trucks parked nearby ready to take us to our respective towns, all the boys waited to learn whether they were hired for the whole summer. Mr. George walked around assigning numbers, and I hoped my gang would be included. Suddenly Mr. Kelly approached me. When he said the superintendent wanted to see me, I felt like my head was hit by a rock. As I dragged myself toward the Main Cabin, I whispered to myself, "This is it. You screwed up big time. You're not hired for the summer. And probably the whole gang won't be hired."

When I entered the Cabin, Mr. Williams was seated at his desk scanning sheets of paper. He didn't even look up. With a tone that I thought said 'it's all over,' he asked, "Explain what happened with Mr. George."

With my fists clinched by my side, I stared at Mr. Williams' forehead as he continued looking down at papers on his desk. I explained that in my opinion Mr. George seemed to be picking on me and my gang all week. To give him some idea of what I meant, I shared a few of the events that happened, like the time he spotted one sucker that had not been removed, and the time he spotted one leaf that should have been picked. I took a deep breath, glanced up at the ceiling, held my hands together, and glanced at Mr. Williams who was now staring at me. I decided I'd better own up to what happened today. "I know I did the wrong thing today when I told Mr. George to stick the leaf he spotted up his ass." I couldn't believe what happened next. A slight smile crept across Mr William's face, as he lowered his head and scanned papers.

After what felt to me like a very long minute, he raised his head and looked at me. "Santo, I know Mr. George has questions. But Mr. Kelly and I have had a chance to see your gang work the Forty Bender at Four Corners. It seems to us that you and your gang do good work. All of you are hired for the summer. But you have to control your Italian temper."

My head jerked up in surprise. I did not hear the arrogant tone that I expected, and realized that I had made a mistake when I first saw him step down from the truck on Monday morning, imagining that he was like a landowning Baron who thought he was of nobility. "Thank you, Mr. Williams. I know me and my friends will show you that we deserve to be one of the Fast Gangs." I stepped out of the office into the Central Lot, and my gang stared at me with looks on their faces that said it was all over. Eager to give them the news, I quickly walked toward them and gave them a message, using an age-old gesture. I extended my arms with the palms of my hands turned upward. "*Ancora, semu di la stissa caccociula.*" ("We are still of the same artichoke.") With relief everyone in the gang stood up on their toes, clenched their fists, and pushed their arms out.

At that moment Mr. Williams stepped out of his cabin and approached Mr. George, pointing in our direction. Mr. George walked over, and with a tone of disgust, assigned me a number. "Santo, keep in mind I expect fast gangs to pick at least 150 bends a day. That's the least. So we'll soon find out if your friends can do it."

By now I had collected myself and responded with a very

friendly tone, enjoying the opportunity to convey that I won the first round. "Thank you, Mr. George, I'm sure we can." Each member of my gang grinned, or made a comment with the same tone of exaggerated friendliness, when he was assigned a number.

Sitting close together on the truck as we rumbled back home, my gang chatted, joked, and then burst out singing an ancient Sicilian folk song: "*C'è la luna nmezz'u mari*" ("There is a moon above the sea.") When we finished the song, Brian Coleman turned to me. "I've always liked that song you Guineas sing, and I'm glad you and your guys made it." When the truck reached the area under the bridge, everyone jumped off and scampered toward their neighborhoods.

My friends and I walked along the Connecticut River toward our neighborhood. I raised my arm to get everyone's attention. "Even though Mr. George gave us a lot of trouble, we showed we could do it."

Tony placed his hand on my shoulder. "Maybe because we're the new fast gang, he was testing us to see if we have what it takes."

"Tony has a point there," Bart added. "And, I think we passed this week's test."

Louie made a fist. "Don't kid yourself. I think we're going to get a lot more from that jerk."

"Well, I know he's going to try to get me." Bongi gasped, tugging on the rope around his waist. "He's going to say I bruised a lot of leaves because I'm like a bull charging down those rows."

At this point we reached the foot of Green Street which was located about twenty five yards from the bank of the Connecticut River. Bart stopped and stretched his arm towards the river. "Never mind that jerk, Mr. George. Look! When the sun is setting, I always feel fantastic. It's like a gigantic red sheet hanging from a clothes line stretched across the sky." Everyone paused and stared at the sun. The bottom edge was dipping behind shrubs on the other side of the river.

Vito turned away from the sunset and looked up at the tenement houses that lined each side of Green Street. "It is a beautiful sunset. But I have to get home."

"Me too," Angelo added.

Musca pushed his arm out, pointing. "Hey! There's my mother buying fish from Nino, the-Fish-Man. Boy does he yell."

Mr. Amenta, who was called the-Fish-Man, had parked his truck near the foot of Green Street and the corner of Rapallo Avenue. While waiting on Musca's mother, who had come outside to purchase fresh fish, he repeatedly yelled, "*Pesci! Pesci!*" (fish) "*Mirruzzu! Mirruzzu!*" (cod) "*Calamari! Calamari!*" (squid) and the names of other items on his truck. He always continued screaming to inform everyone on the street that he had arrived and was ready to serve them.

"I'd better run home and make sure my mother knows the Fish-Man is here!" Pesci exclaimed. "I'd love to see what he's selling today."

Bart grinned. "Well hurry up, Pesci. After all, you're the fish. Maybe he'll sell you." Everyone laughed.

Vito, Angelo, Musca and Pesci began walking toward Green Street. Vito turned around and waved. "Maybe we'll connect tonight." Then he looked up at the sky. "But I'm not sure. From the look of those clouds coming in over there, it seems like it might rain."

"Let's see, Vito," Tony called back. The rest of us continued walking toward the foot of Ferry Street which was the next street over and very close.

Like Green Street, Ferry Street was also narrow. On each side were tenement houses three or four stories high. Some of these buildings were of red brick and others of wood painted dark brown or green. Although the sun was setting for the day, heat was still trapped between the buildings and radiating from the narrow paved road. At this time of day, as usual, several men were sitting in chairs set up on the sidewalk, chatting while waiting for dinner. Clusters of children were also talking and joking while sitting on the street curb.

A tower of three or four decks was located at the back of each building. At least two clotheslines stretched from each deck to a pole some distance away. A wide variety of items hung from each clothesline and flapped in the breeze: table cloths, bed sheets, towels, overalls, dark blue pants and shirts, dresses and blouses of different colors, underwear and socks. The patch of ground behind each building was too small for vegetable gardens, with only a couple of exceptions. Because of this, the immigrants kept gardens along the river where they grew tomatoes, peppers, eggplants, basil and parsley.

As we walked up Ferry Street, Melo smiled and pointed. "Hey, there's my uncle. He's at it again."

Mr. Giuliano was sitting on the steps that led into Mr. Biagio's butcher shop located on the first floor of a three story, tenement house. With his head hanging low, he was strumming his mandolin and humming.

"Hey, *Zio!*" ("Uncle!")

Mr. Giuliano looked up, nodded, smiled, and continued playing.

Melo grinned with pride. "One of these days I'm going to learn to play that." Suddenly he burst out laughing and pushed his arm out, pointing at the large window above his uncle's head. "But when I do get to play a mandolin, I hope I have a better audience than that." Melo was pointing at the freshly butchered products Mr. Biagio always hung from a board that strung across the large window of the shop, announcing what was for sale. "Today a pig's head, five chickens, a long rack of pork chops, and four big Genoa salamis are watching my uncle play!"

Bart grabbed Melo's shoulders with one hand and stretched out his other arm, pointing. "Look!" Everyone paused and turned. "Ok! Melo's uncle is playing the mandolin in front of a pig and chickens, but look at what my father is doing again."

Mr. Marino, Bart's father, was carefully sweeping the sidewalk in front of the next tenement house with a large straw broom. In Southern Italian homes, especially in Sicilian homes, everything was kept as clean as possible. Cleanliness was the symbol of a solid family, and for these immigrants, the sidewalk was included. Each day, therefore, several women and men could be seen sweeping sidewalks and picking up any pieces of paper that happened to collect along the curb.

"Hey, Papa!" Bart called out. "I said I would do that before we ate."

Mr. Marino stopped sweeping, looked up and smiled. "*Ciao, figghiu miu.*" ("Greetings, my son.") Holding the handle of the broom in one hand, he quickly walked over, hugged Bart, turned around and continued sweeping.

We paused before the tenement house where Bart lived. "Maybe we can hang out for a little while after dinner," Melo remarked. He looked up at the sky. "But like Vito said, we may get one of those summer rain storms."

Bart scanned the clouds overhead. "If it does rain, what if we meet at the pool hall for an hour or so and just hang out and celebrate? After all we're the fast gang."

Melo slapped Bart's arm. "That's a good idea, don't you think? Today's Friday, so maybe there'll be some action tonight. Do you think your cousin, Smiles, might be there, Tony?"

"I don't know, but it's possible. Anyway if it's raining, let's check out what's happening there. Everyone bring at least a dime in case there's something to bet about."

Dominic took a quick step toward Tony with a look of concern. "I don't know if my parents will let me stay out too late."

His brother Bongi snapped back. "Dom, it's Friday. I think they'll let you go with us for a little while. If they don't, they don't."

"We better get going," I called out. "Isn't anyone hungry?"

Tony chuckled. "*Sugnu affamatu.* (I'm starving.) If it's raining, we'll connect at the pool hall. If it isn't we'll meet at our hangout by Vinci's Bakery." The group spread out, and everyone walked toward the tenement house where they lived.

Tony and I entered an alleyway that separated two buildings and led to the back entrance of the first floor apartment where our family lived. We opened the screen door and entered the kitchen. Every time we stepped in, we were touched by the wonder of what surrounded us. Our mother, Giuseppina, was standing to the left facing a large black, wood burning, cast iron stove. Her dark wavy hair bobbed when she turned her head and smiled, greeting us. As usual, she wore a dark print dress that reached inches from the floor and a braided necklace she had brought with her from Sicily years ago. Her oval face, decorated with dark, large, bright eyes, full lips and warm smile, regularly invited family members, relatives and neighbors to interact with her. In terms of Sicilian standards, Mamma was of average height. But in terms of standards in the United States, she was relatively short, only about five feet tall. She was frying and slowly stirring, in an open pan, pieces of prosciutto, and thinly sliced onions, crushed tomatoes, and freshly grated Romano cheese, all floating in olive oil. The aroma of this delicious topping for pasta, and the aroma of freshly baked loaves of bread recently removed from the oven, filled the room.

Tony and I loved our kitchen. From the entrance to the other side, five, dark, wooden beams stretched across the white ceiling. And as usual, the rough, plaster walls had been washed clean. Above the stove, and along the entire length of the left wall, stretched a thick, wooden shelf on which were stacked pots, pans, glass bowls, dishes, glasses, and silverware. Straight ahead, at the far end of the kitchen, and to the left of the door leading into our parents' bedroom, hung a large, mechanical clock housed in an ornately carved wooden cabinet. Its pendulum swayed rhythmically to the left and right, and a steady, soft-ticking sound seeped out of the cabinet. To the right side of this door stood another tall, wooden cabinet. The top contained a Victrola, where phonograph records by Enrico Caruso were played almost every night. Beneath the Victrola was a large radio. On the right hand wall were three doorways. The one farthest away led into the bedroom shared by our sisters, the next led into the bathroom, and the one nearest the entrance to the kitchen led into the bedroom Tony and I shared with our younger brother.

A long wooden table was set in the center. The backs of each chair surrounding it displayed a column of overlapping diamonds that had been carved by our mother's brother. He also had carved the legs of the table which looked like miniature Doric columns of a Greek temple. The table was covered with a white cloth Mamma had woven with the needle point technique which was her favorite pastime, whenever she had a half hour or so to relax. As usual, appetizers had already been placed on it for everyone to nibble on before dinner. A bowl filled with pieces of oranges sprinkled with red wine and crushed garlic was set next to a plate of sardines. Another plate was filled with pieces of homemade bread dipped in olive oil.

Tony burst out, "Guess what? We and our buddies were hired to be a Fast Gang! And Santo is the strawboss!"

Mamma turned away from the stove, and exclaimed with emotion, "*Maronna*!" (Dialect for Madonna, the Virgin Mary). This expression was the Southern Italian way of declaring that something deserved special attention.

At the same time our sister, Filomena, who was setting the table, paused and threw her arms around Tony and me. Filomena was eighteen years old, and the same height as Mamma. Her sparkling dark eyes, broad smile, jet black hair that hung just above her shoulders, and the dress printed with flowers that covered her slim legs and hips, all together made an attractive picture typical of Southern Italian women. She was home for the summer from Teachers College.

Teodoro, who was eleven, and short for his age even in terms of Sicilian standards, said, "Oh really," with a tone that I thought expressed a mixture of congratulations and jealousy over the victory of his brothers. He had mentioned several times that he wanted to try to get a summer job at the Goodrich Farm, but preferred to hang around at a neighborhood garage because he was fascinated by anything mechanical from washing machines to cars. As a matter of fact, a few weeks ago he repaired the engine of the washing machine in the apartment on the second floor. Because of this talent, Papa decided that by watching and getting tools for mechanics who worked in a nearby garage, Teodoro could learn a lot that would serve him in the future.

Gloria, another sister, who was sixteen, looked very much like Filomena, almost like a twin sister. She was busy making cake batter in a large bowl.

"What are you doing?" Tony asked.

"I'm making another marble cake," Gloria answered with pride.

"That's good. If you keep making those marble cakes, we could build another Coliseum with them."

Gloria stopped twirling the spoon in the bowl and glared at

Tony. "Very funny, maybe you won't get a piece for dessert." Then she smiled with a sense of victory. "And by the way, *Picchi nun ti vai a cercari n'atra casa?*" ("Why don't you find another house to stay in?")

Just then the door opened. Anna, who was almost twenty years old, entered the kitchen, returning home from her new job in a bakery. Upon hearing the news, she congratulated me and Tony with a hug. Anna was also slender and carried that attractive Mediterranean look, but was a couple of inches taller than her sisters. Moreover, her smile was broader, and the tone of her voice louder and more raspy.

Mamma asked Anna, "*Com'è la giobba?*" ("How is the 'job'?") Sicilian immigrants had translated a number of English words into their dialect: the word for job became *giobba*; for car, *carru*; for store, *storu*; for the toilet or backhouse behind the tenement house, *baccausu*.

"Really good. I brought a bag of some of the biscotti."

At that moment, our father, Sebastiano, arrived from his job operating a weaving loam at a local textile mill. Noticing extra commotion in the kitchen, he asked what was going on. When he heard the news, he hugged Tony and me and kissed each of us on the cheek. Papa stood only about five feet six inches tall which was average for Sicilians. But his very broad shoulders, muscular arms, and soft, raspy voice expressed confidence and power in a quiet way.

Mamma grinned, walked over and kissed Papa. Then she stepped toward the long wooden table, raised her arms with palms turned upwards, inviting everyone to be seated. "*E' ura di mangiari.*" ("It's time to eat.") Her tone and gesture expressed the view of Mediterranean people that sharing food and interacting during dinner was the cord that tied family members together.

Papa placed a record in the Victrola, turned it on, and the soft voice of Enrico Caruso filled the kitchen. Everyone took their usual seats, an arrangement that had become one of the family's rituals. Papa sat at one end of the table and Mamma at the other end. The girls sat on one side of the table, on Mamma's right and Papa's left. Anna, the oldest sat next to Mamma, Filomena sat in the center, and Gloria, the youngest, sat next to Papa's left. The boys sat at the opposite side of the table, Tony, the oldest, sat next to Papa, I in the center, and Teodoro on Mamma's left.

Following another family ritual, Papa scanned a row of eight glasses that had been lined up on his end of the table, one glass for each member of the family. He always began with the glass assigned to Teodoro, the youngest member of the family. As if he were beginning a ceremony, Papa carefully positioned the glass, extended the index finger of his left hand, and placed it flat on the tabletop against the side of the glass. At the same time, he took a pitcher filled with homemade wine with his other hand and, with an air of ceremony, carefully dribbled wine into the glass until the level reached the top of his finger. He passed the glass to Tony who handed it to me, and I handed it to Teodoro.

Then Papa took the next glass which was mine. Because I was older, he set his index finger on its side against the glass, rather than placing it flat on the tabletop, and poured wine to the top level of his finger. He filled Tony's glass to that same level, but added two very small splashes of wine because Tony was slightly older than I was. Tony, however, did not yet qualify for two fingers of wine. But this was the case with the next glass which was Gloria's. Papa carefully held his index finger and middle finger together, placed them against the glass with his middle finger against the table top, and poured wine to that level. With the fifth and sixth glasses, Filomena's and Anna's, he placed three fingers against the side of the glass. In this family, when you reached your seventeenth birthday, you graduated to having three fingers of wine at dinner. Last, he poured wine into Mamma's glass and his, without measuring the level with fingers.

After the wine had been distributed, another family ritual, always took place at the start of dinner. Papa reached out with his right hand, took hold of Tony's left hand, and reached out with his left hand to take hold of Gloria's right hand. At the same time, Mamma took hold of Anna's right hand and Teodoro's left hand, while Filomena and I took hold of the hands of those sitting at our sides. For a few seconds we held hands, forming a circle around the table, and whispered, "*Famigghia*" (Sicilian dialect for family). Now the entire family began talking, laughing and feasting on lentil soup, pasta with tomato sauce, and a tomato and escarole salad.

Toward the end of every meal something playful usually

happened. The roots of the games we invented were located in interactions each of us experienced with Mamma during early childhood. Near the close of this meal, Anna smiled and turned to Mamma. "Remember when Filomena, Gloria and me were kids, and you played games that challenged us to figure things out?"

Gloria interrupted. "One of my favorites, Ma, was when you filled a pan with some water. Remember how you set three or four empty pans of different sizes next to it, and asked us to pick which pan the water would fit in."

Filomena began laughing. "I know that was your favorite, Gloria. But once what happened was hilarious. I don't remember how old you were. You pointed to a pan. Anna and I said we thought you picked the wrong one. But you insisted the water could fit. Remember? We got in an argument. To prove you were right, you poured the water in the pan that you picked, and it spilled all over the floor."

Mamma reached out and touched Gloria's arm. "*Non era male*" ("That wasn't bad").

Embarrassed, Gloria looked down at her plate. "I guess I screwed up that time. But I was good at the hide-and-seek spoon game. I could figure out a lot of Mom's hiding places." Years ago while preparing dinner, another game Mamma played involved hiding spoons throughout the apartment. My sisters searched for them, competing to see who found the most spoons.

Tony slapped the table. "Oh, you girls are all about cooking and pots and pans. How about the game when Santo, Teodoro and me played that we were fish trying to get a bite of the biscottu that Mamma tied at the end of a long string." Another game our mother played years ago involved only my brothers and me. She sat on the steps at the back of the tenement house holding a long piece of string on the end of which she had tied a homemade biscotti cookie. Crawling around on the ground a couple feet below from where she was sitting, we pretended we were fish swimming in the ocean, as Mamma playfully jiggled the line and each of us took a bite of the cookie.

Clearly annoyed because she had been interrupted, Anna tapped her fingers on the table. "Alright, I remember the water game, and the spoon game. But what I just asked Mamma was to remember the game she played with us that challenged us to figure things out." Anna smiled, slowly turned, and looked at Mamma with an expression that combined affection and challenge. "I know when you were a kid, Ma, a school was finally set up in your village, and all of you kids were supposed to go to school. But you told us the parents refused, and none of the kids went."

Anna was referring to a moment in Italian history that became a landmark. In 1877, seven years after Italy became a unified nation, once the Papal State finally decided to include itself, the government, which was dominated by the politics of the North, passed a law that made formal education compulsory for all children between the ages of six and nine years. This law was strongly resisted in Southern Italy, especially Sicily. To cope with the many invaders who had occupied Sicily over the centuries, Sicilians developed the custom of protecting their own culture, namely the family, by keeping the influence of *stranieri* (strangers) at a distance. Sicilians who were already experiencing other conflicts with the politics of Northern nationalists, therefore, felt that the law of compulsory education was an attempt by this new government to erase *la via vecchia* (the old way), that is the Sicilian way of life and its rules of the family. Sicilians believed the new government would accomplish this goal if it could successfully influence children over a couple of generations while they attended school. I heard that in some villages the resistance to this new law of compulsory education was so great the *contadini* (peasants) rioted and school houses were destroyed.

Anna continued. "What I want to do, Ma, is show you a puzzle I found in a store." With a dramatic flair she flopped, on the table, two long nails twisted together like pretzels. She thrust her shoulders back and commented in a challenging tone, "Ma, even though you didn't go to school, let's see if you can do this. Look, if you twist these two nails around in the right way, you can take them apart. It took me a while, but I did it." Anna laughed, "See, Ma, we learn in school how to work out tough problems. I bet you can't untangle these."

Mamma studied the nails for about a minute while everyone watched in silence and with intense interest. Then she picked up the nails, holding the head of each one with the thumb and forefinger of each hand. After a few quick twists and turns of her wrists, she held up the pretzeled nails each freed from the other. A broad grin of pride spread across her face while she dangled the separated nails over her head. As we cheered, Papa asked us to notice that there is a solution for every *imbrogliu* (tangle).

The mention of tangles in life immediately reminded me of what happened this week with Mr. George. Tony and I exchanged glances, and then he blurted out, "Taking those nails apart is nothing compared to the *imbrogliu* Santo and us guys had to deal with all this week at the farm!"

"*Ch'è successu, figghiu miu?*" ("What happened, my son?") Papa asked. "*Si po' sapiri chi ti fa smaniari? Dimmi.*" ("Can we find out why you're upset? Tell me.")

Anna slid her arms across the table toward me. "Santo, I know sometimes you look like you're thinking about really deep stuff. But right now you look like something is worrying you a lot."

I glanced at Anna and then looked into Papa's eyes. Almost whispering, I described several incidents that occurred during the week to show how Mr. George seemed to be picking on me and my gang.

Tony interrupted, "I think he's trying to get all of us fired."

Everyone looked at me with expressions of concern and support, and that made me feel good. Without thinking, I immediately shared today's event, and admitted I was ashamed of myself, when I told Mr. George to stick the leaf he spotted up his ass.

Now, instead of looking at me with concern Papa glared at me, pressed his lips together, and commented with an angry edge. "*Tu sbagghiasti, figghiu miu.*" ("You made a mistake my son.")

Tony dared to interrupt. "Papa, Santo didn't make a mistake. This Mr. George is an asshole. *Ma chi dici, Papa, ca semu stunati?*" ("But what are you saying, Papa, that we're stupid?")

I looked at Tony, tried to convey that I disagreed with what he just said, and turned to Papa. "I know that was stupid of me. *Chi puteva fari?* ("What could I do?") The guy gave me no choice. I could only take so much."

Papa reached out, placed his hand on my wrist, glanced at everyone and said, "We need-a talk-a about *la famigghia* and *omertà* (family and patience)."

Filomena was always turned on by topics that had to do with

customs and pushed her hand out. "Papa, I know you don't mean *omertà* like the newspapers say when a gangster keeps a code of silence and won't squeal on anyone."

Glancing at Filomena, and then at each of us, he slowly folded his hands on the table, commenting in a very soft tone, "*Sì, Sì.*" (Yes). Everyone sat back and stared at him since we understood he wanted to get into a discussion, especially about Sicilian history which he enjoyed very much. Speaking as usual with a mixture of broken English and Sicilian dialect, he agreed with Filomena that people in the United States think *omertà* is only about gangsters. He emphasized that to understand what *omertà* really means to Sicilian peasants, people need to remind themselves of particular parts of Sicilian history. With his hands still folded, he reviewed details we had heard before many times. For hundreds of years the peasants of Sicily had to deal with different foreign groups that invaded the island: Phoenicians, Greeks, Romans, Vandals, Arabs, Normans, French and Spaniards. While most of these groups exploited and oppressed the peasants, many believed that when Spanish rulers occupied the island, beginning in the 1500's, they started the darkest time for Sicilians that lasted almost three hundred years.

Now Papa placed his hands on the table with palms turned upward which meant something like, "wait until you hear the next thing, you won't believe it." He went on to explain that, even before Giuseppe Garibaldi defeated these Spanish rulers in 1861, there had been a ray of hope for Sicilians. A congress met in Vienna in 1814 and legally ended the feudal system, dividing Italy into eight provinces. Each province, however, except Piedmont in northern Italy, was ruled by a different country. And what shattered the hope of Sicilians was that the Bourbon dynasty of Spain was allowed to continue ruling southern Italy and Sicily. Although Sicilian peasants were now supposed to be free legally from the tyranny of feudal lords, this turned out not to be the case. Papa paused, frowned and added that the peasants were still in a very difficult situation. They had no tools, and especially no land, because all the land was still owned by absent *latifundisti* (rich land owners) most of whom were from Spain. This Bourbon dynasty ruled what was called the Kingdom of the Two Sicilies from its capital in Naples. One reason why this period of time became very dark for Sicily was the fact that the government appointed Viceroys to govern the island. Each Viceroy ruled for only three or four years, and answered only to the Monarch who was on the throne in Naples.

Tony couldn't hold himself back. "Wow! Every time I hear this it reminds me that the *contadini* (peasants) had to put up with many bosses. And each one of these bosses had his own axe to grind."

Papa nodded and added that from the 1500's until the Bourbons were defeated by Garibaldi, more than sixty of these Viceroys had ruled the island. Since all of them were selected from noble families in Spain, they were concerned mostly with preserving their privileges of royalty, keeping the island calm, and collecting as much tax as possible from the Sicilian people. Eventually the office of Viceroy developed the reputation of being one of the best paying positions in the Spanish service.

Papa raised his right arm, pointed at me and continued, emphasizing if I thought Mr. George was being oppressive and unfair, I should keep a few things in mind that the Bourbons did to Sicilians. For example, if a Viceroy rode by in his wagon, the peasants along the road were expected to bow. What the peasants found even more ridiculous was the fact that they had to pay taxes if they owned a mule, which was the peasant's lifeline. Cows, on the other hand, which were usually the property of landowners, were not taxed.

I couldn't hold myself back and interrupted, throwing out my hand. "God, Papa, I thought I had it tough with Mr. George. Every time I hear this history I realize that what my gang put up with is nothing compared to what our ancestors had to put up with."

"How did our ancestors survive, dealing with all this shit?" Teodoro asked. "Besides I don't know how, after your parents got killed, you and your brothers and sisters made it."

Sadness poured out of Papa's dark eyes. He took a long look at Teodoro, glanced at the rest of the family and sighed. Teodoro's question, he pointed out, takes all of us back to what he meant when he said we all need to talk about family and *omertà* if we want to learn how to deal with someone like Mr. George. "My brothers and sisters and the *contadini* (Sicilian peasants) survived, and shaped who they were, by developing a custom that declared there was only one social reality. That world was *la famigghia*" (family). We already knew what Papa added. The family, he explained, meant not only the mother, father, brothers and sisters, but also *cugini* (blood relatives). In addition, peasants developed a system of *comparaggio* (Godparenthood) which extended the family by carefully selecting for each child a *compare* (Godfather) and *comare* (Godmother) who were also viewed as important members of the family. The peasants survived, he emphasized, not only because they made the family their country, but also because they followed the rules of the family (*l'ordine della famiglia*). And one of those rules was *omertà*.

"Papa, what are all of these rules about, anyway?" Teodoro asked.

Gloria glanced at Mamma and then Papa, asking for permission to answer Teodoro's question. "I know them by heart, Teodoro. I'm sure you've heard everyone talk about one or another of them."

Filomena interrupted. "Gloria, may I please explain the rules to Teodoro?"

Gloria frowned. "Of course, Filomena, you're the teacher."

Gloria and Filomena stared at Papa. Looking at Gloria, he nodded in Filomena's direction, and Gloria understood he had made a decision. "Okay, Filomena, that would be good. You really know a lot about all of this."

Filomena turned to Gloria. "Thanks. I realize I get worked up when we're into discussions like this." She focused on Teodoro. "One rule is that you have to be loyal to the family. I'll bet you'll recognize the words of the other rules that you might have heard the grownups discussing. There's the rule of *onore*. You must honor the family. There's the rule of *rispetto*. You must respect everyone in the family. There's the rule of *serietà*. You must be committed to the family. And there's the rule of *omertà*. You must be patient and have self- control."

Papa thanked Filomena and added that although these rules were never written down, they were discussed often in family gatherings, as Gloria and Filomena just mentioned. And, of course, these rules made clear that the family is the center.

Anna smiled, deciding to step into the discussion. "So now,

Teodoro, it's my turn to share what I think these rules are all about. If you lace these rules together, you can see that they ask every member of the family to stay connected with the family and to keep trying to do what could help it, no matter what the price."

Since Anna inserted herself, Gloria stepped in with enthusiasm. "Now I want to have a turn. You can see, Teodoro, these rules are supposed to guide the way each family member relates to other family members, and make clear what each family member is responsible for. Like did you notice, Filomena interrupted me and asked if she could explain the rules?"

"I noticed that."

Tony immediately added. "Me too."

"But I noticed that you seemed upset," Teodoro continued. "And you and Filomena both looked at Mamma, and Papa, to find out who can keep talking about the rules."

Papa raised the palms of his hands, pleased that we noticed what happened a few minutes ago. What we are talking about now, he emphasized, relates to the fact that Sicilian peasants saw the mother as the center of the family and the father as the head. If there were disagreements between persons in a family, the father decided how to settle it. And if there were disagreements between people in different families, the father of each family had a discussion and solved the problem. When they couldn't, they would go to the *Capo* of the village or neighborhood who everyone accepted as the leader. The *ordine della famiglia*, he reminded us, was brought pretty much unchanged to the United States by all the immigrants from Sicily.

Almost shouting, Teodoro called out, "Papa, all of this reminds me of what happened last week. Remember when I was playing marbles with Vito's little brother, Roberto? And Gino walked by and kicked our marbles all over the street. Roberto started screaming."

What Teodoro just recalled caused me to feel a surge of embarrassment. "And I almost hit Gino. I couldn't control myself when I saw him picking on you."

"I'm glad I was with Bart across the street, and I stopped you," Tony commented. "Roberto's father must have heard him screaming because he came running outside and got into a big argument with Gino's father."

Gloria added, "That Gino can really be a *testa dura* (hard head) sometimes."

"You're right!" Tony barked. "He always thinks he's joking when he does something like that, but he really gets out of hand."

Teodoro stepped in again. "Well, like I said, what Papa was just talking about reminded me of what happened. Roberto's father and Gino's father got a hold of Papa, and they got into some kind of heavy discussion over there near Joe-the-Jew's store."

"I heard some of it," Gloria commented. "I heard Papa telling Gino's father he's got to do more to help Gino have respect for other kids, especially kids littler than him."

Papa looked at Teodoro, grinned and thanked him because what he just remembered is a good example of what the rules of the family are all about. Then Papa starred at Tony and me, pointing out that now we can talk about the family rule that's especially relevant for how we should deal with Mr. George. This rule, he emphasized, which helped the peasants keep their culture alive while they were invaded time after time, is called *omertà*. Papa turned his head a little and looked at Teodoro. "What did Filomena say that *omertà* means?"

"She said it means having patience and controlling yourself."

Papa nodded, smiled and added that we can see why *omertà*, in particular, helped peasants deal with persons who abused them with their power. He elaborated that when the person in power was taking advantage of a peasant, or his family or friends, in ways that were clearly disgusting and disrespectful, it was important that the person stomach the insult, and wait for the right moment to get the justice and respect he deserves. For Sicilians, then, Papa emphasized, *omertà* became the ideal of manliness. But this ideal had nothing to do with what the Spanish called machismo, or Americans called a really tough guy. It had to do with the person being strong enough to wait and plan for the best time to say or do what the person should say, or do, that protects family and friends, and insures the respect and security they deserve.

Anna grinned in a way that said she had something special to say. "I heard Uncle Gaetano say that you guys call the person who can do this *uomo di panza* (a man of the belly) and *uomo di pazienza* (a man of patience)."

Papa smiled and nodded in appreciation. "When someone is insulting you and taking advantage of you, don't give this enemy more ammunition by getting scared or by getting mad. You look the other way. You keep reminding yourself that the right time will come when you have your turn to protect your respect, and your family's. So another way we call this person," he added, "*is un uomo che pensa alla sua casa*" (a man who knows how to keep in mind what his family and home need).

Papa summarized that in Sicily the people and their culture survived because they kept the family as the center, and because everyone tried to follow the rules of the family that came from that center. He grinned, looked again into the eyes of each of us, spread open the palm of his right hand, and placed it over his stomach. "Now everyone can understand," he continued, "why the family is so important in Sicilian culture, and if a person has no family attachments, Sicilians call that person '*un saccu vacanti*' (an empty sac) and '*un nuddu miscatu cu nenti*' (a nobody mixed with nothing)." He also reminded us that if we looked around, we will notice that these family rules, which evolved over the centuries, have been extended into groups of friends and gangs. And if we wonder what friends who are not Sicilian think about all this, it may help to keep in mind that "*L'ordine della famiglia è omertà, nun è di tutti lu capiri.*" ("The rules of the family and *omertà* are not for everyone to understand.")

Papa paused, turned to me and slowly slid his hand over the table in my direction. "Now do you understand that you did not use *omertà* enough when you told Mr. George to stick the leaf up his ass? I agree he's *veramenti nu svergognatu, sfacciatu e sguaiatu* (really shameless, brazen and rotten). But you must try to use *omertà* to protect the respect you and your friends deserve. I'm sure if you hold his *merda* (shit) in your *panza* (belly) you will eventually have your turn to pay him back. And if you find yourself losing your *omertà*, there is something you can do that might help." Papa demonstrated something we all knew. He stood up, clinched his right fist and bit the knuckle of his index finger, pointing out that this helps to get some of the anger out, but *cu silenziu* (with silence).

Tony was really turned on. "Papa! I did that a lot last year when that High School teacher I told you about was really on me all the time. Everybody knew he hated Italians, Germans and Japanese because of the war."

Gloria reached across the table. "Tony, I remember you really had to work hard to handle all that stuff that teacher gave you guys without losing your *pazienza*. You and your buddies stomached a lot. You really stuck it out and ..."

"You know what?" Teodoro yelled before Gloria finished what she had to say. "I finally understand what Tony was telling me last week at the feast about the guys trying to catch the pig. They were dealing with the impossible and had to have a lot of patience."

Anna slapped the top of the table. "That's right Teodoro. That's what that pig game is all about at the Feast of Saint Sebastian. It's putting up with the impossible until you finally win."

Filomena pointed to the window. "Hey! Look everybody! It just started to rain!" A heavy shower, typical of early summer, was pouring down. "Remember how it began to rain just when the guys were trying to catch the pig last week."

I burst out laughing as the whole event flashed through my mind. " Can you imagine that? The pig was already covered with oil, and then it got covered with water. Talk about dealing with the impossible and not giving up.""That really was hilarious watching those guys trying to catch that *porcu* (pig) in the rain," Anna squealed as we all continued laughing. "It kept slipping away, but the guys stuck with it. It took them a lot longer this year to catch it."

We were referring to one part of the annual celebration of the feast of Saint Sebastian that takes place in our community on the third weekend of May. Saint Sebastian had been a Captain in the Pretorian Guard of the Roman Army during the reign of Emperor Diocletian. He was also a devoted follower of the teachings of Christ. Because Emperor Diocletian persecuted anyone who followed the Christian religion, Sebastian secretly practiced his faith. More than that, he decided to take on the dangerous task of visiting Christians in prison, and encouraging them not to give up their faith in Christ, even in the face of torture and death. Imperial investigators eventually discovered what Sebastian was doing. Although he now faced threats of torture and death, he refused to deny his Christian faith. As a result he was tied to a tree and shot to death with arrows.

According to history, in 1414 a ship crashed on the Eastern coast of Sicily very near the location of the village from which my parents and other parents in this neighborhood had emigrated. In the wreckage that washed ashore was a chest containing a statue of Saint Sebastian. The villagers experienced the arrival of the statue as a divine message and, therefore, developed their own way of maintaining a commitment to the Church, in spite of the animosity that had mounted between the people of Southern Italy and the Catholic Church. This animosity related to the fact that the Church allied itself with landowners who exploited the peasants, and also owned large estates of land until Italy became unified in 1870. In addition, many clergy in the upper hierarchy were related to aristocratic families who owned vast estates. For these various reasons, the peasants of Sicily viewed the Church as another world-wide aristocracy, so they tried to keep customs of family and family rules at a distance from the power of the Church.

The peasants of the village from which my parents emigrated kept a distance from the church but also maintained a commitment by declaring Saint Sebastian the patron saint of the village, and the third Sunday of May as his feast day, because the statue was discovered on that day. They also developed their own customs and rituals to celebrate, eventually building a church near the site where the statue was discovered. Several hundred years later, Mr. Marchese was among the first peasants from this village to immigrate to the United States and help establish the Sicilian neighborhood located in Middletown along the Connecticut River. A few years after arriving, he sculpted a replica of the statue of Saint Sebastian, which the immigrants had left behind in their village in Sicily, depicting him tied to a tree with arrows stuck to his chest. Each year, during the feast day, the statue Mr. Marchese sculpted was carried aloft through the streets of the neighborhood, and immigrants pinned paper money on ribbons that were draped over the statue, or placed coins at its feet. With the money collected over several years, the immigrants purchased material needed to build their own church in honor of Saint Sebastian. Local Sicilian stone and tile masons, brick layers, carpenters, painters and laborers donated their time and skill. By 1935 they completed the construction of the church which, stone for stone, was nearly a replica of the church they left behind in their village.

Sicilians who had immigrated to Middletown also replicated events that had taken place for centuries to celebrate the feast of Saint Sebastian. One event is called "I Nuri" (The running nudes). Before sunrise parents and children, holding lighted candles, slowly walked to the church. In ancient times this part of the celebration involved each father carrying a son on his shoulders toward the church, or having a son walk along side. The father and child did not wear clothing because, according to legend, Saint Sebastian was nude when he was tied to a tree and shot with arrows. At the turn of the twentieth century, most fathers and sons who participated in this event began to wear some clothing, and mothers and daughters joined in, walking toward the church holding candles.

With another event that started about noontime, the statue of Saint Sebastian is carried through the streets for everyone to worship, accompanied by a marching band of musicians from the neighborhood. During the afternoon, the celebrating continues in an open area by the shore of the Connecticut River where stands are set up to serve traditional foods, such as *cuddurunu* (a Sicilian style pizza topped with broccoli or potato), *calamari* (squid), *arancini* (deep fried rice balls stuffed with peas and tomato sauce), *capocollo, mortadella* (salami), sasizza (grilled sausage), *sfingi* (crispy balls of dough fried in olive oil and dipped in honey), gelato, and various Sicilian cookies.

The event Teodoro mentioned with excitement involves men competing to catch a pig which takes place late afternoon. Several of the immigrants maintained small farms just outside of town, and each year one of them agrees to transport a pig by truck to the area where the celebration takes place. When it is time for this particular event, the pig is covered with olive oil and released. About fifteen or twenty young men volunteer to chase after the pig to see who could catch it. Whoever catches the pig, and holds it in his arms for at least half a minute, is declared the winner and celebrated as a hero.

Last week, several minutes after the pig was released, it began to rain. This time the pig was not only covered with olive oil but also with water, a combination that resulted in the pig being very slippery. Each time one of the young men caught the pig and tried to hold it in his arms, the pig slipped away in a matter of seconds. The crowd roared with laughter, cheering the pig on. Of course, each time the pig was caught and held for a few seconds, some of the oil and water on its body rubbed off onto the shirt and trousers of the man struggling to hold onto it. Eventually Marco caught it, held it for the required length of time, was declared the victor, and carried about on the shoulders of the contestants.

When Filomena mentioned the feast of Saint Sebastian, Papa turned to me. "You know the reasons why Saint Sebastian died. You also know he showed *omertà* when he was tied to a tree. He stayed calm and looked straight ahead. He believed in his faith the same way we believe in the rules of the family. He understood that we all must be willing to sacrifice *u nostru sangu pir lu nostru sangu*. (our blood for one's blood relatives and family.) So like Saint Sebastian, we understand that all of us must be willing to sacrifice for the family."

When Papa paused, Mamma raised the palms of her hands. "*Basta per ora*." ("That's enough for now.")

"Sì," Papa responded, "*É' fatta la jurnata*." (Yes, our day is done.)

Tony folded his hands, turned to his right, and stared at Mamma. He had a way of lowering the lids of his eyes that conveyed he had something to ask which fell within Papa's authority. In response she nodded, and Tony looked at Papa with extra respect, probably because of the discussion we just had. "Papa, Santo and I and our friends decided that if it's raining, we would like to meet for a little while at the pool hall and watch games that might be going on. You know, because it's Friday, some big game might get started."

Tony's presentation got me excited. "And because it's Friday, I'll bet Smiles will be there. So we probably can watch some big action to celebrate that we're the fast gang this summer." My cousin, Smiles, was the eighteen year old son of Papa's brother, Gaetano, who lived across the street. Smiles had been named after his father. But ever since he was a kid his nickname became "Smiles," because his smile looked like a bright, flashing light.

70

Papa grinned, turned his palms upward and flipped his fingers, granting permission.

I grinned in return. "Thanks, Papa. We won't stay late."

Tony looked at Teodoro. "We'll be back in a little while. But hit the sack if you want to."

Teodoro stood up and stepped toward the radio. "I'll see you later. I think Jack Armstrong is on now."

Filomena glanced at the clock on the wall with its long pendulum rocking back and forth. "Teodoro, I think The Shadow is on now." She stood up and began clearing dishes from the table, assisted by Gloria. Mamma took bowls down from the long shelf along the wall and began placing food that had not been eaten in them.

Anna walked to the sink, turned on the facet, and started to fill a large pan with water to wash the dishes. "Tell Smiles hello for us. I think we'll see all of them on Sunday, right Ma?" Mamma nodded yes.

"Okay, we will. I wonder if anyone will have the guts to take him on with a bet."

Filomena chuckled. "Not if they're from the North End. Maybe some guys from out of town will, if they show up."

Shooting pool was very popular among older teenagers and young men who lived in the North End. The pool hall was located in the basement of a building that housed a market located on Main Street, a block away from where the top of Ferry Street connected with what the neighborhood called the American district.

Especially on Friday nights, young men, who had become skillful pool players, rented one of the six tables and competed, while others from the neighborhood watched. Of course, there was much bantering and joking by the boys in the audience as they evaluated which of the players was becoming a champ. Occasionally men from a neighboring town would show up and challenge local players.

When Tony and I arrived, games were taking place at each of the tables, and the pool hall was crowded with spectators. Bart and Melo had already arrived, and quickly walked over. Melo whispered with excitement, pointing to the far end of the room. "Guess what? See those guys on Table 5, they're from Wethersfield. They keep saying their friend, the one with the blue shirt, is really good, and they want to set up a match."

Tony stood on his toes and stretched his neck, trying to look over the crowd. "Where's Smiles?"

Bart pointed. "He's been playing with Nino on Table 6 next to those Wethersfield guys. He must have gone to the bathroom, or maybe he's getting some chalk for his cue stick. Everybody is saying those Wethersfield guys have been watching him and Nino."

"Oh there he is," Melo whispered. "He's back."

"Let's get closer, Santo," Tony whispered. "We should let him know we're here." We edged our way through the crowd to the other side of the room and stood near Table 6. Nino and Smiles continued their game of eight ball which was nearly finished.

"Hey!" Melo was now more excited than before. "Did you notice that? Smiles missed another shot."

Roberto, a guy from our neighborhood, leaned toward Melo. "It's obvious he's letting Nino beat him. Those guys have been taking long looks at them for the last half hour. We think Smiles is trying to set them up."

Tony turned to Roberto. "Have these Wethersfield guys been here before?"

"Never seen them."

"Well, if they take Smiles on, they'll be blown away by what they got themselves into."

While Nino was preparing to take a shot, Smiles walked to the other side of the table and caught a glimpse of us. He grinned in that wonderful, warm way that led to his nickname, raised his right hand, holding his cue stick in the other. "Hey, *cuscini* (cousins). We're coming over Sunday. Boy will we feast!"

I waved back. "Can't wait."

Tony jabbed his arm out. "Smiles, you didn't see it. Nino just missed dunking the eight ball."

Smiles turned and scanned the table. He had two more balls to sink before he could take a shot at the eight ball. One of them was about four inches to the right side of the corner pocket at the other end of the table. He leaned over, his chin inches from the table and bushy, black hair hanging down his forehead, slowly positioned the tip of his cue stick, took careful aim, and quickly jabbed the stick forward. The cue ball spun clockwise toward its target and struck the ball which, however, hit the cushion next to the pocket instead of sinking into it. He looked down at the floor. "Shucks. You're on again, Nino."

Nino leaned over and immediately sank the eight ball, winning the game.

The three out-of-towners, who had been playing on the next table, interrupted their game and watched Nino and Smiles finish theirs, as did most of the men who were not playing. When Nino sank the eight ball, one of the visitors turned to his friend, who was holding a cue stick, and mumbled, "It took them forever to finish their game."

Nino and Smiles began to collect the balls from each pocket and place them in the rack. The stranger who had just made the insulting remark faced the audience. "Hey everybody, I'm Frank Scanlon! My buddy and I are from Wethersfield." I wasn't surprised when the other players interrupted their games, and spectators stopped talking. We all turned toward this visitor with interest because we knew what was coming up. Mr. Scanlon pointed to the young man at his side, who was standing still and glancing at the ceiling, while holding his cue stick. I'm not sure he realized it, but he was also pushing his chest out. "This is Jerry. He wants to get into some competition. He's looking for a challenge. He heard there are guys here in the North End who are pretty good." Grinning, the visitor continued. "Jerry's never had a chance to compete with you Dagos." Several North End men smiled. They understood that this visitor was exploiting the moment to slip in an ethnic slur, and allowed him to continue since everyone guessed what was about to happen. "So, who wants to take him on?"

Still holding their cue sticks, several of the North End men, who had been playing, looked back and forth at each other, but did not step forward. While playing their games, they had glanced on occasion at the visitors, and must have realized that the one called Jerry was very skillful. All of the spectators were now crowded by Tables 5 and 6, and knew that Smiles had a reputation in the neighborhood of being a superb, pool shark. More than that, everyone realized that Smiles had been playing well below his ability, because he knew the visitors were watching him along with all the other players.

After a long pause, during which North End players continued to look back and forth at each other, Smiles slowly raised his right arm and the pool stick he was holding. His head slightly lowered, he took a step forward. The North End crowd grinned.

"Oh, you?" Frank Scanlon mumbled. "I've watched you some. You're okay. I mean you're good. I thought your buddy there would want to take Jerry on." Smiles did not move nor did Nino. "Are you sure you want to do this? You know Jerry is really good."

Maintaining a serious expression, Smiles looked at Frank Scanlon, nodded, and then stared at the floor.

"What's your name?"

"Gaetano." Smiles was still looking down at the floor.

Bart nudged my side with his elbow and whispered, "Wow, can he act."

Frank Scanlon scanned the crowd. "Okay, then. To juice up the game, instead of betting one buck for every buck anyone of you puts up, I'll bet two bucks Jerry wins. I know you guys like your friend here, but I'm making up for the handicap." He grinned, tapped his hand on Table 5 where he and his buddy had been playing, and looked around. "Come on! Who's got guts. I'm giving two to one."

Emilio Galanto from the North End stepped forward and slowly spread out a one dollar bill on the pool table. Frank Scanlon reached into a box in which Jerry kept his cue stick and took out a stack of dollar bills. It was clear that these guys were out to make a killing, and thought they had it made because they believed Smiles was an average player. Holding the bundle of dollar bills in his left hand, Mr. Scanlon ceremoniously placed two one-dollar bills across Emilio's dollar. While glancing at each other, several men from the North End took turns slowly stepping forward and placing a dollar bill on the pool table. Of course they weren't absolutely sure Smiles would win, but they were willing to take the gamble. Mr. Scanlon matched each dollar placed on the table with two one-dollar bills. Whenever this type of situation developed with visitors from out of town, everyone from the North End became very excited but remained quiet.

While the betting ceremony was going on, Bart, Tony, Melo and I moved to a spot behind the crowd and pooled the change we had brought with us. Bart quickly approached one of his relatives, handed him the change, and asked him for a dollar bill. Bart walked to the table with the dollar bill dangling from his fingertips, set it down, and stood there watching Mr. Scanlon match it. Bart quickly stepped back next to Tony, me and Melo and whispered, " I hope he gets creamed."

The top of Table 5 was soon covered with a blanket of dollar bills. Mr. Scanlon chuckled, "Okay, everyone, you can keep an eye on which two bucks is yours while you watch the game. But it won't matter, because you'll soon see that all of those greens are mine. Let's go, rack those balls."

While one of the men racked the balls on Table 6, Smiles slowly walked to the far end of the room and returned with a suitcase that once held a clarinet. Everyone watched in quiet excitement. Smiles placed the suitcase on the edge of the table that was covered with dollar bills. Several North End men began to grin.

Mr. Scanlon laughed, "Hey, Gaetano! What are you doing? Do you plan to play a song? I thought you agreed to take on Jerry in a game of eight ball. Look, I know you're nervous, so let's say you go first, and the striped balls are yours."

Smiles did not pay attention to Frank Scanlon. Instead he slowly opened the case, removed two pieces of a cue stick, ceremoniously inserted the base of the stick into the top half, and slowly twisted the two together.

Frank Scanlon's jaw dropped. "Hey, that's a professional stick. What are you doing with that?"

Smiles continued to ignore Mr. Scanlon while carefully sliding his hand up and down the cue stick as if he were touching a strip of silk. Then he turned and faced Mr. Scanlon. "So you said I could go first, right?"

" Yeah. I guess I did. But what are you doing with a pro stick? I saw you shoot a few decent shots but ..."

Smiles stepped to one end of the table which caused Mr. Scanlon to immediately stop his commenting. Many from the North End continued to grin. Smiles gently located the cue ball on the table, leaned over, positioned his cue stick, and stared at the triangle of balls at the other end, as if he was lost in another world. Then he slowly and rhythmically moved his right arm back and forth like the pendulum of a clock and thrust his right arm forward. The tip of his cue stick struck the cue ball which spun forward and crashed into the cluster of balls, splattering them in all directions. Two balls clattered into pockets. A very serious look covered Smiles' face, as he stood up straight with the cue stick hanging from his left arm. For a minute he scanned the table and studied the position of each remaining ball in terms of the position of the cue ball. Then he slowly sank each of the remaining balls, in turn, always pausing for a minute after each shot to study the position of the cue ball and decide which ball presented the best possibility.

During each pause, or while Smiles leaned over swinging his arm back and forth rhythmically, Mr. Scanlon made some comment. Like a few minutes ago he said, "Wow, this grease ball's good." And before Smiles took the next shot, he said, "Maybe this Gaetano made that last one because of all the pizza he ate." Smiles, however, did not flinch, nor did he even glance at the visitor.

Tony leaned towards me and whispered, "What an ass. He's trying to shake up Smiles."

"I know. It's obvious."

Melo grinned. "Who's he kidding? He'll never ruin Smiles' aim."

After Smiles sank all the striped balls, he smashed the cue ball against the eight ball which clunked into the pocket he had selected, declaring him the winner. Everyone cheered.

With a broad grin covering his face, Emilio Galanto, who had placed the first bet, walked over to the table and picked up his three dollars. Everyone who had placed a bet did the same.

Mr. Scanlon's eyes were still glaring with surprise. Smiles looked at him. "So do you want to play another game? It's your buddy's turn to shoot first in the next game."

Mr. Scanlon choked on his words. "Uh, well, uh, no. That was good, Gaetano. Jerry and I have to get back. Maybe we'll see you next Friday." He and Jerry quickly placed their cue sticks in their cases, walked to the doorway and left.

The men who had been playing returned to their tables, quietly joking about what had just taken place. One of them turned to Smiles who was carefully returning his cue stick in the clarinet case. "Good going, Smiles. I don't think we'll ever see them again."

Emilio walked over. "Thanks, Smiles. You helped a lot of us earn two bucks tonight." Tony and I stood very close to Smiles and felt a surge of pride.

"Gee, Smiles," Melo commented, "you carefully measured every shot while that ass was making wisecracks. He was obviously trying to shake you up and piss you off."

Emilio placed his hand on Melo's shoulder. "You're right kid. Smiles held it all in his *panza* (belly) during all those wisecracks. He's really *omu di pacenzia* (man of patience)."

Bart looked up at Smiles with admiration. "Where did you get all that *pacenzia*?"

"You know, Bart. Like you're getting it from your family and relatives, I'm getting it from my family, and from Tony's and Santo's family. And I know you hear your parents saying all the time, you're an empty sack, a nothing mixed with nothing, if you don't stay connected to the family. It really pays off when you're shooting pool."

"It pays off all the time when we're dealing with someone's shit," Emilio commented. "We all need to keep family connections and *omertà* growing."

Grinning, Smiles turned and placed one hand on Tony's shoulder and the other on mine. "I know you have to get going. When you reach eighteen, you can stay longer. See you Sunday."

Tony, Bart, Melo and I stepped out of the pool hall onto Main Street, and started running toward Ferry Street, while the rain splattered on our heads and the sidewalk.

Melo took a deep breath as he jogged along. "Boy, your cousin really crushed that guy who thought he was going to make huge bucks off everybody."

"I'm going to keep filling my sack with *omertà* so it won't get empty," Bart gasped. "Maybe I won't get into so many fights."

Each of us waved as we headed for our appartments.

Second Picking

A Man is Wealthy When He Has a Good Mother and Good Friends; It Doesn't Matter If He Has No Money

First Picking was finished by mid-June in all of the fields of the Goodrich Farm. This Monday morning several gangs, including mine, stood waiting to begin second picking in the fields that strung along the Connecticut River. The straw boss of the Wethersfield gang, Sammy, was nearby. I met him last year but didn't know him very well. He seemed like a nice guy, and I decided to chat with him for a minute, because I was curious to find out if he had learned that this year I was the straw boss of the North End fast gang.

As I walked toward Sammy, Dominic scanned the rows of tobacco plants which now stood about five feet tall. "Hey, I'm glad these guys got taller since we were here a couple of weeks ago. Now I can finally kneel down when I pick, instead of dragging my ass down the row."

When I approached Sammy, he pointed over my shoulder. "Look what your friend is doing."

Melo was scowling and slowly passing his fingers, over and over again, through his thick, brown hair, each time glancing at the sweat covering the palms of his hands. Angry, he looked down at Dominic who was several inches shorter. "Oh, that's great for you, Dom. But I'll still be on my ass."

I whispered to Sammy, "He sweats a lot, and he's always been very fussy about his hair!"

Bart turned to Melo. "We'll be lucky if we can kneel during Third Picking."

Melo and Bart were the tallest pickers of the gang. If they crawled on their knees during second picking, they would have to arch their backs forward for a long time as they picked their rows. During Second Picking, then, pickers their size still used a sitting position and had to wait until third picking before they could kneel.

Melo continue staring at his hands. "It isn't even eight

o'clock yet, and my head is sweating already. Damn it, my hair is all sticky!"

At that moment Bongi yanked on the rope around his waist and glared at his brother. "Dom, who cares about kneeling? Don't you feel hot, already?"

Dominic pressed his hand against his forehead. "Yeah, a little."

At the same time Vito tugged on his T-shirt under his armpit and held his fingertips at eye level. "Bongi, look! I'm already sweating a lot too."

While Vito examined his fingers, Sal looked up at the sky. "There isn't even a cloud to block some of the sun. Wow! Look! It's like a giant, round furnace starting to crawl up the sky. When it gets overhead, we'll all be roasted."

A picker from the Wethersfield gang who had been standing nearby stared at us. He obviously had heard all of what my gang had been saying. "Why are you guys worrying now that it's hot? Worry this afternoon. Besides we're right next to the river, and it's always hotter here."

Another picker from the Wethersfield gang smiled and stared at Bongi's belly that rolled over the rope around his waist. "Maybe if you weren't so fat you wouldn't feel so hot."

In a flash, the whole situation switched from joking to an explosion. With clenched fists, Bongi lunged toward this boy and hurled a vigorous punch. "I'll show you what these fat fists can do!" The boy stumbled backwards and fell on his back. Bongi leaned over, raised his fist, and was about to throw another punch, when I raced over.

Tony happened to be standing a couple of yards away and also rushed over. "Bongi, you're losing it, stop!"

At the same time, three pickers from the Wethersfield gang charged toward Bongi in anger. They immediately froze to a halt, however, when Bart and Melo, side by side, stepped before them with postures that conveyed, "We dare you to come closer."

I threw my arms around Bongi's shoulders, and pulled him back. "*Basta*! Enough! Don't be a jerk!"

The straw boss of the Wethersfield gang also raced over,

reached down and helped his picker stand up. "Let's save our steam for those long rows we'll be picking by the river!"

Jimmy Lewis and his gang were clustered several yards away watching the battle, as did Brian Coleman's gang which was engaged in a discussion down the road. Both groups became motionless and did not step into the fray.

Confrontations like this were almost a daily occurrence among pickers and haulers, especially those from different cities. On occasion, as was the case today, some debate or teasing exploded into a fist fight. Strawbosses were expected to separate the gladiators involved, negotiate the disagreement, and prevent a major battle from erupting. Strawbosses knew, as did everyone else, that if a disagreement got out of hand, their gangs could be docked, and the boys directly involved in the argument might even be fired.

Mr. Kelly was standing further down the road by a pickup truck and saw most of what had happened. When he noticed that the situation had been brought under control, he decided not to step in. He called out, "Santo! Your gang will work today in that section over there where the forty-five benders are." He then assigned sections of the field that contained thirty benders to Brian Coleman's and Jimmy Lewis' gangs and the gang from Wethersfield. He slowly scanned all of us and, given what had just happened, tried to help which is one thing I always liked about Mr. Kelly. "Look, I know it's going to be a hot one today. Take a deep breath, and be sure to keep your caps on. You don't want the sun beating down on your head."

Each gang entered its section of the field and began picking. The three or four leaves that had reached the size that qualified for Second Picking were now about eight inches from the ground at the lowest portion of the stalk. The haulers chatted for a few minutes along the road, waiting for their pickers to harvest leaves. Then they pulled their baskets into the field and began lifting butts off the ground, placing them in their baskets. As everyone penetrated the field, I stepped into Bongi's row. "Santo, I guess I got carried away. Sorry. I'm glad Mr. Kelly was around and not Mr. George."

"Try not to lose it. You're the one who keeps mentioning that you're fat. So what if that guy said something about you feeling hot because you're fat."

"Okay, I get it. But I can't wait for water time. It's just that I feel a little dizzy."

His partner, Suggi, expressed his concern. "Gee, we just got started! Is there something the matter with you today? It won't be water time for a while."

Bongi and Suggi were referring to the ritual of "water time" that happened every morning at about 10 a.m., and every afternoon at about 3 PM, when the field foreman called a fifteen-minute break. All pickers and haulers came out of the field to take a drink of water. The water was transported to the field in a large, wooden barrel mounted belly down in a wooden frame that was set on a two-wheel trailer, and pulled to the field by a pick-up truck. A pipe with a spigot protruded from one end of the barrel. Boys lined up and took turns, pushing the lever of the spigot and drinking for a number of seconds, under the watchful eye of a foreman. After a boy took a drink, the foreman said, "Next," in order to give each boy a chance to have a drink within the minutes allowed for water time. In this way the line of boys slowly crept forward.

When Bongi added that he was feeling a little dizzy, I became concerned and decided to help him, picking one column of plants while he picked the other. "Bongi, what did you eat before coming to work this morning? Maybe you ate something that's making you extra thirsty."

"Nothing different. I guess I'm thirsty this early because it's extra hot and humid already." Bongi held out his hand which was covered with sticky tobacco juice. "See!" Typically, as the plants warmed up, when a picker harvested leaves, his fingers and the palms of his hands, became stained dark brown.

I turned around toward Bongi. "Look at my hands. They're already black and sticky too. You know that all of us get that tobacco juice on our hands. Besides, we're right by the river so there's a lot more dew here."

Bongi tilted his body to one side. "I know. Look at my ass. My pants are already caked with mud."

"Don't focus on the mud. Try to think about something else, like you'll be splashing in the river this weekend." I continued picking leaves in Bongi's row because he was a full bend behind the gang, and tried to joke with him. Everyone else was close to finishing his row.

Suddenly Bart ran over to me, leaned down and exclaimed, "You won't believe it! When I finished my row, I took a minute to chat with a picker I know from Wethersfield. He told me the word's going around that Mr. George filled up a pan with water from the tank two different times and gave it to his dog. He's got his dog with him again! What an ass!"

Bongi heard what Bart just said and yelled, "The damn dog is getting a drink and we can't!"

I did not respond to Bart or Bongi immediately because I was focused on a scene that flashed on today's stage in my mind, as soon as Bart shared what he had learned. The scene was Mr. George's large dog lapping water from a pan. But in seconds, the dog changed into a horse lapping water from a large wooden bucket, and another story that involved my grandfather was performed on that stage in my mind reserved for yesterday's events.

———————

Villagers reported to Antonio that, on several occasions, they had seen the son of the Baron, who owned a *latifondo* (large estate) just outside the village, pull up a bucket of water from the well located in the village piazza, and place it on the ground for his horse to drink. Peasants were outraged since in this village, as well as many others in Sicily, drinking water was a scarce commodity, and, therefore, used with care and appreciation. When the Baron's son rode his horse into the piazza, villagers who happened to be milling about, or carrying their water buckets toward their stone houses, expressed their outrage by looking down at the ground as if they did not see him, while others clinched a fist and bit the knuckle of the index finger.

During one of these visits, while the Baron's son drew water out of the well, a villager dared to object, reminding him that water was scarce. The Baron's son, who had the reputation of being haughty, told this peasant to mind his own business or else he will learn the hard way who is superior. On another occasion, one of Antonio's *amici* (friends) approached the Baron's son, tried to explain that the water in that well belonged to the villagers, and he should water his horse at his estate. This peasant even dared to add that if the Baron's son did not stop watering his horse at the village well, he would ask his friend, the *Capo*, for help. He was also rudely dismissed.

One day in the early afternoon, Antonio was talking with villagers near the piazza in front of the large, stone oven which everyone used to bake bread and roast chickens. A peasant came running to Antonio shouting *"u riccu, testadura, ancora tira l'acqua di lu puzzu po su cavaddu!"* ("The rich one, that hard head, is again drawing water from the well for his horse.") Hoping to resolve the problem, Antonio quickly walked into the piazza. There, by the well, stood the Baron's son, watching his horse drink from the bucket, and ignoring the villagers who were milling about, staring at him.

Antonio approached him. "As you know, sir, this is the only water people of this village have to survive." Everyone in the piazza stood motionless, but some moved closer to Antonio so they could hear what was going on.

"Mind your own business!" snorted the Baron's son. "You're lucky to have this well available to you."

At this moment Antonio demonstrated that he had developed, to a high degree, Sicilian *omertà*, the strength to stomach insult from someone who believed he had absolute power. He also showed the ability to express what looked like indifference. Antonio turned his head and looked to one side, commenting with a low, calm voice, *"Ma tu 'unn hai né rispettu, né maneri."* ("But you have neither respect nor manners"). "Young man, do you know who I am?"

The Baron's son made clear he intended to dismiss this *contadino* (peasant) who had dared to propose with his question and tone that his presence was important. He slowly turned away from Antonio, looked at another peasant standing nearby, and asked with a condescending tone, *"Allora, come si chiama questo?"* (Well, then, what is the name of this person?)

84

Grinning the villager replied, "*Non ha un nome veramente, ma la gente locale l'ha sempre chiamato Paraceddu*" (He doesn't have a regular name, but the locale people always call him Paraceddu – he flies like a bird.)

The Baron's son startled, suddenly realizing who was standing before him. In an effort to placate and seduce Antonio, he raised his head, stretched out his arm, and began speaking rapidly. "I think I know who you are. I hope you understand that my sense of honor and pride comes from the fact that my family has been nobility here for many generations. And I'm sure you know that over the years we have hired peasants from your village to be our gardeners and servants. And you must know that we have had parental relationships with some of the peasants who have worked for us. And..."

Antonio immediately pushed the palm of his right hand in front of the face of the Baron's son, knowing he would continue constructing a list of reasons that justified what he was doing. "I do not take issue with your nobility, and I know you have hired villagers from time to time. What I'm taking issue with is that your horse is not more noble than we are and should not be using our water which you know is scarce."

Because his comments failed to stimulate some sort of submissive response from Antonio, the Baron's son now showed evidence of the haughty reputation that followed him wherever he went. "My horse is noble. A noble horse never stoops to pull a cart. And a noble horse has the privilege of drinking..."

Before the Baron's son finished what he had to say, Antonio interrupted him again, still maintaining *omertà*. "I am the *Capo* of this village. I'm asking you for the last time not to take water from this well for your horse. You have your own wells."

Still struggling to maintain his position of superiority, the Baron's son shouted. "Do you realize we probably own the land your village sits on?" With a very condescending tone he added, "And do you realize how fortunate you are, *Capo*, that we don't tax you for this water. As a matter of fact if you and your villagers don't stop harassing me, I might ask my father to tax you for this water. And..."

Antonio interrupted the Baron's son once again, "*Disidiri la morti?*" ("Do you want to die?"), raised his rifle from his shoulder and shot at the ground near the bucket of water which toppled over. The horse reared high on its hind legs, and the Baron's son startled and stood motionless.

Antonio glared at him. "You are now free to walk back to your *latifondo* (estate). Yes, I said walk. If I see you riding this horse, I will shoot it. My name is Antonio. Your father knows who I am. Describe to him what happened, and tell him there will be a bigger price to pay if you continue to take water from this well. If you insist, and there is a next time, you will pay for water with your noble horse. After that, if there is another next time, well, you know."

Pulling his horse in tow, the Baron's son slowly walked out of the piazza. Obviously very frightened, he frequently turned his head and looked over his shoulder at Antonio. Several villagers approached Antonio, and others grinned, quietly continuing with their chores.

———————————

The drama that was taking place on the stage in my mind reserved for yesterday immediately stopped when Mr. Kelly stepped into the row I was picking. "Santo, it's water time." Suddenly a different scene jumped into my mind on the stage reserved for "tomorrow." While all the boys are waiting in line for a drink, Mr. George is holding a pail under the spigot, watching the water slowly dribble in until the pan is full. His dog is jumping around, holding his head high and vigorously wagging his tail. A long line of pickers and haulers stand still, glare in anger, and cannot believe what is happening. I march towards Mr. George.

This drama immediately faded out of my mind when I stood up and called out to my gang that it was water time. Each picker walked out of the field with arms held tight to his sides, and one shoulder pushed forward, so as not to bruise any leaves. Each hauler set down his hauler's hook, carefully stepped over the basket he had been pulling, and walked the same way. Everyone immediately formed a line leading to the water barrel. After about twenty boys had taken a drink, and were milling about near the barrel, Jack Kane leaned over and pressed the lever of the spigot, but no water poured out. Surprised, he turned and stared at Mr. Kelly. "What the hell!"

Mr. Kelly pressed the water spigot up and down several times, but no water dribbled out. The boys who were still in line, including Bongi and me, stared in disbelief. Mr. Kelly removed the large cork that plugged the opening at the top of the barrel and peered in. "Shucks guys, its empty. That's too bad. We'll try to get the barrel filled before noon. Let's get back to work for now."

Mr. George was nearby and quickly walked over. "I wonder how that happened." Everyone glared at him, and Mr. Kelly stared into his eyes as if to say, "Why would you do something like that?"

Bongi stormed off very upset. "I don't believe this! The dog did get water, and I didn't!"

I was gripped by what just happened, and for a moment imagined I was with my grandfather looking at the Baron's son. "I've got to do something," I thought to myself, as I walked over to Mr. George who was writing in his notepad. I stopped inches away from him and looked up with disgust. "Mr. George, if you didn't use water for your dog this morning, there would be enough for all of us."

Mr. George could not believe what he just heard. He glared down at me for a long moment, and stormed off. Mr. Kelly, and the driver of the pickup truck that hauled the water trailer to the field, grinned in silence and winked at me.

After lunch break, everyone continued harvesting and hauling. Mr. George walked by several times to inspect my gang as they moved along, clearly showing their skill as fast pickers. At one point he called out in a sweet tone that I knew was a cover up. "Santo, come over here, please."

I realized that Mr. George's use of the word "please," and the tone in which he expressed it, spelled trouble. At that moment a saying I heard my parents, and relatives express many times came to mind. *"Un ti fidari di 'na vucca duci."* ("Don't put your trust in a mouth that's extra sweet"). I walked through several rows of plants and found Mr. George standing a few yards behind Dominic. "What do you want, Mr. George?

"Do you see what I see, Santo?"

"See what?

"This boy is nearly one bend behind everyone in your gang. I've noticed that he's always behind, and you and your buddies are always helping him finish so he can keep up with the gang."

I pushed the palm of my right hand toward him, almost hitting his stomach. "What's the matter with that?"

"What's the matter is that he's supposed to be a member of a Fast Gang." Mr. George barked back. "If a guy can't do it on his own, he can't be paid thirty cents an hour. I'm going to report to the superintendent that Dominic should not be paid the wages of a fast picker."

"Wait a minute, Mr. George. Since the beginning of summer, we've been getting the work done that a Fast Gang should do. And Dominic is getting better and better."

Mr. George shot back, pushing his index finger back and forth at me. "That doesn't matter, my boy. The Fast Gang is getting it done, but Dominic isn't."

I glared at him, lifted my head as high as possible, stretched my shoulders back, and thrust my index finger at him. "I think you're pissed off because I said something this morning about you giving water to your stupid dog. So now you're giving me and my gang shit. Go to hell!"

With a sigh of victory, Mr. George scribbled in his book. "You're docked two hours my boy, and say goodbye to Dominic being in your gang." A flood of tension rushed through me. I realized that once again I had failed to practice *omertà*.

At the end of the day, while everyone congregated in the Central Lot waiting for trucks to take them to their neighborhoods, I was called into the superintendent's cabin. Mr. Williams was again seated at his desk before a stack of papers, and Mr. George was standing to one side, grinning. "Santo, Mr. George gave me his reason why a kid named Dominic should be taken off your gang, and a faster picker put there in his place. He thinks Dominic is in your gang only because his brother is in your gang.

I know you know that a picker in a fast gang is expected to pick at least 150 bends a day. Mr. George thinks a couple of guys in your gang, like Dominic, meet that requirement only because they get help. What's your take on this?"

I stiffened my posture and slowly rubbed the sticky tobacco juice covering my left arm with the palm of my right hand, which was also covered with sticky juice. "Yes, Mr. Williams, Dominic is a little slower, and doesn't have as much experience as the rest of us. But my gang has been getting it done as a Fast Gang. Every picker is finishing at least 150 bends a day, even Dominic, who gets help from other guys like Bart and Melo, who are the fastest." I took a deep breath. "Mr. Williams, if anyone in my gang doesn't keep up, like when he doesn't feel good, he gets help too! For us, a gang is like a family. Everybody helps everybody."

Mr. Williams looked at Mr. George, then looked at me, and again glanced at Mr. George. "These are good guys. I like the way they help each other. Let's leave the gang the way it is." Mr. George clinched his fist around his notepad and pressed it against his stomach.

I was so surprised, my jaw dropped. I expected Mr. Williams to fire Dominic. "Thank you, Mr. Williams." I glanced at Mr. George, who looked furious, turned around, walked out and ran to the truck that was assigned to transport pickers to Middletown's North End.

"What's the matter?" Tony asked. "Why did you have to see the superintendent?"

"Nothing's the matter. I'll tell you about it later. I just need to keep working on building up *omertà*, like Papa said the other day."

When Tony and I walked from the river to our neighborhood street, uncle Gaetano and Papa were sitting on the front steps of our tenement house with Teodoro and Gloria by their sides. Gaetano was Papa's older brother and my *patrozzu* (godfather). He was a few inches taller than Papa, carried the same broad shoulders, and had always taken special interest in my experiences at school, work and in the neighborhood. "Hey, Santo. Hey, Tony. *Comu siti*?" ("How are you?")

"Good. Good," we announced in chorus.

Uncle Gaetano asked us to sit by him and Papa for a moment and share how things were going at the farm. I didn't want to get into any of the trouble we were having. "Things are going okay, pretty much. And we are still the Fast Gang."

Apparently Tony felt differently and immediately dumped out the mess we were in. "Yeah, but tell Papa and *Zio* (Uncle) about that asshole, Mr. George."

With a look of disgust Gloria commented, "What again! What happened now with that jerk?"

Papa quietly asked, "*Ch'è successu?*" ("What happened?")

I shared the day's events that had taken place with Mr. George and concluded with the comment, "Papa, Zio, he's really a *vergogna* (outrage)."

Teodoro jumped up from the step he was sitting on. "He keeps picking on you guys!"

"You're right," Tony commented. "He's been giving Santo and our gang a lot of trouble from the beginning of the summer. We can't figure out why."

I looked at Papa and felt that I had screwed up again and disappointed him. "Papa, *mi dispiaci* (I'm sorry). I tried to use my *omertà*. I guess I've got more work to do to get stronger about that."

"Do you think it's because of the war that he picks on you?" Gloria asked.

"You could be right, Gloria," Tony replied. "Italy is an enemy like Germany and Japan. Maybe he's picking on us because we're Italians."

Gaetano looked back and forth at Tony and me with concern, turned to Papa, and placed a hand on his arm. "*Frati* (brother), do you think we should share with them what happened?"

Papa looked down, sorting out his thoughts. "Yes, I think you're right. It might help them understand what is going on. And it might help Santo deal with this *vergogna* (outrage)."

Uncle Gaetano turned to me and Tony. "Senti (listen), it is important that you understand something that happened last year so you can handle this boss of yours." He went on describing how last summer Mr. George hit Emilio, Mr. Biagio's son, with a hauler's hook.

I interrupted, shouting, "I know that!"

Tony immediately became as anxious as I did. "So do I! We were working in the field and heard Emilio swear at Mr. George! We learned later that Mr. George caught Emilio taking a swim in the river at lunchtime and wanted to dock him the whole day's pay. Emilio swore at him, told him it was lunch break, and he could do whatever he wanted."

I was swept away as much as Tony was. "And we heard Mr. George call Emilio a Wop and dock him. We couldn't see them because they were about a bend away from us. We heard Emilio yell. Later he showed us a big bruise on his shoulder."

"I remember that," Gloria joined in. "You and your buddies talked a lot about it."

I turned to Gloria. "Remember? Emilio told us it almost got into a fight, but he held back. We know Emilio's a big kid. Like when he's helping his father in the butcher shop, he shows us he could lift half a cow. He told us he didn't raise his fists or throw a bunch. He just told off Mr. George for docking him."

Uncle Gaetano interrupted us. "Yes, I know. Emilio got hit with one of those hooks you guys use to pull a basket. When he came home he told his father what happened. Mr. Biagio didn't know if he should call the police, and talked to your father about what to do."

Now Tony and I were really turned on, because we were learning something we had no idea happened, and Tony shouted, "What happened, Papa?"

"I thought about it a lot. I decided it wouldn't help to tell the police because they probably would not believe Emilio's story. They would only believe Mr. George. I decided your uncle and I should go see this Mr. George."

Uncle Gaetano shared that at noontime a couple of days later, he and Papa went to the Central Lot and talked to one of the field foreman who pointed out Mr. George. Later, they walked through the field looking for him, while keeping a distance from pickers and haulers, and eventually spotted him. "Your father said to him, 'You hit the son of a friend of mine with one of those steel hooks."

"What did Mr. George say?" Teodoro was jumping up and down with excitement.

"He said, 'That's a lie. What are you guys doing here anyway? You're not allowed in this field' or something like that."

"Then, what happened?" Gloria was as excited as Teodoro.

"Your father told this guy, 'Do you see that river? Do you want to end up in it? If you don't, then never touch one of these kids again."

Gloria, Tony, Teodoro and I jumped up, glanced at each other, grinning, and surrounded our uncle.

"Mr. George said something like, 'Who do you wops think you are?' And he said he would even call the police. Your father told him his name, to check around who he was, and then decide what to do."

Gloria shared what I already knew. "Emilio's sister told me Mr. George did not dock him. And she said that jerk left Emilio alone the rest of the summer."

"Wow!" Tony exclaimed, "That's why he's picking on us. He left Emilio alone, but now he's taking it out on us. But he's trying to be careful because he knows we have friends."

Gloria stretched her arms out. "Yeah, Mr. Biagio was really glad that Papa helped him out."

"Sì (yes)," Uncle Gaetano whispered. "*E' riccu l'omu quannu c'avi amici, 'un ci fa nenti s'unn 'avi dinari.*" ("A man is wealthy when he has good friends; it doesn't matter if he has no money.")

I stared at Papa and wanted him to realize what I just learned meant to me. "That's another good example of *omertà*. I'll keep trying."

Gloria leaned forward, looked into uncle Gaetano's eyes with eagerness, turned to Papa, and went on talking a hundred miles an hour. "A few weeks ago all of us had a talk after dinner about family rules, and the rule of *omertà*, and how a guy can be the best. But, what about us girls? In a few months I'm going to be seventeen, you know. I'd like us to have a talk about family rules that have to do more with us girls. Look at all that Mamma and us girls do every day."

Uncle Gaetano grinned. Papa gazed at Gloria with affection. "*Figghia bedda*, ("My wonderful daughter") let's talk about that *stasera dopo pranzo*." ("tonight after dinner.")

"Great! Now I'll go help Mamma get dinner ready." Gloria ran into our apartment.

At the same time Papa commented, "*Basta per ora*." ("Enough for now.") And everyone stood up.

Uncle Gaetano hugged Tony, Teodoro and me. Then, following an ancient Sicilian custom, he and Papa hugged and kissed each other on each cheek. Gaetano slowly walked across the street toward his apartment, paused and turned, facing us. "*Domani*." (Until tomorrow.)

Papa, Tony, Teodoro and I walked into our appartment. Mamma was at the stove stirring *stemperata di pollo* (pieces of chicken, eggplants, green bell peppers, chopped celery, olives, capers, garlic and olive oil) with a large spoon. What she did next, she has done before many times. She dipped her index finger into the *stemperata*, placed it on her tongue, smacked her lips together, and whispered, "*delizioso*" (delicious). Filomena, who was by her side, did the same. "Ma, it is! It came out really good!"

Anna and Gloria were folding laundry they had taken, a short while ago, from the clotheslines located at the back of the building. "That *stemperata* really smells great even from over here," Anna called out. "I can't wait to taste it."

Mamma turned to Papa. "I learned from Gloria that you and Gaetano helped Tony and Santo understand why that boss at work keeps giving them trouble. Maybe now they can handle themselves better."

"And guess what?" Gloria shouted from the bedroom. "Papa said that tonight we can talk about the rules of the family that have to do with us *fimmini*." (women)

Mamma grinned. "*Bellissimo*." (Wonderful).

"It'll be good to help these guys understand what we're all about," Anna declared, raising her hand from which draped a towel.

Filomena joined in with less drama. "Well, Tony and Santo are getting old enough to add to how they see us girls."

Soon everyone sat down at the table in their usual seats. Again, Papa poured wine into a row of glasses, while placing his fingers against each glass, carefully measuring the amount designated for the person's age. After he poured wine to the level of one finger in my glass, Tony commented, "Hey, Papa, pretty soon Santo is going to be fourteen years old. Why not put one extra splash in his glass."

I leaned toward Papa and tried not to sound frustrated, "Yeah, you're about to give Tony the usual two extra splashes. I know he's a year and a half older than me, but why can't I get at least one extra splash?"

Tony stepped in again, this time thrusting his chest out, and then his arms, as if he were giving a speech. "Papa, when you pour the wine in our glasses, a lot of times you mention that Sicilian saying, "*Un giorno senza vino è un giorno senza sole.*" ("A day without wine is like a day without sun."). So why not give Santo a little more sunshine since he's getting older?"

Anna laughed. "But we don't want him to get sunburn, do we?"

Gloria chuckled and joined the joke. "If he wears a shirt when he's drinking the wine, then the sun won't burn him."

Papa slowly raised the palms of his hands, asking for everyone's attention, and commented that while he understood what Tony was saying, there were reasons why it was important that parents measure how much wine their children drink. "One reason is you want to help someone not get sunburned, like Anna just mentioned. But there is another, more important reason. '*Lu biviri non misuratu fa l'uomo asinatu.*'" ("Drinking that is not measured, or regulated, makes a man an ass"). Now everyone chuckled.

Imitating Papa, I slowly raised the palms of my hands. "I'll wait until I turn fourteen. One thing is for sure. I don't want to become a *sceccu*" (donkey).

Mamma shook her head in amusement, got up, took the pan of stemperata from the stovetop and began serving some in each plate. At the same time, Anna and Filomena got up, took the pan of manicotti and placed it on the table.

Tony stabbed his fork into a piece of *manicotti*, stuffed it in his mouth, and chewed vigorously, "Delicious, Ma."

Anna scooped some *stemperata* from her dish with her spoon, slowly lifted it to her lips, and poured it into her mouth. "The taste is even better than the delicious smell. Filomena, did you and Ma do anything different this time?"

"No." Filomena dipped a piece of crusty homemade bread into her plate of *stemperata* and munched on it. Everyone continued eating with gusto while exchanging comments, laughing, and sometimes arguing over some issue.

When the meal was nearly over, Gloria turned to Papa. "Could we talk now about family rules that have to do with *i fimmini* (the women), like you said we would? Remember, a few days ago we talked about *omertà* which had mostly to do with guys."

Filomena placed a hand on Gloria's shoulder and immediately got into her teacher mood. "Well, not exactly, Gloria. *Omertà* is patience and not letting somebody get the best of you. It's really a rule that everybody in the family is supposed to follow." Papa nodded in agreement as Filomena continued her lecture. "Maybe because the custom of *omertà* got started when peasants had to deal with invaders and land-owning Barons from other countries, it was mostly the fathers who had to develop patience when dealing with these strangers, because they had to find work. But I know about one part of Sicilian history where mothers used *omertà*. They wouldn't tell the army where their husbands were hiding in the mountains."

"I get that," Gloria replied, resting her arms on the table. "But I thought we should talk about a family rule that has a lot to do with us gals." Then with a look on her face that said, 'I really need this,' Gloria placed her hand on Filomena's arm. "You know, Filomena, I'll be turning seventeen in a few months, and I'm wondering about things like that."

Papa immediately got into what Gloria wanted. He reminded all of us that for Italians, but especially Sicilians, "The mother is the foundation on which everyone in the family stands. Why do you think Sicilians always say we are from the same artichoke?"

When a question like that was asked, Filomena could never hold back. "Papa, I really love that Sicilian saying. I shared it

95

with my classmates at school, and they loved it too. That saying means ..."

Mamma turned the palms of her hands up, interrupting Filomena which was not at all usual for her. "That saying says it all. It reminds us that each person in a family is like a petal of an artichoke, and that each of those petals is connected to the heart, to the center of that artichoke."

Papa looked at Mamma for a long moment, spreading the fingers of his hand over his chest. "*E u cori da famigghia è a matri.*" ("and that heart of the family is the mother")

Mamma smiled, leaned forward, and commented she had a few more thoughts to share. She reminded us of the many times we have talked about how, although Sicilians were abused by tyrants, the family was their world, not the politics that had control. She asked us to look around and notice how many persons believe they are successful because they have connections with politicians and money, like Mr. Salemi in Sicily who thought he was *un pezzu grossu* (a big shot) because he had established connections with the viceroy from Spain. And later Mr. Alba thought the same thing when he agreed to be the *gabelloto* (superintendent) of the estate owned by a politician in Turin. Mamma continued talking in a way that reminded me of how Filomena lectures. She added that for Sicilians, and for most people in the *Mezzogiorno* (Southern Italy), it was the opposite. Who a person was, and how much a person felt worthwhile, came from the family. That's why, she added, the heart and center of the family was so critical if everyone was going to survive and do the best they could.

Filomena had to join Mamma's lecture. "Mamma, that's why if we get upset about something, or need help about something, we say '*Mamma mia*' (my mother). We say that because we know Mamma is the heart, the place in the artichoke where you can get help."

Mamma grinned, nodded and leaned forward. Both Anna and Filomena, without realizing it, placed the palms of their hands together as if in prayer. Gloria spotted them and did the same. We boys stared at Mamma as she continued in her soft voice. "A few days ago, we talked about how, for Sicilians, the

96

men, especially the fathers, were expected to build their *omertà*, their patience, so while they worked, they could deal with insults of foreigners who ruled, and also protect the family. Well, for the same reasons, the women, especially mothers, were expected to build their *serietà*."

Teodoro did not hesitate to ask his question. "What's *serietà*, Mamma?"

"It has to do with a person, especially a mother, being serious and committed to helping everyone in the family grow close together and stay connected all through life. This was important because, like we have said to each other many times, the family was the only world for the peasants, not the government or the country."

Anna jumped in quickly because she wanted to get ahead of Filomena who had just raised her hand and was about to say something. "You know, Teodoro, *serietà* for a mother includes doing a good job with all the chores that need to be done like preparing delicious meals, washing clothes, hanging clothes on the clothesline and cleaning the apartment. But it's much more than that. It's how a mother cares about everyone in the family, especially someone who might be sick or needs help for some reason."

Gloria stared at her sisters. "So a woman who's only about romance, or only about looking perfect like they show in the movies, does not necessarily have *serietà*." She turned toward Mamma with a look on her face that said she was bothered by something. "Ma, I don't mean to be disrespectful, but Sophia's mother is never around. Sophia told me her mother is always lost in that job she took seating people at tables in that restaurant up town. And she's always carried away about looking right."

"That's why Sophia's brother, Gino, kicked the marbles I was playing with. His mother is never around." Teodoro declared.

Filomena gestured in that particular way whenever she was being a teacher which Anna ignored a few minutes ago. "Ma, we call a mother like that *mala fimmina* (bad woman)?"

"You are correct. For Sicilians, *mala fimmina* is not a woman who is promiscuous, but a woman who can't do, or doesn't want to do, her job being the center of the family."

Gloria jumped in again. "Gee! I'm glad we're having this talk. What a woman, a mother, does has to do with things that are a lot more important than sex and cooking. She has to do things that keep everyone of those petals of the artichoke connected and devoted to each other."

Filomena grinned, still in her teacher mode. "But good cooking is one way of helping the family grow close together." Everyone agreed, smiling.

"Hey!" Gloria was even more excited, carefully adjusting the sleeves of her red blouse. "When we were talking outside with Zio Gaetano and Papa, Zio Gaetano mentioned that Sicilian saying, 'A man is rich when he has good friends. It doesn't matter if he has no money.' Well guess what? I'm adding to that."

"What are you adding?" Tony asked.

"I'm starting a new Sicilian saying." A wide grin covered her face. "It doesn't matter if a man doesn't have any money. A man is rich if he has a good mother with a lot of *serietà* and good friends."

Everyone applauded, laughing. Papa pointed to Gloria. "What you added to is brilliant."

Several days later at the Goodrich Tobacco Farm, pickers and haulers were scattered in clusters along the edge of a field, while taking a drink during water time. As usual, everyone was engaged in vigorous discussions. Occasionally these discussions resulted in arguments about whose neighborhood or town was better in terms of some unique feature. Boys from one town, for example, insisted that their high school football team was better then that of another town. Bart was engaged in such a discussion with a boy from Hartford. Because Bart and the other picker were shouting, a crowd gathered around them. Their argument related to another major interest and concerned which of two professional boxers was the best. " I'll say it one more time!" the boy from Hartford yelled, placing his hands on his hips and thrusting his face at Bart. "Sandy Smith is the greatest!" Sandy Smith came from Hartford.

Bart pushed his clenched fist forward with the index finger

extended, almost stabbing the other boy. "And I'll tell you again, Willie Pep is the best!" William Guglielmo Papaleo, was also a professional boxer who came from Middletown. More than that, he came from the very neighborhood where my gang lived. Willie had already achieved national attention because last year he became the world's featherweight boxing champion.

As the argument continued, the boy from Hartford screamed, "Your Willie Pop-lay-o, or whatever the hell his name is, sucks! He only throws a lot of little rabbit punches. That Dago can't throw a good knockout punch to save his ass!" The boys surrounding them moved closer, watching with intense interest.

I thought Bart wouldn't lose it when he yelled back, "You don't know what you are talking about. Willie is featherweight champ of the whole world." But then he exploded. "And here's a rabbit punch from a Dago, you asshole!" Bart whacked the boy in the chest, knocking him flat on his back.

Sprawled out on the ground, the boy screamed, "You hit me! You dirty bastard!"

Mr. George, who happened to be nearby talking to Mr. Kelly, ran over, pushed his way through the crowd, and startled when he saw the boy lying on the ground. "What's the matter?"

The boy pointed to Bart. "He hit me. I didn't touch him."

Mr. George immediately turned to Bart and asked with a very stern tone, "Aren't you in Santo's gang? Give me your number. You're docked today's pay."

With deep sighs of "Wow!" and "Unbelievable!" all of the boys were surprised, as was I. Everyone felt Bart's punishment was too severe. Being docked the wage of one full day was very rare and took place usually when a picker or hauler did something carelessly that injured many tobacco plants or leaves.

Without reflecting for even a second, I quickly pushed my way over to Mr. George, stood before him, and yelled, "Hey, wait a minute! That's not fair! The argument they had is their business not the farms!"

Mr. George thrust his arm. "Shut up, Santo, or you'll be docked too."

Mr. Kelly had also entered the crowd of boys. He stared at

me and jerked his head to one side, advising me to walk away.

I spotted his message, whispered to myself, "*Omertà, omertà*," and turned away.

Bart's argument with this boy remained the topic of discussion for the rest of the day. Even more than baseball, Friday night, professional boxing matches, that were held throughout New England and in New York City, played a major role in the pride everyone felt. The career of Willie Pep got a lot of attention from my gang, and he was our hero. On some occasions after a workout, he walked down the street of our neighborhood, dressed in a very sharp, zoot suit and polished shoes, and sat on the street curb or the steps at the entrance to a tenement house. Kids of all ages huddled around him and chatted about his latest match, or the boxing matches that took place every Sunday in our neighborhood by the river.

In Middletown's North End, boxing was a major recreational pass time. On Sundays, after everyone returned from attending Mass at Saint Sebastian Parish, boxing matches among boys of the neighborhood took place in an open area by the Connecticut River. Many adults came to watch these matches and usually paid about five cents admission. Every boy who boxed had a "manager," either a teenager or young adult. Managers negotiated among themselves arranging matches for a particular Sunday. Boys were usually matched by age and also in terms of size and experience. Mimicking the professional sport of boxing, typically a manager received five cents, from the money collected, for each round of a match his boxer fought. In turn, the manager gave his boxer two or three cents for each round he boxed. The adults cheered boys who happened to win on a given day, and also encouraged boys who did not win to continue developing their skills.

The day after Bart was docked one full day we were in the Central Lot waiting for assignments. Suddenly a large, shiny, black, Buick sedan slowly rolled into the compound. Everyone paused and stared, since it was very unusual to see a car like that in this location.

Bongi spotted the car and shouted with excitement and surprise. "That looks just like my cousin's car. It is his car!" Bongi and Willie were cousins.

Tony also recognized the car, as did other members of my gang. "My God! I don't believe it! Why is he here?"

The door of the sedan opened, and Willie stepped out smiling. He was only about five feet two inches tall and slender. Although his nose was scared and somewhat flat, he still presented a handsome appearance. His head was covered with wavy, black hair, and his dark eyes sparkled under a canopy of thick, black eyebrows. His smile, his very sharp zoot suit and polished shoes, and his way of walking with confidence, always led everyone to stare at him.

All of us from the North End watched in silence, but a boy from the South End shouted, "Look! It's Willie Pep!" In seconds a crowd rushed toward him chanting, "Willie, Willie, Willie!" Standing off to one side, Mr. George remained still, glaring at him. Mr. Kelly, however, quickly walked over, shook his hand, and jogged toward the Main Cabin to inform Mr. Williams.

Because he apparently had heard the commotion and chanting, Mr. Williams was already stepping out of his cabin as Mr. Kelly approached. "What's going on?" I moved closer to the Main Cabin so I could catch some of what might happen.

"That's Willie Pep over there. Wow! I don't know why he's here." It was great to see how proud Mr. Kelly felt that Willie Pep was here.

"You mean the professional boxer?" Mr. Williams was also very surprised and pleased.

"Yes that's him, the world featherweight champ." Thrusting his shoulders back, he added. "And he's from Middletown."

I noticed that Mr. George had not moved from where he was standing when Willie arrived.

Mr. Williams eagerly pushed his way through the crowd of boys, and I followed with Tony a few yards behind. When Mr. Williams reached Willie, he extended his arm for a handshake. "It's a real honor to meet you. What brings you here?"

"May I please speak with you privately?" Willie shouted, because by now the crowd of boys was cheering loudly.

"Of course, come in." As Willie followed Mr. Williams, he spotted my gang and gave us a quick wave.

Everyone from Middletown milled about the superintendent's cabin. I stood as close as I could because I was eager to learn what this was all about. While Tony, Bart and I chatted, boys from the South End and from Wethersfield kept shouting. "Do you believe that? I saw Willie Pep in person." "Do you believe that, I shook Willie's hand?" The boys from Hartford drifted to the opposite end of the Central Lot.

Several minutes later Mr. Williams and Willie stepped out of the cabin. Everyone stood still and stared. Mr. Williams called out, "Okay boys, Mr. Kelly will tell you which fields you're working in today. We're losing time. Let's get started."

Everyone began to walk toward their trucks. Willie called out, "Hey Bongi! Hey Dom! Hey you guys! Come over here for a second." All of us trotted over.

Bongi was really turned on. "Wow, cousin. It's great to see you. Are you looking for a job as a picker or a hauler?"

Laughing, Willie placed his hand on Dominic's head. "Actually, Bongi, I applied for a job to train your kid brother to be the best picker. Then he can show up all you guys."

Dominic beamed with pride. "Gee Willie, thanks. I'm definitely going to ..."

Bart did not wait for Dominic to finish. "Holy mackerel. We didn't expect to see you here."

I gasped, "*Madonna* (wow), this is a long way from Ferry Street! What the hell are you doing here?"

Willie placed his hand on Bart's shoulder. "Your parents and Santo's father told me what happened yesterday with that kid who said I throw rabbit punches. We decided that getting docked a whole day was unfair." He went on to explain that my father thought it would be a good idea if he came here to help the superintendent understand why it wasn't fair, and added with a smile, "Mr. Williams just decided that you're not docked for what happened yesterday." Willie turned and looked in the direction where Mr. George was still standing, watching us, and we turned and stared at him. Willie raised his right hand, extended his index finger and small finger, while clenching the middle fingers against his palm, and aimed the extended fingers at Mr. George.

"That jerk deserves the horns," Melo whispered. "It's the best way to tell him to go to hell."

Mr. George spotted Willie's gesture, grimaced and walked away.

Willie slowly turned and faced us. "I know you guys will keep it up and show them we Dagos can do it."

Willie's dark eyes glistened with confidence, and I wondered what a boxer, who was in the ring fighting him, must have thought when he looked into those eyes. "Sometimes that Mr. George can be a real asshole. But even though he's much taller and bigger than you are, Willie, you threw him a knockout punch today. It's great of you to come and help."

With his hands on the shoulders of his cousins, Willie leaned forward and quietly reminded us, "Hey everybody, always remember, *E' riccu l'omu quannu c'avi amici; un ci fa nenti s'unn'avi dinari.* ("A man is wealthy when he has good friends; it doesn't matter if he has no money.") And today I had a chance to show that."

"You sure did!" Bart exclaimed. "And today I'm really rich, thanks to you."

"You're more than welcomed, Bart." Grinning, Willie shook the hand of each member of the gang and slowly walked toward his car. He turned, smiled, gave us a wave, climbed in his car and drove out of the Central Lot. We stood still and slowly turned our heads, watching the car disappear into the distance.

At the end of the day all of the boys were still very excited because they had seen Willie Pep in person, and some of them even had a chance to shake his hand. While riding the truck home, Jack Kane called out to Bart, "Gee, you guys have it made. I mean Willie Pep comes from your neighborhood."

Brian Coleman shouted, "Wow! That he would take the time to come here and help you. That's unbelievable."

Bart grinned. "You're right. It's great when friends help you out."

That Sunday our apartment was crowded by noon. While Southern Italians typically maintained the custom of having the entire family for dinner every night, the major meal of the week took place on Sunday. Since most adults and teenagers were not working, Sunday provided the opportunity to have a larger gathering of *la famiglia* and relatives. Sunday *pranzo* usually began mid-afternoon and continued into the evening.

Uncle Gaetano, aunt Concetta, and their children, who lived across the street on the third floor of a tenement house, had already arrived. Uncle Gaetano immigrated to the United States first, and Papa followed two years later. Their older brother, Aurelio, and three sisters chose to remain in Sicily. As they chatted, Uncle Gaetano and aunt Concetta were wishing, with much emotion, that their oldest son, Sebastiano, could be here today, enjoying the *pranzo*. He carried the nickname "Lucky," had been drafted shortly after the start of World War II, and was now serving in the South Pacific. Their youngest son, Alberto, was sixteen years old, not that much taller than I was, but his dark hair was much more curly. He and I sat at the far end of the kitchen chatting. Alberto's other brother, Gaetano, who was named after their father, carried the nickname, "Smiles" and was one of the best pool players in the North End, which he demonstrated a couple of weeks ago. He was eighteen years old and sat chatting with Tony. Uncle Gaetano's and Aunt Concetta's daughters, Isabella and Olivia, who already finished high school, were chatting with Anna and Filomena. Isabella was a little older. Her smile and eyes sparkled in a dramatic way and her face was framed by long, jet black hair. Olivia was a little shorter, but more lively and animated, and was constantly joking about something. Her hair was not as dark as Isabella's but, in my opinion, she still had that attractive Sicilian look. Both of them were working in a textile mill where army tents were being sewn, and thought it made sense to work there until they decided what they really wanted to do.

Uncle Vito, Mamma's older brother, his wife Aunt Felicia, and their children had also been invited, but had not yet arrived. Uncle Vito was very short, even for a Sicilian, and almost bald.

He had served as a captain in the Italian army during World War I. He immigrated to the United States and set up what became a successful one-man business, making and repairing shoes. Although I experienced Aunt Felicia as a nice person, she struck me as very quiet compared to my mother, Aunt Concetta and my sisters, but especially Olivia who always expressed herself with intense feelings and vigorous gestures.

Aunt Felicia's and Uncle Vito's son, Filippo, was born in Sicily, immigrated to the United States with his parents, and was now serving in the US military. Their daughter, Sofia, who was in her twenties, was also born in Sicily. From birth she had a physical disability, but I wasn't clear exactly what her problem was. All through her childhood she needed help with walking. When she approached her teenage years, she began to use a wheelchair Papa was able to obtain for her so that she could move about the neighborhood more easily. Maria, their other daughter, was Tony's age. Uncle Vito's family lived one block from Ferry Street on Rapello Avenue in one of the small tenement houses very near the Connecticut River.

When Uncle Vito's family arrived, Tony and Smiles immediately went outside, lifted Sofia out of her wheelchair and carried her up the stairs into the kitchen, while Alberto and I carried in the wheelchair. Everyone from each of the three families hugged and kissed each other, exclaiming, "*benvinutu*" (welcome).

Mamma interrupted the hugging, kissing and laughing. "*E' ura di mangiari*." ("It's time to eat.")

Each parent took a seat at the long table, and each child took a seat at one of the three smaller tables that had been placed in a row, while Anna and Filomena helped Sofia out of her wheelchair and guided her to a chair. Then they took a seat with the adults. Each of the men and boys tucked a cloth napkin into the collar of his shirt, but most of the women held a cloth napkin in one hand.

Typically, the atmosphere of this Sunday pranzo quickly swayed back and forth between joking and arguing, while Enrico Caruso's soothing voice, singing the ancient Neapolitan song "*O Sole Mio*" drifted up from the nearby record player and filled the kitchen. I turned and spotted Smiles tilting his head back and holding a slice of cantaloupe, wrapped in prosciutto, over his wide, open mouth. "Wow, do I love prosciutto and melon." He stuck half of the slice of melon in his mouth and began munching with his eyes closed and face radiating with happiness.

Tony took what Smiles just did as an invitation to compete. He reached out to a plate of anchovies, picked up one with his fingertips, slowly tilted his head back, opened his mouth wide, raised his arm with the anchovy dangling, dropped it in his mouth, chewed with delight, and sighed, "Aaah, I love anchovies." I wondered why my brother was being so ridiculous.

Olivia was holding three large green olives in one hand. "You guys are being jerks. You better stop, or you'll get our fathers mad."

For some reason I began to act silly too. I smacked my lips, and vigorously munched on a piece of provolone cheese. "Olivia, they're just kidding. By the way, why do you keep eating so many olives? You know your name is Olivia, not *olivi* (olives)."

Isabella burst out laughing, while picking up a slice of Genoa salami and wrapping it around a piece of cheese. "Santo, maybe she should change her name to '*Oliva*.' She must eat a dozen olives at one time."

Alberto had been watching Tony drop the anchovy into his mouth with interest. "Watch this, Tony. I'll bet you can't do it."

"Do what?"

With ceremony, Alberto reached out and picked up an anchovy with the fingertips of each hand. He paused for a moment, and flipped one anchovy almost three feet up in the air, tilted his head back, and the anchovy spiraled down into his wide, open mouth. Munching with exaggerated delight, he immediately did the same with the other anchovy. While it twirled down, I thought to myself, "Wow, that's really great." But I was quickly brought back to reality when Uncle Gaetano shouted with an edge of anger, "*Figghiu miu! Basta! Chi fai, sì pazzu?*" ("My son! Enough! What are you crazy?)

At the same time, Uncle Vito shouted, "*Tutti stunati siti!*" (You're all stupid!")

And Papa called out with a tone that was less loud but expressed more anger, "*Basta, non quannu mangiamu.*" ("Enough,

106

not when we're eating.")

Mamma quickly turned toward Papa and placed a hand on his arm. "*Caru maritu, iddi stannu schirzannu.*" ("My dear husband, they are only being funny.")

Alberto now felt nervous because of what he had done. He placed his hands together. "*Zio Sebastiano, mi dispiaci.*" ("Uncle Sebastiano, I'm sorry.")

"*E puru a mmia, Papa.*" ("And me too, Papa.") Tony added.

"*Grazzii. Mangiati, mangiati.*" (Thanks. Eat, eat.")

Suddenly Uncle Gaetano yelled at Alberto, "Figghiu miu." All of us looked up wondering whether he was about to announce some punishment for Alberto because of what he did. Knowing he had our undivided attention, Uncle Gaetano pointed to a long plate set in the center of the large table on which was curled a pan-roasted eel. "Alberto, maybe you can throw *st'ancidda nta l'aria* (this eel in the air) *e acchiapparla ca vucca* (and catch it with your mouth)." Everyone burst out laughing.

Tony flipped his hand up high. "Great idea, Alberto."

While the joking continued, Mamma gestured toward Aunt Concetta and Aunt Felicia and pointed to the stove. They walked over to the stove, and each took hold of the handle on one side of a large metal pan, lifted it off the stove, and carried it to the long table. Mamma carefully scooped soup into bowls, as Aunt Concetta and Aunt Felicia served one to each of us.

Teodoro immediately dipped his spoon into his bowl and lifted it to his lips. "I really love *pasta e fasoli* (bean soup)."

Alberto grinned. "I'm glad you do, Teodoro. Always remember that song." Waving his spoon, Alberto began singing, and we all joined in. "Pasta e fasoli make-a the weak-a man-a strong. Pasta e fasoli make-a you live-a very long."

Isabella had already poured a spoonful of soup into her mouth. " So I'm as tough as you guys."

While everyone feasted on the soup, Tony and I shared with excitement the news that Willie Pep visited the farm to help Bart. During a brief pause, Uncle Gaetano commented "I have some good news too!" and focused on my sisters, brothers and me.

"What news?" Filomena asked.

I noticed Papa grinning. Isabella laughed and shouted, "You mean your father hasn't told you yet! We found out last night."

Anna looked more puzzled than Filomena. "What are they talking about, Papa?" I knew it couldn't be bad news because Papa was smiling, but I was really confused too.

Placing her hand on Papa's shoulder, Mamma commented, "Iano (my father's nickname came from the last four letters of his name, Sebastiano), this is a good time to tell them."

Smiling with pride, Papa looked at all of us. "I was appointed a supernumerary policeman. I got the news late yesterday, but I wanted to announce it today so we could celebrate."

Uncle Gaetano lifted his glass of wine, "*A tutti salute!* (Everyone, congratulations!). That's what we are celebrating today."

Everyone raised their glasses and shouted, "*Salute, Papa!*"

"What's a supernumerary cop?" Zio Vito had an edge of anger in his tone and eyes.

Filomena, of course, couldn't resist the opportunity to do some teaching. "I think it's a part time job. It's somebody they add to the police force for a particular reason. You know, to do something that the other cops can't do."

Tony surprised me when he yelled with his face twisted in confusion, "Papa, a cop! I don't get it. Why take a job like that?"

Alberto immediately joined Tony. "Yes! Zio, I never heard of this."

Mamma and Aunt Concetta ignored what was being said and began serving pasta with crab sauce, a summer dish everyone relished. While we continued eating, Papa shared that because the Sicilian population in Middletown had grown big before World War II started, the police department decided they needed someone who could speak Sicilian. With this help they would be better able to communicate with immigrants who did not understand English too well.

Anna still seemed confused. "How did you get this job?"

Papa explained that Mr. Russell told him about the position. Mr. Russell was the owner of the Russell Manufacturing Company, a textile mill located in Middletown where Papa had worked for several years operating weaving looms.

Anna continued. "Why did he tell you and not someone else?"

"During the past years I gave him a lot of help. I trained new Sicilian immigrants to operate looms, and explained other jobs, like moving and storing supplies."

Olivia usually came up with really clear ideas when our families were having discussions. "So because you helped him, he decided to help you?"

Papa twirled pasta with the tip of his fork, "Sì (yes). Mr. Russell introduced me to the commissioner of police. The commissioner and the chief of police talked to me and decided to give me the job."

Uncle Vito immediately pushed his fork forward and, with a tone of disbelief and intense anger, interrupted Papa. "Our ancestors hated the government and their soldiers and police! Our ancestors didn't trust them because of all the *sfruttamento* (exploitation) they experienced." Now Uncle Vito waved his fork over his head to emphasize details about his past experiences that we had already heard many times. For example, when he was in the Italian army during the last World War, a lot of our *paisani* (neighbors) didn't like that, because they expected him to hide in the mountains like a lot of the other men did to avoid being in the army. He glared at Papa and brought up another detail I had never heard about. "Iano, if you want another reason why we should stay away from police, remember what happened in Colorado just before you arrived in this country? All the paisani here were talking about it when they heard the news."

Uncle Vito went on describing in detail that in 1914 Italian immigrants lived in a tent colony and worked for the Rockerfeller-owned Fuel and Ironworks near Pueblo, Colorado. Because they were dissatisfied with wages and working conditions, they held a demonstration. The company called in state militia to subdue the strike. Troopers shot at the demonstrators and burned the entire tent camp to the ground. Several men were killed, and two women and thirteen children burned to death.

Suddenly, Filomena jumped in with vigor because she wanted to prevent the discussion from becoming an explosion.

"Zio Vito, because that happened, it doesn't mean we should be against all soldiers and police."

Olivia surprised me, and I think everyone else, when she called out with an edge of anger glaring from her dark eyes. "Are you kidding, cousin? You're in college now. You can look up the *sfruttamento* that went on in Sicily for centuries. We've talked a lot about it, right?"

"Okay, You're right." I was surprised to see Filomena look so apologetic. She turned to Uncle Vito. "*Scusa, Zio.* ("Excuse me uncle.) I know our ancestors had reasons to hate the government and the soldiers and police. But don't you think there are a lot of other ways that soldiers and police have helped people?"

Mamma stepped in to see if she also could quiet things down. "*Basta tutti. Sintiti a Sebastiano.*" ("Enough, everyone. Listen to Sebastiano.")

But Uncle Vito did not give Papa a chance to continue, nor did he consider what Filomena said. While munching on a mouthful of pasta, he continued pushing his point by bringing up a topic that was painful for everyone. "Like I said a moment ago, our ancestors did not trust the *pulizzia* (police). They hated them." He slammed the palm of his hand on the table so hard some dishes rattled. "Iano! We know what they and those soldiers did to your father and mother in our village! Then why did you take the job?"

Everyone took a deep breath, glanced back and forth at Uncle Vito and Papa, and remained silent for a long moment.

"*Caro* (dear), Vito." Papa's voice was more soft then his usual raspy tone. He paused, sat back in his chair, and exchanged glances with his brother. Neither one of them showed that he was hurt by Uncle Vito's reminder that their parents had been shot years ago by soldiers in the piazza of their village. I had heard many times that when my grandparents were killed, Sicilians were rebelling against what they experienced as unfair laws imposed by the recently established Italian government dominated by Northern Italians. Papa lifted his fork to ensure everyone's attention. "Gaetano and I are very happy now because our Papa and Mamma gave their lives for what I plan to do. I took the job because, instead of working on only one side of the street to help

Acculturation not Assimilation

our paisani, with this extra job, I can help them from both sides of the street."

Mamma glanced at Papa and Uncle Gaetano with warmth and sympathy in her eyes and stared at her brother with an expression that scolded him. As she shared her thoughts, my sisters, brothers and I were proud of the sense she made of Papa's becoming a policeman. She reminded all of us that by taking this part time job, Papa would be in a stronger position to help families in the neighborhood continue developing *l'ordine della famiglia*, (the rules of the family) as they handle the American ways. "Like he could help paisani understand that they must maintain respect not only for family members, and other families in the North End, but also for the city of Middletown. He could help our neighborhood have *campanilismo* for Middletown."

Introducing *campanilismo* into the discussion caused Uncle Vito to lower his head and clutch his hands in deep thought. In Southern Italy, especially in Sicily, *contadini* (peasants) did not identify themselves with the country of Italy. They defined themselves in terms of their relationships with parents, siblings, relatives and the village in which they lived. Southern Italians called this loyalty to the village or region *campanilismo* which stems from the word *campanile*, a church steeple or belfry. Accordingly, the roots of this loyalty were symbolized by the distance the sound of the bell traveled which defined the boundaries of a village or neighborhood. So *contadini* who could not hear the bell because they lived beyond this area, where not *paisani* (neighbors). Especially in Sicily, then, each village developed unique customs and dialect. I remember, for example, how my parents and relatives joked about the fact that peasants who lived in Sortino, a village only about five miles from Melilli, pronounced some words in their own unique way. So whenever a peasant from Melilli happened to encounter another peasant, while walking his mule into the hillside, and they engaged in a brief conversation, the peasant from Melilli knew immediately he was talking to someone from Sortino, and the peasant from Sortino recognized he was talking to someone from Melilli.

After bringing up the Sicilian notion of *campanilismo* as it

111

related to the argument that was going on, which was insightful, Mamma paused and scanned everyone. "There's one more thing. Because the United States is at war with Italy, it is very hard for many *paisani* to maintain respect for the United States because they are confused." She pointed to Tony. "Like you noticed several minutes ago, even Tony showed how confused he was about whether to have respect for the city's police department?" Tony squirmed a little. Mamma turned, stared at her brother, and reminded him how often he has talked in a disrespectful way about the local government and the United States, especially since his son, Filippo, enlisted in the United States army. "Like I said, maybe with this new job Iano can help you, Vito, and our *paisani* to have *campanilismo* for Middletown." At this point Mamma raised the palms of her hands to indicate she was finished expressing her thoughts. "Now it's time to serve *baccala* (swordfish), *ancidda* (eel), *sparaci* (asparagus) and *miringiani* (baked eggplant)."

While Mamma, Aunt Concetta and Aunt Felicia retrieved the next course and placed the items on the table. Filomena decided do some teaching to add to what Mamma had just said. "There's something else. You know how in Italy prejudice has always separated northerners and southerners. To northern Italians, southerners, especially us Sicilians, are really inferior. We have our own customs, and they think we refuse to speak proper Italian. Well, if Papa is a policeman, he will help to melt that prejudice away."

His eyes wet with tears, Uncle Gaetano, again raised his wine glass. "*Salute* to Sebastiano on this side of the street where he is *Capo* and can help paisani with their problems. And *salute* to Sebastiano on the other side of the street where he is a policeman and can help *paisani* become a part of Middletown."

"Salute!" everyone exclaimed, tapping their glasses.

Papa grinned with obvious appreciation. "*Mille grazzii.* ("A million thanks.) But you know what? To do the best job on the side of the street where I will be a policeman, I have to learn to speak better English and to write English."

Isabella surprised everyone when she yelled, "Zio, you have a daughter who is going to Teachers College, you know. Now you can be a student, and she can be the *Capo*."

Everyone, including Papa, burst out laughing.

Anna must have thought she had remained quiet too long and used this moment to jump in. "Come on, Filomena. Let's watch a brief lesson while we're eating our fish."

Filomena smiled and could not resist the invitation to hold a class before this audience. "Okay, Papa, put down your fork, fold your hands, and look into my eyes. Say, 'I am.'"

Papa faced Filomena and folded his hands. "I-a am-a." All of us laughed.

"Papa, say 'I' not 'I-a'."

Papa burst into song, as if he were an opera singer "I! I! I!" Everyone exploded with laughter.

Filomena folded her hands, leaned forward and tried to take on a serious tone. "Now we're going to say the word job."

"Giobba," Papa whispered. Some of us slapped our thighs, laughing.

"Papa, listen. The first sound is 'Ja', 'Ja.' You know like the first sound of Giuseppe. Then add an 'a' sound, and then a 'b' sound."

"Gia, gia, ba, ba. I mean-a giobba."

Uncle Gaetano laughed so loud the walls seemed to vibrate.

"Okay, Pa, it's going to take time." Filomena tried to be reassuring. "Let's try another word. What if you have to stop a car? Say car."

"Carru,"

"What if you have to go into a bar? Say bar, bar."

"Barr-a,"

As everyone continued chuckling, Filomena looked into Papa's eyes with an expression of hope. "Well, we have a lot of practicing to do. I know you, and all your paisani, have to add the 'a' sound to nearly every English word. Go ahead and eat your baccalà. We'll have another lesson later."

Mamma grinned, and congratulated Papa with a big hug. Extending her arms, she added she was pleased everyone was enjoying the meal and asked everyone to remember, "*Lu megghiu pastu è la suddisfazioni.*" ("The best meal is a person's satisfaction.") Suddenly the expression on her face changed from pleasure to concern. "But I have something to share that has spoiled my sense of satisfaction. I apologize for disrupting the happiness you are sharing, but there is a problem that really disturbs me."

Papa placed his fork down and looked at Mamma with a confused expression, "*Chi? Dimmi 'na cosa.*" ("What? Please tell me.")

Mamma explained that when she went to get some groceries today at "Joe-the-Jew's" store, he mentioned to her that he would appreciate very much if he had a chance to talk to Papa. The look on Joe's face made clear that he was scared. The only thing he told her was that a *carogna* (scoundrel) visited him and threatened him.

On Ferry Street, right in the middle of this Sicilian neighborhood, was a grocery store owned and operated by Joseph Epstein. All the *paisani* affectionately called him, "Joe-the-Jew," who was very much admired by everyone. He was outgoing, friendly and very generous. When a mother entered the store, if accompanied by her children, he typically exclaimed to them, "Hello. *Mangia! Mangia!*" (Eat, Eat). While the mother was deciding what to buy, he always asked the children if they wanted something to eat. If a child asked for olives, he scooped several out of a large barrel sitting on the floor. If the child asked for cheese, he asked what kind, and then cut a piece from one of the large cheeses hanging by a rope from the ceiling.

When Papa heard Mamma say that Joe had been threatened by a scoundrel, he stood up immediately and asked if the store was still open. Anna looked at the clock. "I'm sure it is. Joe always stays open late on Sunday." Papa announced that he would be right back and urged everyone to continue enjoying dinner.

About a half hour later he returned. We stared at him in anticipation, while continuing to eat. For some reason I couldn't wait to find out what was going on. "Did you catch Joe? What's the matter?"

Papa took his seat. "Joe-the-Jew told me two Italians from Portland visited him."

"Why did that upset him?" Anna asked.

"They said they were selling insurance."

Since Teodoro had remained quiet for a long time, except to

laugh, he surprised me when he spoke up." Why would that upset him?" Tony nudged Teodoro with his elbow and glanced at all of us sitting at the small table. We knew what Tony had in mind.

"*Aspetta, ora lu spiegu* (Wait, now I will explain.)" Papa went on to say these men told Joe that if he paid them for their insurance, they could guarantee that nothing would happen to his store. But if he didn't pay, something would probably happen.

Filomena threw her arms out. "That extortion stuff is disgusting."

Anna slapped the table. "Why doesn't he call the police?"

I was a little confused by Papa's response. "If Joe did call the police, that might make things even worse." Now Papa was talking almost in a whisper. "Those men will do some damage to the store, or they could break in at night, and take away groceries."

Tony frowned. "Joe is such a good guy. Look how he gives us kids something to eat every time we go in that store."

"And look how he gives something every Sunday for Mamma and us girls to take to the families by the river," Gloria shouted.

"What can we do to help Joe?" Teodoro asked.

Papa shared that Joe-the-Jew described the two men and, from that description, he knows who they are. They operate out of Portland across the river.

Uncle Gaetano stared at Papa. "They're not our *paisani*, are they?"

Replying that they came from Naples a few years ago, Papa continued with a tone that expressed a lot of determination. "I plan to visit these men to help them understand *che sunu pazzi*" (they're crazy.) for trying to bring their business to this neighborhood. I will tell them that Joe is a big and good part of this neighborhood and a paisano. I'm sure they will understand."

Tony was very excited. "Hey, Papa! It's great you can help Joe from our side of the street."

"But wait a minute," Isabella joined in, chewing on a piece of asparagus, one end of which was protruding from her mouth. "He is also helping Joe from the other side of the street as a supernumerary."

"Well, let's say he's helping him with a foot on each side of the street," Alberto added.

Everyone became involved in animated and vigorous discussions about Joe Epstein's predicament and the problem with extortionists. At one point, Papa interrupted the conversations, commenting that we might be interested in hearing about a problem the city of Middletown was having.

Uncle Vito chuckled with disgust. He was still holding onto his opposition to government which he usually expressed whenever our families got together. "What problem is Middletown having that we should care about? Middletown doesn't care about our problems." From this sarcastic remark, he mentioned an issue all of us had heard him bring up many times. When Sofia reached her tenth birthday, after they arrived in the United States, Uncle Vito went to the town hall several times to try to get help for her, including a wheelchair. But for reasons no one could understand, weeks passed without Vito receiving any response. One day Papa arrived at their door with a wheel chair. The neighborhood noticed that their *Capo* again solved another problem.

Because Uncle Vito had repeated this detail numerous times, everyone must have drifted away into private thoughts. I know I did. But he recaptured our attention when he shifted to a topic we had not heard him complain about before. He reminded us that his son, Filippo, had enlisted in the military shortly after World War II broke out, rather than wait to be drafted, and he asked to be sent to the South Pacific, not Europe, because he was born in Sicily and grew up there. Uncle Vito's anger exploded when he reminded us that the military still sent him to Europe.

Anna thrust her arm out. "But, *Zio* Vito, with all respect, when Filippo came home on leave for that week, he explained to all of us why he was being sent to Europe."

"I don't care!" Vito interrupted with anger still pouring out of him. "Now there's talk about invading Sicily, and there's my son over there. *"E' statu pigliatu pir fissa."* ("He's been taken for a fool.") When he's looking through the sight of his rifle, and he sees one of his own cousins, what is he going to do?"

Filomena slapped the tabletop while still holding her fork. "Come on, *Zio*. Instead of shooting his paisani, Filippo's helping them. Remember? He explained when he came home on leave that the government needs guys in the military who speak English and Sicilian really good. He's not carrying a gun. He's working with people who are making plans. So if the Americans do go into Sicily, maybe Filippo's job will be to help make arrangements with villages that will help Americans."

Papa placed his hand on Vito's arm. "I understand why you feel the way you do. But maybe those feelings are blocking you from seeing problems Middletown is having." Papa captured everyone's attention again, including Vito's, when he added "*Ognunu avi la so' malatia.* (Everyone has his own problems.) Then he did something he always liked to do which was to come up with a Sicilian saying that clinched his point. He emphasized that all of us should do what we can about problems family, friends and neighbors have because, *morti ci stamu assai, e vivi picca.*" (We stay dead a long time and alive just a little while.)

"Where's the problem Middletown is having?" Sophia asked while scooping up a piece of eggplant with her fork. I wasn't at all surprised that she would step into the discussion now, after remaining quiet for a long time, since it had to do with helping people with problems.

Papa explained that the problem does not have to do with the Sicilian neighborhood. It concerns another group of people who are kind of isolated from the city like the Sicilians are.

"What people are you talking about?" Anna asked.

"This afternoon, while I was at the police station, I learned the city could not find anyone who would take the job of driving the Books-On-Wheels into the South End." We all knew that a group of African Americans had established a community in the South End over the past twenty years.

"What's the Books-On-Wheels?" Sofia asked, "I never heard of it."

Filomena glanced at Papa, conveying with eagerness that she wanted to address Sofia's question. Papa nodded. She went on to explain that a couple of years ago, before the war started, the politicians of Middletown did something really good. They noticed that some of the black kids were not going to school, and that the grownups were not using the library. So they decided to bring the library to them with a huge van that had shelves built in it on which were stacked books for kids and grownups. The truck went into the South End about once a week.

I stuck my fork in a piece of eel. "Filomena, didn't you ride on that truck sometimes to help out?"

Tony joined me with excitement. "Yeah, before you left for college, you asked Santo and me about books kids might like."

"You're right, guys. The city had two or three high school students go with the truck to show books to the kids, read books to them if they wanted, and loan the books out if anyone asked. I was one of those high school students who volunteered. It was a lot of fun."

Mamma apparently noticed that everyone had placed their forks down, so she decided to clear the table and bring out desserts. Aunt Concetta and Aunt Felicia joined her, carrying plates to the sink.

While the tables were being cleared, Sofia stayed focused on Filomena. "Wow, that's great. I would love to see that truck someday. I know you brought me books to read, because I'm stuck in that darn wheelchair and can't go to school or the library."

Anna pointed at Papa. "I don't get it. Why can't they find anyone to drive the truck? "

"No one will take the job because white men are afraid to go into that neighborhood."

Filomena sat straight up in her chair and seemed upset by what Papa just said. "Nothing like that ever happened when I volunteered on that truck. Besides why don't they give the job to a black guy?"

Papa spread out his hands. "I don't know why the job is not open to Blacks. I told them I would drive the truck."

Maria surprised everyone when she jumped in. "Aren't you worried about that fighting stuff between black and white guys? Some white guys might give you trouble, because they're against the Blacks."

Papa explained he understood why Maria would ask that question. But she should keep in mind that the people in the South End know who he is, and Blacks and Sicilians have always gotten along. Everyone nodded.

Uncle Vito stared at Maria. "*Figghia mia* (my daughter) I know we will never forget what happened in Louisiana when those crazy people hung our *paisani* because they let black people in the store and treated them good"

Anna walked over to Maria and hugged her. "We Sicilians feel for Blacks because we know what it's like to be put down. So you can see why Papa offered to drive the Books-On-Wheels."

While this conversation went on Mamma, Aunt Concetta, and Aunt Felicia had been placing dishes filled with almonds and walnuts on the tables. On other dishes they arrayed biscotti (almond cookies), *cannoli* (tube-shaped shells of fried pastry dough filled with ricotta cheese blended with pasticcio nuts and wine), and bunches of red grapes.

Papa reached out, took two walnuts and squeezed them together. While peeling the shells away, he explained that when he volunteered to drive the Books-On-Wheels, he had a plan in mind. He wanted the children to help. Because Filomena will be a teacher, her job would be to show books to the grownups and help all of us learn the best way to urge kids to pick out books they could borrow. He added that because some of us had summer jobs, he would take the truck out for a couple of hours on some Saturdays or Sundays during the rest of the summer. He appointed several of us to go on Saturday and others on Sunday.

During all the excitement, I spoke up even though I realized everyone knew what I was sharing. I described experiences I had in school with my friend, Jimmy Lewis, from the South End, and emphasized Tony and I were friends with the South End gang. While listening, Tony and Alberto crushed nuts against the tabletop, and placed them in a plate for anyone to nibble on. Everyone also munched on a biscotti cookie, or *cannoli*, or grapes.

About a half hour later, Mamma reminded her daughters and nieces that it was time to deliver meals. My sisters and Isabella and Olivia immediately wiped their lips with their napkins and stood up. Mamma was referring to a Sunday ritual that developed years ago. Mamma, Aunt Concetta and Aunt Felicia, and other mothers in the neighborhood, prepared food for families in need. Several families that lived in poorly constructed sheds located along the Connecticut River were very impoverished. And a few families that lived in tenement houses were also in need, usually because the fathers could not find enough work, or had been ill.

Food given to these families was donated each week by other families in the neighborhood who had a reason to thank Papa for helping them with an issue or problem. Any day during the week, a neighbor would come to our apartment, open the door, which incidentally was never locked, and place a bag, filled with various food items, on the kitchen floor. Sometimes no one was in the kitchen, but Papa and Mamma usually could tell, by what was in the bag, who was saying thank you. If someone happened to be in the kitchen, that family member would simply say hello and continue with what she or he was doing, understanding that the person leaving the bag was showing a sign of respect and appreciation. Each week food items were also donated by Joe Epstein.

Every Sunday Mamma and her friends carefully wrapped food items and placed them in paper bags. When the bags were carefully arrayed on the kitchen floor, Mamma began her ritual. She scanned the bags, pointed to two or more of them, called out the name of a family in the neighborhood, and the name of one of her daughters or nieces. Whoever received the assignment picked up the bags, quickly ran off to deliver them, and returned to make another delivery.

Mamma paused, turned away from scanning the bags, and looked at Tony and me. "Did you check Mrs. La Bella's basket today before we started pranzo?"

"Yes, Ma," Tony quickly answered. "Santo and I we're going to check it again when we finish our dessert. Her note said she wanted some provolone cheese, bread, and a bottle of olive oil. We're going to Joe-the-Jew's to get them for her."

"Very good." Mamma pointed to a bag. "That one has chicken in it. Take it to her with the other things Joe will give you. Be sure to shake the rope so the bells ring loud."

I was chewing on a cannoli. "We always do, Ma. We'll go when the girls start the deliveries."

Mamma's question and request related to another ritual she put in place a year ago. Mrs. La Bella lived alone in a small two-room apartment on the third floor of a tenement house located at the end of Ferry Street along the shrubs that bordered the river. She was approaching her six-fifth birthday. Because she was slightly physically disabled, walking up and down three flights of stairs several times a day was difficult for her. More than that, because her husband died a year ago, and her relatives were still in Sicily, she had to rely on neighbors for assistance. When her husband died, Mamma organized a ritual. She gave Mrs. La Bella a long rope. One end was tied to a chair in her apartment on the third floor. The rope passed over the windowsill and down the side of the building to the sidewalk. Bells were tied to the rope just a foot or two under the window. A basket was tied to the other end of the rope near the sidewalk. Each day Mrs. La Bella placed in the basket several coins and a piece of paper on which she scribbled the names of items she needed, and slowly lowered the basket to a level just above the sidewalk. Mamma had assigned Tony and me the responsibility of checking the basket on a daily basis. One of us scanned the paper, ran to Joe Epstein's store with coins in hand and purchased the items. Usually Joe Epstein added something such as olives or two oranges as a gift. We placed the items in the basket, took hold of the rope, and shook it to ring the bells tied near the window at the third floor. Usually seconds later, Mrs. La Bella heard the bells ringing, opened her window, and slowly pulled up the rope and basket into her apartment.

When Mamma asked Tony and me to be sure we shook the rope well, Gloria raised her arm. "Hey, everybody, what us girls are taking to families, and what Tony and Santo are taking to Mrs. La Bella, got me and my sisters to invent a new Sicilian saying the other day."

"What saying?" Isabella asked.

"We all know the one about a man is wealthy if he has good friends." A wide grin crawled across Gloria's face. "We invented that a man is also wealthy if he has a good mother. And now I am adding something else. The woman is not only the center of the family, all of the women are the center of the neighborhood." Mamma, Aunt Concetta and Aunt Felicia smiled with pride.

Anna's smile gleamed as she slowly turned around, and took a long look at Papa, Uncle Gaetano, and Uncle Vito who were sitting at the table carefully watching the women perform their

121

Sunday ritual. "So Papa, like Gloria said, we all know everyone is rich if they have you guys as good friends. Right? But now don't forget what Gloria just said. You are also rich because you have a good wife. And we are all rich because we have good mothers." Everyone cheered.

Papa raised his glass. "*Sì, Salute! E' riccu l'omu quannu c'avi amici e na bedda mamma.*" ("Yes, congratulations! A man is wealthy when he has good friends and a wonderful mother.")

As Mamma assigned bags to a family and one of the girls ran off with the delivery, everyone applauded, and I stood up. "Tony, I'll take the bag to Mrs. La Bella's basket. You can get the other stuff at Joe-the-Jew's."

"Okay, Santo, we're all very rich."

The next day at the Goodrich Tobacco Farm, the four gangs from Middletown were assigned to complete Second Picking in the fields that spread along the river between Cromwell and Rocky Hill. By midday the temperature had already climbed more than ninety degrees Fahrenheit. What made matters even more difficult, a temperature of ninety degrees meant that under the nets that draped over the fields, the temperature was more than one hundred and ten degrees. For this reason most of the boys, even those who usually could tolerate high temperatures, were soaked in sweat. I was picking leaves on one side of Bongi who, because of his weight, had become extra exhausted, and was experiencing more difficulty than usual keeping up with the rest of the gang. "How are you doing, Bongi?"

Bongi stopped picking and sat for a moment. "*Sono stanco.*" ("I'm tired.")

Several yards away someone whispered with a frantic tone, "Santo! Santo!"

I peered between the tobacco plants surrounding me. But I could not see anyone.

Bongi stoped picking. "Who's calling you?"

I jumped up and looked around. "I don't know. But whoever it is, something has to be wrong." Again I heard a whisper and walked in the general direction of the voice, carefully pushing plants to one side. "Who's calling me?"

"It's me. I'm over here." Now I recognized the voice, adjusted the direction in which I was moving, and located Brian. He was kneeling on the ground several yards away from the rows Pesci and Musca were picking.

"What's up, Brian? Why are you whispering? And why are you crawling on the ground?"

"Mr. George is somewhere around here. I don't want him to see me talking to you."

I quickly knelt down confused, since I had never seen Brian act this way. "What's the matter?"

"Four of my guys don't feel good today. Mr. George kept checking because we're way behind. He said that if we don't finish the section we got assigned by five thirty, we might get docked for the day. He doesn't care that the guys are not feeling good. Or maybe he doesn't believe it."

"I know he can be rough." I leaned within inches of Brian. "How can I help?"

"I needed to talk to someone even though I know Mr. George is against gangs helping each other. But I'm in a jam. Like Jim Murphy, he's a really good kid. His parents need the money. If he gets docked, he's in big trouble."

"Brian, wait, let me think. You're right. If he catches us helping you guys, we'll all get docked." I paused for several moments and looked down at the ground. The possibility of getting some revenge against Mr. George gave me a thrill and caused a bunch of thoughts to tumble into me head. I struggled to sort them out and suddenly got excited. "I've got it! Here's what we'll do!"

Brian's head quickly twisted toward me, flipping his long blonde hair. "What are we going to do?"

"It's almost three o'clock, so it's near water time. While everyone is taking a drink, I'll have Bongi fall to the ground and pretend he fainted. Mr. George will have to drive him to the First Aid Cabin. So he's going to be away for an hour or more. Bart and anybody else who's done with their rows could go over and help pick your section of the field."

Brian's jaw dropped. "Wow, that's great! Hope it works."

"Get back quick. Tell your guys."

Brian crawled to his section of the field, and I crawled to mine. Bart had already finished his row and so did his partner,

Melo. When I reached them, they were trying to decide whether they should help Bongi first, because he was behind everyone, or help his brother, Dominic, who was always behind everyone.

Melo barked at me. "Where the hell have you been? Look how far behind Bongi is. Even his kid brother caught up to him."

"I know. Bongi's been behind all morning. But we've got a bigger thing to deal with. Listen." I quickly explained the predicament Brian Coleman's gang faced, and outlined the plan I had cooked up to help.

Melo threw his hand toward me. "But what if Mr. Kelly spots us helping Brian's gang? He's the field boss today. I know he's a cool guy, but he'll have to report us, unless he knows what's going on."

Bart's eyes were gleaming because he was really turned on by the challenge we faced to outsmart Mr. George. "What do you think, Santo?"

Tony had walked over a minute earlier because he spotted us engaged in a vigorous discussion. "Santo, I think you should explain the whole thing to Mr. Kelly. We can trust him. If he thinks it doesn't make sense, then we shouldn't do it."

"You're right. Maybe you could go with me and tell him what our plan is, and why we set it up."

Bart placed his hand, which was covered with sticky tobacco juice, on Tony's shoulder. "Can I go with you too? I've talked to him about his son whose getting ready to go to high school in the fall."

I nodded and turned to Melo. "While we're doing that, you help Bongi."

Tony, Bart and I hurried and located Mr. Kelly who was talking to several haulers. When he spotted us, he paused. "What's wrong, guys? You look worried."

Tony described Brian's problem and the plan we thought could help. I stressed that I knew Mr. George's rule that gangs can't help each other, but thought that sometimes it's unfair.

Mr. Kelly looked away from us. His forehead wrinkled a little, like he had really mixed feelings. "I know what you mean. He sometimes gets carried away and is really heavy on you guys. But Mr. George is the super boss, you know." I got nervous because I thought Mr. Kelly didn't seem to think we should go ahead with our plan.

Bart quickly stepped toward Mr. Kelly. "He sure is a super boss. But like you told me once at lunch time, your son is getting help this summer to make it to Choate Prep School. So it's kind of the same. Brian Coleman's gang needs help to make it. You know that Brian's gang is not always behind, and they certainly aren't always making trouble. They deserve help." Tony nudged me with his elbow because he was impressed with what Bart said, just like I was.

Mr. Kelly turned, looked at each of us, and grinned. "Okay guys. I understand. Your plan is tricky, but I like it. Let's play it out."

I reached out and shook his hand. "Thanks a lot."

Tony, Bart and I raced back to our section of the field. I explained to Bongi what we wanted him to do at water time, and walked from row to row explaining the plan to each of the other members of my gang. Everyone was excited because they wanted to help Brian Coleman's gang, and that Mr. Kelly agreed, but especially because they had a chance to outsmart Mr. George and get some revenge. He always made it clear that if a gang did not finish the section of the field they were assigned, in the time that he decided the gang should get it done, that gang could get docked.

A short while later, Mr. Kelly yelled, "Water time." Everyone walked out of the field, formed a line leading to the water barrel, and edged forward, chatting while each boy took a drink. When Bongi approached the barrel, he suddenly fell on the ground, choking and gasping for air. He pulled his knees against his stomach and clutched his throat with his hands.

I ran over, dropped to my knees, held my face inches above his, yelling, "What's the matter? What's the matter?" Then I whispered, "You're doing great, keep it up." Bongi loved to be dramatic.

Bart shouted, "Mr. Kelly! Quick, there's something really bad here."

A group of boys had already gathered around Bongi, watching him gasping for air. Mr. Kelly pushed his way through the crowd, knelt down and joined the drama. "What's going on?"

I pulled on Bongi's shirt which was wet with sweat. "I don't know. He just fell over, choking. He's been sweating all day because it's so hot. But look! Now he's fainted."

Bongi had stopped choking and was lying motionless on the road with his eyes closed and his arms stretched out.

Bart joined in as if he was acting in a movie. "What are we going to do? We've got to get help!"

Mr. Kelly winked at me. "It looks like he passed out. I'll have Mr. George get his pickup truck. We'll need some guys to lift him in it." He raced over to Mr. George.

"What's going on over there? Why is that gang standing around the water barrel?"

"A kid fainted. He's got to be rushed to the First Aid Cabin. This is really serious."

Mr. George jogged over to his truck, jumped in, quickly started the engine and drove to where Bongi was lying. Tony, Bart and Mr. Kelly picked up Bongi. "This kid is really fat. I mean heavy," Mr. Kelly commented with a grin, as they struggled to carefully lift Bongi into the back of the truck.

Mr. George leaned out of the truck's cabin and yelled at me. "Pick one of your gang to go with him." I pointed to Tony, who jumped on the back of the truck and sat next to Bongi. With the engine racing, Mr. George clutched the steering wheel and again leaned out of the cabin. "As soon as water time is over, everyone back to work!" Then he sped off, dirt spitting out from under the tires.

I glanced at Mr. Kelly. With his fists near his waist, he gave me thumbs up. When I turned and looked at Brian Coleman, he also thrust his thumbs up. Everyone understood what needed to be done. Brian's gang returned to their rows, and my gang immediately started at the end of their rows, working toward Brian's pickers. I was pleased to see that while Brain and I moved from row to row helping pickers who were the farthest behind, my gang seemed to be picking at a speed, and with rhythm, that was even faster than their usual fast pace. Everyone was mobilized by the challenge we faced and by the opportunity to outsmart Mr. George.

About two hours later, before the trucks arrived to take everyone to the Central Lot, Mr. George sped up the road and screeched to a halt. I ran toward the truck as Mr. George and Tony stepped down. "How is Bongi?"

I was pleased to see that Mr. George seemed a little worried, or at least he didn't show any sign that he was suspicious. "It's probably heat exhaustion. I left him in the First Aid Cabin. The nurse said it looks like he'll be able to get back to work tomorrow." Then he glanced over his shoulder in the direction where Brian's gang was working, shouting, "I'm going over to check on the Regular Gang!" and walked at a very fast pace down to the other side of the field. Tony and I exchanged glances and grins and entered the field. "It worked!" Tony exclaimed. "Bongi can sure act."

"What happened?"

"The nurse was really nice. She said she doesn't know why more of us guys don't pass out in this kind of weather. She cleaned Bongi's forehead, face and chest with a wet towel and gave him a special drink. She even gave one to me. She talked to us just like a mother. She even talked about her kids, and said when they get a little older, she isn't sure she'll want them to work on the farm." Tony paused, "What happened with Brian's gang?"

"We helped them get all caught up."

I learned later from Brian that Mr. George looked around in disbelief and said with an edge of sarcasm, "Well, Mr. Coleman, looks like your guys got all caught up. I can't believe it. How did you do it?"

Brian told me he worked hard to hold back a grin and said something like, "We knew we had to push hard to catch up. We just kept pushing and pushing."

Brian was sure Mr. George struggled to understand what he saw because he said something like, "I still don't get how the hell you did it. I mean you guys would have been here till seven o'clock to get your section finished." But when he glanced at his watch he realized it was time for trucks to take everyone to the Central Lot, so he walked away.

While sitting next to me on the truck that transported us to the Central Lot, Brian shared with pleasure what had happened between him and Mr. George, and made clear he appreciated what we did for his gang. "Thanks a lot. You and all your guys, especially Bongi, were great to help out."

Bart munched on a sandwich of cheese and prosciutto which he had not eaten at noontime. "No sweat, Brian. I think it's great that our plan worked."

Brian was still turned on. "When Mr. George got back from the First Aid Cabin, he was sure he would find us way behind, but was shocked, even disappointed, that we finished our section. Thanks a lot!"

While the truck rumbled on, Sal shouted, "Hey Brian, you know how Sicilians have a rule."

"What rule?"

Sal turned to me, "You tell him."

I felt charged up. "Well Brian, you know we Sicilians are all about the family, all about friends helping friends and helping the neighborhood. When it makes sense, that's the way we feel about our town. And you guys live in our town, so we were glad to help you."

"It's more than you guys living in our town," Ancio chimed in. "Remember, Brian, when you told me my family lives in the tenement house your grandfather lived in a long time ago? So Brian that means, even though you're Irish, you're still a part of our Dago neighborhood. But you better color your hair dark brown or black." Everyone laughed.

When the truck arrived in the Central Lot, everyone jumped off and rushed toward Bongi who was standing with other boys.

"You did great!" Brian shouted. "Thanks a million."

"What happened in the First Aid cabin?" Pesci asked.

"It was great! I think I'll faint every couple of days." Everyone laughed. "The nurse felt just like my mother."

Tony patted Bongi on the back. "I know."

"The way she was talking to me and putting that cool, wet cloth on me, like I was a little baby." Now the laughter grew louder. And I wasn't surprised when a number of guys wished they had received that treatment.

Suddenly Tony shouted, making clear he had something serious to say. "Hey guys, listen to this!" I didn't know what was on his mind that was so important. "You know we were talking on the truck about Sicilians, and family, and friends. While what Bongi just said about that nurse reminded me of a saying my sisters invented ."

I interrupted. "Actually, they invented a piece and added it to one of those sayings Sicilians always mention."

"What's the saying?" Brian asked.

Tony stretched his arms out. "A man is wealthy when he has good friends and a good mother. It doesn't matter if he has no money."

At this moment a foreman shouted and pointed to the trucks assigned to transport workers to Middletown. As we ran, a number of the guys laughed, throwing up their arms, "I'm rich! I'm rich! I'm rich!"

Late that evening, we were nearly finished with dinner. Suddenly a lightning bolt rippled overhead, and seconds later the crash of thunder rattled across the sky. Teodoro shouted, "Wow! Did you hear that?" Heavy raindrops began to slam against the ground.

Anna, who was leaning over the table toward Tony, quickly sat up in her chair. "I was so into what Tony and I were talking about, I didn't hear the thunder."

I looked out the door. "It's another big summer rain storm."

Filomena turned to Tony. "From the sound of it, aren't you glad we didn't get caught out there?"

"Yeah, we're all in here enjoying delicious manicotti."

While everyone continued chatting, Mamma asked Teodoro whether he had played along the river before dinner, like he said he was going to do, with his friend, Joe Vinci.

Teodoro grinned and pushed his chest out. "Yes, Ma. Joe and I had a blast crawling through the bushes looking for river rats to throw rocks at."

Mamma looked at Teodoro with concern and asked if he wore a *cammisa e cappeddu* (a shirt and hat).

Teodoro's shoulders sagged and a troubled look covered his face, making clear he realized he had broken a rule. "No, Ma. I know I should have. But it was really muggy so I took my shirt and hat off." He paused and looked down. "I know you don't think that's a good thing to do near the end of the day, because there might be a lot of *pidocchi* (lice) on those bushes near the river."

Mamma held her palm up toward Teodoro. "*Figghiu* (son) I'm glad you and Joe had fun. But I want to check your scalp just in case. Maybe I'll even look for *pidocchi* (lice) in Tony's and Santo's hair. You know, this time of year, I want to check at least once a day."

She got up, walked to the doorway of our bedroom, placed two chairs there, sat down and gestured to Teodoro . He sat down in front of her, and Mamma slowly examined each square inch of his scalp with her fingertips, pushing his dark wavy hair to one side, commenting in a low whisper, "*bonu, bonu.*" ("good, good.")

While Mamma examined Teodoro's scalp, Papa stood up, slowly walked to the doorway which was wide open, looked outside, and took a deep breath. Rain was still pounding against the ground. He quickly turned around, faced everyone, and pointed over his shoulder. "Quick! Look! Remember how we talked about serietà, how the mother is the center of the artichoke?"

Every one of us got up, rushed over and huddled around the doorway. Papa directed our attention to an area of tall weeds at the corner of the fence that bordered the patch of ground. There stood a large cat, and from her mouth dangled a very small kitten by the back of its neck. With one paw raised, the cat was turning its head from side to side, frantically looking for a safe haven from the downpour. Suddenly the cat raced across the patch of ground into a barrel that had tipped over. The cat emerged from the barrel without the kitten in its mouth, ran back to the corner of the fence, picked up another kitten buried in the tall weeds, and again raced to the barrel.

While everyone stared and marveled, Anna commented, "There's an excellent example of *serietà.*"

Teodoro grinned and placed his arm around Mamma's waist. "And here's another one! She just checked my head again for *pidocchi.*" Tony and I turned and also hugged Mamma.

Filomena burst out with excitement "What that mother cat just did says what *serietà* is all about, more than a thousand words can."

Gloria couldn't control herself and screeched, "With that mother cat, those kids are really, really rich!"

Everyone turned toward Mamma, and cheered.

Third Picking

The Road of Life is Full of Pitfalls
It's Not Smooth

In early July gangs from Middletown and nearby Glastonbury were assigned to Crow's Hill which was ready for Third
Picking. When we arrived, a boy from Glastonbury stepped
toward Ancio, who was only a few yards away from me, and
said something that, for some reason, was becoming popular.
"Hope your day goes good, you know, Day-Go." From the way
this boy used the words "day" and "go," it was obvious that he
was joking with an ethnic slur frequently used to refer to Italian
Americans, especially those from southern Italy. Even though this
boy was grinning, Ancio did not take it as a joke. He clenched
his fists and stepped toward the boy.

Sensing that an argument could erupt, I quickly walked over,
and whispered, "Ignore the jerk. Don't let him hook you." Ancio
turned away and walked to the edge of the field.

Minutes later Mr. Kelly assigned each gang to a section of
the field and encouraged everyone to do a good job. Dominic
stood still at the start of his row, while others began picking, and
looked up and down several times at the plants on his left and
right. "Hey guys, I can stand up now when I pick. I just have to
lean over a little." Leaves that qualified for Third Picking were
located on the stalks approximately three feet above the ground.
Since Dominic was short, he could stand and bend over to harvest
the leaves, instead of kneeling down.

A few rows away, Bart had already started picking with his
rapid and rhythmic style. "That's great, Dom. Guess I'll have to
wait for Fourth Picking. I'm still going to be on my ass once in
a while." Although most pickers knelt down to harvest leaves
during Third Picking, because Bart was very tall, he found that
his back was less stressed if he alternated between crawling for
several bends, and then sitting and dragging himself forward.

I called out to my gang because I wasn't sure they knew we
faced a challenge from the Glastonbury Fast Gang. "Looks like

these guys want to show us up. If they finish their piece before the day's up we, have to finish ours. Let's do it!" I was pleased to see that my gang took in what I just said, and everyone, even Dominic who had gained experience since the start of summer, moved with a smooth rhythm.

Throughout the morning I walked from one row to another, checking stalks, picking a few plants for one picker and then for another, and sometimes joking with someone to keep him connected to the gang, which I enjoyed doing. Because I believed the rules of the family should be followed, I felt that my job was to cultivate loyalty, respect, honor, patience and commitment among gang members. As I walked toward Angelo, he leaned over and picked up a butt of leaves that had just been set down by Pesci. "I've always liked Third Picking." I wasn't sure what he meant.

Vito was hauling nearby for Bart and Melo who, as usual, were almost a bend ahead of him. While quickly picking up a butt, he asked the question that crossed my mind when I heard what Angelo said. "What's so great about Third Picking?"

"Well, because the stalks don't have any leaves near the bottom, now it's easier to see the butts."

Also hauling nearby, Louie paused for a moment. "That's right, Angelo, you can spot the butts better. But with Third Picking, the leaves are bigger and heavier. The last basket I pulled out was tough."

I was about to go over and help Dominic who was kneeling a couple of bends away, when Mr. Kelly approached me. "Santo your guys are really rolling. Good job. They'll be glad to know it's time for lunch."

I shouted out to my left and right, "Okay its lunch time! Haulers, before you walk out, check around for any butts."

Filippo yelled back, "Okay, Santo. I know! I know! The last thing we want is for Mr. George to spot a butt!"

Pulling his basket out of the field, Tony gasped, "He's always checking during noontime. If he finds one, all of us haulers would probably be docked."

"It's you haulers that would get docked, not us pickers,"

Baggi chuckled, as he followed Tony out of the field.

Each member of the gang retrieved his lunch pail, sat under trees on the edge of the wooded area that bordered the field, and began munching on apples, oranges and sandwiches, while chatting.

Sal took a bite of his Genoa salami sandwich and chewed with obvious pleasure. "Hey, Louie, I heard you guys talking about how the leaves are heavier now. Can you haulers really tell the difference from Second Picking?"

"Yes, we can," Tony joined in, holding one of his favorite sandwiches which consisted of a thick piece of baked eggplant between two slices of home-made, crusty bread. "It's not that the first basket you pull out is heavy. But after a dozen or so, you can really feel the difference."

Suggi glanced at Tony while peeling the skin off an orange, and the expression on his face made clear he was in the mood for an argument. "You haulers have it made. We have to crawl along on our knees for thirty or forty bends, and keep turning back and forth to pick the plants on both sides of us. At least you guys don't have to crawl. All you have to do is walk along, pick up butts, and pull your basket out of the field. And when you walk back in, the basket is empty."

Filippo held a mortadella sandwich near his mouth. He paused before taking a bite, accepting Suggi's invitation to get into an argument. "You're right, Suggi, we're walking not crawling. That may look easy to you. But like Tony just said, after you drag a bunch of baskets out, you begin to feel like a *sceccu* (mule) pulling a wagon loaded with rocks."

Musca's cupped hands held a bunch of red grapes. He turned and stared at Filippo, eager to join in. "Well at least you guys are dragging a basket a half mile on pretty flat ground. You're not climbing a half mile up one of those shafts, tugging a bag filled with sulfur, like my father did when he was a kid." I was impressed how Musca introduced a new angle to the debate by mentioning sulfur mines in Sicily.

Suggi stopped eating his orange and looked up. "I heard my parents talk about those sulfur mines that were operating until

133

a few years ago. One of my uncles worked there." The topic immediately got everyone turned on.

Sal quickly jumped in with so much vigor it was obvious he had a lot on his mind. "My father worked there too when he was a kid. He was one of those haulers, like your father was, Musca. He told me he had to work twelve hours a day following the *picconiere* (pick man) he got assigned to. That pick man kept chopping away at the sulfur rocks. My father put the pieces in a bag, and when it was full, he had to pull it all the way up the shaft, dump out the pieces of sulfur, and go all the way down the shaft again."

Still holding his sandwich, Filippo lowered his hands, resting them on his lap. His tone now became sad. "Gee guys, what you're saying is really getting to me. My parents talk about that a lot, too. My grandfather was one of those picconiere who crawled down those shafts and chopped away all day. And his boss always told him he was behind."

Suddenly I felt the urge to give a lecture. "From what I heard, everybody who worked in those mines was really cheated." My urge came from the fact that a number of pieces of history again whirled around in my mind on yesterday's stage, while I listened to all those remarks about the sulfur mines.

––––––––––––

Since ancient times, the mining of sulfur was a major industry in Sicily, along with producing grain, citrus fruits, wine and nuts. Most of the sulfur mines were owned by families from other countries in Europe who had acquired them even before Italy became a unified country in 1870. While sulfur mines elsewhere in the world eventually began to use modern tools, the mines in Sicily continued to use very primitive methods. As late as the 1930's, workers in the Sicilian sulfur mines hobbled up and down deep mining shafts on foot, whereas elevators had become a common feature in the mines of other countries.

The main worker in these mines was the *picconiere* (pick man) who splintered chunks of sulfur with his pick. A *caruso* (young boy) was assigned to each pick man. The boy's job was to follow the pick man, gather the pieces of sulfur, and place them in a bag. When the bag was full, sometimes weighing as much as 70 pounds, the boy dragged the bag up the shaft from the depth of the mine to the surface, emptied the bag, climbed back down to where the pick man was working, and began filling it again.

Because of the hazardous conditions that existed in the mines, pick men and boys frequently experienced accidents. The Italian government, however, did not seem to become concerned until 1933 when the owners of these sulfur mines were required to submit accident reports. The reports submitted were studied over a four year period and confirmed that many boys and men suffered injuries. On the basis of the information gathered, a government commission was successful in passing a reform law which, however, did not address the hazardous conditions of the mines. Sicilian peasants were stunned when they learned that this law only forbid the owners of these sulfur mines to hire boys younger than ten years of age.

I was successful in preventing myself from giving a lecture on the history of sulfur mines in Sicily. Instead, I stuck my arm out and pointed at Musca who had introduced the topic. "You're right Musca. Our haulers have it made compared to the kids who were dragging those bags of sulfur. I think it was really good that you reminded us of that whole situation."

While chewing on a bite he had just taken from his sandwich, Tony raised his arm. I wondered if he also felt like giving a lecture. "It's easy to forget about all of that even though it was going on only a few years ago. Santo, remember every time our relatives talk about it, they say what happened in those sulfur mines reminds us that the road of life isn't smooth."

"It sure isn't!" Angelo shouted. "But when we think about those sulfur mines, it makes us realize that the bumps all of us have to go over ain't as rough."

Mr. Kelly was standing yards away. He turned and pointed at the pickers and haulers who were finishing their lunches on the other side of the road, and then pointed to us. "Okay, lunch break

135

is over. Let's go. Keep up the good work. See if you can finish the section you got assigned by the end of today." Everyone stood up, placed their lunch pails in a basket, and entered the field.

I faced my gang and held my arms out with palms turned up. "Like Tony just said, it helps to remind ourselves that what's ahead isn't as bad as those sulfur mines."

"At least I'm not in a dungeon. I can look at the sky," Melo commented.

Grinning, Bart turned to his partner. "Yes Melo, and at least I can hear you singing off key." Everyone laughed as each picker dropped to his knees and began harvesting, while haulers followed behind them, dragging their baskets.

At about three o'clock that afternoon, Mr. Kelly yelled, "Water time!" Everyone quickly walked out of the field and lined up by the water tank.

A teenager from the Glastonbury gang turned to Sal. "Hey! Did your Mafia friends deliver this water? How did your day go, so far, Dago?"

Sal turned to his partner, Ancio, and to Bart and Melo, who were standing nearby. "What is it with these guys and this Mafia and Dago shit?"

Bart immediately stepped within inches of the boy who made the remark, leaned forward, glared into his face, and pressed his fingers against the boy's chest. "Listen, how did your day go? And if I hear that once more, I'm going to show you what the Mafia is about."

"What's the matter with you?" the boy complained. "I was just trying to connect with you guys since we don't see you that much."

While this exchange was going on, Tony whispered into my ear, "We better cool this down."

The boy from the Glastonbury gang, who had made the wisecrack about the Mafia, looked at me and commented with a provocative tone, "I know who you are Santo." Then he pointed at Tony, "Who is that your *consigliere*?" (Advisor).

Bart quickly grabbed the boy's shoulder with his left hand, and raised his right arm with fist clenched. "That did it!"

Tony immediately took hold of Bart and pulled him away. "Come on, use your head! He isn't worth it!"

I gathered my gang across the road from the water tank because I was worried that something big might happen. "Listen. These jerks are from Glastonbury. We really don't know them that good. Don't let them get you to start something." Everyone nodded.

At this moment, Mr. Kelly shouted, "Okay water time is over!" Everyone returned to the field and began working.

About twenty minutes later Tony came running over to me with a very worried look on his face. "Something's really wrong! Dom is very sick!" As we raced over toward Dominic, Tony blurted out, "When I hauled a basket out, I found him stretched out trying to breath."

Dominic was curled up on the ground, choking for air, with his knees pushed up to his chest. His partner, Baggi, was kneeling by his side trying to find some way to reassure him. "It's okay Dom; it's okay."

I put my hand on his forehead and looked him over. For a moment, I imagined that Dominic was faking he had fainted, like his brother, Bongi, did a few weeks ago, because he wanted to see that wonderful nurse. But when I registered that his knees were still pressed against his chest, that his eye lids were crunched together, and his lips twisted in pain, I realized he was not pretending. I spread the palm of my hand on his stomach. "Dom, your stomach hurts a lot?"

"Yeah!"

"When did it start?"

"Right after I took a drink at water time. This guy gave me a drink from a cup. He said it was soda. It tasted sweet."

Tony leaned over. "Santo, whoever it was must have given him some bad stuff. We've got to get him to throw it up. Let me do it. I learned this in school." He pulled Dominic up, stood behind him, placed his fists tightly against his stomach, and pushed in with several quick jerks. Dominic immediately vomited dark liquid.

Everyone had already gathered around us and was relieved when Tony got Dominic to spit out what was making him sick.

With a strong edge of anger, Ancio brought up an issue that had been preoccupying him all day. "Dom, I want you to show us later who the jerk was that gave you that drink. I'll bet it was that ass who keeps asking me how did my day go. Did the guy say anything when he gave you the drink?"

"He asked me, how did my day go."

Ancio pushed his clenched fist against his chest. "I was right! We know who the shit-head is! "

I grabbed Ancio's arm which, of course, was covered with brown, sticky tobacco juice, and wanted to stop what could become a gang fight. "Let's wait. All of the guys from that Glastonbury gang are saying Dago and joking about the Mafia. Right now we can't be absolutely sure which one of them gave Dom that drink. We'll figure this out."

Later that day while we rode home on the truck, Tony turned to Brian Coleman. "Did you notice these days some of the guys on the farm keep calling us Dago, and mentioning the Mafia?"

Brian smiled. "I think they're jealous. Maybe they wish that when they need help, they could call that kind of muscle."

Musca was sitting across from Tony and Brian. "Come on, Brian, you know everyone gets carried away about the Mafia. They make it sound like there's Mafia guys all over the streets."

When the truck reached the area under the bridge, everyone jumped off. Brian Coleman's gang quickly walked from the river up the road that passed the Catholic Church Irish immigrants had built more that seventy-five years ago. Tony called out, "See you tomorrow."

Brian waved and Jack Kane held his arm up high. "Yes, another fantastic day in that hot summer sun!"

My gang walked in the opposite direction along the Connecticut River toward our neighborhood. Bart paused and pointed toward the foot of Rapello Avenue. "Tony, look. There's your father talking to Mr. Milardo."

Tony and I shouted, "Papa!" He turned toward us, waved and smiled, but held the palm of his hand toward us and continued talking.

Tony whispered, "I guess he doesn't want us to come over."

As we continued, Melo pointed, "Look, Santo. Mr. Milardo is kissing your father's hand. He must have done him a favor."

"My parents say he's always doing somebody a favor," Angelo commented. "Did I tell you guys he helped my uncle get a job at the Russell Company?"

Tony's eyes gleamed. "No, you didn't. Great. How's he doing?"

"Really good. My uncle said ..."

As if he did not hear that Angelo was talking, Vito interrupted, obviously turned on about something. "Tony! I didn't have a chance to tell you that your father told off Mr. Messina."

I stared at Vito wondering what he was talking about. "I haven't heard about that one."

Vito looked back and forth at me and Tony. "My father was talking about it the other day. Last Saturday a bunch of them were playing cards at the Garibaldi Lodge. Mr. Messina got into a huge argument with somebody. From what I hear, he's always picking on something and starting fights."

Louie stepped closer to us. "I heard my parents talking about that too."

"But what happened, Vito?" Bart asked. "I didn't hear anything about this."

Vito glanced at each of us, and I became confused because now he looked like he was really nervous. "They called your father over, Santo. Your father asked Mr. Messina to quiet down. But he kept arguing and trying to start a fight. And you won't believe this. He told your father to mind his own business."

Bart's mouth opened wide. "Wow. My parents say he loses it once in a while and doesn't show any respect."

Tony stopped walking. "Well here we are at the foot of Green Street and some of you have to get going. But now I'm all worked up. I want to know what happened before we head home."

While Tony made his request, I immediately tuned out. This always happened to me whenever a kid from our neighborhood would say to me something like "Hey, Santo, did you hear what your father did the other day in that restaurant on Center Street?" or "at the Sons of Italy Lodge?" When I heard anything like that, my mind turned a switch nearly off, so that I could barely hear the rest of what the kid said. I knew that once in a while Papa had to get really rough with a person who was breaking the rules of the family in a big way. Once Tony and I talked to Mamma about this, and she said something like, "You have to keep in mind one of his jobs is to keep the peace. He's a peace maker." That helped, but I still would get nervous when somebody mentioned something about Papa having to be a peace maker. I snapped back when Tony took hold of Vito's arm, and growled that he wanted to know what happened.

Vito mumbled, "Well, Tony, my father said your father told Mr. Messina '*Chi fai, tu disidiri la morti?*' ('What are you doing, do you wish to die?'). And all of a sudden Mr. Messina became very quiet. Your father asked him to leave and come back only when he thinks he has more respect for the rest of the fathers who were playing cards."

When I put my hand on Vito's arm, I was saying, 'stop, enough,' I didn't want to hear anymore. I turned to Tony, "We better get going. See you guys later." A few members of the gang walked up Green Street and the rest of us continued walking towards Ferry Street.

When Tony and I entered our apartment we startled when we saw Mamma crying while she stood at the stove. Both Filomena and Gloria were holding an arm around her waist.

Teodoro was sitting nearby very worried. "I'm really glad you're home."

"What's the matter, Mamma?" Tony asked. I was surprised that she did not respond. She continued stirring tomato sauce in a large metal pan, and sobbed quietly.

Gloria faced us. "Mamma decided to check out the A & P Store in the American district to see the fruit and things they sell there." Mamma stopped sobbing, lowered her head, and wiped the tears from her cheeks with the edge of her apron. Gloria kissed her on the cheek, and whispered, "Ma, it's okay, it's okay."

Filomena finally turned around. Now I realized why she had continued to look straight ahead at the pots and pans on the shelf above the stove. Tears were rolling down her cheeks too.

"You know how Mamma likes to feel the fruit she buys, just like all the mothers around here. It helps them figure out if the fruit is okay. Joe-the-Jew lets them do that all the time."

I interrupted because I didn't think this was the right time for my sister to be a teacher. "But what happened, Filomena? Why is Ma crying?"

Filomena's face and eyes glared with anger. "Guess what! Ma went into the A & P store to check the oranges. This guy in the store came over and told her to take her Guinea hands off the oranges she was feeling, and get out of the store. He even called Mamma a Dago."

Gloria tightened her arm around Mamma's waist. "You won't believe this. He told her to get out of the store because no Wops were allowed. Do you believe that jerk called our mother those stupid names?"

Gloria was right. I couldn't believe what she just said. I placed my hand on Mamma's shoulder and whispered, "That guy really is a *cafuni* (rotten slob)." For a brief moment scenes whirled through my mind of different ways Tony and I could retaliate. I pictured us throwing rocks at the store window. Then I pictured us in the store throwing boxes, cans and vegetables in all directions. Suddenly I felt very confused. I jerked my hand away from Mamma's back, held both of my hands before Tony with palms turned up, and glared, clutching my lips together.

Tony shrugged his shoulders and whispered, "I don't know what we should do. Let's go outside." He stepped closer to Mamma and also placed his hand on her back. "Ma, that sauce you're making smells really delicious." Mamma nodded, but did not turn around.

I put my hand back on Mamma's shoulder and whispered, "Don't let that *cafuni* bother you. Tony and I will be right back."

Tony walked over to Teodoro and placed a hand on his head. Teodoro looked up, his eye lids drooping with sadness. "Can I come?"

"I think it's better if you stay here with Ma." Teodoro glanced at me hoping I would ask him to join us, but I nodded toward Tony.

141

Tony and I stepped outside and stood motionless in the small yard. I felt nervous and mixed up. I stared at the ground with my hands in my pockets, took a few quick steps to the left, turned, and took a few quick steps to the right. While I paced about, Tony walked over to one of the large, metal trash cans that had tipped over at the corner of the fence. I don't know why he bothered, but he lifted it upright.

I stopped pacing, walked over to Tony and suddenly kicked the trash can so hard it toppled over. "Tony, I can't figure out what we should do."

"It's a hard thing to figure out," Tony whispered. "I mean I would like to go up there and throw a rock through the damn window of that store."

"That's exactly one of the things I just imagined us doing. But, better still, I would love to throw the rock at that jerk instead of the window." I began pacing back and forth again. "But we're supposed to be practicing *omertà*. Boy am I having trouble with that."

"Me too, Santo. But we have to find a way to show that asshole that he can't get away with what he did to our mother."

I stopped pacing, turned and stared into Tony's eyes. "Let's go up there."

"Yeah, maybe we'll figure something out that won't get us in trouble."

We quickly walked toward the top of Ferry Street which led to the American neighborhood. "Tony, have you noticed that in the past months we're hearing more and more words like Wop and Dago, and more stuff about the Mafia?"

Tony shrugged his shoulders. "Maybe it's because of the war, and Italy is an enemy on the side of the Germans."

"What the hell is going on?"

Tony stopped walking and threw his arms out. "I wish I knew. And besides we're not the enemy. For God sake, look at what our neighborhood is doing for this country. How about our cousin, Lucky, and our cousin, Filippo, they're in the army fighting for the United States like other guys from our neighborhood. I really hope this war ends soon."

For some reason, I couldn't get into the mess about World

War II. I took a deep breath, and continued walking. "But Tony, what I'm thinking about right now is not that stupid war. Ma couldn't have picked a worse time to go into the American part of town. And she came home crying. She practically never cries."

"I don't know if I've ever seen her cry."

When we reached the A&P store, I stood inches from the large window, and scanned the inside of the store.

Tony also leaned close to the window and looked in. "What are we going to do? If I can't throw a rock through the window, I'd love to go in there and tell that idiot he's an asshole for doing what he did to Ma?"

I found myself remembering all of what we discussed about what I did with Mr. George at the farm. "I'd love to do that Tony, but we're supposed to be practicing *omertà*."

"You're right. Let's think of something to do that's really quiet, but at the same time screams to that guy that he's a big jerk."

I slowly pressed my forehead against the window, and continued surveying the inside of the store. Suddenly an idea flashed through my mind. "I got it!"

"What! "

I placed the tip of my finger against the window. "Look. Do you see that huge pyramid of oranges stacked up on the table over there near the middle of the store?"

"Yeah, I see it. What are you thinking?"

With my forehead still pressed against the window, I answered Tony with a soft but firm voice that reminded me of the way Papa talks about times like this. "Here's the plan. We go in there and grab a couple of oranges with each hand from the bottom. When we pull them out, that whole mountain should tumble down."

"Fantastic! That's a great idea. We don't say a word, but what we do will scream out loud. That's a really good way of calling him an idiot."

We entered the store and walked past a couple of customers toward the display of oranges. Tony nudged me with his elbow and jerked his head toward the clerk. He was wearing a white shirt, white apron, and black trousers, and obviously checking us out. " That's gotta be him."

I glanced at the clerk, and quickly looked down. "I'll bet he can tell we come from the North End."

Suddenly the clerk shouted, "Hey, you kids! What are you doing here?"

Tony and I stopped next to the pyramid of oranges and faced the clerk. Tony spoke out in a quiet tone that surprised me. "Did you tell our mother a little while ago to take her Guinea hands off these oranges?"

The clerk pushed his arm at us with a clenched fist. "Get out of here you..."

Before he finished what he had to say, I also surprised myself when I called out with a firm but quiet tone, "Hey mister, watch what these Dago hands can do." I quickly pushed my hands into the huge stack of oranges and yanked out two with each hand. Tony did the same. Suddenly the pyramid caved in, and dozens of oranges bounced to the floor, rolling in all directions. The clerk looked in shock at the earth quake taking place before him, and jabbed his index finger at Tony and me as if it were a knife. "You little grease balls!"

Tony and I raced to the main entrance and out the door, with the clerk in hot pursuit. As we ran down Main Street, adults who were walking along suddenly stopped and stared at us with puzzled looks on their faces. After running about thirty yards, we turned into Ferry Street which marked the beginning of our neighborhood. When the clerk reached the corner, just a few yards behind us, he suddenly stopped. "Okay, you Wops! I know you're safe now! This is where the Mafia lives, right?"

When the clerk made that stupid remark, Tony and I looked over our shoulders and noticed he had stopped running, so we slowed down to a walk. Tony stopped for a second, turned around, and yelled back, "Yeah, jerk. This is where the Mafia lives!"

I smiled. "He wouldn't dare follow us all the way down Ferry Street. He knows if he did, maybe he will never come back out."

That evening while the family finished dinner, Tony picked up a piece of crusty, homemade bread and carefully passed it over the bottom of his plate, wiping up the olive oil, pieces of roasted red pepper, parsley, oregano and garlic in which sat the grilled shrimp he was eating.

While chewing, Gloria grinned. "Boy, I love shrimp scampi."

Anna joined in. "Ma, it really came out delicious again. There's nothing like shrimp scampi." Like she always did, Mamma smiled and nodded, appreciating the compliment.

Teodoro held up a shrimp stuck to the tip of his fork. "But I'm full. I can't eat this last one."

I don't know why, but I could never deal with food being wasted. "I'll take it."

At the same time, Tony reached for Teodoro's fork and shouted, "I'd love to have it!"

Papa slapped a coin on the table. *"Basta cu stu scrusciu!"* ("Enough with the noise!")

Tony looked at Papa, "Okay, I'll take heads."

"Then I guess I'm tails."

Papa placed the coin on his thumb and flipped it up. The coin tumbled to the table and wobbled still.

Tony leaned over and stared. "Well Santo it's yours."

I grinned, took Teodoro's fork, and chewed the shrimp with exaggerated pleasure. Everyone continued chatting until Filomena interrupted. The tone of her voice made clear that she was upset about something. "Did everyone hear the news on the radio?"

Anna placed her hand on Filomena's wrist. "What news? I didn't have a chance at the bakery to listen to the radio."

Filomena glanced at each of us, and from the look in her eyes something big was bothering her. "Yesterday Sicily was invaded by American and British armies. I'm worried about our relatives."

Tony snapped his head around, looked into Papa's eyes, turned, and stared at Mamma who lowered her head. "Yesterday, July 10, 1943! I'll never forget that date as long as I live."

"Why did they pick on Sicily?" Teodoro asked.

I wondered the same thing and, as everyone looked at each other worried about this news, Filomena mumbled with sadness, "I guess it had to be. If you look at today's paper, they explain that Sicily is really close to North Africa."

Anna reached across the table toward Teodoro. "Since we beat the Germans in North Africa, it makes sense, I guess, to keep fighting Hitler by going from there to Sicily."

Tony interrupted with a strong edge of anger in his voice which surprised me. "I was telling Santo that because of the war, and because Italy is an enemy, we're getting a lot of stuff about the Mafia, and we're being called Wops and Dagos."

I lost it and blurted out, "Even that jerk at the A&P store yelled at us about the Mafia, when he chased us."

Anna reached out, yelling, "Why where you in the A&P store? What jerk?"

Papa stared at me. I knew he was also confused by what I just said. "*Dimmi 'na cosa, figghiu miu.*" ("Tell me about it, my son.")

Tony and I had already shared with Gloria what happened. Before I had a chance to respond, she yelled, "Wait everybody! You have to know that Mamma was really upset about that A&P store when Filomena and I got home."

Now Papa looked very confused and stared into Mamma's eyes. "*Ch'è successu?*" ("What happened?")

Mamma picked up a *biscottu* (cookie) and took a bite. I was relieved that she tried to help herself as she quietly shared what happened in the A&P store. She finished mumbling, "*E' nu sceccu. Unn 'avi né rispettu né maneri.*" ("He's a mule, a stupid ass. He had neither respect nor manners.")

Papa stood up, walked around the table and gave Mamma a hug. "*Mi dispiaci.*" (I'm sorry.) He turned toward Tony and me and spread his hand out, asking us to continue. We described how we went to the store and toppled the pyramid of oranges. I tried to make clear that although we wanted revenge, we still tried to practice *omertà*.

Papa mumbled, "*Così si fa; non di dietro.*" ("That's the way it's done in the open, straight ahead, not from behind.") Then with an expression of concern mixed with some anger he took a long look at Tony and me. I wondered if we did something wrong, even though I felt what we did made sense. "But maybe," he added, "you went too far. You could have thought of a more quiet way to tell the *sceccu* (donkey) off."

146

Tony picked up an apple. "But Papa, when we got to Ferry Street, that jerk yelled that's where the Mafia lives. Why be quiet with that kind of ass?"

I decided to join Tony. "Yeah, what do you mean we went too far? I keep hearing Mafia more and more these days. Why does everyone call us that? Do they think we're all gangsters?"

"*Tutti dui nun capiti.*" ("The two of you don't understand.")

With that comment, Papa now expressed a tone of disgust mixed with disappointment which really got to me. I tried to keep myself calm so I picked up two walnuts from a dish. While crushing the shells against the table top, I turned to Papa. But smashing the shells didn't help because, as I began talking, I noticed I spoke with a tone of frustration and irritation. "Papa, what do you mean we don't understand? Like I just said, we keep hearing all the kids in school call us Mafia guys. They keep teasing us that we live in Mafia Town. *Picchì lu fannu?* ("Why do they do that?") Are you in the Mafia?"

Papa and Mamma exchanged glances of concern.

Tony must have been turned on by what I said, and how I said it, because he suddenly sat up straight, quickly set his apple on the table, cleared his throat, and raised the palm of his right hand, jabbing his index finger straight up. I thought he was about to give a speech. "We mean no disrespect, Papa. It's just some kids keep throwing that word around and make it sound like something bad. Like one kid in school told me he saw a man kiss your hand while you guys were standing on Main Street. This kid said, 'Oh, I see your father is one of those Mafia guys.'"

"For God sake, you know Sicilians do that all the time," Anna yelled. "That guy was just doing what everyone does, *mustrari u so rispettu.*" (showing his respect) But why are you and Santo into all that Mafia stuff? Why aren't you talking about that stupid thing you did at the A&P store?"

While Anna blasted us, Filomena looked at Papa with her lips pressed together. "It's been awhile since you've talked to Anna and me about the Mafia. Don't you think Glory and the boys should hear what you told us? It would help them understand what it's all about."

Papa nodded and turned the palms of his hands upwards. "*Sentiti, figghi*" ("Listen, children"). He spoke with a tone that always meant he had serious business to share, and folded his hands. "*Allura, unni cuminciamu?*" ("Okay, where do we begin?") Everyone placed their forks and spoons down and also folded their hands. We knew that a discussion about Sicilian history was about to begin, which we always enjoyed.

Filomena immediately sat up straight, and slid her hand across the table. "I think we should begin by reminding ourselves of one thing in particular about why the Mafia got started that a lot of people don't know." She must have realized that sometimes she becomes lost in her lectures, because now she paused, scanned all of us, turned her palms up, and whispered, "Shall I continue?"

Gloria grinned. "Signora teacher, I mean Filomena. I know you love to teach, but I thought Papa was supposed to tell us about the Mafia."

Filomena's dark eyes sparkled. "Papa is going to do that, my dear sister. But he just asked where should we begin, didn't he? And, in my opinion, I think to understand the Mafia, it's important to remind ourselves of one particular thing about Italian history. Maybe even Teodoro doesn't know about it."

Teodoro clenched his right hand and tapped it against the table. "Okay, what don't I know?"

Filomena pushed the dish of biscotti toward him. "I wasn't picking on you. I was just trying to say that a lot of people don't know one particular detail about Italian history. I'll bet maybe your brothers don't even know."

Now I was also irritated. "What's that?"

Tony showed even more irritation than I did. "See, even Mr. History doesn't know what you're talking about."

Filomena did not get upset by the way we barked at her. She pushed her shoulders back and asked a question, much like a teacher would, to get students thinking and wondering. "Did you know that as recent as about seventy-five years ago Italy wasn't even a country yet?"

Teodoro munched on a biscotti cookie. "How do you mean

it wasn't a country? That doesn't make sense."

There was an ounce or two of wine left in Filomena's glass. She slowly picked it up, took a sip, set the glass down, stretched her arms out and placed the palms of her hands on the table to tighten our connection with her. "Teodoro, at that time there were eight provinces all across what is now Italy. And guess what? All of them except one were run by other countries. Only one province, way up North, called Piedmont, was run by Italians."

Chewing a bite of apple, Tony seemed to be enjoying the class that was going on. "So in a way, at that time, Italy was eight different countries."

"That's a good way of putting it, Tony."

The stage in my mind reserved for yesterday was already open and very busy. "And with all those countries doing their own thing, I'm sure the *contadini* (peasants) must have had it rough."

Papa nodded in agreement. "*Si, figghiu.* ("Yes, my son.) The paisani faced *tanti sfruttamenti di ricchi.* (a lot of exploitation from the rich) And there was no one who could help them. *Tuttu lu beni c'aiutava allura era la forza umana.*" (The only strength on which they could depend was in their own arms.") For these reasons, he added, the people began to revolt.

Anna glanced at Filomena with that sparkle in her eyes that always made clear she enjoyed competing with the teacher. "You're right, Papa! And with that strength in their arms, people began to revolt because they wanted to push all the foreign rulers out of the country and build one Italy. They kept revolting for more than fifty years."

Filomena accepted Anna's challenge and raised both hands. "And we all know what happened. Italy finally became one country in 1870 after Garibaldi led an army of volunteers from Sicily and freed Sicily and the southern half of Italy."

Anna stayed in the competition. "We should remember that all of those revolts that happened before Italy became one country were called the *Risorgimento.* I think that means like a renaissance. You know, like everything was going to change for the better. But it didn't, did it Papa?"

Papa responded with a sad expression. "*No, Tuttu canciau, má sempri era la stissa canzuna.*" ("No, everything changed but it was always the same song.") He added that a new, unified, Italian country was supposed to free Sicilian peasants from the abuse they had endured for many years from other governments, but instead very big problems developed.

"I don't get it. If Sicilians were now free to run their lives like they wanted to, why did big problems get started?" Gloria asked.

At the same time Teodoro blurted out, "and what does this have to do with the Mafia?"

Still excited by the opportunity to compete with Filomena, Anna reached across the table toward Teodoro. "Wait. You'll soon find out."

Papa liked that Anna and Filomena, and the rest of us, were excited by the discussion that was developing. He explained that problems developed because the province of Piedmont in Northern Italy, with its capital in Turin, controlled the politics of the new country of Italy. But other areas of Italy opposed its control. For example, politicians in Florence were afraid of the power politicians in Turin were developing, and politicians in Milan, preferred the political system in Austria as a way of ruling the new country of Italy. To make matters worse, even the Vatican opposed this new political system.

Anna could not control her wish to show all of us that she could be a teacher too. "And you told us, Papa, what upset Sicilian peasants most of all was the fact that while these politicians argued with each other, they showed little interest in what southern Italy needed, especially Sicily." Slowly peeling an orange, she explained that when Sicilians joined Garibaldi to fight against the Bourbons, he promised them that the new government would break up the *latifondi* (large feudal estates) owned primarily by absentee landlords, who extracted as much wealth from their holdings as they could without caring very much about the *contadini* (peasants) who lived and worked there. And these estates were owned by noble families living in northern parts of Italy and other countries. Anna added what she believed was an especially important issue. Garibaldi promised Sicilians the new government would give some of the estates to them so they could go back to *la via vecchia* (the old way, their own way of living).

Papa interrupted, reminding us with a surge of pride that his father was one of these patriots who joined Garibaldi.

Filomena made clear she wanted to score points before Anna got too far ahead. "But the government didn't give Sicilians any land like Garibaldi promised, right Papa? And you won't believe this. I read in an article I found, in the library at Teachers College, that said by 1910, that's forty years after Italy became a country, more than three quarters of all the land in Sicily was still owned by a few families. And most of them lived in other countries. So you see, that's what Papa meant when he said the Sicilians got exploited again."

Papa clenched his lips in a way that always meant he was disgusted with what he was about to say. "*Si, nun c'è rosa chi spini non teni.*" ("Yes, there's no rose that doesn't have a thorn.") He elaborated that after Italy was unified, these absent, landowners established connections with politicians in Turin and arranged to keep their large estates. Then they hired *gabelloti* (superintendents) to manage these estates. Because most of the local farmers had no land, they were forced to become *giornalieri* (day laborers) herding cows and goats and harvesting wheat for the *latifundista* (rich estate owner).

Thrusting the palms of her hands upwards, Filomena quickly joined Papa's sense of disgust. "And Papa, even though some peasants could get jobs, they were still taken advantage of, right? Like the *gabelloto* usually required a peasant to hand over a part of his wage as payback for being hired."

Papa nodded. "Si, the peasants took for granted the *gabelloto si vagnava u pizzu* (wet his beak)." He explained that the word "*gabelloto*" literally means tax collector, and that landowners, and their *gabelloti*, also used *mezzadria* (sharecropping) to increase their profits. With this system about one hectare (two and a half acres) was leased to a family. But the family was required to pay back 50% or 60% of the crops they were expected to harvest. "*Lu gabelloto, sempri misurava prima la parti chi spittava o patruni.* ("The *gabelloto* always measured first the wheat the landowner

151

received.) *E si l'annata era mala i paisani nun ricivianu nenti.* (And if the harvest was bad the villagers got nothing.) *La 'ngiustizia 'un si po' suppurtari"* (All this injustice is unbearable.")

Filomena was pleased and excited that she was adding to Papa's presentation. "I have a great example of that injustice. My friend, Angela Russo, told me the other day something her father was saying about how those land owners and their *gabelloti* left the peasants *sicchi* (dry – without resources) and *senza speranza* (without hope). When her father was about Tony's age, his father rented a couple of acres of land to farm from the Tudia estate on the edge of Siracusa."

Tony surprised me when he spoke up. "That's the estate that was owned by that Baron from Austria. He inherited it. I heard he was almost never there."

Since Tony spoke up, I decided to join in. "I heard plenty of stories about that jerk."

"Well, Angela shared more with me. Whenever this Austrian spent a few days at the estate, he expected the wives and daughters of the peasants who rented his land to go to the estate and wait on him. More than that his *gabelloto* asked everyone to contribute a dozen chicken eggs for each acre they were renting. And guess what? Her grandfather refused."

Gloria's jaw dropped. "What happened?"

Filomena looked up at the ceiling with disgust. "The next day they got evicted. Angela's father and grandfather had to pack up their stuff and leave the crops behind that they had planted."

Papa took a deep breath in a way that always said there was even more bad news. He described how owners of large estates also used their political connections to get control of water rights and to own most of the roads. Sometimes they charged unfair rates for water, and sometimes they even charged unfair rates if a peasant traveled over those roads.

I noticed Filomena glancing at Anna and grinning. Anna glanced back, flipping up the palms of her hands as if to say, "Ok. I know you're winning." Now Filomena was really on a roll. She pushed out her hand and again interrupted Papa. "I read how peasants were not only abused by landowners, they were also abused by government regulations from Turin." Raising her head, she continued her lecture explaining that after Italy became a unified country, the tax rate in Sicily was 30% higher than the rate that existed when the Bourbons ruled Sicily, because owners of estates used their political connections to arrange new tax laws. Then she shouted, "Guess what? Cows and horses owned almost only by estate owners were not taxed. But mules and goats that peasants needed to survive were taxed."

"That's amazing." Gloria's dark eyes glared.

Papa sighed, looked into the eyes of each of us and held the palms of his hands upwards. "As you see, once again peasants found themselves in the same predicament they were in before Italy became a country. *Ddi genti eranu stanchi e avviliti* (The people were exhausted and debased) *e nun c'era nuddu mezzu c'aiutava* (and there was no one among them who could help)."

I was so charged up, I couldn't control myself, and noticed my tone growled which was not like me. "What did our ancestors do about all this?"

"Santo," Filomena replied " that's why, a little while ago, I said there was one thing in particular that had to do with how the Mafia got started. It had to do with the different ways Sicilian peasants started to fight back because this new country of Italy didn't help them at all, and made things even worse."

Filomena paused because Papa reached out and placed his hand on my arm. "*Ti ricordi chi ti dissi? Tuttu lu beni c'aiutava allura era la forza umana.* (Remember what I said? The only strength on which they could depend was in their arms.)" He spoke each word very slowly to emphasize his point. "What peasants did about their predicament was to rebel against the Italian government, and the government sent an army to Sicily to crush this opposition."

Anna made clear she had remained quiet too long. "Papa, I want to tell the story about one thing that happened that you were talking about with Zio Gaetano and Filomena and me a while ago. It's a horrible example of what this army did to try to crush the opposition of the peasants." Papa nodded, so Anna continued. "Listen to this. You know the village of Caltavuturo. Well this landlord from Spain was initially required by the new government to give some land to farmers in the village to make up for the land he had taken in the past. But this Duke, and his *gabelloto*, used political connections and arranged to keep legal ownership of the land. When the peasants heard the news, they moved on the land and claimed it for themselves."

Tony smiled. "Great! They held their ground."

Anna glanced down at the table. "What happened, Tony, is not happy, it's very sad. The peasants were asked to leave. But of course they refused. According to the politicians, what the peasants did was not legal. So government troops were sent to this estate, killed more than fifty of them, and drove the rest off the land."

"Unbelievable!" Teodoro cried out.

Filomena was turned on by Anna's story. "If you think that was disgusting listen to another thing that happened. How about the *vergogna* (outrage) by that Govone?" She stretched her arms out with palms turned upward. "You've heard the old timers in our neighborhood talk about what he did, right?"

Tony decided to answer even though he and the rest of us knew. "I've heard our neighbors talk about him, and they call someone who's a dirty, rotten bastard that name.""

Filomena slammed the palm of her hand on the table. "Wait until you hear this story. What Govone did is another reason the Mafia got started."

Teodoro gasped, "A guy had that name, wow!

Filomena's dark eyes were now very wide and glaring. She turned to Papa, excited over what she had just introduced. "Tell them about General Govone."

Papa nodded and explained that a good example of a *vergogna* is what happened in another village in Sicily when peasants also rebelled because they did not get the land they were promised. This time the government in Turin sent someone named General Govone and his army to put the rebellion down. Before he arrived, most of the men and older boys of this village, who were involved in the rebellion, escaped into the mountains. What this General did is hard to believe. To get information about where the men of the village were hiding, he ordered that whole families be held hostage, and he cut off the water supply. Papa paused and remarked with

154

a tone of pride, "But these Sicilians did not betray their families."

Filomena interrupted. "Yes, *l'ordine della famiglia* is a very powerful force."

I gasped and slapped the table wondering to myself what on earth could have happened that was worse than what happened at Caltavuturo. "What happened, Papa?"

"Because General Govone was not getting any information from the families, he had some mothers and children tortured and others put to death."

"Disgusting!" Gloria screamed. Tony, Teodoro and I turned our heads back and forth in disbelief.

Filomena stared at Papa and thrust her fist out. I could tell she was about to share something that she knew would blow us away. "I heard how when the fathers and older boys came back from the mountains, some of them found their wives, mothers, and kids with their heads cut off, or their guts cut out, or burned so bad they could hardly recognize them."

Anna's eyes drooped with sadness. "Filomena and I were talking about that. What these fathers and older sons saw made them so crazy they started like suicide attacks. They attacked every soldier they could find, charging at them with knives, since a lot of them didn't have guns. They didn't care whether or not they got killed. They wanted revenge. The way these guys attacked even scared the soldiers who had a lot of experience."

I was very surprised when Mamma broke her silence and whispered with very sad eyes, "*Era un turmentu e si chiamava vita.*" ("It was a torment, but it was called life.") Then she asked everyone to keep in mind that "*La via della vita è china di valanchi. È pocu chiana.*" ("The road of life is full of pitfalls. It's not smooth.")

Papa looked at Mamma and nodded. "If all of you think what General Govone did was bad, something else happened that was even worse." He added that after all of this took place, the Italian parliament in Turin held a meeting and accused him and his troops of committing acts of cruelty.

Papa obviously had more to say, but Anna yelled, pointing to us boys. "Guess what? Listen to this! During this meeting, General Govone did not deny doing what they said he did. He explained to the Italian Parliament that since Sicilians were not

155

civilized, they deserved the kind of treatment he gave them."

Tony, Teodoro, Gloria and I screamed in disbelief.

Papa held his palms up toward Anna and Filomena, and both of them sat back in their chairs. "What's really very sad is the fact that most soldiers and policemen who were sent to Sicily to maintain order saw Sicilians in the same way."

Papa had more to say, but Filomena was so charged up she could not remain quiet. "Things that happened, like what we just said, is one reason some people in Italy, and now even some people in the United States, think all Sicilians carry knives and are uncivilized. More than that, they think Sicilians aren't really Italians."

Tony was clearly frustrated. "All right, Filomena, and you too, Anna. All this history is very interesting. But let's get back to the question Santo asked ten minutes ago. What did our ancestors do about all of this?"

As Papa was about to respond, Filomena stared at him and turned the palm of her right hand up. He understood she had something urgent she wanted to say, and nodded. Filomena looked into Tony's eyes. "What's the word Mamma and Papa and all the Sicilian immigrants here use for shovel?"

Obviously annoyed, Tony looked down and replied almost in a whisper, "Come on, Filomena. Why are you pushing so hard to be the teacher? What is this, a language class? And why are you avoiding the question Santo asked?"

Anna chuckled. "Tony, wait, I know why Filomena asked you that question. It answers Santo's question about what our ancestors did to handle all the abuse that went on. She and I talked about this with Zio Gaetano and our cousins the other day."

"So what's the word, Tony?" Filomena asked again with a calm, teacher-like tone.

Still annoyed Tony looked up. "Okay, Miss Teacher, the word is *sciabola*. For God's sake everyone knows that."

"Right," Filomena replied still smiling. "Now listen to this. The Italian word for sword is the same. It's *sciabola*."

Anna jumped up and slapped the palm of her hand on the table. "You see, Tony. That's the answer to the question about what our ancestors did, that's how our ancestors handled all the abuse dumped on them. They made the shovel, they made working hard, their sword, their way of fighting back."

Papa nodded, smiling, obviously pleased with what Anna and Filomena just brought up. He emphasized that it was really helpful to bring up our word for shovel because that word says a thousand things. To deal with all the abuse and prejudice, peasants worked hard and fought back by starting a movement that became known as the *Fasci Siciliani* which spread across the island in 1893. Later it eventually became known as the Mafia. Papa paused, stared at us and slowly asked, "*Capissci la parola fasci?*" ("Do you understand what the word fasci means?")

Teodoro quickly sat up straight in his chair, obviously eager to have a turn defining a word. "Since this is a language class, Papa, I want to tell you I know that word. When we play by the river, sometimes Mamma asks us to bring back *nu fasciu*, you know, a bundle of dried branches all tied together, so she can start the fire in the stove."

"*Hai ragiuni, figghiu.*" ("You are correct, son.") Papa smiled at Teodoro, adding that one *fasciu* is a bundle of sticks all together, like a family, and a *fasci* is a lot of bundles of sticks, like a village. So the word *fasci* became the symbol of bringing together all the families in the village. He elaborated that each village had its own *Fasci*, or league, and a *Capo* (chief) of that league. The goal of this league was to help peasants become aware of how landowners were exploiting them, and find ways of coping. Papa's voice now became raspier, as he emphasized that when peasants needed help they did not go to the government. Instead they turned to the village *Capo*. For peasants their *Capo* was not a bandit. He was a person who wanted to give them the justice that law and landowners failed to give them.

Anna interrupted with excitement. "Look what happened in the sulfur mines near our village that our grandfather took care of." She described what we already knew. The men working there were chopping away in tunnels from early morning to almost night time, and boys were dragging bags filled with sulfur all the way up those shafts that sometimes were a mile long. Then she mentioned a detail I did not know. One time the owner decided the *giornalieri* (day laborers) didn't produce what they were supposed to, so he cut everyone's pay. That's when our grandfather organized a strike. He gathered the laborers before the estate, and when the landowner stepped out to see what was going on, all the peasants threw down their picks and shouted, "Do the mining yourself." The landowner changed his mind.

Mamma surprised everyone when she spoke up, reminding us that because our grandfather was the Capo of the village, and respected by all the villagers, they sometimes called him 'Don,' and ..."

Before Mamma finished what she wanted to say, Filomena apparently couldn't wait. "The word 'Don,' comes from the Latin word 'dominus' which means 'sir,' or 'master'."

Tony interrupted Filomena. "That's it for language lessons. Papa, let's get back to what you called *Fasci Siciliani*. What did the *Fasci* have to do with the Mafia?"

While Papa glanced up at the ceiling to collect his thoughts, Anna could not control herself, glanced at Filomena and stepped in more vigorously than before. "Tony, wait. You'll soon see the connection. The *Fasci Siciliani* was in fact what Filomena and I, and our friends like to call the Old Mafia."

What Anna just said confused me, so I was surprised when Papa nodded, thanking her. He explained that the peasants began to call what these *Fasci* Leagues did 'Mafia,' and called the *Capo* who provided help '*u Mafioso*'. While he and Mamma shared a grin, he asked in Sicilian, "Why do you suppose peasants used the word *Mafia*? Guess what the word *Mafia* means?"

While Tony, Teodoro and I glanced at each other looking for clues, Gloria commented. "Here goes the language class again. But, I've often wondered, Papa, where that word came from. It's very different than the word *Fasci* that Sicilians use to remind themselves they are connected like sticks in a bundle. What does *Mafia* mean?"

Papa turned the palms of his hands up, and the look that covered his face at this moment meant he had something special to say. He pointed out that the word 'mafia,' as used by Sicilian peasants, came from the Arabic word *mahjas* which means a sanctuary, like a place of refuge, a place where you can get help and protection. He emphasized that the word '*mafioso*', then, means someone who can give you that help or refuge. He elaborated that the word *mafia* was probably taken into the Sicilian dialect because when Arabs invaded Sicily they built irrigation systems, gave peasants small, pieces of land and were interested in helping them develop their way of life. But when Normans invaded, they plundered the island and peasants became slaves, so they hoped they could find a mafia, a place of refuge. Papa paused. "*Ora capisci la parola mafia?*" ("Now do you understand what the word mafia means?") We all nodded.

Papa's face again expressed he had something special to say. "*Senti.*" ("Listen to this.) He added that as part of its war against the *Fasci* League, the government planted an army of occupation in Sicily, asked the prefect of each province to turn in a list of all of the persons involved with the *Fasci* League, and the army was ordered to arrest anyone suspected of *Fasci* activity. The prefect of the province of Siracusa, where Mamma's and Papa' village is located, reported back that if he did make a list of everyone involved in the *Fasci* League, he would have to include the names of all the males in the province older than seventeen years. All of us burst out laughing.

Filomena pointed to Tony, Teodoro and me. "Now you can see why Anna and I, and our friends, call what the *Fasci League* did 'the old Mafia'. And now you can see that in the beginning, the Mafia was a movement against a government that favored owners of sulfur mines and *latifondi* (feudal estates) and allowed peasants to be abused."

Anna looked preoccupied, and surprised everyone when she spoke almost in a whisper. "A lot of people don't realize what Filomena just said. That's what worries me. A lot of people, like that A&P guy who chased you, or like the kids at the farm, think the Mafia is only about gangsters. Today's gangsters are what Filomena and I call the New Mafia."

Papa interrupted Anna. I was confused because he usually waited until a person finished. He pointed out that if we recall the talk we had a few weeks ago about *l'ordine della famiglia*, we can see why these same rules were used to shape the *Fasci* in each village, or the *Mafia* as it was called later. Since these rules developed over many years, so families could deal with invaders who abused them, it's easy to understand why these same rules became part of the *Fasci* League. With these rules, each *Fasci* maintained loyalty, honor, respect, commitment and patience with other *Fasci*, so they could deal with abuse from the government and outsiders. Papa emphasized that if we look around, we can see these same rules operating in our own neighborhood and even in gangs like mine.

Anna spotted a chance to match Filomena. As soon as Papa finished, she spoke up like she was giving a lecture. "Let's go over these rules of the family again, everyone. Remember in addition to the rules of *omertà* (patience), and *serietà* (commitment), which we discussed a few weeks ago, there are the rules of loyalty, *rispetto* (respect), and *onore* (honor). And if families disagreed, usually the father or mother of each family went to the person everyone in the village accepted as *Capo* of the village, or *Fasci*, for help in settling the problem."

Mamma surprised all of us again when she spoke up with a tone louder than her usual way. But her pride about what she had to say was familiar. "Your grandfather held this position in our village, and your father holds this position in our neighborhood." We all looked at Papa, nodding with respect, and he nodded in return.

Anna wasn't finished, stretching her arm out toward Papa. "When you told us that the *Fasci*, or the *Mafia*, followed the same rules of the family, we know that gangsters began to follow those rules too. Like I said before, that's what Filomena and I call the New Mafia." Anna gestured to Filomena to continue the topic even though, to this point, they had been competing. Now they gave the impression they were performing something they had discussed many times.

Filomena nodded, accepting the invitation. "Anna and I talk a lot with our friends about the New Mafia in this country. That's what's upsetting. We need to remind everyone that Sicilians do not call these gangsters, Mafia, like the newspapers do. Like Papa often says, Sicilians call them *a Manu Niura* (the Black Hand)."

Anna again took a long look at Tony, Teodoro and me. "Maybe now you can see what we mean by the old Mafia and the New Mafia."

"I get it," Tony whispered.

"You know Tony," Anna continued, "after 1920 when the prohibition law was passed, these *Manu Niura* guys of the New Mafia began to make and sell liquor. But maybe you don't know that in 1929, the year Santo was born, these gangsters, from several cities in the United States, held a convention in Atlantic City to discuss how to run their business of extortion. Since a lot of these gangsters were Sicilian they followed the rules of the family because they knew those rules help."

Papa held up his hand toward Anna, interrupting her. "*Spetta,* (wait) Sicilians know these gangs have nothing to do with what the Mafia was really about in the beginning. But I have to remind us that a few Sicilians, and *Capi* of the *Fasci*, also built strong connections with politicians, and they became greedy."

Anna totally lost control of herself, bringing up a topic that caused all of us to feel pain. "That's like Mr. Salvatore Alba in your village when you were a baby, right Papa? And he helped get your father and mother killed?"

Papa stared at his hands as he clenched them together. "*Sì.*"("Yes") He added how much he regretted that here in our state, and in other places in the United States and Sicily, the New Mafia is operating, but it's important to keep in mind that the Old Mafia is also operating, and helping people, not exploiting them."

Filomena must have noticed that Papa did not stick with Anna's reminder of what Mr. Alba did, and she probably thought it would help if we talked about this *gabelloto*. "Papa, I think Tony and Santo have heard a little about Mr. Alba from talks you've had with our relatives. But Teodoro probably doesn't know much about him."

Teodoro did not feel slighted. "I've heard the name. I know he was a really bad guy."

Tapping her fingertips on the table, Filomena stared at Papa. "Can I please tell one particular story about Mr. Alba, because he's a really good example of what you're talking about? He belonged to the *Fasci* your father was the *Capo* of. But then took the side of the estate owner."

Papa glanced at Filomena, nodded and turned his palms up. He knew which story she had in mind.

Filomena paused to collect her thoughts, but Anna couldn't hold back. "Filomena! What an ass that Mr. Alba must have been! I heard so much bad stuff about him!"

"You're right, Anna, but with the story I have in mind, I want our brothers to be clear about why Mr. Alba is a good example of those members of the *Fasci* League who started what you and I call the New Mafia."

Anna did not seem to get it that Filomena had something in particular to tell us. She pushed her arms up and down, shouting, "For a couple of years he kept trying to get everyone to agree that he should be the *Capo*, not our grandfather. Everybody thought that was ridiculous because our grandfather had helped a lot of people. So when Alba couldn't get support to be the *Capo*, he joined the owner of an estate."

Teodoro wondered, "What did he do?"

"Like Anna just said," Tony commented with disgust, "he took the job of *gabelloto* of the huge estate owned by this guy who lived in Austria."

"Wow!" Teodoro shouted. "That's really switching sides."

Tony was still agitated about what Anna had brought up. "I also heard he asked peasants who were farming on that estate to pay him more than they were supposed to."

"What do you mean?" Teodoro screeched.

Anna jumped in to answer the question. She explained that, like Papa was saying a little while ago, a peasant could rent a piece of land on the estate to grow crops, and the *gabelloto*, like Mr. Alba could raise the rent. Anna came up with an example that involved one of our neighbors. "Teodoro, Mr. Milardo likes to tell the story of how Mr. Alba told his father the rent for his little piece of land was ten bushels of wheat. When it came time to collect at harvest time, he looked around and said he changed his mind. The rent now was fifteen bushels. Everyone knew he raised the rent because he noticed the crops were extra good that season."

With an expression on his face that said I can't believe this, Teodoro yelled, "How the hell could he do that?"

Anna placed her hand on Teodoro's arm. "Mr. Alba said if Mr. Milardo's father didn't pay the extra five bushels, something was going to happen. And if he wanted to make sure everything stays safe, he should pay the rent."

"What happened? Did he pay?"

"Mr. Milardo asked our *nonno* (grandfather) for help. And the story goes that Mr. Alba changed his mind and went back to the ten bushels for rent."

Filomena reached out and pushed Anna's hands down. "That's a small thing compared to the story I asked Papa, a little while ago, if I could tell. All the old timers like to talk about it because it says a lot about the New Mafia getting started."

Anna finally understood what Filomena had in mind in the first place. "You mean the story about the well water?"

"Yes."

"I'm glad you're going to talk about that," Tony commented. "Different people talk about it when they're sitting outside after dinner. But I've never heard the whole story."

Filomena was pleased that she finally had everyone's attention. "The owner of the estate Mr. Alba was managing arranged with the government in Turin to have control of the big well just outside the village so he could sell water to the villagers."

"Disgusting!" Again, Teodoro couldn't stop himself from shouting.

Mamma calmed him with a hand on his arm. "*Senti.*" (listen)

Filomena continued explaining that there was a well in the piazza of the village that belonged to the villagers, so they did not have to pay for water. Leaning over the table toward Teodoro, she stressed "And because it was small, everyone was very careful with how they used water."

"Teodoro, you won't believe what happened," Anna blurted out. Because she had just interrupted Filomena's story, she apologized to her with a nod.

Filomena accepted the apology, nodding in return. "Once in a while, some people in the village spotted a guy, who worked

163

for Mr. Alba, taking water out of the village well. It was clear he was trying to get the well dried up so people would have to buy water from the Baron's well. Now guess what happened?"

Mamma glanced at Teodoro and then glanced at Tony and me. "What happened shows how, sometimes, to deal with this kind of *vergogna* (outrage), a *Capo* has to retaliate in a big way."

Filomena reached across the table and placed her hand on Teodoro's. "The story goes that each time they spotted this guy, they told our grandfather. And each time our grandfather talked to Mr. Alba to help him see why what he was doing was not fair."

Papa interrupted with a tone that made clear how he felt. "Alba *era nu stunatu* (was stupid, out of his wits), *svergognato* (shameless), *e sfacciatu* (and brazen)."

Filomena leaned over with a look on her face that said "you won't believe this" and continued. "At night villagers still spotted this man pulling buckets of water up from the village well. And a couple of times the well got empty. So people had to buy water from that Baron."

Teodoro shouted again, "Wow! So he didn't listen!"

Filomena still had her hand on Teodoro's because she knew what she was about to share might be painful for him. "Teodoro, you'll be interested in how our grandfather solved the problem. This is the part of the story people talk about all the time." She shared that the man who worked for Mr. Alba was found dead in the big *puzzu* (well) of the estate, and our grandfather told Mr. Alba, '*mi dispiaci*' (I'm sorry) but somehow he slipped in. He also told Mr. Alba that if he didn't stop taking water from the well that belonged to the people, he might slip in the big well too.

Papa looked at Filomena with appreciation. "I think it was a good idea to share that story. It's a good example of how some persons turn their backs on the rules of loyalty, honor, respect, and commitment for the family and village." He stressed that a *cafone* (rotten person) like Mr. Alba, and other *gabelloti*, turned those rules around to get more power and money for themselves. And some of these crooks brought that way of operating to the United States.

Anna joined in. "They sure did. Not only did they get rich selling liquor to people in nightclubs, when it was against the law, but they went to stores and asked the owners to pay rent to make sure that no damage will happen to the store. You know that's what happened with Joe-the-Jew right here a few weeks ago, and Papa took care of it."

Papa tapped the table top with his hand. "Iu ci strazzai a cammisa e ci dissi d"un riturnari mai." (I tore his shirt and told him never come back.) He stressed that, as Anna and Filomena mentioned earlier, our neighborhood does not use the word Mafia when they talk about this kind of crook, but call this person, *manu niura* (black hand).

Filomena turned toward Papa, and again the look in her eyes made clear she had something to say that she thought was important. "You told Anna and me many times that, if you want to do something for someone who is being treated unfairly, it helps a lot to follow the rules of the family. Well, I read something at college in a history course this past spring that really blew me away. In my opinion what I read said that the colonies who started the United States were trying to follow the rules of the family." With much drama she asked, "Did you know that a phrase in the Declaration of Independence, which was drafted for the thirteen colonies when the United States was getting started, came from something an Italian wrote. It's a phrase kids hear all the time in school."

"What phrase?" Gloria asked.

"The phrase is 'all men are created equal'."

Anna held her arms out. "Everybody should listen to this. Filomena told me about it when she got back from school. The newspapers never write about it. They just write about Italian crooks."

"Are you saying an Italian wrote the words 'all men are created equal'?" Tony asked in disbelief.

"Not exactly. But those words did come from something an Italian wrote. Listen." Filomena continued acting like a teacher which she loved, and so did all of us. She went on to explain that before the thirteen colonies of the United States revolted against Britain, because they felt they were being abused, an Italian named Filippo Mazzei had moved to England and set up a business that imported Italian wines, cheeses and olive oil. While he

165

was there, he met Benjamin Franklin who convinced him to go to Virginia and try to set up a farm. Mazzei arrived in Virginia with Italian peasants and a bunch of different Italian vines, trees and plants. While doing his experiments, trying to get different crops started, he became really upset by the way the British were abusing the colonies, and he urged them to rebel.

We wondered how Mazzei urged the colonies to rebel.

Filomena elaborated that Mazzei wrote a bunch of articles that were published in the Virginia Gazette. Of course he couldn't write in English. The articles were translated by another one of his friends, Thomas Jefferson. At this point Filomena grinned since she was getting to the climax of her story. "Well, there is a part of one of Mazzei's articles that I memorized. He said, 'all men are by nature equally free and independent. Equality is necessary in order to create a free government.'" Now Filomena shouted. "That's what Sicilians have been saying for hundreds of years! That's what the *Fasci* League was all about!" She placed her hand on Anna's arm. "I told this to Anna. Those words by Mazzei that I just quoted became part of the Bill of Rights that the colony of Virginia issued. But when the Declaration of Independence was drafted in 1776, Thomas Jefferson changed them to read 'all men are created equal'. Even though Mazzei knew that Jefferson changed his phrase a little, he still made public that he agreed with the Declaration and urged the colonists to secede from England as soon as possible."

"That's amazing!" Tony shouted. "That was never mentioned in my high school class last year about American history." Since I loved history, the same thought crossed my mind as Filomena told her story, and I wandered why I had never run across this fact. Tony continued shouting, "So Mazzei saw that the colonists were being treated unfairly, and reminded them that the rules of the family say everybody should be treated as equals. You're right, Filomena, that's what the *Fasci* League was all about. Look at all the different ways Sicilian peasants were abused instead of being treated as equals."

Anna reached out across the table. "Yes, Tony, but unfortunately gangsters in Italy began to use those rules of the family when they organized themselves, and they took advantage of people instead of helping them. And gangsters in the United States are using the same rules."

Filomena continued her teaching adding that maybe people are fascinated by these crooks because they are fascinated by the aura of *l'ordine della famiglia*. She emphasized that it's too bad many people seem fascinated by crooks who use these rules instead of being fascinated by someone like Mazzei. "My God every time you turn around the newspapers have another story about some Italian gangster."

While Filomena was making her comment, Anna jumped up, raced to the girls' bedroom and returned, clutching a newspaper. She loved to match Filomena's teaching when she had a chance. "Listen to this article in last Sunday's Hartford Current. Filomena and I were discussing it yesterday." Anna remained standing, so everyone looked up. She carefully spread out the newspaper before her face in a very dramatic way and began reading slowly. "One part of this article says, 'Authorities now report they have enough evidence to declare that the *Capo* of each Mafia family of cities in the Northeast held a conference in New York City. They also believe a main item on the agenda was to discuss who was qualified to be the *Capo* of all the Capos, so that disagreements can be negotiated among families. There is not enough evidence yet that indicates who was selected.'" Anna lowered the newspaper and shouted, "Isn't that ridiculous! They call a gang of crooks a family and the head of those crooks a *Capo*."

With a look of disgust on her face that I had never seen before, Filomena reached up and touched the newspaper Anna was holding. "And newspapers forget that even though these gangsters use the ideals of the family to run their businesses, it doesn't mean that the rest of us Sicilians are all gangsters too. The newspapers have it all turned around."

Anna knew she and Filomena really had something going. "You're right! The newspapers don't help. They keep using the word Mafia for every crook, and they make it sound like only Sicilians are crooks in the New Mafia."

As Filomena glanced at Anna and began to speak, I imagined that they were on a seesaw taking turns going way up. "How about the famous Al Capone? He isn't even Sicilian. He came from Naples."

With what happened next, Anna went really high up on their seesaw. She slapped the table hard enough to rattle the dish in front of her, imitating Papa. "How about gangsters like Meyer Lansky. He isn't even Italian. But because the newspapers keep using the word Mafia about guys like him, everybody thinks all criminal gangs belong to one big Mafia family or organization, and they're Sicilian."

"Wait a minute, Anna." Filomena's expression said she felt mixed up. I couldn't wait to hear what was on her mind. "Since we got into that gangster stuff again, what Lucky Luciano did for the United States a little while ago makes everything very confusing."

I also felt mixed up so I had to say something. "What are you talking about? He's in prison. It was all over the news months ago. He's going to spend thirty to fifty years in maximum security, if he lives that long, and ..."

Tony interrupted me. "Filomena, what's Luciano doing for the United States except sitting in prison?"

Filomena glanced back and forth at us. "Something happened a few months ago that seems really strange, at least to me and Anna."

Tony and I recognized that the look on Filomena's face now said she just entered a topic she should not have trespassed. But Tony asked, "What happened that's strange?"

Filomena took a nervous glance at everyone. I was surprised because she stumbled and even looked scared. "Well, well, you know how Anna and I have been making a big deal about the difference between the Old Mafia and the New Mafia. What happened is very confusing. Like, uh, it's a strange mixture of the old and the new."

Anna saw what we all saw, that Filomena was not herself. She turned to Papa and stretched her arm on the table in his direction. "Gloria and the boys don't know what our cousin Filippo was asked to do. Is it okay if we tell them?"

"What your sisters are going to tell you stays in this family.

Capisci (understand)?" Each of us nodded, leaned forward, and held the palms of our hands together. From the tone of Papa's comment, the expression on his face, but especially his eyes, each of us realized that something very important, like a family secrete, is about to be revealed.

Filomena continued with a soft tone. "You're right, Santo, Luciano was in a maximum security prison. But when our cousin Filippo came home on leave for that week this past spring, he shared something with us. First I should tell you that Anna and I noticed that Filippo was having meetings with Papa, Zio Vito, Mr. Battastini, Mr. Corvo and Mr. Russo. One day we walked past where Mr. Russo lives. They were in the basement. But the window was open so we heard them arguing."

Tony couldn't resist stepping in. "I figured something was going on, because of the way Filippo was acting. Like something was really bothering him."

I had to join in. "Tony and I thought it was because Filippo was on leave for just a short while and..."

Tony, suddenly became very anxious, slid his arm across the table toward Filomena and interrupted me. "So what do you want to tell us? Is he okay?"

"Yes, yes," Filomena replied patting Tony's hand. "Like Papa just said, this is our business, so you can't tell even your friends. We told Filippo we heard the argument that was going on in Mr. Russo's basement. He knew he could trust us. He shared that, a few months ago, Lucky Luciano was moved from that maximum security prison to the Great Meadows Penitentiary. They moved him there because it would be easier for military people to visit him in plain clothes."

Tony's eyebrows pushed down in confusion. "Why were they meeting with that gangster? Didn't you say he was one of the *Manu Niura*?"

"Yes, he was, I mean is. But this is what Anna and I think is confusing. From what Filippo told us, Luciano, that *Manu Niura*, was being more like an old Mafia guy with the United States government because he wanted to help." Filomena explained that when combat in North Africa was ending, the American and

169

British armies were figuring out how to take over Sicily and set up a military base there. But the island was crawling with Nazi troops who had set up a very strong defense. "Filippo told us the American military people were meeting with Luciano in the Great Meadows Penitentiary because he was helping to set up connections with the *Capo* of each village. So when the Americans and British invade Sicily, they would have help from the inside, you know, from the villages."

Tony interrupted. "Like I said before, I'll never forget the date. They invaded Sicily on July 10th just a few days ago."

"Well before they invaded," Filomena continued. "The United States Army set up a special unit that met with Luciano and got assigned to go to certain villages to meet with their *Capi*, operate behind enemy lines, and set things up to destroy German units from the inside. Of course these undercover agents had to speak Sicilian, and know Sicilian ways. Filippo was one of them. And so were the sons of Mr. Russo and Mr. Battastini and Mr. Corvo."

I glanced at Papa and blurted out, "So that's what all that fuss was about a few months ago?" Then I tried to talk with a softer tone. "Papa, remember when I came home from school, you and Zio Vito were arguing?"

Tony tried to support me. "I remember you telling me about that."

Filomena stepped in again. "Anyway it was settled. They went over there, but no one's gotten any letters yet." She looked at all of us and raised her hands. "You can see now why Anna and I are confused. What Luciano did to help the United States get ready to invade Sicily and defeat the Germans is a weird mixture of a New Mafia guy being an Old Mafia guy."

From the expression on Papa's face we knew we must not say a word about this family business. He extended his index fingers and set them side by side, a gesture we all knew very well. Then he thanked Filomena and Anna for sharing their ideas and added, "*Sta parola, Mafia, nun è di tutti lu capiri*" ("This word, Mafia, it's not for everyone to understand.")

At that moment Isabella burst into the kitchen, and every one of us spun around, surprised. "*Zia Giuseppina! Zio Sebastiano!*

170

Mi dispiaci aiutu subitu, subitu! ("I'm sorry; help, quick, quick!) My mother is screaming!"

Mamma and Papa immediately rushed out of the kitchen and raced across the street to Aunt Concetta's and Uncle Gaetano's apartment. All of us followed a few yards behind. As we entered the building and galloped up to the third floor, we could hear Aunt Concetta screaming, and Uncle Gaetano trying to reassure her. When we pushed our way into the kitchen, Aunt Concetta was on her knees sobbing, her face only inches from the floor. I became very nervous and wondered if she was sick. Uncle Gaetano was kneeling beside her, gently rubbing her back with one hand while Isabella, Olivia, Alberto and Smiles stood nearby with their heads hanging low. In his other hand, Uncle Gaetano clutched a sheet of paper. Mamma immediately knelt beside Aunt Concetta consoling her and asking why she was so upset. Uncle Gaetano reached up and handed Papa the sheet of paper, and he spread it open.

Anna was standing next to him, looked down and gasped, "It's a telegram! Oh my God! It says, 'This is to inform you that Sergeant Sebastian, No! It can't be! Lucky was killed in action in the Southwest Pacific on July 18, 1943." When I heard that, I froze.

Aunt Concetta screamed, "*Me figghiu! Me figghiu! Non è possibbili! E' nu sbagghiu!*" (My son! My Son! It's not possible! It's a mistake!") Mamma raised Aunt Concetta's head, gently tucked it on her shoulder, and held her in her arms much like a mother would do with a child.

Filomena and Anna immediately threw their arms around Isabella and Olivia. Tony, Teodoro and I surrounded and hugged Alberto and Smiles. Suddenly Teodoro fell on his knees sobbing and choking. "My godfather is dead! My godfather is dead! I can't believe it." Smiles, Alberto, Tony and I, with tears streaming down our cheeks, knelt down around Teodoro and placed our arms on each others shoulders forming a circle.

Isabella and Olivia quickly walked into their bedroom followed by my sisters, and they sat on the edge of the bed. All of us boys also walked in and stood before them, forming what seemed like a wall that provided protection. Isabella gasped, "When they delivered that damn telegram, and Smiles read it, I screamed. I really got furious. I never dreamed this would happen!" With her fists clenched on her lap, she burst out crying. Anna quickly picked up a towel and gently dabbed the tears on her cheeks.

Olivia cried out, "So much for his nickname! God, he sure wasn't lucky this time!"

Filomena hugged Olivia with one arm while stroking her head with her other hand. "I know, Olivia. I know. No one can find a better brother and cousin than Lucky."

Several minutes later Aunt Concetta, who apparently had regained her composure, walked to the doorway of the girls' bedroom. "*Per favore, vieni in cucina.*" (Please come in the kitchen.) All of us immediately walked into the kitchen. With tears still rolling down her cheeks, Aunt Concetta slowly knelt down. Everyone joined her, making the sign of the cross, and praying that Lucky would find peace in heaven.

Mamma hugged Aunt Concetta and whispered in her ear, "*Curaggiu. Sapemu ca la via di la vita è china di valanchi.*" (Have courage. We know the road of life is full of pitfalls.) and suggested that we go to our apartment and share espresso coffee, biscotti and gelato which Lucky loved. "We can also share our memories of Lucky." Uncle Gaetano took Aunt Concetta by the arm, walked out of the kitchen, and we followed in silence with our heads hanging low.

Before sunrise the next morning, with lunch pails in hand, Tony and I stepped out into Ferry Street. Tony paused and pointed across the street. "Santo look, Zia Concetta already hung a black banner from their window. Mamma was getting ours ready just as we were leaving."

I looked up. "Tony, banners are hanging already from the second and first floor windows too."

"That's great," Tony whispered, "and Mamma said she, Anna, Filomena and Gloria are going to wear their black dresses."

My eyes felt really heavy with sadness. "Tony, did you notice this morning that Papa already had a black arm band around his shirt? All of Ferry Street is going to be in black for days." With our heads hanging low, we continued walking toward the area under the bridge where the trucks pick us up. With every step, I felt as if a huge stone was tied to each foot. Several members of our gang were already there. Melo and Bart waved, but Tony and I did not respond. Instead of approaching them, we walked a few yards to one side and scanned the river. I could hear some of the conversations.

Suggi almost growled. "Why are they standing over there?"

Bart placed his hand on his shoulder. "They're really sad. Didn't you hear the news? Their cousin, Lucky, died in the war. Last night it spread all through the North End."

Suggi was shocked. "He did? I never heard that. I went to bed early last night because I didn't feel good."

Vito whispered, "I just want them to know we realize how tough this is, and we'll do anything for them." What he said made me feel better for a moment.

When the truck departed for the farm, Tony and I sat close to each other, hunched over, with our heads hanging low. Each of the boys in our gang, as well as boys from Brian Coleman's gang, occasionally glanced at us with sympathy.

As the truck traveled over the river, I whispered, "Tony, you know how I'm always lost in these ideas and pictures that spin around in my mind."

Tony raised his head. "But sometimes you get really good ideas. Like that paper you wrote for Ms. Press just before school ended. Some of our buddies still talk about it."

"Thanks, Tony. But, did I tell you that this summer, when we cross over this bridge every morning, I get these twisted feelings in my legs like they're tied up? Then I get the opposite feeling like I want to start running. It's weird. It goes back and forth from being tied up to leaping ahead."

Tony looked down again. "There's a battle going on in you."

"And I get this feeling that going over this bridge is like trudging along over the road of life, from First Picking to Last Picking."

Tony jerked his head up. "That's like from the beginning to the end. Maybe it has to do with Lucky getting killed."

"You're right. This morning I'm feeling that when anyone

173

travels on that road, he's bound to lose someone he's really close to before he gets to the end."

Tony took a deep breath. "We just lost Lucky. And, God, Papa lost his mother and father when he was a baby, when he was just beginning to travel on his road."

My head sagged even lower. "Losing someone you're close to is really, really tough."

During the entire morning, I found it difficult to keep focused, as I walked through the field checking plants and occasionally helping Dominic pick his row. Thoughts and memories that tumbled into my mind wobbled and froze instead of spinning around. Like a few minutes ago, I found myself remembering how one day, a couple of years ago, Lucky burst out laughing as he ran up and down Ferry Street playing kick-the-can with Tony and me and other kids. A lot of people didn't know that for us the game kick-the-can was a little like the game of soccer, except we used a large tin can instead of a soccer ball. The picture of Lucky laughing and kicking the can spun into my mind and then froze to a stop. I also noticed that my body felt heavy, as if it was carrying huge stones.

Later at lunch time, Tony and I stood by ourselves at the edge of the field, talking quietly. Our gang slowly approached us. Bart placed one hand on Tony's shoulder and one on mine. "All of us are worried. I know the news about Lucky must hurt a lot."

Tony looked down at the ground. "You have no idea. He was a really special cousin."

The gang stepped a little closer forming a tight cluster around Tony and me. "I know he was your favorite," Bart continued quietly. "Everyone on our street thought he was a really cool guy. Remember how he coached me for a bunch of Sunday boxing matches."

I placed my hand on my forehead. For some reason, I could barely speak. "Yes, I remember."

A slight grin crept over Tony's sad face. "And remember how Lucky always joked that someday you're gonna be the world heavy weight champ?"

Bart was touched by this reminder. He lowered his head and whispered, "I know."

Angelo was standing to one side of Tony. "But how about when Lucky saved my kid brother from drowning."

Angelo referred to an incident that occurred before Lucky was drafted and that had become a legend on Ferry Street. It was eventually learned that Angelo's younger brother, and another boy, organized a secret mission for themselves. They decided to construct a raft. When the construction was completed, they planned to surprise everyone by paddling across the Connecticut River. For weeks they were occasionally seen collecting scraps of wood, and when asked what they were doing, their response triggered laughter. They were collecting wood to sell it.

Later it was learned that they carried the wood to an area by the river that was covered with thick bushes. This spot was many yards away from where children typically played and fished, so their mission remained a secret. When they finished constructing the raft, their plan was to launch it on a Sunday, and display their accomplishment. They knew that most adults and children from the neighborhood were always by the river every Sunday to participate in, and watch, the boxing matches that took place. A captive audience, therefore, was guaranteed for their launching and journey across the river.

When Angelo mentioned the incident involving his brother, Bart's head spun around. "I'll never forget it. There I was waiting to start my match with Franco, and Lucky was giving me tips about how to handle him."

"Pesci jumped in with excitement. "Angelo, remember how Suggi spotted your brother and his buddy on the raft in the middle of the river."

Suggi became even more excited than Pesci. "I was waiting for Bart to start his boxing match. I happened to look out across the river, and there they were, standing up on the raft waving their arms. I yelled!"

Angelo's brother and his friend had paddled their raft almost half way across the river. When Suggi screamed, everyone looked up and were amazed by what they saw. But disaster struck. Seconds after the two boys waved vigorously at their audience, Angelo's brother slipped into the river and his father screamed for help, since he knew his son did not know how to swim.

Angelo thrust his hand up. "It's a good thing you spotted them, Suggi. And it's a good thing Lucky was a great swimmer, or my brother would have drowned."

"In seconds, Lucky kicked off his shoes." Bart sounded as if he was back at that moment. "He said to me you can box with Franco next Sunday, and dove into the river."

When Lucky reached the raft, he found Angelo's brother franticly trying to hold onto the edge of the raft, while his friend lay flat on his chest, sobbing. Lucky helped Angelo's brother climb on the raft, and then pushed the raft toward the shore. The boys helped by paddling with their hands because the boards they used as paddles had been kicked into the water. When they reached the riverbank, everyone cheered.

Angelo sighed and looked up at the sky. "God, my mother and father will never forget what happened. You know last night they lit a candle for Lucky when they heard he was killed in action."

Bart stared at Tony and me. "Lucky was the greatest. Like I said, I'll never forget him."

At this moment, I felt as if Bart's arms, and everyone else's, were around Tony and me. "Thanks."

"And you know what else?" Now, Bart looked very worried. "There's something that makes me even more sad and scared?"

I felt a surge of fear. "What?"

"I had this dream that my brother Carlo was going to meet Lucky in the South Pacific. Now I'm nervous about whether anything will happen to Carlo."

Tony glanced into Bart's eyes. "Let's all hope he'll be okay."

At that moment a field foreman shouted, "Hey you guys over there! Did you hear me? I said lunch break is over. Let's get back to work."

I turned to my gang. "It helps a lot to have you guys talk about Lucky. Okay. Let's do it."

As I entered the field, I noticed the heavy, twisted feeling I had all day was not as heavy now. And as I walked up a row behind Suggi, I felt my legs moving more freely and smoothly.

More than that, I noticed when I scanned a plant, I immediately spotted a leaf Suggi had missed.

At the end of the day, after Tony and I finished bathing, we lingered outside in the back of our tenement house. Gloria stepped out of our apartment and approached us. "I've got to show you something that's weird."

"What's weird?" Tony asked.

"I'll show you. It's over here by the fence."

We followed Gloria, and Tony quickly looked up and down, scanning the boards of the fence. "I don't see anything weird."

Gloria pointed to the ground. "Not the fence, Tony. Look down here."

Tony and I looked down. About ten dead flies were lined up in a very straight row.

Tony grunted, "What the heck is that?"

Gloria whispered, "I saw Teodoro whacking flies with a fly swatter. I was watching him from the kitchen window. Every time he swatted a fly, he brought it over here."

"That's really strange, isn't it Santo?" I did not respond, because I had become lost in many thoughts.

"I went outside and asked him what he was doing," Gloria continued. "He said he was making a cemetery."

I leaned over. "If you look close, there's the sign of the cross scratched in the dirt in front of each fly."

Gloria whispered, "Wow, I didn't notice that."

At the same time, Tony exclaimed, "What the hell! Now that's really, really weird. I think we should say something to Mamma and Papa. Is he cracking up?"

I pointed at the flies. "Wait! Wait!"

Tony wondered why I didn't agree with him . "What? Why wait?"

"Don't you think it has to do with the news that Lucky died? Lucky played with him a lot, and he was Teodoro's Godfather."

Gloria joined me. "I know. Teodoro loved him."

Suddenly all three of us turned around because we heard someone. Teodoro slowly walked toward us with a stride, and look on his face, that said he was very proud about something.

"What do you guys think about my cemetery?"

"It's really nice," I whispered.

Gloria turned to Teodoro, and her eyes were filled with tears. "Yes it is."

"Those flies were buzzing around like they were in battle, so I thought I would bury the ones who got killed. See I'm putting them in their nice cemetery, not just throwing them away."

Tony placed his arm around Teodoro's shoulders. "That's really good, brother."

"I've been really down, and it makes me feel really good when I bury another fly."

I glanced at Gloria and Tony. "I know what you mean. We've been feeling sad too about Lucky getting killed."

Now Tony pressed the fingers of one hand against Teodoro's chest. "You know what? You feel sad. But I've been feeling more mad than sad that Lucky got killed."

Teodoro looked up at Tony and kicked the fence. "Guess I feel more sad."

"I know, Teodoro," Tony mumbled with a reassuring tone. He must have noticed what I did, that Teodoro kicked the fence when he said he felt more sad. "Remember last night you were crying and holding onto that special rock you and Lucky found along the river a long time ago. Later I heard this bang. You must have thrown it against the wall."

With tears in his eyes, Teodoro looked up at Tony. "I guess I was all mixed up before I fell asleep. Am I weird?"

I placed my hand on Teodoro's shoulder. "No. When somebody you care a lot about dies, anybody could feel sad and mad at the same time."

At this moment we all spun around because we heard someone step into the yard. Papa just arrived from work. Teodoro immediately pointed to his cemetery. "Look, Papa. I made a grave for every fly that got killed. See, I even put a cross in front of each one."

Papa quickly walked over, scanned the ground, carefully scraped the dirt around each fly, and whispered, "*Bonu, bonu.*" (Good. Good.) He stood up and looked at each of us. "*Comu siti?*" (How are you doing?) Each of us looked down, and no one said a word. I noticed Gloria rubbing her stomach with the palm of her hand, and Tony stamping his foot several times. With tears in my eyes, I looked up at Papa and shrugged my shoulders.

He realized none of us had anything to say. "Let's help Teodoro build his cemetery. Search for *petri nichi* (small stones)." Then he knelt down and carefully scratched a boarder around each grave site, and Teodoro joined him. Gloria, Tony and I returned with rocks and helped Teodoro locate one at the head of each grave site.

Once the project was completed, Papa stood up, slapped the palms of his hands together to shake off the dirt, and whispered, "*Ora partemu p'u sciumi*." (Now we leave for the river.) We walked quickly down Ferry Street toward the river.

Tony turned to me as we hurried behind Papa. "Remember how today I swore at that kid in Brian Coleman's gang because he bumped into me when we were getting on the truck? I've been in a bad mood all day."

"So have I. I screamed at those guys from Hartford at lunch time and called them assholes. That isn't like me."

Gloria rubbed her stomach as she hurried along. Papa glanced at her hand and slowed down his pace. "*Chi c'è, vi fa mali a panza?*" ("What's the matter is your belly sick?")

"I don't know, Papa. It's just a tight feeling in my stomach. It started last night. Maybe it's something I ate."

When we reached the river, Papa stopped and slowly scanned the water as it rippled south toward Long Island Sound. Papa bent over, picked up a rock leaned back and yelled, "Ahh!" as he flung the rock, which spiraled through the air and flopped into the water. "Okay, Let's see who can throw *chiù luntanu* (the farthest)."

Each of us immediately imitated him, hurling one rock after the other as hard as we could. Laughing we frequently paused to evaluate who was throwing a rock the farthest. After about fifteen minutes, Papa commented that we should all return home because it would soon be time for dinner.

When we approached our tenement house, Mamma called out from the doorway, "*E' quasi ura di mangiari*" ("It's near time to eat.")

Gloria took Teodoro's hand. "Let's go guys."

Filomena and Anna were in the kitchen helping Mamma prepare dinner. Papa immediately shared what we had just done at the river, and that Teddy had built a nice cemetery in the back yard which they could look at later. Mamma turned away from the stove, smiled and touched each of us on the head.

Filomena stepped towards Papa with a look on her face that always meant she was wrapped up in some important issue. "Because Aunt Concetta lost Lucky, Mamma, Anna and I were talking about last year."

Papa asked what each of us was wondering. "What do you mean?"

"Remember how bad the United States government treated her and other *paisani* in our neighborhood about that alien and radio stuff?"

Anna jumped in with vigor. "Papa! We were talking about how even though that terrible thing happened, she gave this country one of her sons!"

At that moment, what Filomena and Anna were referring to immediately tumbled on that stage in my mind reserved for events of the past.

Last summer Tony, Teodoro and I sat on the curb listening with interest to Papa and two of our neighbors, Mr. Marino and Mr. Colavito, who were sitting on chairs lined up on the sidewalk and engaged in vigorous discussions. They got into the dilemma all of the parents in our neighborhood were facing whose sons had enlisted in the military, or had been drafted, weeks after President Roosevelt issued a declaration of war against Japan the day after the Japanese attacked United States naval and air bases located at Pearl Harbor on December 7, 1941. What upset them, and all the adults in our neighborhood, was not so much that Hitler's Germany, which had an alliance with Japan, declared war on the United States four days later on December 11, but because Mussolini and Italy did the same. Mr. Colavito was shouting to emphasize that before immigrating to the United States, he and his parents and all the other *contadini* (peasants) had little use for the Italian government, or for any government. Yet, when he and our neighbors immigrated to the United States, they gradually developed loyalty to the United States government. This loyalty, he believed, was clearly shown by the support everyone gave their sons who enlisted, or were drafted, into military service to help defeat fascism in Europe, but especially in Italy. He went on with issues I had heard before several times. Mussolini, and his party of fascism, rose into power more than a decade before World War II began in regions north of Rome which benefited most from his public works projects. But, for the most part, Sicilians opposed Mussolini and his political party.

Papa got into a topic that my brothers and I often heard and realized how much it made all the adults furious. President Roosevelt had signed a proclamation that designated as enemy aliens more than a half a million Italians who were living in the United States but were not citizens. Papa shared how his brother Gaetano's wife, our Aunt Concetta, cried when she received that ID card in the mail weeks after her son, Lucky had been drafted.

The reminder of the proclamation that designated many Italians as enemy aliens caused Mr. Colavito to express the rage that was rolling throughout the neighborhood. He brought up that a few months ago, in February, 1942 President Roosevelt signed another executive order authorizing that enemy aliens be relocated in internment camps. Japanese Americans, many of whom were U.S. citizens, were affected most by this decision. But what a lot of people didn't know was that many Italian Americans who were not citizens were also confined in camps. A few men from our neighborhood, including Mr. Colavito's brother, were arrested and sent to one of those camps. It was not until June of 1942 that the government permitted these Italians and some Germans to return to their homes. Mr. Colavito was relieved that his brother returned home a few weeks ago, had not been injured and was not ill.

Even though the adults in our neighborhood were furious over the fact that some of them were designated as enemy aliens, they still supported their sons who entered the United States military but had to pay a painful price. The price was that although

181

most Italian Americans in the military were assigned to serve in the South Pacific, some were serving in units stationed in Europe. This meant that they might have to participate in killing their *paisani* and maybe even some of their relatives.

At one point during this discussion, Mr. Marino, who worked on a night shift in a textile mill, turned to Papa with a troubled look in his eyes, reporting that earlier today he had seen two men walking into different apartments in the neighborhood. Mr. Colavito and Papa looked at Mr. Marino with concern and wondered if he had asked the strangers who they were and what they wanted. Mr. Marino shared that these men showed him a badge, told him they worked for the government, and wanted to see papers that proved certain people were now citizens of the United States. Papa commented that maybe these men were in the neighborhood because of another law that has confused the neighborhood and made all the adults very angry. Authorities were ordered to take away short wave radios, and flash lights from non-citizens, and to issue ID cards because of "military necessity."

Tony and I startled when suddenly Olivia came running across the street yelling for Papa that men were trying to take away their radio, but her mamma wouldn't give it to them and was going crazy.

Papa immediately jumped up and ran across the street with Mr. Marino and Mr. Colavito close behind. Tony and I followed, and Teodoro ran into our apartment to tell Mamma and our sisters what was happening. When we reached the third floor, we saw Aunt Concetta standing in front of the family radio throwing wild punches at a man no one recognized. Another stranger was trying to restrain her. Aunt Concetta was screaming in Sicilian that her son went into the United States Army a few months ago, and she could not understand why she could not have a radio. The whole scene made me feel scared and confused.

I remember how Papa immediately stood in the face of the man who was trying to restrain her and shouted with confidence, "Hey! Stop!" while Aunt Concetta continued screaming. The two men made clear that they were the authority, pushing their badges in the faces of Papa, Mr. Marino and Mr. Colavito, while Olivia hugged her mother and tried to quiet her down.

At this moment Filomena burst into the kitchen followed by Mr. Marino's son, my friend Bart. Now I felt some sense of relief. "Papa! What's the matter!" Filomena yelled, "Why are these strangers trying to take the radio?"

Papa was still standing in front of one of the men who continued to hold his badge out. "*Non sacciu*" ("I don't know.")

Filomena quickly walked within inches of the two men and glanced at the badges they were holding. "What! You guys are from the OSS! What are you doing here?" I had no idea what OSS meant.

One of the men pointed to Papa. "Who is this?"

Filomena mumbled to Papa in Sicilian, "Let me find out what this is all about." She glared at the two men and expressed herself with confidence. That relieved me. "He's my father. He understands English but does not speak it well. I'm asking you again who are you, and what are you doing here? Look what you've done to my Aunt."

One of the men stiffened his posture, tilted his head back and spoke in a tone that I never liked because it sounded so elitist. "We are from the Office of Strategic Service. An order has been issued that if one of the heads of a family does not have citizenship papers, that family can not own a radio. We are trying to tighten up security and…"

"Are you kidding?" Filomena interrupted with anger. " For God sake! My cousin Lucky, this women's son, is in the United States Army. So what if my Aunt isn't a citizen yet."

"An order is an order. We can't make exceptions." I remember wondering to myself why was this agent barking like that.

Filomena glanced at Papa and quickly explained to him in Sicilian what the agent just said.

At this moment Uncle Gaetano burst into the room, "*Ch'è successu*? (What happened)?"

Papa explained the situation with a few brief sentences in Sicilian and asked Uncle Gaetano to remain quiet. Then he turned to the OSS agents, "*Per favore*. I mean-a, Please. We take-a walk-a. Filomena you come-a with-a us-a."

The two agents walked down the steps followed by Filomena and Papa. While Uncle Gaetano hugged Aunt Concetta,

Mr. Marino and Mr. Colavito sat at the kitchen table with Bart, Tony and me.

Mr. Marino blurted out a comment I had heard many parents say ever since the war started. "*Io non capisciu. Stu munnu è pazzu.*" ("I don't understand. This world is crazy.")

Bart's eyes were glaring with anger, when he turned to his father. "You're right. Guys from this neighborhood fighting for this country, and we still have to put up with all this shit." Tony got into a vigorous discussion, wondering how could our aunt and uncle's son fight for the United States, but they can't have a radio."

About ten minutes later Papa and Filomena entered the kitchen. "*Unn'è a polizia?*" Mr. Marino wondered. ("Where are the policemen?")

I noticed a slight grin on Filomena's face. "They decided to leave. And Zio, they said it's okay if you keep the radio, even though Aunt Concetta isn't a citizen yet."

"*Comu lu facisti?*" ("How did you do that?") Uncle Gaetano asked Papa.

"I help them understand. *E' fatto.*" ("It's done.")

Uncle Gaetano hugged his wife who had stopped sobbing, and whispered the Sicilian saying familiar to her and to everyone. "*La via di la vita è china di valanchi. E' pocu chiana.*" ("The road of life is full of pitfalls. It is not smooth.")

While the last scene of last year's episode was being performed on that stage in my mind reserved for yesterday, Filomena grabbed my shoulders. "Santo, where did you go? Mamma just said let's sit down and eat."

"Oh, sorry. When you mentioned that you were talking about that radio thing that happened last year to Aunt Concetta, I got lost remembering all of what happened as if it is happening now."

Apparently Anna could tell that I had a lot of mixed feelings whirling around in me. She put her arms around me and then gathered Gloria, Tony and Teodoro into the embrace. "I'm glad you went to the river and flung rocks. It helps to let out those feelings."

Filomena joined the circle. "Teodoro, I can't wait to see the cemetery you built. Each of us has to find ways to handle losing Lucky."

Anna cleared her throat. "And all of us have to find ways to help Aunt Concetta, Uncle Gaetano and their kids feel that Lucky is still with us."

Smiling with pride, Mamma and Papa joined the crowd. We all whispered *"famigghia"* (dialect for family) and sat at the table for dinner.

The next day, while waiting in the Central Lot to learn which field we were assigned to pick, I shared with my gang the flashbacks I experienced about what happened last year, and we vigorously discussed our confusion about why apartments throughout the neighborhood had been searched and radios removed from a few of them?

"I still can't believe it!" Pesci exclaimed. "My Uncle Nunzio has been here since I was six years old, working his ass off digging ditches for the city to put water pipes in the ground. And those bastards took his radio away!"

"I guess that was the rule. No citizen, no radio," commented Melo.

"That's stupid!" Angelo muttered. "So my uncle was not a citizen yet. What's that got to do with having a radio?"

Vito pointed vigorously. "Well you won't believe this! My Aunt Sofia had her apartment searched, and she had citizenship papers."

"Why did they search her apartment?" Ancio wondered.

"I'm not sure. It was something about my Uncle Rosario. They said he joined some organization when he came to this country a couple of years ago. A club that was on some list the government was keeping."

When I heard Vito mention something about his uncle being a member of an organization, I listened carefully. All the adult males in our neighborhood belonged to the Garibaldi Society.

"For Christ sake. So what if your uncle belongs to a club," Sal joined in, reflecting the outrage our parents expressed when some of them were classified as enemy aliens, and the government decided to investigate organizations. "He's got two sons in

185

the United States Army. I guess that doesn't count."

"What club?" Louie asked. "The only club I know about that our parents and relatives belong to is the Garibaldi Society."

Tony yelled out something I was thinking about while hearing all this stuff about Italian clubs. "What the hell, my father helped start that club!"

I was about to step into the discussion and learn more from Vito when one of the foreman approached me. "Santo, Mr. Williams wants to talk with you for a minute." I felt nervous because I expected the foreman to tell me which field my gang was to pick.

Louie was standing nearby chatting with his pickers, Sal and Ancio. "Now what's the matter?"

"Nothing's happened with that jerk, Mr. George, right?" Sal asked.

"Not that I know of. I'd better see what's up."

I quickly walked to the Main Cabin and stepped in. Mr. Williams was standing by his desk talking with Mr. Thomas. I immediately recognized him. He supervised the inspecting, sewing and hanging of tobacco leaves that took place in sheds. Now, the whole scene of what went on in a tobacco shed whirled through my mind.

There were a number of huge barns, or tobacco sheds as they were called, located on the edge of some fields. The sides of a shed included rows of long, wooden slats on hinges which were flipped open so air passed through the walls into the shed to help dry the tobacco leaves. Inside, tiers of beams were strung across the entire width and length of the shed from the roof down to a distance of about ten feet above ground, each tier separated by about seven feet from the one below it. Three main activities took place with the tobacco leaves brought to a shed. They were "inspected," "sewn," and "hung to dry."

Long tables were set up on each side of the shed. On the back side of each table stood a row of teenage girls facing the center of the shed. Baskets of tobacco leaves were carried into the shed by older boys and placed at one end of each table. "Inspectors," removed and examined the leaves, placing to one side any leaf that had been bruised. The leaves that passed inspection were

186

picked up by boys, carried to the girls, and placed in front of any one of them who was ready to "sew".

Each girl, called a "Sewer," followed a routine. She placed a wooden lath about six feet long on the table, threaded a needle at one end of a long piece of thick string, and tied the other end to one end of the lath. She quickly and carefully picked up a leaf by the base of its stem with her left hand, and with her right hand pushed the needle into the stem. Then she switched the needle from her right hand to her left, and with her right hand carefully dragged the leaf along the string to the far end of the lath. After sewing the maximum number of leaves the lath could hold, the sewer quickly removed the needle and tied the string to the left end of the lath. During this process, a good sewer gracefully swung her arms back and forth sewing a lath in about two minutes. The lath now was much like a curtain rod from which hung a number of small curtains. If these curtains, or leaves, needed to be spaced better, the sewer gently pushed them an inch or two to the left or right along the string. When the sewer nodded or said, "Okay," a boy, standing on the other side of the table, immediately grabbed the lath with one hand. If he was not already holding a lath in his other hand, he waited until another sewer completed a lath. Once he had a lath in each hand, he quickly walked over to one end of the barn and handed the laths to boys who were called "Servers".

From this point on, the next job was much like that of a relay team. Each Server stood on beams, forming a column to the top of the barn. The first Server stood on beams closest to the ground. The second stood on beams about seven feet above the first Server, the third on beams above the second Server, and so on. With this arrangement a team of five or six Servers formed a column with the last Server near the roof of the shed.

There was another feature that distinguished what these Servers did from a relay team. In a track race, each member of a relay team passed a single baton only once to the next runner until the last runner crossed the finish line. In contrast, the members of a team of Servers were required to pass many laths, one after the other, until each lath reached the finish line. Also, each Server was required to be skillful enough to stand on beams, and maintain his balance, as he reached down to take a lath from the team member below him, and quickly pass it up to the team member above him.

The finish line was crossed when the Server at the top of the column handed the lath to the boy who was called the "Hanger". Straddling two beams, the Hanger took the lath from the Server below him, leaned over, and placed the lath at his feet so that each end of the lath rested on a beam. Of course, a steady stream of laths was being passed up by Servers. This meant the Hanger had to step backwards on the beams, as he located each lath at his feet, and make sure that the leaves were not pushing against the last lath he set down. Of course, as the Hanger slowly stepped backwards on the beams he was straddling, each Server beneath him was also required to step backwards slowly and steadily, so that the column of Servers remained positioned under the Hanger. In this way the entire column of Servers, and the Hanger, crept inch by inch across the tiers.

Once the tiers at the very top of the shed were hung with laths, the Hanger and his team of Servers continued to hang laths on the next tier below, until they reach the last tier. At this point when the shed was full, everyone moved to another shed were the inspecting, sewing and hanging continued.

As I stood in the Main Cabin, with all these thoughts about what happens in a shed whirling through my mind, I became confused since my gang did not have anything to do with what goes on in a shed. Mr. Williams interrupted his discussion with Mr. Thomas and turned to me. "We've got a problem. Two of Mr. Thomas' Servers are out today because they're sick. Mr. Thomas just started a new shed. He needs one more Server to get going."

Puzzled, I looked back and forth at each of them. "I don't understand what that has to do with my gang."

"Mr. Thomas just told me that a few times Melo was a Server last year when someone was sick."

"I remember Melo talking about that. He said he served a couple of days for Giorgio." I got nervous. "Don't you think it's risky for him."

Mr. Williams leaned back in his chair. "Santo, Mr. Thomas just told me Melo was really good. He said Melo is tall for his age, kept good balance, and moved those laths in a really smooth way." Mr. Williams paused. "It's Giorgio's gang that needs a Server."

"Oh, Giorgio, he's from our neighborhood." My tone quickly changed from concern and opposition to being an ally. "I remember Melo said he liked being a Server. Last year he told me it reminded him of being on a relay team."

Mr. Williams interrupted me. "Santo, if Melo works as a Server today, can your gang keep up with its job?"

I raised my hand. "Yes, of course. Vito and I can pick Melo's rows. Besides, Melo's partner, Bart, is the fastest picker in the gang, and he can help too. I know we can get our job done."

Mr. Williams grinned. "Please tell Melo what's going on."

I quickly walked out and approached my gang. Louie was anxiously waiting. "What's up? Now what did Mr. George say we did wrong?"

"No, nothing." I gestured to everyone in my gang. "We've been asked to help with a problem." I explained why Mr. Williams wanted Melo to be a Server.

Melo looked around at all of us and stretched his shoulders back, "Okay. I'm cool with that. It'll give me a break from picking. Besides, swinging those laths up is easy and fun."

"Oh yeah," joked Bongi. "There goes Batman Melo again, flying through the beams." Everyone burst out laughing.

Musca thrust his arm up, pointed to the sky and yelled, "Look! It's a bird! No! It's a plane! No! It's Super Melo!" Again everyone roared with laughter.

Mr. Thomas approached us so we stopped laughing. "Melo, I guess Santo told you you'll be a Server today."

"I'm all set." Melo grinned and stepped up on his toes.

"We're starting a new shed, and Giorgio wants you to handle Station Five. Is that okay?"

Mr. Thomas was referring to the position of each Server when a shed was started. The Hanger, of course, stood on the top most tier. The Server on the first tier above the ground was sometimes referred to as handling Station One. The next Server handled Station Two, and so on. Mr. Thomas, then, asked Melo

189

to be the server who passed the laths to Giorgio.

"Sure," Melo replied, "I can get back in the groove easy. I know Giorgio really good. His younger brother and I go to school together." Still grinning, Melo turned, waved to us, and walked quickly toward the truck. "See you later guys."

"See you later, Batman," Dominic shouted.

Moments later the rest of my gang was transported to a field. At the end of the day, we milled about in the Central Lot waiting for a truck to take us to our neighborhood.

"Where's Melo?" Pesci asked stretching his neck and looking around.

"Don't worry," Bart responded. "The shed guys should be here any minute."

"There he is!" Sal shouted, pointing toward Melo who was walking quickly in our direction.

"How did it go, Batman? I mean Melo-man!" Pesci yelled.

"What was it like?" Jack Kane asked. "Man, aren't you scared to stand up there on those beams?"

"It was okay. I got in the groove. Actually, it was kind of fun being up there. It's like a bunch of guys in a circus act, balancing and swinging."

Tony stared at Melo. "Well, I'm glad you like it. I would never, never go up there."

Sal grinned. "That's because you're not Batman, Tony." Everyone exchanged jokes.

The next day Melo went to the shed and again took on the job of Server. At noon my gang, and the others, sat on one side of the road that bordered the field. As usual we were joking as we ate our lunches. Suddenly a pickup truck sped up the road and screeched to halt. Everyone looked up with concern, clutching their sandwiches.

The driver of the truck ran toward a foreman who pointed in the direction of my gang. "He's over there?"

The driver ran toward us yelling, "Santo?"

I immediately noticed the worried look on his face. "Yes. That's me. What's up?"

"Come with me, quick."

"Why? What's the matter?"

"This kid, Melo, needs you. I'll explain on the way."

The rest of my gang, as well as other boys sitting nearby, stood up in alarm. I jumped in the pickup truck.

As the driver sped toward the shed, he explained to me that when lunch time arrived, Melo climbed down the tiers, slipped, fell to the ground and bumped his head on a beam. He was unconscious for a few seconds, and when he recovered he asked for me. The driver reassured me that there were no cuts on Melo's head or body, and the nurse had checked him and said he was okay.

The truck screeched to a stop in front of the shed. I jumped out and raced inside. Melo was sitting on the ground with his back against the side of the barn. Mr. Thomas, Giorgio, and one of the inspectors stood nearby.

Everyone moved to one side when I approached and sat next to Melo. "Are you okay?"

"Yeah."

"What happened?"

"I was coming down for lunch break. The beam wobbled, and I slipped, and my head hit a beam before I hit the ground. They said I passed out for a few seconds."

"Wow! Lousy luck."

"Maybe I wasn't as careful as I should have been."

"Where does it hurt?"

"Here." Melo placed his hand on the back of his head. "It feels just about the same as when you get a good whack to the head when you're boxing."

I placed my hand on Melo's shoulders. "I'm glad you're okay."

Mr. Thomas stepped over. "Mr. Williams said you could take the afternoon off."

"What about Giorgio's gang?" Melo asked.

I stared at Melo. "You can't climb up there again this afternoon. Not after what happened."

Mr. Thomas interrupted. "Melo, Giorgio's gang hung three tiers this morning. So this afternoon he needs only four Servers."

Giorgio stepped closer. "Melo, I heard what you said. My guys can handle it. I feel really bad that you slipped. Thanks a lot for helping us yesterday and this morning."

Melo looked up. "Thanks, Giorgio. I told Santo I feel like I just got punched in one of those boxing matches we have on Sunday. But this time I got whacked hard."

I tried to reassure him. "Melo, you'll be okay for many, many more rounds."

Giorgio knelt down before Melo. "You know what our parents keep saying. The road of life isn't smooth. Our parents and grandparents had to travel on some really rocky roads. And sometimes even our roads get rough."

I looked back and forth at Giorgio and Melo and clenched my fist. "And we're going to make it, like our parents did, and like their parents did."

Giorgio placed a hand on Melo's shoulder. "Yes we will."

That evening at dinner time, while everyone was engaged in conversations, pictures flashed across my mind a number of times. Melo is standing on a beam. Suddenly he loses his balance and tumbles to the ground where he lies stretched out, unconscious. Each time this scene flashed before me, I felt a wave of tension, realizing I too will have to deal with unexpected challenges and disasters as I try to continue walking ahead on my road of life. I surprised myself when I blurted out, "Hey! There's something I have to say!" Everyone immediately interrupted their discussions and looked at me with concern.

Anna slid her arm across the table, gently removed the fork I was holding and wrapped her hand around mine. I felt a surge of relief. "What's the matter? You seem very upset."

Tony stared at me. "I know what Santo has to share. He's been thinking and worrying about what happened to Melo and what it means."

Gloria's eyes glared with concern. "Is he alright? What happened?"

Tony continued helping me, describing what happened to Melo and emphasizing that he and I talked all the way home about how Sicilians always say the road of life isn't smooth, and why it's important to follow family rules so we can keep going and be the best we can be.

When Tony paused, Mamma slowly raised her hands to capture everyone's attention. "When Tony said everyone felt like it was all over when they learned Melo had fallen down from the beam, I found myself remembering two things that happened in Sicily years ago."

Filomena couldn't wait. "Ma, I'm not sure what you mean. We've talked about many different things that happened in Sicily that got the *contadini* (peasants) to understand why the road of life isn't smooth, and you have to keep going."

Mamma raised her hand, making clear she had not yet expressed what she had in mind. She emphasized she was referring to two particular events that happened when she and Papa were kids that made everyone feel as if all of Sicily had fallen down. But then everyone worked hard to get back up and find ways to continue on the road of life. She stared at Papa and asked him to share the disasters that occurred at Messina and Mt. Etna.

Papa emphasized Mamma was right that these two events are great examples of what we are discussing.

"What happened at those places?" Teodoro yelled. Mamma took hold of his hand.

Papa reminded us that in 1908, when he was nine years old, one of the worst disasters in Italian history took place. An earthquake devastated Messina, north of his village, and thousands of *contadini* (peasants) were killed. Many of those who survived travelled south and some located themselves on the hills surrounding his village. As soon as Papa mentioned this event, we remembered that our parents, aunts and uncles frequently discussed how they and other children of the village were asked to bring water and food to the peasants crammed on the hillsides.

Teodoro interrupted, "What about Mt. Etna?"

Papa shared that two years later, in 1910, Mt. Etna erupted and again thousands of peasants were killed. Like when the earthquake took place, some survivors rushed south and a number of them set up camps on the outskirts of his village. Again all of the families reached out to help, sending children to the camps with food and water.

Mamma raised her hand and Papa nodded, agreeing that she should now continue to make her point. Mamma emphasized that whenever she and her brothers and sisters brought food and water to the survivors during both of these tragedies, they also spent time talking with the children, and noticed everyone felt like it was all over. Mamma paused. "But the grown ups, and even some of the children, kept reminding themselves. *La via di la vita è china di valanchi. È pocu chiana* (The road of life is full of pitfalls. It's not smooth). Mamma stretched her arms toward me. "They also said whenever you fall down, you have to get up and keep fighting the problem, so you can move ahead."

Of course, every time we discuss lessons from history and our ancestors, Filomena could not resist jumping in with the last word. "Tony! Santo! When Mamma said the villagers always said you have to keep fighting the problem you're facing, what weapon did they use to fight? Remember our discussion?"

A wide grin crept across Teodoro's face as he pushed his arms up. "Teacher! I learned from that language lesson we had they used a *sciabola* (shovel) which for them was the same as a sword. They kept digging hard to fight back and solve the problem."

Everyone smiled at Teodoro while Mamma's eyes reached out to me with affection. "*Ora comu ti senti.*" (Now, how do you feel?)

"Ma, I feel a lot better now, and I know we're going to work hard to move ahead on the road of life."

Fourth Picking

Although the Road is Sometimes Rocky,
We Were Fortunate to Find This Pathway of Life

Early one morning a few weeks later, near the end of July, the sun was already glaring on the Central Lot. My gang and several others were waiting for assignments.

Musca always got nervous when our routine changed. "Do you think we'll be sent to the Cromwell Meadows today or to-morrow to begin Fourth Picking?"

Before I had a chance to answer, Melo joined in. "That would be great. Then I can finally stay standing."

Pesci, Musca's partner, walked over and looked up at Melo's face. I had noticed this summer that Pesci was beginning to show he was self- conscious about his height. Although I was not that tall when I was 14, he was much shorter, and so was his partner. When the two of them stood before Melo, they looked to me like midgets.

As soon as Melo expressed relief that he could now stand up during Fourth Picking, the expression in Pesci's eyes, the tone of his voice, and what he said, made clear my guess was right, that he was jealous. "If you weren't a giant, you could have stood up all the time during third picking, like Musca and me."

I nudged Melo with my elbow because I didn't want an argument to start this early in the morning. He got my message and grinned. "I know, Pesci. Me and Bart had to crawl on our knees, while you squirts had it made, dancing down every row."

At this moment, Suggi ran toward us and interrupted the bantering. I wondered what the problem was because he had a very worried look on his face. "Santo! Bart wants to talk to you! Quick!"

I turned and scanned the Central Lot. Tony heard what Suggi just said, pointed and whispered, "He's over there with the South End gang. I'm going with you." The two of us immediately ran across the lot.

Bart always enjoyed socializing while everyone waited for

195

their assignments. Apparently, he had walked over to where workers from Middletown's South End were gathered. As Tony and I approached, Bart was engaged in a big discussion with some guy whose back was toward me, so I couldn't tell who he was. I wondered why Bart was leaning so close to him with his face only inches away, jabbing his right arm back and forth, and pushing his fingers against that guy's chest.

When we got closer to the crowd, a boy I recognized from school spotted us and stretched his arms out. "Hey, where the hell have you guys been all summer? We hardly ever see you garlic balls." Everyone chuckled.

I whispered to Tony, "That's Adam Smith, he's cool," and yelled back, "Where have you and your chocolate buddies been?"

Tony couldn't resist raising the ante. Imitating Adam, he threw his arm up and pointed to the sky. "Look, Adam! That sun up there is already hot." Then he pulled his arm down, pointing at several boys. "And look at all those Hershey bars standing around you. If you guys don't get your shirts on, you're all going to stand in a puddle of chocolate pudding." Now the crowd burst into a roar of laughter.

"But it'll be delicious, right?" Adam shouted back.

The roar of laughter caused Bart to stop talking and look up. The boy facing him spun around. It was Jimmy Lewis the straw boss of the South End gang whom I knew very well. "Hi Jimmy. How's it going?"

"Hi, cousin."

As soon as Jimmy called me "cousin," an incident that occurred during the last weeks of school, when we were completing eighth grade, whirled into my mind. Before I got involved in this incident I learned what had happened from discussions Papa had with Mamma, but especially with Uncle Gaetano, because the incident involved helping a black family. These are the scenes that flashed on yesterday's stage like a movie.

––––––––––––

Near the end of this past spring, a crew of the Middletown Water Department was digging a trench in a narrow dirt road

196

that joined Ferry Street and Green Street. A pipe that connected a tenement house to the water main was clogged and needed to be replaced. Papa was standing on the road looking down into one end of the trench. Mr. Misenti, one member of the crew, stood in the trench, leaned on the long handle of his shovel with his head tilted back, and looked up at Papa as they conversed. The other members of the crew continued working, rhythmically slamming their picks into the hard, crusted dirt, shoving their shovels into it, and heaving it up onto the road.

Papa thought Mr. Misenti wanted to ask him something but, for some reason, was holding back because he went on and on about different minor details concerning his family. At one point Papa flipped the palm of his hand toward Mr. Misenti to let him know it was time to get down to business. "It's nice to hear that news about your family. But why did you say you needed to talk to me?"

His head still tilted back, Mr. Misenti jerked it to one side toward one of the men who was digging several yards away. "*Ddu niuru dda havi bisognu du vostru aiutu,*" (The Black man over there needs your help) because you are the *Capo* here, and you know cops on the Police force. Maybe you can help him."

Papa leaned over and whispered, "What's the matter? Was his son arrested?"

Mr. Misenti shrugged his shoulders. "*Non sacciu. Sulu mi dissi ca so figghiu ebbi na granni sfurtuna.* ("I don't know. He only told me his son had a huge misfortune.) *Na scola ha sempri statu incasinatu* (In school he was always in a jam) *era na minchiata.*" (it was a stupid thing.") Now, Mr. Misenti showed how nervous he was trying to justify why he had asked to see Papa. He began talking one hundred miles an hour. "His name is Mr. Lewis. He's a really good man. He's one of the Blacks in the Water Department everybody likes. He thought you would help because word is going around that this summer you'll be driving *Libbri cu roti* (Books with wheels) in the South End."

Mr. Corvo, one of the residents of the tenement house toward which the men were digging, had been watching the crew working. When he noticed that Mr. Misenti was engaged with

Papa in what seemed to be a very serious discussion, he walked over to the edge of the trench. "What's the matter? Is something wrong with one of our *paisani*?"

Clearly annoyed, Mr. Misenti stared at Mr. Corvo. "*Fatti i cazzi tuoi!*" ("Mind your own damn business!") Mr. Corvo glanced at Papa, who was still focused on Mr. Misenti, and quickly walked away.

In an effort to reassure Mr. Misenti, Papa showed he was not bothered by the interruption and slowly turned the palms of his hands up, "I'll talk to him for a minute, *Non c'é problema* (It's all right)."

Mr. Misenti turned and called out to Mr. Lewis. "Hey! The Capo is here!"

Mr. Lewis left his shovel sticking up from the ground, quickly walked over, and looked up at Papa. "Hello sir. I appreciate you taking the time to talk with me."

"What big problem is your boy having? Is he in trouble with the police?"

"No, he's in trouble with passing to the next grade. His whole class got a writing assignment, but my boy didn't get it done. The teacher told him if he doesn't turn it in before the last week of school, he won't pass."

"What grade is he in?"

Mr. Lewis became very anxious, "Eighth grade. That means he won't go to the high school in the fall." He clenched his teeth and slammed his fist into the palm of his other hand. "Look! I want him to finish school! I don't want him to be a ditch digger like his father!"

"I know what you mean," Mr. Misenti interrupted with a tone of compassion. "The same with me. I want my son to be more than somebody who digs ditches."

"Some of it is my fault," Mr. Lewis continued. "I got my boy a job working on Saturdays and two nights a week at the Bunces store, sweeping floors and emptying trash buckets. Maybe he didn't have time to do his work." I remember Papa telling Uncle Gaetano that at this moment he thought Mr. Lewis had something embarrassing to share, and wasn't sure if he should, because he kept wringing his hands together. "But maybe he does have a problem. His mother noticed this year that every time the teacher gave the class something to write, he sat for a couple of hours holding his pencil. And he'd write only half a page."

Papa turned the palm of his hand up. "I understand. I know you don't want your boy to dig ditches. If he's in eighth grade, my boy must know him, because he's in the same grade. So I'll talk to him to see what can be done."

Mr. Lewis took a deep breath. "Thank you, *Capo*." With his head lowered, he slowly walked away, grabbed the handle of his shovel, and continued digging.

That evening after dinner Papa shared with me what Mr. Lewis told him. I got very excited. "Papa, I know Jimmy Lewis. He's a really neat kid. He loves to joke around, and boy can he run. I'll bet he makes the track team his freshman year. I'll talk to him about this tomorrow."

The next evening Papa asked, "Did you get a chance to talk to Mr. Lewis' boy about his problem?"

"Yes, it's all set. I'm going to his place this Sunday and we're going to get it done. Jimmy told me where he lives in the South End."

"Do you want me to take you there?"

"No, it's okay. Some kids in my class come from there."

Early in the afternoon on Sunday, I knocked on the door of the Lewis apartment. Mr. Lewis opened the door, smiling. "Hey, boy! It's really great you could come here today."

Jimmy stood behind his father with his mother and sister on either side of him. Mrs. Lewis also smiled. I was really amazed how her teeth sparkled, and her eyes glistened. "Come in Santo. Jimmy's told me a lot about you." She anxiously turned her head back and forth, glancing at the walls and ceiling. "Please excuse our place."

I wasn't sure what she was apologizing about. "It's okay. It's about like ours, except a little smaller."

Mr. Lewis pointed at the table set in the middle of the kitchen. "You guys can sit here to do whatever you're going to do. I know you Italians like grapes, so I put a bunch there. Help yourself." He placed his hand on Jimmy's shoulder and gave him a reassuring look. "We're going to take a walk. See you in a few hours. Okay?"

"Sure Dad." Jimmy seemed nervous, and he jerked his shoulder back when his father placed his hand there.

I sat down at the table, reached out, and plucked a couple of grapes from the bunch. Two pads of paper and several pencils had already been placed on the table. "Jimmy, have a seat. I think we can get this done in a couple of hours." Jimmy sat to the right side of me, picked up a pencil and clutched it in his left hand. "Do you remember what Miss Press wanted everybody to write about?"

Jimmy squeezed his pencil very hard. "Yeah. We're supposed to pick something we talked about in social studies and fit it into something that happens to us."

Even though Jimmy still seemed to be nervous, I wanted to get started. I picked up a pencil and slowly pushed one of the pads in front him. "That's about it. So what do you want to pick from what we talked about?"

"Santo, I decided to get into that James guy Miss Press told us about. She was really into him and spent a lot of time on his stuff."

"She sure did, maybe because he wrote one of the first books about psychology. I think it came out in 1890. I remember it because when Miss Press told us, I said to myself, 'Holy smoke, that's just a few years before my father was born.'"

Jimmy not only squeezed his pencil but tapped it hard against the table. "Well my grandmother was a kid then. Boy, she really bent my ear about the days when she was a kid."

Without thinking, I reached out and placed my right hand on Jimmy's left wrist to hold his hand still. "Anyway Jimmy, what about that James guy? What part did you want to get into?" Jimmy stared at my hand on his wrist and jerked his hand away. Even though in my family we're always putting our hands on each other to say something, for Jimmy this wasn't working.

Jimmy sat back, held his hand still for several moments, and continued to clutch the pencil. "Well, if I got it straight, I wanted to get into the part where Miss Press told us that this James guy said the stuff of who we are comes from all the things a kid does with the people he lives with."

I took a deep breath and searched for things to say that would help him feel less nervous. "You're right, Jimmy, that's one of the things, and I used that to start my own paper. So what are some of your opinions about it?"

"Well, I know I hate to write. Even when we were writing alphabet letters in first grade, I hated to drag a pencil across a piece of paper. So I thought I would write about it, since my hand has to move the pencil."

Grinning, I took a long look at Jimmy. "That's really good. That's just what Miss Press wanted. We're supposed to connect something James said with what we notice. Why don't you start with what you just told me and make those your first sentences."

I was amazed to see how much Jimmy struggled. He clutched his pencil and slowly pushed his hand along, as if a fifty pound weight was pressing down on it. I leaned over and read aloud each word Jimmy printed, because I thought it might help him be less afraid. "I really hate to write, even when I was a kid when I had to write alphabet letters."

Jimmy stopped, sat back and gasped with irritation. "Santo, that took me a long time! See what I mean? Shit!" Suddenly he slammed his right fist on the table.

Again without realizing it, I did what we always do at home. I placed my hand on Jimmy's shoulder. "Easy. Let's not give up." When I felt him jerk his shoulder back, telling me "Hands off," I quickly removed my hand. I was desperate to make some kind of a connection, so I slowly read again each word he had written. Then a plan flashed into my mind. "I got an idea. What if you say the sentences and I write them down? Maybe things will start to roll."

Jimmy closed his eyes. "Okay Santo. We can try that."

I slid the pad in front of myself and picked up a pencil. "Okay, what were you going to say next?"

Jimmy leaned toward me, pointing at the pad of paper. "Well, after I wrote that, I was going to write 'but I don't know why I can't get my arm to move this pencil.'" Suddenly Jimmy again slammed his fist against the table, which startled me.

I collected myself and continued struggling to find a way to help him. "Gee, Jimmy, I know you must really be pissed off about writing. Since you're slamming the table, I just got a crazy idea. What if you slam the table first and then write what you want to write?"

Jimmy smiled. "You know, every time I try to write I want to punch somebody, I mean something."

I burst out laughing, "Well punch whatever you want, except don't punch me."

Jimmy chuckled and playfully punched my arm with his fists, as if he were hitting a punching bag. Apparently he decided to do what I suggested. He picked up the pencil with his left hand, stretched his right arm straight up and slammed his hand against the table. Then he slowly printed, 'but I don't know why.' Suddenly he raised his head and yelled, "You know what? I just remembered something!"

"What?"

"When I was a little kid and used crayons, my grandmother always whacked my hand with a wooden spoon."

"Why? That's ridiculous!"

"She took care of me while my mother worked. When she saw me picking up a crayon with my left hand, she always hit my hand with a wooden spoon, and put the crayon in my right hand. Even in first grade when we were learning the alphabet, she'd whack my left hand, if I held my pencil with it."

"Gee Jimmy, that's terrible. What the hell was the matter with her?"

"I don't know. She was a witch. She said it was bad to be left handed. But thank God she went back to New Orleans. So then I could use whatever hand I wanted."

"Well Jimmy, the hell with her. Let's finish our paper."

For the next two hours sometimes Jimmy dictated sentences for me to print, and at other times, he elected to print a sentence while slapping his right hand on the table. We were nearly finished when Jimmy's parents and sister returned. "How did you guys make out?" Mrs. Lewis asked.

Jimmy carefully picked up five sheets of paper with the thumb and forefingers of his left hand, turned in his chair, faced his parents, and waved the pages.

A very wide smile covered Mr. Lewis' face. " Great!"

Mrs. Lewis again flashed her sparkling white teeth. "Wonderful!"

The way they reacted made me feel really good. I stood up, pointed to the pages dangling from Jimmy's hand, and wanted to say something to let him know he did really great. "You just got a couple more of your ideas to write down, and then you cross the finish line. Jimmy, I'll bet next year in track, you're going to cross the finish line first a lot of times."

Jimmy raced into another room and returned. "Santo I know you're a rock freak. You're always collecting rocks. Here's one my grandmother brought from New Orleans." He placed a small stone in my hand.

I didn't know what else to say. I grinned, "I'd better get home."

The next day at Central School we were waiting for class to begin, and Miss Press was at her desk, looking over sheets of paper. Jimmy entered, walked to her desk and slowly stretched his paper in front of her. She glanced at Jimmy and quickly looked over each page. "You got it done!" Jimmy turned and looked at me. I placed both of my hands on my desk with each index finger extended and set next to each other.

Suddenly Miss Press called out, "Okay, school's in session! It's time to begin!" Jimmy walked to his seat, and everyone focused on Miss Press.

At the end of the school day, I was standing in the hallway chatting with friends. Jimmy came running over. "Santo, guess what? Miss Press just told me that what I wrote, I mean, you know, it was okay. I got a passing grade."

"Fantastic! You crossed the finish line." The boys with whom I was talking playfully slapped Jimmy on the back, congratulating him.

Jimmy turned to me, extended the index finger of each hand and pressed then together. "When I gave Miss Press the paper, you put your fingers together like this. What were you doing, Santo?"

Ancio grinned. "That means guys are connected together about something. You know it's like their secret mission."

Jimmy stared into my eyes. "I've been wondering, why did you help me? It took a piece of your Sunday."

I returned Jimmy's gaze. "Jimmy, Mr. Misenti works with your father, right? And he is like a cousin to my father. I mean, he's not a blood cousin. But for us Sicilians, close friends are like cousins. And whenever you need help you can ask them. Your father asked Mr. Misenti for help, and he asked my father."

Jimmy nodded with a grin of victory. "Boy, I'm glad for the cousin connection."

Later I learned that Tony was waiting for me with a group of boys near the entrance to the school. Three black boys approached them and yelled, "We just heard that nigger word from over there!" They stepped before Tony, hoping to start a fight.

Jimmy was standing yards away, witnessed what just happened, and raced over. "Wait guys! They wouldn't say that. I know this guy's brother. He's a good friend of mine. "

At that moment I came out of the school's main entrance, spotted Tony in the middle of a crowd, and raced over. "What's the matter?"

I was surprised when Jimmy placed his hand on my shoulder. "Nothing, cousin, everything's cool."

The boy who had confronted Tony looked down, mumbled, "Sorry, man," and walked away with his friends.

I wondered why Tony was here at the Junior High. "What are you doing here?"

"Mamma said I should pick you up because we have a bunch of things to do." Tony turned to Jimmy and held out his hand. "Thanks."

Jimmy grinned, reached out with his left hand, quickly pulled it back, stretched out his right hand, and shook Tony's. "Cool man. After all we're cousins." Then he glanced at me. "We're almost through with school. Maybe I'll see you at the farm."

"Let's hope we get our jobs again, Jimmy."

The story racing through my mind on yesterday's stage suddenly stopped when Tony and I reached Bart and Jimmy. Now I focused on what was happening on today's stage, and stepped in front of Bart. "Suggi said you wanted to see me. What's the matter?"

"Jimmy's gang is in big trouble."

Tony looked back and forth at Jimmy and Bart. "What do you mean?" My brother liked to be behind the scenes, trying to figure out how to solve a problem, and imitating our father.

"Jimmy's gang is having a tough time with Topping."

Topping was a routine that took place near the end of July. By this time most of the tobacco plants were almost six feet tall, and a small cluster of flowers had grown at the top of each stalk. The job of snapping off this cluster of flowers was called "Topping." By removing these flowers, the growth that continued to take place during the next weeks resulted in larger leaves for both Fourth Picking and Last Picking.

Tony was confused. "But what do you mean they're in trouble?"

Bart glanced back and forth at Tony and me. He wasn't sure whether he should report to Tony or me, so I nodded toward Tony. Bart faced him. "Yesterday afternoon the boss told Jimmy that his gang screwed up because they're way behind."

Jimmy hurled his arms out. I was surprised to see him explode with so much anger. "Hey man, three of my guys felt sick all week! They got some kind of infection!"

Bart placed his hands on Jimmy's shoulders to settle him. I noticed that Jimmy did not flick his shoulders to make Bart remove his hands, and was glad to see that Jimmy was getting used to how Sicilians always talk with their hands. "They told Jimmy that because his gang wasn't getting it done, guys from Hartford might finish Topping. If they do that, maybe there won't be any more jobs for Jimmy's gang this summer."

Jimmy clinched his teeth. "Shit, if that happens, me and my guys are really behind the eight ball. We need the dough."

Now Bart squeezed both of Jimmy's shoulders and shook him a little. "I told you, Jimmy, I would find out if my cousins could help."

Tony placed his hand on Jimmy's arm. "Jimmy, don't get worked up. Santo and I will see what we can do."

Suggi, who had followed Tony and me after locating us, was standing a few yards away. "Wait, Santo! What do you mean you'll see what you can do? Why are you going to help them? They're niggers. They've never done anything for us."

Tony, Bart and I spun around and stared at Suggi. Tony grabbed each of Suggi's arms. "Listen! You're not going to get to know these guys unless you walk with them?"

Bart was furious over what Suggi just said and pushed a clenched fist against his chest. "When you get older, you'll have some of these niggers in your class, and you'll run into them on the street, so better that you get to know them now."

Suggi shoved Bart's fist to one side and turned to me. "But what if I need help, Santo? If you guys are helping those niggers, you can't help me!"

Now Tony glared at Suggi. "Then if that happens, suck on your fingers like you did when you were a kid."

Suggi glanced at the three of us and looked down. "Okay. I trust you know what you're doing."

Bart, Tony and I turned our backs on Suggi and faced Jimmy. Tony was still trying to help Jimmy feel he was with friends. "Forget what Suggi just said. He's a kid."

"No sweat," Jimmy responded with a look of appreciation.

I thought it would help if I used a sign Jimmy had learned. I extended the index finger of each hand and held them close together.

Jimmy smiled and turned to Bart, "Did you see what Santo just did with his hands?"

"Yeah, Jimmy, why are you asking?"

"Do you know what he's saying?"

"Are you kidding, of course." A smirk covered Bart's face. "It's an old Italian gesture."

Jimmy glanced at me. "Santo used it when I turned in the

essay he helped me write, and told me it means we are on a secret mission."

Bart flexed his broad shoulders. "That's what it means. So now we know we're on a mission that's our business."

Tony and I turned jogged toward the Main Cabin and stopped a short distance away. "Tony, let me ask Mr. Williams if our gang can join Jimmy's to finish Topping."

"That should work Santo. We're just about finished with Third Picking in the Portland Hills." Tony stared at the ground. "Wait! Your idea would even work better if you ask Mr. Williams if Brian's gang, along with our gang, can join Jimmy's. Then Topping would be finished in a day, and we can go back and finish Portland Hills."

"Tony, that really makes sense."

At that moment a foreman stepped out of the Main Cabin. I rushed toward him, "Could you please ask Mr. Williams if I can talk to him for a minute. It's important."

The foreman nodded and seconds later he stepped back out. "Okay."

I entered the cabin and found Mr. Williams engaged in a discussion with Mr. George. "What's the big problem Santo?"

I looked down at my hands, and was surprised when my words slipped out in a whisper. "I heard Jimmy is way behind with Topping. You know, his gang is from Middletown too. So we happened to be talking ..."

"I can't hear you very good, Santo. That's true, way behind. But it's none of your business. Why are you bothering yourself with this?"

I became worried when I heard a tone of frustration in his voice, paused, and repeated *omertà* several times to myself. "Mr. Williams, with all respect, I have an idea about what we can do. It's just that Jimmy's gang is from Middletown like my gang and Brian Coleman's, and I ..."

Mr. Williams interrupted me. Now he seemed annoyed. "Getting toping done is what Mr. George and I are talking about."

At the same moment, Mr. George looked at Mr. Williams and growled. "Like I said, I don't think the Middletown niggers can finish the job in time to get all the fields ready for Fourth Picking. I think the Hartford gang can do the job, because they're almost finished with getting the last sheds ready."

I was surprised when Mr. Williams pointed at me. "What's this idea you have?"

I felt relieved. "What if my gang and Brian's gang join Jimmy's? We'd get all the Topping done in one day. "

Mr. George leaned against Mr. Williams' desk, glanced at me, and gripped the edge of the desk with both hands. "But you've got Third Picking to finish in the Portland Hills."

I stared at him and pressed the tips of my fingers into the palms of my hands which helped me to remain focused. "My gang is ahead of schedule. We've got one field in the Portland Hills left. That won't even take us a day. If we join Jimmy like I said, everything will be done in a day or less."

Mr. Williams turned to Mr. George. "What do you think?"

Mr. George was obviously annoyed. "But how are we going to get three gangs to work together and do the job right? Besides we never have black kids working with white kids."

Mr. Williams pointed at me. "What's your answer?"

For some reason, what Mr. George just said offended me. I stood up straight, lifted my head, and expressed myself with a firm tone. "Mr. Williams, Blacks live near the North End. Some of the fathers in my neighborhood work with them in the Water Department, and some of us kids are connected with black kids. It's not an issue for us Sicilians. I know we can work together."

Mr. Williams turned to Mr. George with an expression that said he was taking my side. "In a way, Santo's plan makes some sense. We can put the responsibility on Santo to bring the gangs together. And I just got an idea. If these guys finish Topping, the Hartford gang, instead of Topping, could clear that field we expect to plant next year."

Mr. George looked down at the floor. "Okay. Let's see if this works."

Mr. Williams turned to me. "I'll be right out. Get a hold of Brian Coleman for me."

I stepped out of the cabin and looked around, searching for

Brian. I spotted Tony standing a short distance away, wondering what happened. I gave him thumbs up. He smiled and jogged toward our gang. A moment later Mr. Williams stepped out of the cabin followed by Mr. George. "I just spotted Brian. He's over there."

We quickly walked toward Brian's gang where my gang was also hanging out. Everyone was exchanging jokes and insults as usual, but when we approached, they immediately stood still. "Will one of you get Jimmy and his gang?" Mr. Williams asked.

When Bart saw us walk out of the cabin, he raced toward Jimmy and his gang. In seconds they all rushed over.

Mr. Williams scanned the crowd. "Listen. To get Topping finished I'm asking Brian's gang and Santo's gang to join Jimmy's gang today. All of you are from Middletown, right?"

I heard Suggi whisper to Pesci, "I'll be damned." Suggi still had a problem about working with Blacks.

Bart raised his arm. "Mr.Williams, who runs the three gangs?"

"I want Santo to be in charge of the three gangs."

Mr. George pointed to Jimmy and then to Brian, hoping to stir up opposition. "What do you guys think? That means you both take a back seat."

Jimmy Lewis turned and glanced at his gang. Several of them who knew Bart, Melo and me grinned. "That's okay with my gang. It's really cool with me."

At the same time Brian scanned his gang. Several of them grinned and others gritted their teeth, looked down at the ground, and clenched their lips in frustration. "Well that's okay with me too. My gang and Santo's come here on the same truck, so I guess its okay."

"Okay!" Mr. George barked. "Get on those trucks over there. We've gotta get the Riverway fields done today."

My gang and Brian's ran toward one and Jimmy's toward the other. I heard one of Brian's guys yell, "So now we gotta work for a Guinea straw boss and with Blacks. My grandfather would flip out."

Suggi scrambled onto the far end of one bench. "I've never

worked with niggers before, and we still have to finish Third Picking."

Tony was sitting opposite Suggi, leaned forward to make sure he could hear him over the truck's rumbling, and grabbed his arm. "Listen. I know Santo's plan doesn't make sense to you. But he must have his reasons for wanting to help Jimmy. Decide if you want to join him."

Baggi, who was sitting next to Tony, thrust his hand out. "But I never heard of anything like this."

Bart slammed his hand against Baggi's knee. "Listen you little shit. You don't know any of those guys, right? Do you know that Adam, in Jimmy's gang, is one of the best hundred yard dash guys the Middletown High track team ever had? And it looks like Jimmy is going to be great too, when he gets to ninth grade. When you get to know them, you'll see there's more there than black skin." Bart glanced at Tony and me with concern. "I'll bet Baggi and Suggi don't know about that Louisiana thing our parents talk about."

Tony nodded, placed his hand on Baggi's shoulder and leaned toward Suggi. "Did you hear what Bart just said about Louisiana? What do your parents say about that?"

Suggi looked down at his shoes and mumbled, "I don't know. When they talk about Louisiana stuff with my aunts and uncles, everyone sounds really pissed off."

"It's something that happened with niggers and Sicilians," Baggi shouted. I don't know all about it, but I know from what my parents say, it turned out really bad."

Bart and I held our hands out toward Tony, encouraging him to take advantage of this opportunity, and he continued with a firm tone. "Listen, what happened there has a lot to do with what is happening here, so you should remember the whole story and learn from it. When your parents were kids, before they came to Middletown, a few Sicilians had already reached a town in Louisiana and were working in a store there. You know a lot of Blacks lived in that state."

To dramatize what Tony was about to say, Bart placed a hand on Suggi's shoulder and Baggi's and shouted, "Guess what these

Sicilians did? You won't believe it. They let the Blacks in the store and treated them the same as Whites. Can you imagine doing that where Blacks had to stay in their own place. They couldn't even walk down some of the streets that Whites used."

Tony jumped back in. "The people in this town said what these Sicilians did was bad. Just like you guys are saying that it's bad for Santo to want us to help Jimmy's gang." Suggi and Baggi lowered their heads. Tony continued, "And I'm sure you heard from your parents what happened, because the whole village of Melilli talked about it for years. The police arrested those Sicilians and threw them in jail."

Melo, who was sitting next to Baggi, was obviously very turned on and interrupted. "But putting them in jail wasn't enough for those white jerks! They pulled the Sicilians out of jail, grabbed a couple of other Sicilians who had moved into the town, and hung all of them."

Suggi raised his head. "That hanging stuff is the part I always hear about, and my parents keep saying *era na vergogna* (It was an outrage)."

Baggi looked at Tony. "I get it. If we help Jimmy's gang with topping, that's like those Sicilians who let Blacks in the store and treated them like *paisani*."

Bart leaned over and placed one hand on Baggi and the other on Suggi. "You'll see that Blacks in this country are treated a lot like Sicilians were treated in Italy. That's one reason why we find it easy to make friends with them, and why fathers from our neighborhood like to work with them."

All of the gang had been listening, and since the point Tony, Bart and Melo made was now clear, Sal changed the subject. "Suggi, if we work with these Blacks, at least we get a break from picking."

"Yeah," echoed Fillippo. "And us haulers get a break from pulling those damn baskets."

When the trucks arrived at the Riverway fields, and everyone jumped off, the teasing that had been going on before we left the Central Lot continued. "Hey man!" called out Adam Smith of the South End gang. His thick lips and wide nose framed a broad smile that revealed sparkling teeth. "Did your gang bend as much spaghetti as it's supposed to since First Picking?"

"Never mind how much spaghetti did us Wops bend since First Picking," Melo shouted back. "How many watermelons did you cotton pickers eat since First Picking?"

With the tempo of a blue grass song, Joseph Harris, another South End boy, sang and jerked his hips back and forth, "Ha! Ha! Ha! Ha! Very funny, never mind the Wops. How many four leaf clovers did those Harps pick?"

"Okay kiddies," Mr. George snarled. "Recess is over. We got a lot of Toping to do. Santo get these guys started. I'll be back later."

This was the first time that I was in charge of such a large group. More than that, I was nervous because having the three gangs work together was my idea, and I hoped it didn't fail. For a few seconds I struggled with how I should begin. "Okay. Listen. I'm giving each of you one row to top at a time, not two rows."

"Here goes the Italian boss," mumbled a boy from Brian's gang.

"Wait, Santo! I don't get it," Jimmy called out. "We always did two rows at a time, like you guys pick leaves from two rows at a time."

"Last year buddies of mine figured out that Topping one row, instead of moving back and forth between two rows, goes smoother and quicker. And you make less mistakes because you concentrate better."

Jimmy placed his hands on his hips. "I guess that makes sense."

I hoped he didn't feel like I put him down. Suddenly I got an idea. "Jimmy, some of Brian's gang and my gang have done only a little topping. So show these guys the best way to do it."

Suggi was standing a few feet away. "Pesci, I think we can learn from that nigger." Tony heard what Suggi said, stepped next to him, and patted his arm.

Jimmy was turned on by my asking him to take the lead. He grinned, stepped into a row of plants, pointed to the top of the plant, glanced at the gangs, and then looked up at the flowers,

"See, you look really good at this bunch of flowers, and snap off the skinny stalk just under them." Jimmy demonstrated. Then he took a step forward. "Now look here at this next plant. If I grab the stem lower, like right here, I'd snap off too much." Jimmy again demonstrated. "You gotta snap it right here."

"Good job, Jimmy. Does everyone get it?" The boys who had not topped that much before nodded.

Dominic stepped into a row and reached up. "Wait, Santo! Look! I can't reach the top of some of the plants."

Melo grinned. "Well, we can get you a ladder." The crowd burst out laughing.

Dominic glanced at Melo, lowered his head, and bent his knees, which made him appear even shorter than he was. I quickly tried to find a way to help him feel useful. "I know Dom. You're not tall enough to top all the plants. I think you can still help. If a guy is behind, you can help him by topping the shorter plants in his row that you can reach."

Dominic glared at Melo. "But I'll take the ladder anyway. Then I can jump on Melo's head and crack it." The laughter continued.

I remained serious because I didn't want anything to spoil our plan. "Dom, wait and do that after we finish Topping. I want to show Mr. Williams that the Middletown gangs can get it done." Without realizing it, I assigned rows first to my gang, then to Brian's, and then to Jimmy's.

Once everyone was busy topping, I stepped into a row that had not been assigned, stood motionless, and stared at the plants. I surprised myself when I felt a lump in my throat and noticed my chest and arms tighten. These sensations were similar to the ones I sometimes experienced this summer when riding over the bridge. But now a different fantasy crossed my mind. There, instead of plants, stood Tony, Bart, Vito, Filippo, Louie and Angelo, in a straight row. Each of them had turned fourteen, many months ago, and on each of their heads rested a yellow crown. I reached up and gently touched the cluster of flowers on Tony's head, and on the heads of the others, whispering to myself that the crown of childhood was a wonderful thing. Then I snapped off the flowers from each plant, imagined that the bliss of child-hood was gone and whispered, "Now, you are on your own, choose which way to go, and deal with the grown up world."

"Santo!" Dominic yelled with alarm.

I snapped out of my trance and raced in the direction of Dominic's voice. "What's the matter?"

"Look, I guess I wasn't tall enough for this plant. I think I broke the stalk."

I examined the top of the plant, and another set of thoughts tumbled into my mind. If a boy is not yet ready to take a step forward, he should wait until he's ready. "Dom, I don't think you destroyed leaves that would make it to last picking. Try to be careful."

"Okay, Santo. If I can't reach the top, I'll call for help, and let someone else top it."

At lunch break, Brian Coleman's gang and my gang sat along one side of the narrow dirt road that bordered the field, and Jimmy's gang was scattered along the other side.

Pointing to something that Louie was taking out of his lunch pail, Harry Morrison, of the South End gang, grinned and shouted, "Hey man, what the hell is that? Is it a baseball?" The boys chuckled.

Louie grinned and held the palm of his hand wide open with a round object wobbling on it. "No, it's not a baseball. It's an *arancinu*. It's better than a baseball." *Arancini* were deep fried, rice balls stuffed with peas, tomato sauce and little pieces of veal or pork.

"You're right man. These Dagos eat some really weird stuff," laughed Danny O'Neil. "Look at what this guy over here is eat-ing. Hey Tony, what are all those things stacked in that sandwich that looks like a four story building? "

Tony raised his sandwich and slowly pointed to each of the layers of meat stacked between two slices of homemade bread. "This is *capocollu*. This is *mortadella*. This is *prosciutto*. And this is *provolone* cheese in between them."

"Wow! That's not a four story building, that's like a ten story building," exclaimed Al Powell of the South End gang. Everyone laughed.

Jimmy Lewis yelled, "What Bart is holding over there is my favorite! What the hell do you call that again? Something like 'scratch out'." The laughter grew louder.

Bart raised his arm, holding a large piece of Sicilian *schiacciata* over his head. "No, Jimmy, listen to how I say it – ska, cha, da." While laughing, everyone repeated the sounds Bart just expressed. "You see it's like a pizza, but there's a layer of dough at the bottom and a layer at the top. And in between it's stuffed with cooked broccoli. You can put other stuff in there like spinach, or ..."

Jimmy Lewis yelled from across the road, "Okay Bart, thanks for the lesson on Dago cooking. But you know what, Santo? I heard your sister, and some cousin of yours, were really nice. They showed my sister a bunch of books, and one of them read a little bit to her. You know, my sister doesn't like to read, just like I don't like to write. They even got her to pick out a couple of books to read."

Confused, Suggi snapped his head around. "When did your sister see Santo's sister?"

"You know that book-truck Santo's father drives in the South End on some weekends."

"Oh yeah, that wheel barrel of books, or whatever it's called," Angelo joined in. "Everyone in our neighborhood is talking about that."

Joe Harris of the South End gang stepped in. "Santo, guess what? Remember that Sunday when you and your brother gave comic books to kids who live in the building next to ours? Now, every time I walk by these kids, they're talking about the Batman story they all read."

Another South End boy called out, "Next weekend I'm going to watch for that truck. I gotta see what's in there!" It pleased me to hear that, and I knew it would also please Filomena.

Al Powell, one of the older boys of the South End gang called out to Tony. "That's really cool what your father is doing."

"Yeah, especially when word got around no white guy would drive that truck anymore," added Joe Harris. "Everyone's afraid of going into black territory."

Al Powell continued to look at Tony. "Once your father had a couple of guys with him on the truck, not just young gals. Who the hell were they?"

"Our uncles. My father wanted them to see what he was doing."

"Well my Dad was talking about it with this guy from the South End. He said white guys won't even come near us, let alone come down our streets."

"But the Mafia will come in any time," Dan O'Neil blurted out, laughing. "Why is your father driving that book-truck? Is it some deal the Mafia is working on?"

Tony growled. "It has nothing to do with what you guys call the Mafia."

I thought Tony might have shown too much anger. I held up my hand. "Let me explain."

Still very angry, Tony interrupted me. "Wait! I want to make sure Dan heard me. It doesn't have anything to do with what you guys call the Mafia. Santo, I wish these guys heard the talks we had about the Old Mafia and the New Mafia."

"What the hell do you mean, Tony?" Brian asked. "I never heard of the Old Mafia and the New Mafia."

Given what Tony just said, I decided to return to the exchange. "Listen guys. You've got a lot mixed up about the Mafia. Do you want to know why my father's doing the Books-on-Wheels" Several boys nodded and looked at me with curiosity. "I'll try not to make a long speech. But to tie what my brother meant by the Old Mafia with the Books-on-Wheels, we need to take a look at what us Sicilians mean by having Godfathers and Godmothers."

Bart joined in. "I have a Godfather and a Godmother. And every one of my brothers and sisters have their own."

"Having a Godfather and a Godmother is a special Sicilian custom," Tony added. "Godparents make every family really big. And if everybody has a Godfather and a Godmother from the neighborhood, or the next town, they have a lot of connections that can help you."

Without giving it any thought, I blurted out a Sicilian word.

The custom is called *comparaggio*."

Bart continued to join me. " The word for godfather is *patrozzu*."

Tony raised a clenched fist. "But listen guys, these days people use the word godfather to mean a gangster, especially newspapers. Godfathers have nothing to do with gangsters." Tony was now very excited as well as angry. He took a long look at the boys scattered on his side of the road, and those from the South End sitting on the other side, pushed his arm forward and exclaimed, "When a Sicilian makes someone a Godfather or a *Mafioso*, he is saying that person is smart and patient, and figures out the best way to solve a problem and help."

I glanced at Tony and nodded. He understood I wanted to step in again. "Okay, like I said, I'll try not to give a speech." I explained that to understand what we are saying about Godfathers and Godmothers, everybody should keep in mind that for hundreds of years Sicily was invaded many times, and sometimes the peasants were mistreated. But they didn't have a country or a city to help them. Then I found myself saying something that I realized didn't make sense to Brian's gang or Jimmy's gang. "Even when Sicilians immigrated to the United States in the early 1900's they had to deal with a lot of abuse and prejudice."

Tom Murphy interrupted me. "Are you kidding? We Irish had to put up with a lot of prejudice here way before you did. You know in some cities, the stores put signs in their windows saying that Irish can't apply for jobs. And my grandfather told me when his father got here, they couldn't even go in some stores."

Harry Morrison of the South End gang burst in. "Well, for God sake, I don't have to tell you guys what us Blacks had to put up with, starting with when we came over here as slaves, and still have to put up with it."

I spread out the palms of my hands, eager to make my point clear. "I know what the Irish and the Blacks put up with long before Sicilians got here. But you know what my parents say? At first all the Sicilians who came over here thought this country was *terra maliditta*."

"What the hell is that?" asked Al Powell.

"That means they thought this country was a land that was cursed," Tony replied.

I blurted out another Sicilian word. "But Sicilians didn't let anyone take them for a *fesso*."

"Now what does that mean?" jumped in Dan O'Neil.

"That word means fool," Bart shouted. "Sicilians wouldn't let anyone take them for a fool."

I continued, determined to make my point. "But what I'm getting at is that even though Sicilians thought this was a cursed land, and tried not to let anyone take them for a fool, I always heard my parents and other parents say, '*fu fortunatu truvari sta via della vita.*'" .

"What the hell are you trying to do, teach us Sicilian? What does that mean?" Jack Kane blurted out.

I scanned Jimmy's and Brian's gangs and spoke very slowly because now I was making the point I had set out to share. "That means, I was fortunate, lucky, to find this road of life."

"I don't get it. What road of life?" asked another boy from Brian Coleman's gang.

"That's the point," Melo joined in. "Look guys, Sicilians survived by choosing a certain road of life to follow, and they tried to keep repairing that road."

I stretched my hand out to get back everyone's attention, because now I had a chance to finish the point I wanted them to understand. "That road of life was built by the custom of *comparaggio* we just mentioned. Sicilians survived by making the family the same as their city or country. And that family was really big because it included not only the mother and father, brothers and sisters, aunts and uncles, but also Godmothers and Godfathers. And everyone in the family followed the same rules."

"What rules?" asked Adam.

Vito chimed in and quickly reviewed the rules of loyalty, respect, honor, *omertà*, and *serietà*. "That's why," he added, "we say everybody in a family makes an artichoke. Every person in a family is a petal of the same artichoke, really close together and connected."

Tony pointed to a canvass basket filled with tobacco leaves that had not yet been picked up by the truck. "There's another way to see how the custom of comparaggio hooks up a lot of families together. Look at that basket. All the butts are packed in it close together. Let's say each butt of leaves is a family. That basket is like a bunch of families from the same village, all close together and connected, because each family has Godparents from other families."

I stepped in again, speaking louder than usual. "Vito, I'm glad you mentioned the rules of the family and the artichoke, and Tony that was good to use the basket of butts over there. You see, to give themselves more ways to handle the mess they found themselves in, with different kings and armies taking over, all the families that were connected followed those rules. And in Sicily, what a whole neighborhood or village did with those rules was called the *Fasci* League."

Al Powell grinned, "A faa-she league? What's that some kind of sport?"

"No it isn't," Tony replied, smiling. "But you pronounced that word really good, Al. That's the way it's pronounced. *Fasci* means a lot of bundles of sticks all connected together. One bundle of sticks in Sicilian is called a *fasciu*."

Jack Kane smacked his lips. "Oh, a faa-shoe?"

Tony smiled. "You guys are getting good at saying these Sicilian words."

I was eager to make sure everyone got my point. "Like Tony just said, the *Fasci* League meant that every family in a village was a bunch of branches that was really close to all the other branches, like that basket of leaves. They all followed the same rules, and they had a chief."

Tony was as turned on by this discussion as I was and continued being a teacher, imitating our sister, Filomena. "You can see one way these bundles of sticks were hooked together was the Godmother and Godfather each kid had, who came from different families in the neighborhood. For the kid, they were like another set of parents."

As Tony went on, a boy from the South End slowly raised his head. He looked so sad; I thought he was going to cry. "I wish I was in a bundle of sticks hooked up to a Godfather and

Godmother. I live in that small house in the South End for orphan kids. "

Tony walked across the narrow road, always into helping someone who he thought needed it. He placed his hand on the boy's arm. "I sure hope a Godfather and Godmother come along for you."

As Tony walked back and sat down, Jack Kane yelled. "Bullshit! What you guys are saying sounds so sweet, like frosting on a cake. It's a dream. My grandfather told me when he got here as a kid with his father, he didn't have any aunts or uncles. They all stayed in Ireland. He said it took a long time for him and his father to get connected with other people."

I was really annoyed by what I just heard. "It's not bullshit, Jack. This custom also had other ways of connecting families, if there were no aunts and uncles around."

Tony immediately stepped in again. He wasn't upset by what Jack Kane said, and was still in his teacher mode. "Jack, don't be a jerk. If there weren't any aunts and uncles, the Godparents were picked from cousins (*cugini*), and if there were no cousins around, families were connected by special, close friends they called *amici*, by friends of friends they called *amici degli amici*, and by neighbors they called *paisani*." Tony paused, pointed a finger at Jack, and spoke with a slow, serious tone. "What you need to keep in mind is that whether they were Godparents, or cousins, or special friends, they were all treated with the respect we talked about. And they were all seen as part of the family."

Bart suddenly changed the tone and rhythm when he yelled, "And you have to keep in mind that to be a Godparent, or cousin, or special friend is an honor."

I was turned on by how Tony and Bart handled Jack Kane's criticism and raised my hand. "So you see, the parents of every family had different people they could go to for advice and help. In this way a kid grew up connected to a lot of different bundles or families."

Tony turned, looked at me and nodded. I nodded in return, understanding that he had much more to say. He stood up and turned from side to side looking at everyone as if he were facing a class of students. He pointed out that perhaps everyone could now see how, through the custom of comparaggio, each family not only had connections with blood relatives but also with many other persons throughout the village. So when a family needed help, it was common for the head of that family to contact "*mio cugino*" (my cousin). And everybody understood that sometimes, to get the help the family needed, the cousin who was contacted might have to contact one of his cousins. Tony paused, turned to me and sat down. I nodded to let him know he did a good job.

I looked around at Brian's gang and Jimmy's, trying to figure out if they understood what Tony was getting across. Suddenly I remembered that we got into the custom of Godparents when Tony mentioned the Old Mafia and New Mafia, and thought we should try to make the connection clearer. I raised my arm. "Now, you can see what Tony meant by the Old Mafia. Every family had connections, and every neighborhood picked someone they trusted and respected to be the community leader in charge of those connections. So those connections were the old Mafia that got the help a family needed." Without realizing it, my tone became soft and sad. "Like, if a kid's parents died or got killed, he always had Godparents or cousins to take care of him. Or if a grown up was hurt or sick, he always had cousins to take care of him and his family."

Tony stared at me, worried that I might say something about what happened when our father was a kid, so he interrupted. "Santo is reminding us of something very important. The Sicilian custom of Godparents and cousins came from the ancient custom that was used to help kids who lost their parents. They lived with Godparents or cousins."

I looked down at the ground and took a deep breath. Something my relatives often said, especially my father, jumped into my mind, and I almost yelled it out. "People in our neighborhood not only say I was lucky to find this pathway of life; they also say '*chista è 'na terra d'opportunitati'*."

"Now we need another lesson in that Dago language of yours," Al Powell commented. "What does that mean?"

"It means, 'this is a land of opportunities.' I gave it to you first in Sicilian because the parents in our neighborhood say this all the time. You see, when they brought this custom of Godparents and cousins to the United States, and the custom of the *Fasci* League, they found that, in this country, they were free to keep following that road. That's why Italian neighborhoods are knitted tight together. That's why some people think Italian neighborhoods keep to themselves. It's more about the close ties they hold onto."

Adam Smith scanned my gang from across the road and raised his hand. "Now I get how the *Fasci* works with all its connections. Like your father is hooked up with the police department, and since they couldn't get someone to drive the truck, he figured he'd do it."

"This custom of connections, is cool," Jimmy Lewis added. That's how I finished eighth grade. Everyone grinned. Then he yelled, "Santo, Brian, lunch break is over. We better get in the field before Mr. George gets back!"

Topping was completed by the end of the day. The next morning, the gangs from Middletown and nearby Cromwell were congregated in the Central Lot waiting for their next assignments. Bart and Melo were standing before an audience, thrusting their arms back and forth, engaged in discussions that continued from yesterday. Mr. Williams walked toward us, accompanied by Mr. George, and everyone immediately stopped talking. Mr. Williams called out. "Brian, Jimmy, Santo, come here please." We walked over. The rest of the boys crowded around us. As if he was making an announcement, Mr. Williams stated, "I just want you to know that all of you did a good job yesterday finishing Topping in the Riverway fields. Now we're all caught up."

Brian, Jimmy and I mumbled, "Thanks" at the same time.

Mr. George surprised me when he said, "At first I thought your idea was crazy, Santo. I never thought all of you could get along and work together like you did."

I glanced at Tony, and he made a face that agreed with what I felt. From the way Mr. George made his comment, I assumed he was complementing me because Mr. Williams was there. It turns out that I was right, because a few seconds later, as Mr. Williams walked back to the Main Cabin, Mr. George's true feelings burst out. He gripped the palms of his hands and looked at me with an edge of irritation. "Your guys have Third Picking to finish in the Portland Hills."

I felt a sense of victory, and decided to rub it in. "I know Mr. George. I told you and Mr. Williams we'd get that done easy after we finished Topping."

"Yes, Santo." Now he expressed revenge and barked, "Get in that truck over there. After you finish Portland Hills, you'll take on all of Four Corners for Fourth Picking."

Bart whispered to Melo, "That bastard is laying all of the Four Corners on us." I gestured to Bart to be careful because, if I heard him, maybe Mr. George could hear him.

Mr. George looked at me and my gang with a slight smirk on his face and turned to Brian . "Your guys will start Fourth Picking in the Cromwell Meadows. Jimmy, today your gang can help the Hartford gang get a shed ready. Then maybe you can get into Fourth Picking in some of the Riverway Fields with the Hartford gang."

Later that morning, after my gang completed Third Picking in the Portland Hills, we were transported to Four Corners to begin Fourth Picking. When my gang entered the field, Melo yelled out, "Hey Dom, look, I can stand up now!"

"That's great. But I've been standing for weeks."

"Well Dom," Bart retorted, "with Fourth Picking you won't be able to stand. Now you definitely have to climb a ladder to reach the leaves." Everyone burst out laughing.

Pesci decided to join Bart and give Dominic the business. "It's going to be tough lugging that ladder up and down the row, Dom. And what if the ladder tips over and breaks down a bunch of stalks, you'll be docked a week's pay." Again everyone roared with laughter.

I thought that was enough joking for now. "Okay! Let's get started! I'll help Dom carry his ladder!" Everyone began picking.

Vito placed his hauler's hook on one of the many empty baskets that were strewn along the road. Before pulling it into the field, he paused, and stared into the distance. A huge shed was located on the far edge of the field. He whispered with excitement, "Look! The sewers and hangers are over there getting ready to go in that shed."

Angelo, who was also retrieving a basket, stretched and looked in the direction of the shed. "That's great. This is the first time this summer we happen to be picking near where they're sewing and hanging."

Louie picked up his basket and gasped, "Angelo, maybe we'll get a chance to see some of the chicks!"

Dominic, who was twelve years old and the youngest of the gang, overheard the frantic whispering as he began picking his row. "You oldies are all about the chicks."

I walked over to Vito, Angelo and Louie who were still standing motionless, staring into the distance. "Come on! We've got to get going! Have you forgotten we're supposed to be the Fast Gang?"

"Oh yeah, man, are we fast!" Louie shouted, laughing.

"We are fast as a race horse and hot as that sun," Vito joined in, also exploding with laughter. Then he began singing an old Sicilian ballad, "Oh Maria, Oh Maria." By this time other members of the gang were peering in the direction of the shed, chuckling and whispering.

I became furious. "I'm not going to say it again! Let's go. Save your Broadway show for lunchtime!"

During the next two hours, the leaves of one section of the field were harvested so that the group worked its way in the direction of the shed. At one point Bart and Melo finished picking their rows a bend or more ahead of the rest of the gang. Instead of looking around to see if anyone needed help, they jogged toward the shed with Vito, their hauler. From what I learned later, this is what I pieced together about what they got into as they peered into the shed.

Vito whispered, "Thank God the slats are flipped up. Now we can look in." They stood still by the wall of the barn, leaned forward, and peered inside.

"Wow!" Bart commented. "Look at those chicks swinging their arms back and forth. They make sewing look like they're dancing."

"Never mind their arms," Vito whispered. "Look over there, the one with the red shirt. Now that's a beautiful body."

"Yeah," Melo mumbled. "and how about that one over there on the right, the one with blue slacks and blue shirt. She's really *sapurita* (gorgeous)."

"And look at the one next to her wearing that *cullana* (necklace). What a beautiful face," Bart gasped. "She's definitely *a chiù bedda* (the most beautiful). She looks like Ingrid Bergman. Wow! Remember her in Casablanca?"

"Do I remember? Absolutely," Vito whispered. "Humphrey Bogart was sure lucky to have a chance to kiss her. She does look like Ingrid Bergman!"

At this point Louie, Angelo and Filippo spotted them peering into the shed and came running over with their pickers who had just finished their rows. Soon nearly the whole gang was peering into the shed. I was busy helping Dominic and Baggi who had not yet finished.

Louie leaned down and peered through an opening. "This is better than going to the movies. Some of these gals are gorgeous."

Sal grinned. "The movies are just movies. This is the real stuff."

"Hey," Pesci quietly exclaimed. "See that one over there with the long black hair and white blouse. Look at the way she swings her hips and arms when she's sewing. It's like dancing the boogie-woogie. Wow is she hot. And look at those boobs. Would I love to be on her."

Filippo joined in, "She is really *sapurita* (beautiful), and she dances like ..." Before Filippo finished his comment, Ancio raced over to Pesci and vigorously punched him several times. Pesci tumbled to the ground, as Bart reached out and restrained Ancio.

Just as Pesci tumbled to the ground, I happened to step out of the field and spotted the fight that was going on. I immediately raced over, followed by Tony, Baggi and Dominic. I was very confused. "Stop it! What's the matter with you guys?"

"Pesci said something dirty about my cousin," Ancio shouted.

"I didn't know she was your cousin!"

I was still confused, but my anger exploded. "Pesci get up! Ancio cool down! We gotta get back in the field! If Mr. George catches us standing by the shed, we're in deep shit! You're all screwing up! We'll settle this at lunch break. "

Everyone returned to the field and continued picking. A short while later it was lunch time. The whole gang, still preoccupied with what happened, walked slowly across the dirt road and sat on the ground under nearby trees.

I looked back and forth at my gang and knew it was my job to straighten this mess out. I glanced at Tony, and he nodded, making clear he was there to help. "Okay, let's settle what happened. It's been a long time since one of the gang took a shot at somebody else in the gang."

Ancio immediately pushed his arm out toward Pesci. "Santo, like I said before, he said something dirty about my cousin."

"And like I said, I didn't know she was your cousin," Pesci shouted back. "Besides it wasn't dirty."

Suggi gritted his teeth. "Yes it was."

Filippo turned and looked at Suggi. "I wouldn't call that dirty."

Noticing a tug of war was developing, I yelled, " Exactly what did you say, Pesci?"

"I said this girl was like dancing the boogie-woogie while she was sewing. And I said she was hot. All of us say that when we see a girl who's really *sapurita* (pretty). That's not dirty."

"Oh, really!" Ancio glared at Pesci. "You left something out."

"What did I leave out? That's what I said."

Ancio leaped up, ran a few steps, grabbed Pesci by the shirt and raised his clenched fist. But before he could throw a punch, Tony, who had already jumped up, restrained him. Ancio slumped to the ground and sat still with his head hanging low.

I walked over to Ancio and held my palm out near his head. "Try to quiet down."

Tony joined me, placing his hand on Ancio's shoulder. "Come on Ancio, I know you're really pissed off. But let's figure this out."

Again, I tried to learn exactly what happened. "Ancio, what did Pesci say that you think was dirty?"

226

Ancio raised his head and looked at me. "He said something about her boobs. But even worse, he said he would like to be on her."

"But what's the matter with that?" Pesci whispered. " I just meant it would be great to be close to her."

Ancio smirked. "Oh, really! You meant you wanted to do something sexy."

Pesci's jaw dropped. "Not exactly that. Besides, I remember Filippo said he agreed with me."

Filippo jumped in obviously irritated. "Wait a minute. When Pesci said she looked like she was dancing while she was sewing, all I said was that she was beautiful."

Pesci looked at Filippo with frustration. "But I thought you were agreeing with me."

I surprised myself when I shared something personal. I think I was trying to quiet things down so we could get into a discussion that would pay off. "Look! All of us get turned on once in a while, like I wanted to look in the barn to try to spot Corrina. But I couldn't because of what happened."

"I know, Santo. You've mentioned Corrina to me. You really like her, right?" Melo asked.

Bart raised his clenched fists. "Sometimes for me those feelings are a galloping horse."

Melo turned to Bart. "Well, we all have to find a way to put a harness on that horse."

"I get the galloping horse," Sal commented. Then he turned to his partner. "But Ancio's horse wanted to kick the hell out of Pesci."

Tony was also looking for a way to quiet things down so we could sort this out. I was surprised that he brought up something personal like I did. "Santo, remember what Papa told us a few weeks ago about Gloria?"

"Yeah, it fits here."

Bart's fists were still clenched. "What did your father say?"

"Well first you gotta know what happened," Tony replied. "When our sister went to a store in the American district, some guy made a dirty comment about her. This guy didn't know our cousin, Smiles, was standing a few feet away. He just grabbed this guy; he didn't hit him. The guy begged for mercy."

Ancio spread both of his hands out. "Well I guess I should have just grabbed Pesci by the shirt."

Tony was annoyed by what Ancio just said. "That's not the point, Ancio. My father told Smiles he did the right thing, because the guy only said something dirty. He didn't try to grab her."

Bart waved his arm to his left and right. "That fits with what my father told my brother and me. In a Sicilian family, the sons are expected to handle anything that insults the females of the family, and anything that threatens their safety. But you gotta match what you do with what the insult was."

Sal returned to the discussion. "Sometimes I want to beat up this high school guy from the American district because I hear him always making sexy jokes about the girls from our street."

Tony stared at Sal. "What you just said made me think of something else my father told us about. Did you guys ever hear about the Sicilian Vespers? That's a time when things got way out of control in Sicily."

"I know about that." Bart spread his arms out. "Wow! My parents talked about it a lot."

"What do you mean?" Musca asked. "What's a Sicilian Vesper?"

Musca's question got Tony in a teaching mode again, because he stood up and looked around as if all of us were students in a classroom. "It's not something. It's a name that they gave to what happened in Sicily a long, long time ago." He went on to explain that in the 1200's Sicily was occupied by the French who, like other invaders, were often very abusive and exploited the peasants. On Easter Monday, at the end of March in 1282, peasants in Palermo were celebrating their holiday. While they were walking around, French soldiers searched them for weapons. One French officer apparently offended a Sicilian girl in the presence of her male relatives. Some peasants reported that this officer said something very inappropriate, grabbed the girl, and tried to have sex with her. Tony elaborated that even then, among Sicilians, what the officer did was an offense greater than the political persecution and abuse they experienced from aristocrats. Outraged, the girl's brother, uncle and cousin killed the French officer. The news of what happened quickly spread, and because of this incident, the peasants in Palermo started a revolt that spread across the whole island. Thousands of French were killed and, within weeks, Sicily was cleared of all Frenchmen.

When Tony finished the saga about the Sicilian Vespers, Baggi gasped, "Wow! Unbelievable!" He apparently had not heard of this incident.

"You know what that whole thing makes me think of?" Vito added. "When we were looking in the shed at the girls, every one of them must have a brother, or an uncle, or a cousin."

Bart waved his arm again. "I'm glad all I said was that a sewer looked like Ingrid Bergman in the movies."

Tony looked at Bart and the others who were approaching, or already had reached, their fifteenth birthday. "Well, all of us have to think about how to put a harness on that galloping horse."

"Now I think I know what you guys are saying," Dominic commented. "But my horse can't even gallop yet."

Tony gave Dominic a reassuring look. "Don't worry. When you get a little older, your horse will start galloping."

I announced that lunch break was over. Everyone got up, walked into the field and thought a lot about our discussion.

Near sunset when Tony and I returned from the farm and stepped into the kitchen, we found Teodoro kneeling near the washing machine. The motor had been dismounted and placed on the floor. Bolts, washers, and other parts, along with a rubber belt, were strewn about. Tony pointed at the floor. "What the hell are you doing?"

Teodoro did not look up and continued examining the motor. "I'm fixing the washing machine."

"Where are Mom and our sisters?" I asked.

"They decided to go over to Joe-the-Jew's store." Teodoro continued to ignore us. He picked up a part off the floor and, while carefully screwing it into the engine's casing, mumbled, "This morning Mamma tried to wash some clothes, but this damn engine wouldn't turn the thing in the tub that chugs back and forth and washes the clothes."

"That doesn't mean you can take it apart!" Tony declared with a critical tone.

"Well, the engine was making this grinding sound. I guessed it had something to do with the gears that turn the belt, which turns the ..."

"Never mind," Tony growled. "You better hurry up and put the rest of that stuff back in there. Papa will get the appliance guy to fix it. If they come home and find this mess, they're gonna really get mad."

Still looking down and scanning the parts on the floor, Teodoro whispered, "Yeah, yeah," and continued to slowly assemble the engine parts.

Annoyed, Tony stared at Teodoro. "Suit yourself. Tell Mamma we're going down to the river to check our tomato plants." Almost every family in our neighborhood cleared and cultivated an area near the Connecticut River where each summer they planted tomatoes, peppers, eggplants and cucumbers.

About an hour later, Tony and I returned and entered the kitchen. We immediately noticed that the washing machine was back in its corner, and no engine parts were on the floor. Papa was standing by the stove chatting with Mamma, Teodoro and our sisters. When we walked in, everyone turned in our direction with looks on their faces that I could not figure out.

Tony noticed what I did, because he exaggerated his greeting, which was not usual for him. "Hey, everybody, *Buona sera!*"

Papa stopped chatting, walked over to the washing machine, spread the palms of his hands on its side and asked Tony and me to come over. At the same moment, Mamma slowly walked over followed by our sisters and Teodoro. Because they stopped grinning, and their faces looked worried, Tony and I immediately assumed we were facing a big problem.

I nudged Tony with my elbow, and he whispered, "What the hell! Are they going to believe us?"

When we reached the washing machine with everyone standing around it, Mamma pointed into the inside of the machine , "*Guarda ccà.*" ("Look here.")

Tony and I leaned over and immediately noticed it was filled with water and clothes. Performing an ancient Italian gesture which stated, 'this has nothing to do with me,' Tony raised the palm of each hand toward Mamma and commented, "*non sacciu nenti*." ("I don't know anything.")

At the same time I rattled on apologetically one hundred miles an hour, "Gee Ma, you must have tried to start a load of clothes. I know the machine is broken. It was all Teodoro's idea to take it apart. We told him to wait for the appliance guy. We ..."

Anna raised her hand, telling me to be quiet. "We know that it's all Teodoro's doing."

"Come on, one of you reach down and turn the switch on," Filomena demanded, as everyone expressed concern.

"But it won't work!" Tony exclaimed. "Why turn on the switch? You made your point."

Suddenly I noticed that even though their faces were serious, their eyes sparkled. "Tony," I whispered, "Look at their eyes. Don't you see it's a set up?" He reached down and turned the switch on. Much to Tony's and my surprise, the engine immediately began running, and the agitator in the tub churned rhythmically back and forth. Everyone burst out laughing.

"*Maravigghiusu*, (wonderful)" Mamma cried out.

"It's fixed!" Filomena shouted.

As my sisters and Teodoro cheered, Papa announced that Teodoro is becoming "the fixer" of the family and hopes he continues on that road. Then he announced that to celebrate Teodoro's achievement, he will receive an extra splash of wine tonight at dinner, and one extra biscotta. Tony and I were stunned for a very brief moment, and then quickly joined the cheering, patting Teodoro on the back.

With happiness spread across her face, Filomena pushed her arm up high and shouted "There's something else that just got fixed."

Papa, Mamma, my sisters and Teodoro became quiet and glanced at each other, making clear they had been talking about what Filomena was referring to. But I was confused, and so was Tony. Filomena glanced at Anna, who nodded, turned to Papa who also nodded, and was pleased that they gave her permis-

231

sion to continue.

Tony noticed the silent communicating that was going on, but he couldn't wait another second. "So what else is fixed, Filomena?"

"Italy!" she screamed. Mamma, Papa, my sisters and Teodoro burst out in another loud cheer.

Tony was annoyed. "What the hell do you mean? What's the joke?"

I took hold of Tony's arm. "Wait, it's got to be something they were talking about before we got back."

"You're right!" Gloria screeched.

Filomena quickly jumped in, since she had permission to continue. "It's all over the news! We heard it on the radio while you guys were at the vegetable garden by the river. The dictatorship of that jerk, Mussolini, has collapsed. Don't forget the date, July 25, 1943."

Anna jumped in. "That's the birthday of a new Italy, now that he's out."

I was surprised that Papa interrupted Filomena, but he too was excited. "Like Mamma can now wash clothes clean, because Teodoro fixed the washer machine, Italy can now clean itself and make things better for everyone because Mussolini no longer rules. And now all the boys in our neighborhood who are in the United States army in Italy won't have to shoot at their cousins."

Tony and I joined the cheering, and were swept away by what we just heard.

Two weeks later we were all waiting in the Central Lot for trucks to take us to our fields. Louie turned to everyone. "Well, we're really rolling with Fourth Picking. And when we start last picking, Dom is going to need a really, really tall ladder." Everyone burst out laughing. Moments later a foreman approached and informed me that Mr. Williams wanted to see me. My gang stopped laughing and wondered, as did I, what was the matter now. I ran over to the Main Cabin. Mr. Williams was seated at his desk engaged in a vigorous discussion with Mr. George but immediately stopped talking when I stepped in. I stood still, glancing back and forth at the two of them.

Mr. Williams pushed the palm of his hand toward me. "One moment." He continued his discussion with Mr. George, but I couldn't quite figure out what they were talking about. They seemed to be arguing, and kept mentioning the names of different fields, dates, and things that had to be done. A minute later Mr. Williams turned to me. "Santo, this time we have some catching up to do with Fourth Picking in the Riverway Fields, like we did with Topping. Jimmy's gang and the Hartford gang are not on schedule enough. We needed to take the Hartford gang away a couple of times to clean out some sheds. Now we have to take them away again." Mr. Williams paused and looked up at Mr. George. "And I came up with an idea."

"I don't think it's going to work," Mr. George insisted with an argumentative tone.

Mr. Williams ignored him. "Since your gang, and Jimmy's and Brian's worked really good together to finish Topping, I thought all of you could do the same thing to finish Fourth Picking in the Riverway Fields."

"But I have a little more to do at Four Corners."

Mr. Williams glanced at Mr. George. "We were talking about that. But you're a little ahead of schedule. So if you get the Riverway Fields done first, we can give Jimmy's gang a job that needs to be done. The nets in parts of the Rocky Hill Fields have to be replaced."

I intentionally avoided looking at Mr. George since he made clear a minute ago that he didn't agree. "Whatever you say."

Mr. George nearly growled. "Okay, Santo, get Brian and Jimmy. I'll see all of you in a minute."

I ran out, located them, and we all jogged to the Main Cabin. Mr. George stepped out. "We got catching up to do again in the Riverway Fields. Now it's with Fourth Picking."

"Yeah," Jimmy mumbled. "The Hartford gang hasn't been around very much."

Mr. George turned to Jimmy and sneered. "Your gang should have gotten it done. It's Mr. Williams who thinks we can catch up if we use the same arrangement for a day or two that we used

233

a few weeks ago."

"You mean the three gangs working together again?" Jimmy asked.

"That's right."

"But my guys don't have as much experience picking as Santo's Fast Gang, and even Brian's gang. How are we gonna pick with them?"

Mr. George snarled with that tone I could not stand. "That's what I tried to get Mr. Williams to understand. Anyway it was his decision. Now it's your problem."

Tony happened to be standing near Jimmy and me. "That's okay, Jimmy. We'll work it out. Remember we're all bundles of sticks in the same basket. We'll show them Middletown can do it."

Jimmy Lewis grinned, and several boys from each gang mumbled with confidence.

Mr. George didn't seem to notice what just went on. "Okay, like before, Mr. Williams decided Santo is in charge of all of you." Pointing, he barked, "Those are your trucks."

When the trucks arrived at the Riverway Fields, the three gangs scrambled off and broke up into small groups, discussing or arguing about some issue. While scanning that part of the field that had to be finished, I spotted Bart and Adam, from Jimmy's gang, sneaking into the first pair of rows with Vito following them as their hauler. They immediately began picking leaves. I had no idea what they were doing and yelled at them, "Hey! I haven't assigned rows yet! What are you doing?"

Bart stood up straight, turned around and smiled. "What do you mean what are we doing? We're working. Are you blind?" Everyone chuckled and remained still.

I was still confused. "So what are you saying, Bart? Now you're the straw boss, and you decide who picks where."

Bart stood at attention and gave me a military salute. "No, absolutely not. You're the *Capo*." Everyone burst out laughing. "It's just that Adam and I got into a really good rap session on the truck. So we thought we could finish it while we pick." The look on Bart's face told me, and I think everyone else, that he was inventing a story to make a joke.

While I stared at Bart and Adam, a thought crossed my mind. Even though Bart could be kidding, he doesn't realize that he's giving us a chance to see if we can put our bundles of sticks in the same basket. I really liked the idea of mixing the gangs together. "Okay Bart, if that's what you and Adam want to do, go ahead."

Bart turned around and began picking. Adam, who had been grinning while Bart and I were engaged in our discussion, raised his arm. "Wait. We were kidding. I can't pick with Bart, man, I'll never keep up."

Bart peered between the tobacco plants at Adam and shouted. "Come on! We haven't finished that rap session."

I wanted Adam to feel okay with the arrangement. "I'm sure Bart, and even Vito, will help you. Go ahead and see what happens with the joke you guys are cooking up." A number of the guys smiled while Bart and Adam began picking, which I took to mean they also liked the idea of mixing the gangs.

I scanned the crowd standing around me. "Okay. If any of you want to be partners for any reason, you know, if you're making some joke too, come over here." A few members of my gang stepped over, each of them accompanied by either a member of Brian's gang or Jimmy's gang with whom they had been talking. I assigned each pair a set of rows and a hauler. Then I assigned rows to the remaining members of each gang.

As everyone worked throughout the morning, and I walked from row to row doing my job, I heard some of the boys from Brian's gang and Jimmy's gang express their frustration in not being able to pick rapidly and smoothly, when they compared themselves with members of my gang. At lunchtime while we sat in the shade under trees. I tried to reassure everyone. "We did really good. I think we're gonna finish the job today."

Adam Smith took an apple from his lunch box. "But Santo, even though Bart helped me, and even though Vito helped me when he wasn't hauling, it was really tough for me to keep up."

Joe Harris, who had worked as Melo's partner, opened his lunch box. "Yeah, man. It was hard for me to get into Melo's rhythm. It was like dancing with someone for the first time."

"Well if picking is like dancing," Jack Kane muttered, while taking a bite of his baloney sandwich, "Sal and I were stepping on each other's toes."

Laughing, Tom Murphy waved his arm. "How about me and Ancio. He was doing the tarantella, and I was doing the Irish jig."

Tony munched on his sandwich of Genoa salami and provolone cheese. "Well, every one of us is from a different bundle of sticks. Remember that word? Every one of us is from a different *fasciu*. So picking and hauling together this morning gave us a chance to see that it ain't easy to fit into somebody else's bundle."

Vito carefully held a large piece of pizza covered with pepperoni. "What we're talking about reminds me that it takes time for two guys from different bundles to get connected."

"If two guys want to be in the same bundle," Jack Kane commented, "and learn the same dance, they have to practice for a long time."

I was really pleased with the conversation that got started on its own. I especially liked what Joe Harris said about needing to find someone's rhythm when you dance with them, and Jake Kane emphasizing it takes time to make that connection.

Harry Morrison set his sandwich on his lap, looked to his left where his buddies were sitting, and noticed that most of the black boys were sitting together. Then he looked to his right where most of the white boys were sitting and yelled, "Hey, do you think you could ever get black sticks and white sticks in the same bundle?" Everyone laughed.

"How about can you ever get four leaf clovers and garlic balls in the same bundle?" Tom Murphy asked. Again everyone laughed.

Joe Harris of the South End gang jumped up and connected his fascination with dancing and what Tony said about bundles of sticks. Dancing across the road, he sang out, "How about one of you guys try to boogie-woogie with me. Then you can join my bundle." Now the crowd exploded with laughter. Everyone clapped their hands in rhythm as he continued dancing.

"Hey, Santo!" Vito called out. "What about the Garibaldi Society your father and my father helped to get started? Doesn't that show another way our parents fit their bundle of sticks together when they came to this country?"

Louie raised a chunk of cheese above his head. "You're right, Vito, The Garibaldi Society is a beautiful example."

"The Society is where I learned to box," Bart announced with pride. "That's where Lucky started to be my manager."

Joe Harris stopped dancing. "What the hell are you talking about? What society?"

Bart jumped in. "Listen, the Garibaldi Society shows how our parents figured ways to fit families together and help families who needed help. Like we said, when they first got here, they felt they didn't have a city or country that wanted to help them. So about twenty years ago a number of men from the neighborhood decided to organize a society."

Vito made clear he had something very important to say. "You'll see why I brought up this Society. Once you hear what it does, you'll understand how this Society had its roots in the *Fasci* League, and in the custom of Godparents that we talked about a few weeks ago." Vito was really turned on, and continued sharing details, like the Society has a small gym where boxing matches take place, a large hall where families meet to celebrate holidays and watch puppet shows, and rooms where families play card games, and sample the wine each of them made, which they bring to the club for everyone to taste.

Jimmy Lewis interrupted. "I hear people in my neighborhood talk about that place. You Dagos have a lot of fun there."

"But it's more than a place for fun, right?" Louie called out. "Tony, since your father is really involved, and now is the president of the Society, tell these guys the other stuff they do for all the *paisani*."

Tony was pleased that he had a chance to be a teacher again. He explained that if the head of the family is sick and can't work, the Society gives the family enough money to get along. And if someone dies, and the family can't afford the funeral expenses, the Society helps. More than that the Society is considering helping families pay for college tuition, if one of their children is accepted into a college.

"That's great!" Tom Murphy exclaimed. "Where does the Society get the money to do all of these things?"

Tony continued his lecture explaining that if members of a family are working, that family pays dues, and families that can't afford to pay dues chip in whenever they can.

"Speaking of college, you won't believe this." Jimmy Lewis commented. "Santo's sister is going to Teachers College in New Britain."

I looked at everyone with pride. "That's right. She just finished her second year, and the Society is paying for some of the tuition."

Vito jumped in. "The whole neighborhood talks about it. Santo's sister started college when she was only sixteen years old. She's going to be eighteen in a little while, right Santo? My sister and her are really good friends." Laughing, Vito added, "My sister just finished high school."

"How the hell did she start college when she was only sixteen?" Tom Murphy asked. "I just made sixteen, and I've got two more years of high school left."

Tony couldn't resist another chance to do more teaching. "Never mind her age. I don't know of any Italian American girls from our town who have gone to college yet." He added that a lot of our parents had a strange way of thinking about education, and they brought this opinion with them from the old country. As far as they were concerned, since you can't trust the government, you can't trust schools.

Adam Smith stopped chewing on his sandwich. "I don't get that. Why were they against schools?"

Tony leaned over so he could take a good look at Adam. "I know it sounds strange. They didn't trust schools because over there, in Sicily, they felt the schools were all for the government. They felt the government set up schools to get kids to give up Sicilian customs."

"Okay then. Did anybody hear me?" Tom Murphy asked again. Like I said, how did she get in college when she was only sixteen?"

Tony explained that teachers at Middletown High School noticed that our sister was really ahead of her class and thought she should apply for college. They offered to graduate her early if a college accepted her. A couple of years ago, just before World

238

War II broke out, our father came home and said that he had a surprise. The Garibaldi Society voted to give our sister a scholarship if she accepted the offer from the High School. "Because the Society gave her confidence," Tony added, "she applied to Teachers College in New Britain and was accepted."

Vito joined in again. "What Santo's sister is doing is really great. Italian American girls don't go to college. But now some of the girls in the neighborhood are thinking about going. Even my sister said she's thinking about going , after she visited Santo's sister at that college."

Tony raised both arms. "Now you know why our parents like to say, 'I was lucky to find this path of life.' Remember when we shared that a few weeks ago? They feel lucky because they could build the road they walk on with tools like the Garibaldi Society and Godparents. And you can see how the families of a neighborhood get tied together. That's how Vito's sister is thinking of going to college."

While Tony was talking, I pulled the watch the farm loaned me out of my pocket and noticed that lunch break was over. I regretted we had to stop, since we were having such a great discussion. "Okay, I have to break this up now. We gotta finish the Riverway Fields." When some of the boys stepped toward the rows I assigned to them, I was thrilled to see them joking and dancing the boogie-woogie, or the tarantella, or the Irish Jig.

On the next day, we finished Fourth Picking in the Riverway Fields before noon. Trucks took us back to the Central Lot where we eat lunch before each gang returned to jobs they had been assigned. All of us walked to the edge of the Central Lot and sat under trees. Joe Harris approached me. "Hey man. What's that game you guys play sometimes at lunch? You know flipping your fingers and yelling numbers."

"Let Louie tell you about it. He's the expert."

Tony yelled at Louie. "Hey, tell Joe Harris about *Morra*."

"I'll be happy to. I'm the champ of all the kids at the Garibaldi Society." He strutted over to Joe Harris and stood before him, flexing his shoulders back and forth. "This is how we play it. You stand there, and I stand right here just a few feet away." Joe positioned himself and waited. "Each guy holds his hand down his side or behind his back."

As Joe placed his right hand along his leg, the South End gang and Brian Coleman's gang gathered around with interest.

"Why do you have to keep your hand behind your back?" Al Powell asked.

"So the guy you're competing with doesn't see what you're doing with your fingers." Louie continued, "Each guy throws out any number of fingers. And while you throw out your fingers, you yell out any number from two to ten. Lets' try it."

Joe Harris and Louie stood in silence. Each of them held his right hand behind his back while staring into the other's face. Everyone grinned and chuckled. Louie called out, "Okay!" When each of them thrust his hand forward with fingers extended, Joe called out the number four, and Louie called out the number two.

Louie explained, "You see Joe, you threw out two fingers, and I threw out one finger. That's three fingers. And you yelled four and I yelled two, so we're both wrong. We keep throwing fingers out and calling numbers. When a guy calls out the right number, he wins that round."

Joe Harris pushed his hand down. "But that's just a game of guessing."

Louie remained very still and became more serious. "Not really. Some of it is guess work. But the trick is you gotta learn what the other guy's pattern of numbers is by concentrating on several things." Louie explained that you watch the expressions on your opponents face while his hand is behind his back, because he might make a certain face just before he throws a certain number. And you watch whether he throws a certain number after a certain number without realizing it. "So you gotta concentrate on all of that while throwing out your fingers. Let's try it."

With their bodies only about a yard apart, Louie and Joe Harris leaned toward each other. Then they threw fingers out in a rhythm every couple of seconds, each time yelling out a number. More than fifty percent of the time Louie called out the correct number of fingers that had been thrown .

Suddenly, Joe Harris stopped throwing out his hand and stood up straight. "How the hell are you doing that, man? I won only once, and you won a bunch of times. I guess I don't have it."

"We told you Louie is the expert," Tony declared.

Louie grinned. "Joe, if I tell you how I do it, then I won't beat you again."

Joe Harris threw his arms out, searching for some way to retaliate. "Well maybe you won the finger game, but us Blacks are the real winners. You know, we're the winners of what really counts."

Louie was more than pleased to get into a sparring match. "The winners of what?"

A broad grin crept across Joe's face. "Well, man, our Mr. Jones everybody talks about. He shows you guys who the winners really are." Joe pushed his hips forward toward Louie with a provocative jerk.

"Oh, will you Blacks stop it already." Vito threw both hands toward Joe Harris. "Why does everybody always have to say something about Mr. Jones and his long thing? They make it sound like he's one of those Greek myths we learned about in school this year."

"For God sake," Tom Murphy joined in. "Never mind his long thing. How about, he's also got a couple of front teeth missing. And his eyes are always marked red."

Mr. Jones, an African American in his late forties, loaded baskets onto trucks. When he laughed, he displayed a fiendish grin which contributed to why white boys saw him as some kind of special, devilish figure. But the main reason why a legend had been constructed about him had to do with boys imagining that his penis reached down to his knees. Whenever this was challenged, someone always stepped in with an attempt to verify the myth by reporting what someone else saw when he spotted Mr. Jones urinating in the woods, or at the edge of a field. These stories constantly whirled about in the fields.

"Like hell it's like a Greek myth," Joe Harris retorted. "Filippo, tell these guys what you told Jimmy."

Louie spun around, and his jaw dropped. "What, Filippo? What did you tell Jimmy?"

Filippo glanced up and down several times and clutched his

hands, embarrassed. "Well, this morning I had to take a leak really bad. So I went behind the trees over there. When I finished, I saw Mr. Jones walk over there. I hid behind a tree and watched him. He took a leak. It really squirted far. I think I saw his dick. It was really, really long."

Louie became very angry. "You think you saw it. No matter what was there, you're going to see what those stories say you're supposed to see. Was it longer than your father's?"

"Come on Louie," Filippo shot back with irritation. "Don't bring my father in this."

Rather than backing off, Louie pushed forward, while the rest of the boys listened with intense interest. "Well, was it down to his knees like everybody says, or not?"

Filippo lowered his head. "It seemed that way. I only got a glimpse."

Joe Harris turned toward Louie and shouted, "You see! Like I said, white guys win the finger game, but us black guys win where it counts."

Angelo clenched his fists and stared at Joe Harris. "Bull shit. Do you want me to get a ruler and measure everyone?"

Sensing that an intense argument could develop, and possibly even a fight, Tony jumped in with a firm tone. "Bart and a bunch of us older guys were talking about this the other day. You want to hear what we think? We noticed that every time this argument comes up about who's got it, and who doesn't, some guys laugh, some guys get nervous and some guys get mad."

Melo pushed his arm out, pointing at Joe Harris. "Like you! After you lost that finger game you got nervous and mad."

Jimmy Lewis stepped forward, scanned the members of his gang, threw his shoulders back, and raised his arm. "All this stuff is about who a guy thinks he is, and how a guy has to get rid of what's in his way. That's one of the things Santo and I wrote about in the paper I turned in at the end of school."

Filippo turned to his left and right with his jaw sagging. "I still don't get it."

I faced Filippo. "A guy could get nervous and mad because something happened to him that makes him feel he didn't do good at all. And he feels he doesn't have what it takes."

Louie pointed at Joe Harris. "Just like when you played the finger game with me."

"That's the way I felt when the school year was coming to an end," Jimmy continued. "Because I have a hard time writing, I definitely felt I didn't have what it takes. I wrote that in my paper."

Tony jumped up and took a long look at Jimmy. "Once this past spring, I really felt like I didn't have what it takes. A big deal happened in high school." He paused, stared at the ground, and slowly sat down.

I knew the big deal Tony just referred to, and was impressed that he would even mention it. When Tony glanced at me, I gestured urging him to tell his story. Bart happened to notice what I did. He opened the palm of his hand toward Tony. "Why don't you tell the younger guys what happened."

Tony looked up and down several times. "I don't think it would make sense for everybody."

Angelo jumped up and stared at Tony. "Bart's right. If you tell what happened, guys like Joe Harris will see there's a lot of ways a guy can show if he has it, besides the really long thing Mr. Jones is supposed to have."

I tried to use a reassuring tone. "Tony, go ahead."

Tony took a long look at everyone. "Well, school was over for the day. I walked down the hall with Bart, Melo, Vito and Angelo. These guys started bugging us again."

Bart interrupted, wringing his hands. "They were all from the upper part of town near Wesleyan University. Every chance they had, they yelled 'Hey do any of you Wops have guts? Who wants to bet?'"

Melo thrust his arms forward. "Those guys were always calling us names to piss us off and get us to bet on something."

"I know," Vito added. "Once I got into a fight with one of them. The principal said if I don't cut it out, I'll be expelled."

Musca jumped up. "I told my parents that I didn't want to go to high school because of shit like that."

Bart spread out his hand. "Anyway, these guys wanted to bet that one of us would not have the guts to climb out of the second floor window and stand on the stone ledge for fifteen minutes."

"Listen to this!" Vito yelled. "The ledge is only about a foot wide. They kept teasing us, saying you Dagoes don't have it."

Tony slowly stood up. "I don't know why, but I got really mad. I told them I would go out there, and to put up or shut up. They each put up a quarter."

Bart thrust his arm out. "I tried to get Tony to walk away, but he wanted to prove to these guys that he had it. He climbed out the window onto that ledge, and stood with his back against those bricks. We went outside, scared"

"In a few minutes, a bunch of kids were standing on the sidewalk, looking up at Tony," Vito added.

Now everyone stared at Tony completely lost in imagining what they were hearing. Jimmy Lewis' gang and Brian Coleman's gang quietly expressed their amazement.

Musca mumbled, "Wait until you hear what happened. The whole neighborhood was talking about it."

"What happened?" Joe Harris called out, his mouth wide open with amazement.

Tony grinned, "I told those jerks that I was not coming back in the building unless one of them came out on the ledge with me."

"Wow!" exclaimed Dan O'Neil. "You put them on the spot. Did one of them take you on?"

"No!" Angelo yelled. "Tony was standing up there for a long time, and those guys kept arguing with each other. But no one would step out on the ledge with Tony."

Vito threw his arms up. "By now there was a big crowd with us on the sidewalk. We yelled at Tony to come back in."

"And guess what?" Bart shouted. "Even a teacher yelled at Tony to get off the ledge. But he didn't move."

Jimmy Lewis' gang and Brian Coleman's gang were leaning forward gripped in suspense.

Tony pushed his chest forward. "I really wanted to show those ass holes, who kept calling us names, that they didn't have it. But we did."

"What made you come down?" yelled a boy from Jimmy Lewis' gang.

Tony turned to me and gestured, inviting me to answer the question.

"Wait till you hear this!" Suggi yelled. "Our whole street was laughing about it."

I grinned. "Vito ran like mad to Central School and told me what was going on. So I ran like mad to the high school. And there was my brother, way the hell up there, standing on a stone ledge, gripping the bricks behind him."

"How did you get him to come in?" Joe Harris wondered.

"I yelled that if he didn't get off the ledge right away, I was going to run and tell Papa." Everyone burst out laughing.

At this moment a foreman approached all of us. "Do you realize lunch break is over? The trucks are over there to take you to your other jobs."

As everyone stood up, Jack Kane exclaimed, "Let's all play that fingers game and start a tournament! That'll decide who's got it."

"Yeah!" Brian Coleman yelled. "And the winner gets to pick the sandwich he wants from anybody's lunch."

"Not if you guys keep bringing those peanut butter sandwiches," Tony commented with an expression of disgust. Everyone burst out laughing.

That evening while my family was sitting around the kitchen table, chatting and eating fruit and biscotti for dessert, someone knocked on the screen door.

"Who could that be?" Tony asked. "No, *paisano* would knock."

Anna quickly stood up. "I'll see." She walked over, opened the screen door and looked out into the small yard.

"Excuse me, Anna," a man called out in a soft voice.

"Hi, Mr. Epstein. What brings you here? And who's watching your store?"

"The store is closed, Anna. Do you think I could talk to your father for a minute?

Anna turned, poked her head into the kitchen, and called

245

out, "Papa, it's Joe-the-Jew. He wants to talk to you."

Papa stood up with a look of surprise, walked to the door and stuck his head out. "How-a com-a you-a here Joe?" I wondered if Papa would ever learn to speak English without adding an "a" to almost every word.

"Can we please talk in private?"

Papa glanced at us as he stepped outside.

Anna was concerned. "I wonder what's the matter. Something must be worrying him from the look on his face. Maybe someone in his family is sick."

Gloria flipped her hand out. "But he wouldn't come here for that. I don't know if he would use the herbs and stuff we use when someone gets sick."

"We'll soon see what the story is," Filomena commented.

Minutes later Papa walked back into the kitchen. "*Ch'è successu?*" ("What happened?") Mamma asked. Papa explained that a close friend of Joe Epstein, whose name is Miller, owns and operates a small grocery store across the river in Portland. A few months ago he agreed to pay insurance to Giorgio Luppo to keep his store safe. But Mr. Miller doesn't have the money to pay the insurance for this month. Today he shared with Joe-the-Jew that Luppo came by the store with two of his men, and told him it was unfortunate, but he had to teach him a lesson. If a person agreed to a business deal, he had to keep it, and if he did not pay the rent for the month, he might lose everything in the store. Papa paused, "Because I helped him a little while ago, Joe-the-Jew wondered if I would help his friend."

Anna jumped up. "Papa, a guy I work with told me about Luppo and his gang! He's a rotten jerk! Whenever he can, he threatens store owners to pay rent. That extortion stuff really upsets me."

"I agree." Filomena looked up at Anna. "It's stuff like this that really disgraces us Italian Americans."

Papa glanced at Anna and Filomena. "I agree too." He added that the Mr. Miller's predicament is disgusting, and knows Luppo has tried many times to extort Italian immigrants.

Anna slapped the table. "Papa, I'm surprised Mr. Luppo is trying to do business with Mr. Miller because he's a close friend

246

of Joe-the-Jew. And everyone knows Joe-the-Jew is respected by the North End."

Mamma spoke out with vigor which was unusual for her. She agreed with Anna and added that everyone realizes how much Joe-the-Jew has done for the Sicilian community. Not only does he give children olives and pieces of cheese, but as everyone knew, he donates things every Sunday for the bags of food she and her friends distribute to families in need. "I'll bet you don't know that Mr. Miller sometimes gives food to Joe-the-Jew for Sunday sharing."

Filomena turned to Mamma and touched her hand. "Ma, some of us know that." Then she looked at Papa. "What are you going to do? Can you help Joe-the-Jew's friend deal with Mr. Luppo's operation across the river?"

Papa spread his hands open. "I'm a close friend of Mr. Adorno, the *Capo* of the *paisani* in Portland. Most of them are from Naples." He paused. "I plan to talk to him. I'm sure he'll solve the problem."

The next day when we sat down for dinner, Mamma announced she had something to share. All of us stopped chatting, joking, and arguing. We could tell by the tone of her voice she had something to say that was important. Papa smiled.

"Why are you grinning, Papa?" Anna asked.

At the same time Gloria wondered, "What do you want to tell us, Mamma?"

Mamma explained that today when she went into Joe-the-Jew's store to buy some vegetables, he told her he had some exciting news she must share with Papa. Mr. Miller visited Joe earlier today and told him that Mr. Luppo came to his store to say he did not have to pay rent anymore. Mr. Miller thanked Joe for his help, gave him a basket, and asked him to give it to the person who helped solve the problem. As she was speaking, Mamma walked to the corner of the kitchen and lifted a piece of cloth. There stood a basket filled with oranges, apples, bananas, dates, figs, vegetables, boxes of pasta, and several bottles of olive oil.

We all screamed. "Wow!"

Teodoro pointed at the basket. "I wondered what was under

there. I thought it was a pile of clothes to be washed."

Anna spread her hands out. "That was very nice of Mr. Miller to show his appreciation for what Papa did. He must have known Joe had connections in this community, and those connections had cousins across the river." Everyone walked over and relished the items in the basket.

Gloria placed her hand on Mamma's shoulder. "The Amenta family could use some of these. I was talking with Maria, their daughter, and she happened to mention they needed food."

Mamma selected some of the items and asked Gloria to take them over as soon as dinner was finished, adding that the other items will be used on Sunday when the bags are prepared.

Teodoro took a step toward Mamma with a very worried look. "But not those figs. You know how much I love figs." Smiling, Mamma put her arm around his shoulders and reassured him that the figs were his personal treasure.

———————————

The next day at the Goodrich Tobacco Farm, while all the boys from Middletown were waiting for trucks to transport them home, Tony shared the story about Mr. Miller and the rent he no longer had to pay.

Danny O'Neil looked upset, but I wasn't sure why. "Tony, that's a good story. It makes you guys look like heroes. I don't mean to hurt your feelings, but I heard my father saying that a friend of his, who has a carpentry business, needed to figure something out about what he was building. He asked this Italian guy, who was good at it, for help. This guy refused because my father's friend was Irish."

I was surprised to hear Adam Smith of the South End gang elaborate this theme, growling when he spoke. "I heard another story about this Dago, I mean this Italian guy. Someone from the South End was digging a little place by the river because he wanted to grow tomatoes and stuff like you Italians do. Somebody from Williams Street told this guy he was digging in a place only Italians use, and told him to find a spot nearer the South end."

"That's the kind of shit that goes on," Danny O'Neill continued with a strong edge of resentment.

Tony threw out a clenched fist. "Look, I know that kind of stuff goes on. But we said it takes time for people to get connected."

Angelo stepped in. "We told you that Joe-the-Jew, who Tony was talking about, has had a store in our neighborhood for years. And we told you what he does for the neighborhood. So people in our neighborhood see him as one of their own, even though he's a Jew."

Tony waved his hand back and forth, pointing to everyone. "Look at us. We know each other, but we had to work at being in the same gang when we were topping and picking. It's taking a lot of time to fit our sticks in the same basket."

"You said it, man," Joe Harris mumbled. "I don't know if we'll ever end up in the same basket." I was really disappointed in what Joe Harris just said, especially when I saw several boys from each of the gangs nod in agreement.

Bart did a good job when he changed the atmosphere from a disagreement to a joke. He grinned and pointed to Dan O'Neil and Joe Harris. "But look at how you guys like our lunches. I'll tell you one thing. I'll agree to join your neighborhood, except for one thing."

"Except for what?" Jimmy Lewis asked.

"As long as I don't have to eat those crappy lunches you Irish and Blacks bring to work." Everyone roared with laughter.

Tony shouted to capture Jimmy Lewis' attention. "Never mind the lunches we all bring. If you want to visit our neighborhood, I got an idea. It has to do with Jimmy asking me about all those dishes he spotted down by the river last Saturday."

Joe Harris lit up with excitement. "I was with Jimmy when he spotted them. We were down by the river near the edge of the Dago neighborhood. Those dishes had bright, red stuff in them."

A broad grin covered Jimmy's face. "From where we were, it looked like somebody sprinkled red dots from an airplane all along the edge of the river."

"What are you guys talking about?" Tom Murphy asked.

Tony spun around. "Tom, I guess you haven't been by the river in our neighborhood during this part of the summer."

249

"No, I haven't. What does Jimmy mean about red dots sprinkled all along the riverbank?"

"Every August, our parents make *strattu*."

"What the hell is that?"

"That's the Sicilian word for tomato paste that we use to make tomato sauce, you know for pasta dishes."

"I don't get it. What's that got to do with red dots sprinkled by the river?"

Tony raised his hand, glanced at Jimmy and Joe Harris, and then faced Tom Murphy. "I explained this to Jimmy Lewis. *Strattu* is sun dried tomato paste. It takes a lot of work by the whole family to make it." He quickly described how our parents take fresh tomatoes we grow near the river and grind them up to get buckets of tomato sauce that looks like tomato soup. Then they take out a whole bunch of dishes and put a couple of scoops of the tomato sauce in each one. Tony paused at this point, noticing that everyone was focused on him. I really liked the job he was doing explaining this custom. "That's when us kids come in. Early in the morning we carefully carry the dishes down by the river and put them on the ground where it's kinda flat, so the tomato sauce is under the sun. It slowly dries up and turns into a thick paste."

"But why do they make all those dishes of it?" asked Joe Harris.

Tony continued, enjoying being a teacher with this new subject. "You see, when the tomato sauce turns into paste, our parents stuff it into ceramic jugs which they keep in the cellar. This way they have the paste all winter long to make tomato sauce for different pasta dishes." Tony paused and shared that he had explained to Jimmy Lewis one important thing. The tomato sauce in each plate had to be stirred with a spoon about every fifteen or twenty minutes so the sun dries it all, kind of even. "That's what all of the kids do. They walk around and stir the sauce in each plate." Grinning, he added, "And the kids hope that it doesn't start to rain. Man, if rain clouds drift in, the kids have to hurry and carry all the plates back in their houses, because the rain will ruin the tomato sauce."

I was impressed with how Tony now extended an invitation to Joe Harris and Tom Murphy to step into our neighborhood or bundle of sticks. He poked a finger at each of them. "When Jimmy said he spotted the dishes along the river, I told him if he wants to get an inside look at the North End, he can come this Saturday and help us stir the sauce. There are many, many plates, and some families that don't have a lot of kids could use the help. Why don't you come and help?"

Jimmy Lewis spoke up and encouraged Joe Harris to accept the invitation. "Tony, remember? I told you I'll be there. I've seen those plates from far away. Now I can get close up, and maybe for the first time I can swim in tomato sauce." The crowd roared with laughter.

Bursting in song, Joe Harris, who loved to bring dancing into everything we talked about, began jitterbugging along the dirt road. "Well, I'll be there too, and I'm going to dance all around those red plates."

As Joe Harris continued singing and dancing, Bart yelled out, "Well, Mr. Dancer, if you happen to hit a plate with your foot and spill the sauce, whoever owns that plate will make sure you limp for the rest of your life." The laughter grew louder.

Apparently Tom Murphy was encouraged by what just happened. "Well, Brian and me are going to try to show up and help out too."

At this point Brian Coleman looked up. "Here come the trucks! We gotta get going."

As everyone raced toward the trucks, Tony called out, "See you guys tomorrow. Don't forget to bring your sticks."

I discovered later that Jimmy Lewis, Joe Harris, Brian Coleman and Tom Murphy met on that Saturday morning on Main Street, as they had planned. They knew that Tony and I would be surprised and pleased when we saw that they arranged to come and help with stirring the tomato sauce. They walked down William Street to the river and then followed the narrow dirt road along the Connecticut river that connected with the streets of our neighborhood. They passed dozens of plates of many different shapes and sizes that had already been distributed along the riverbank, each covered with freshly ground tomatoes. Every few steps, they paused and scanned the children who walked about with spoon in hand, slowly stirring the tomato sauce in one plate for a few seconds, and then turning to another.

Their attention was immediately captured when Tony yelled and waved, "Hey, guys, we're over here!" They slowly made their way toward him, carefully stepping between plates. "I'm glad you could make it."

When I heard Tony call out, I looked up, spotted Jimmy Lewis and the others, and made my way toward them, also stepping carefully between dishes. My sisters and Teodoro trailed behind me and warmly greeted them. Chuckling, Teodoro joked, "You guys are a little late. This whole thing started at seven this morning."

Gloria smiled, clutching several spoons in her hands. "It's great you guys want to help. Tony and Santo told us a lot about you. Take a spoon." Our visitors were nervous about whether they should go ahead, but then reached out and took a spoon.

Anna also noticed that they were nervous because she stepped forward, stretched her arm out, and moved it slowly from left to right. "See, all those plates from that bush over there to that bush, they're ours. Doesn't that make a beautiful picture, like red flowers in the sun?"

Filomena, who of course could not resist being a teacher, also took a small step forward. "I know you know what we're supposed to do, but let me show you." Kneeling down next to a plate, she demonstrated. "See just take your spoon and move it slow like this, and push the sauce that's near the bottom up to the top, so the sun can dry it."

"I get it," Jimmy Lewis whispered, "This is going to be neat, and I promise I won't swim in the plates." We all laughed.

Gloria chuckled. "Tony told us that you said that."

Tom Murphy thrust his hand against Joe Harris' chest. "And you promised you won't dance around the plates, right?" Everybody again burst out laughing.

Joe Harris placed his hands on his hips. "Well maybe I'll dance here after the dishes are taken away."

"You should do that," Anna commented. "We've got a lot of good dancers."

With his hands still on his hips, Joe Harris continued looking into the faces of my sisters. "You know what? I noticed nobody is staring at me because I'm black."

"Are you kidding. Look over there." Filomena pointed to her left. "See that guy? He's nearly as dark as you are. Some Sicilians are really dark. We don't get into color."

Joe Harris turned and faced Tony. "Remember how I'm always joking about black sticks can't fit in. Being here today helps me not worry so much about that."

Tony and I nodded making clear we liked what he just said.

Filomena interrupted. "Okay everybody. We've got to get going. There are families who could use help because they don't have enough kids to do the stirring. Two of you guys could go help them with Tony and Santo. And two of you guys could help me, Teodoro and my sisters." Joe Harris and Tom Murphy immediately volunteered to accompany Tony and me.

While we were standing there talking, mothers, fathers and kids, who were stirring tomato sauce, occasionally lifted their heads, smiled and nodded. I felt gripped by the whole situation. Here we were, Tony and I with two black kids and two Irish kids surrounded by hundreds of plates of tomato sauce and people from our neighborhood. The situation caused a lot of what we had talked about on the farm to tumble into my mind.

I waved my arm in a full circle. "Look! Isn't that fantastic? Hundreds of plates filled with tomato-sauce jewels, sitting under the sun. And how about all those kids, laughing and having fun, stirring the tomato sauce. Now you can see what we meant when we said our parents changed their minds after they got here and set up their own way of life, deciding that the United States was the land of opportunity. Do you realize in the old days in Sicily, when they made *strattu*, they couldn't put their plates where they wanted to."

Gloria chuckled, "You're right, Santo. The Duke who owned that estate would probably charge them rent."

"But I have much more to say, Gloria. I know in some other parts of town, and other parts of this country, we couldn't be standing here together. We're showing that it's possible to mix together sticks from very different bundles."

Anna quickly raised the palm of her hand and interrupted me. "Santo, I'm not sure what you're talking about with your friends. This is not the time to make a speech. Like Filomena just said, it's time for us to get to work and turn all these red jewels into tomato paste." Each of us began stirring tomato sauce in one dish after the other, chatting and joking.

The next day, Papa and Mamma, along with Uncle Gaetano and Aunt Concetta, decided to take the families to Seven Falls which had become a family ritual on Sundays, during the summer. We loved to go to this public park on the outskirts of town where a rippling brook poured over many, large stones into a small pond. In this location the town made available picnic tables and fireplaces scattered under a large grove of trees. Sicilian families loved to make use of this park during the summer because it gave them an opportunity to eat outdoors, and get a good taste of the countryside, which was routine in Sicily but very limited in Middletown by the tenement houses they lived in. Although the Sicilian neighborhood maintained vegetable gardens by the Connecticut River, the landscape did not provide families the opportunity to picnic in comfort.

When we arrived at this park, each family member carried some item related to the Sunday *pranzo*. Papa carried a bundle of branches and small logs. Mamma carried boxes of pasta called *orecchiette*, because the shape of each piece of pasta was like a little ear. *Orecchie* is the Italian word for ears. Anna carried sausage and chicken cutlets. Filomena carried basil, parsley, and other herbs for seasoning under one arm and a bag with several loafs of homemade bread under the other.. Tony carried a large pan for cooking the pasta, and in it was a watermelon. Teodoro carried a bag filled with clams, and Gloria carried a basket of fruits and nuts. Uncle Gaetano, Aunt Concetta and their children were also carrying items that everyone would share.

Because this park was visited by many families during the summer, one important ritual everyone practiced upon arriving was to have a family member run ahead and place an item, such as a bag or pan, on a picnic table. Typically, the item indicated to others, who might be looking for a table, that this particular table and the fireplace near it were reserved. I had run ahead to locate and claim two tables. When everyone arrived at the tables I had reserved, Tony commented, "Oh darn it, we didn't get the tables I like." For some reason, which I never learned, a particular area of the park and its tables were Tony's favorite.

I was a little annoyed by his comment. "Tony! I ran over to your favorite tables as soon as we got here. They were taken, so get over it."

Anna overheard Tony's comment. "This is a really nice part of the park, Tony. These aren't our favorite tables, but even Mamma just said she feels lucky."

Everyone immediately began unwrapping items to prepare the Sunday *pranzo*. Suddenly, a girl standing several yards away waved to Isabella, calling her to one side. She was upset and talked very fast for several minutes. Isabella ran over to Uncle Gaetano who was busy setting up the fireplace. He stopped what he was doing, leaned over, and became very involved, listening to Isabella.

Filomena was preparing herbs nearby and turned to Isabella. "What's the matter, Bella, you seem upset? Does that girl have a problem?"

"She's a friend of mine, one of the Carnavale girls. You know the family lives on Washington Street."

"Yes, I know. What's the matter? Why was she upset?"

Papa looked up and noticed that everyone had stopped making preparations and were staring at Isabella. He walked over and asked if there was a problem. Isabella looked at her father, conveying he should explain what she had just shared. In response, Uncle Gaetano gestured, encouraging her to go ahead and discuss the matter with her uncle.

Isabella pointed to a group sitting at a table under a nearby cluster of trees. "Zio (uncle) that girl is one of the Carnavales. They live on Washington Street." Papa nodded, indicating that he knew the family. "Well, her father's friend, his name is Mr. Pagano, just told him something that he was really upset about, and didn't know what to do."

Papa placed a hand on Isabella's shoulder. "I know the Pagano family. They emigrated from Sicily a couple of years ago just before World War II broke out. What was Mr. Pagano upset about?"

"A little while ago, he put a pan on a table to claim it, and went back to his family to help them carry things. When they got to the table, there were three, young guys with their girlfriends, or wives, sitting there. He looked around, and his pan was on the ground under a bush."

We were all very upset by what Isabella just shared, and Filomena let it out. "What! That's ridiculous! He shouldn't put up with that!"

Isabella raised her hand, asking Filomena to wait and be quiet. "It gets even worse. Mr. Pagano can't speak English that good, but he tried to tell one of the men that the pan on the ground was on the table, and the table was his."

Tony stepped close to Isabella and guessed what we all expected. "The guy gave him shit, right?"

"More than that, he said something like go back to where you belong, you Dago, and what are you doing here? You're supposed to be helping Hitler."

Filomena exploded. "That's disgusting!" What can we do for Mr. Pagano?"

Papa asked everyone to calm down and acknowledged what happened was disgraceful. He also reminded us that this was a time to practice *omertà*, and think about how friends can help friends.

Tony turned to Papa. "Ever since that talk we had weeks ago, Santo and I have been trying to practice *omertà*. We gotta think of a cool way to get that table back for Mr. Pagano."

Everyone calmed down, and Papa asked if anyone had an idea. Each of us turned and looked around to see who would step forward. During this pause, I found myself staring at something that suddenly appeared on the stage in my mind reserved for yesterday. Last fall Tony took me to a high school, football game. During one particular play, Ed Palermo, from our neighborhood, crashed through four or five guys from the other team, raced down the field and scored a touchdown. Just a little while ago,

I spotted Ed when I raced into the park to claim a table for us. Suddenly, an idea flashed into my mind.

"Papa, when I ran over to get our tables, I went by the Palermo family. They're over there." I pointed. "You know, Ed Palermo is the fullback on the high school football team. He's built like Tarzan. What if we ask Mr. Palermo to have his son go over to that table and just stand there, and help those people understand the table was taken? Maybe if we send just one guy, it won't come across like a gang fight is starting. That might straighten things out."

Everyone thought what I had suggested was a good idea. It really pleased me how something that happened yesterday connected with what's happening today. Papa and I walked over to the table were the Palermo family was seated. As we approached, Mr. Palermo called out, "Hey *cugino* (cousin) *comu stai* (how are you)?"

Papa smiled. "*Bene, bene* (good, good)." Mr. Palermo stood up, and in keeping with Sicilian custom, they hugged and kissed each other on each cheek. Papa quickly explained to Mr. Palermo and his family the problem and insult that Mr. Pagano experienced and described my suggestion. Mr. Palermo agreed with the plan, and so did his son, Ed.

Ed smiled. "Hey Santo, I'll really enjoy helping those people understand. They can't talk to us like that. You're right. Maybe if I put a pan on the table, and then just stand there, they'll realize the table was taken." He paused and pointed to another table about ten yards away. "But wait. I just got an idea. My friends, the Alessi brothers, are over there. They could come with us. Maybe the three of us could make these people understand even better."

I glanced at Papa and wondered if he thought it would look too much like a gang fight. But I couldn't hold back my excitement. "Wow, that's Joe and Nick Alessi, the halfbacks on your team. That means we'll go at that table with the whole backfield. You'll be the fullback, Ed, and Joe and Nick will be the halfbacks."

"But that gives me another idea, Santo. You'll be the quarterback." A broad grin spread across Ed's face.

I flexed my shoulders and also grinned. "And you guys can

be the muscle." Ed's invitation made me feel very powerful for a second.

Papa stepped in and quietly reminded Ed and me to practice *omertà* when we approached the table. Ed nodded as a sign of respect. "Okay, Santo. Let's just tell these jerks we're all cousins. You do the talking, and I'll bet we're going to score a touchdown and win this game." Ed ran to the Alessi brothers and quickly explained the situation. They were thrilled with the opportunity to help deal with an example of the kind of insult Sicilian immigrants have been exposed to from time to time, but especially since World War II broke out.

Flanked by Ed Palermo and the Alessi brothers, I slowly walked toward the table that Mr. Pagano had claimed earlier. When we arrived, we stood in silence for a moment. I looked around and noticed a large metal pan under a bush only a couple of yards away. Three young men and their female companions, who had been chatting and eating, looked up and stared. One of the men spoke out with a strong tone of irritation. "What do you guys want? Get lost."

"Wait a minute, sir." I was pleased with how I used a calm voice and the word 'sir.' "Our cousin, Mr. Pagano, said he put a pan on this table to claim it for the afternoon." Ed Palermo and the Alessi brothers stood beside me and stared straight ahead, trying not to grin.

I barely made my comment when the man who just spoke out shot back. "What pan? Did you hear what I said you little shit? Get lost!"

I tried not to show any fear or anger, and slowly pointed to the pan that was under the bush. "That pan. Besides, our friend Mr. Pagano said you said some really nasty things about us Italians."

"Oh I get it. There are more of you Dagos here. Well ..."

At this moment, Ed Palermo and the Alessi brothers took one step forward toward the man who was speaking. Ed, who in fact was really built like Tarzan, emphasized his physique by flexing the muscles of his arms and chest. At the same time, each of the Alessi brothers placed their hands on their hips with palms turned out, showing they were ready for action.

I was pleased that I was still talking with a calm voice. I gestured toward Ed and the Alessi brothers. "My cousins are here to help me help you understand. So I'm asking you again whether you understand that our cousin, Mr. Pagano, claimed this table first."

The young man's jaw slowly dropped, and his eyes widened with fear as he scanned Ed and the Alessi brothers. "Okay. Okay." At the same time his friends quickly stood up and began gathering their items.

I couldn't resist saying more. "And if I were you, I would think twice before saying nasty things about us Italians, like helping Hitler. Do you realize we all have cousins in the United States Army and Navy. Anyway, why aren't you guys in the service?"

While I was speaking, Ed picked up the pan under the bush and, with a bang, dropped it on the table. The three couples hurried off.

The Pagano, Palermo and Alessi families, as well as Uncle Gaetano's family and mine, were clustered together about ten yards away and had witnessed the whole event. When Ed Palermo, the Alessi brothers and I walked toward the crowd, we were greeted with hugs.

Mr. Pagano stepped toward Papa and kissed each of his cheeks while shaking his hand. Then he did the same with Uncle Gaetano, Vincent Palermo, Ed's father, and Salvatore Alessi the father of Joe and Nick. Staring at everyone, Mr. Pagano commented that since arriving in the United States about three years ago, he and his family had experienced rejection and insult at times, much like what happened today over the picnic table. He admitted that sometimes he wondered whether he had made a mistake immigrating to the United States, even though conditions in Sicily were not good and opportunities were very limited. Mr. Pagano paused. With a troubled expression, he shared that he has often asked himself, "*comu a stu munnu 'un ti pò abituari?*" ('Why can't you get accustomed to this world?')

At this moment, Papa stepped forward and took Mr. Pagano by the hand. He acknowledged that, when they began to arrive here in the early 1900's, every family in the North End had been insulted and discriminated against on occasion. But over time, he emphasized, most of the families have learned that the United States is *'na terra d' opportunitati* (a land of opportunities). And most families, he added, do feel *fortunatu truvari sta via da vita* (fortunate to find this road of life). They feel fortunate, Papa elaborated, because here they can continue *la via vecchia* (the old way of life with ancient Sicilian customs), and continue to experience that *l'omu è riccu guannu c'avi amici* (a man is rich when he has friends). The big and very tough job everyone faces, he added, is to learn how to keep building that road so it fits with, and uses, what the United States has to offer.

I wasn't surprised when Filomena stepped forward since all of what just happened was like a lesson. "Don't you think every family that came to this country, Blacks, Irish, Jews, Germans and people from Asia, all have to face that job? Nobody has it easy."

Tony couldn't resist bringing up some of what we talked about at the tobacco farm. "And people have to realize it takes time to fit sticks from different *fasci* into the same basket or neighborhood."

Papa glanced at Filomena and Tony, appreciating what they just said. Then he placed his hand on Mr. Pagano's shoulder, reassuring him that he will eventually find different ways of fitting in the good parts of the old Sicilian ways with what the United States makes available.

Everyone yelled, *arrivederci paisani* (until we meet again, neighbors), walked to their tables, and began feasting.

Last Picking:

To Have a Life that is Ensured,
We Must Find Another Road.
But Whoever Completely Leaves the Old Way for a New Way
Knows What He Is Losing,
But May Not know What He will Find.

In mid-August my gang lingered along a field that bordered the Central Lot, waiting for today's assignment. Baggi stepped into the field, and looked up and down at the stalks. I wondered what he was up to. Before I called him out, he placed his hand on his hip and shouted, "Hey, remember when we started First Picking, the plants were only this big?" Then he stretched his arm up high. "Now, they're up here, and got only a few leaves left for Last Picking. Then it's over."

When Baggi yelled, "It's over," I said to myself, "No, it isn't over." I don't know why I protested and became lost in a fantasy. I imagined that the plants were like children. During First and Second Pickings, they experienced the surge of growing bigger and taller. With Third Picking and Fourth, they experienced having their royal garments of childhood slowly removed, one part at a time. Now with Last Picking, each plant stood tall with three or four leaves remaining near the top, and each plant must understand where he's come from and where he's headed. I was jolted back to the present when Mr. Kelly raced toward me. "Mr. Williams wants to see you for a minute."

Louie was nearby. "We didn't do anything wrong." The rest of the gang also looked confused and quickly stepped toward me.

I tried not to look worried and raised my palms. "Let's see. I'll be back in a few minutes." As I walked toward the Main Cabin with Mr. Kelly, I examined the expression on his face looking for a clue. When I couldn't find one, I pushed him to give me a hint. "Why do you think he wants to see me?"

"I don't know. He didn't say anything to me."

I pushed harder. "I mean did he look pissed off?"

"There was a stranger in the office when he asked me to get

you. I know you'll like why he's here." I felt relieved by what he said and his tone.

When I entered the Main Cabin, Mr. Williams was talking to a man wearing a dark suit, white shirt and necktie. I thought, "Wow! He really looks like someone from the King's Palace." I felt confused, wondering why Mr. Kelly decided I would like that this kind of guy is here.

Mr. Williams interrupted his conversation. "Santo this is Mr. Wendell. His job is to locate prisoners of war where they can work. The Goodrich Farm was allotted twenty-five Italians. They arrived yesterday."

I learned later that more than fifty thousand captured Italian soldiers were interned in camps throughout the United States. Several thousand of them were located in Connecticut and Massachusetts, and, for the most part, the United States War Department kept this a secret.

Mr. Williams explained that the prisoners of war assigned to the Goodrich Farm were housed in a nearby shed which was fixed up like an army barrack, and that they had been checked out and did not need to be guarded all the time. Accordingly, they will be assigned to work on projects like replacing or fixing lose poles, chopping plants down and removing nets when Last Picking is completed. Mr. Williams paused, "But there is one problem. Only a couple of them know a few words in English. I know most of your gang can talk Italian, so I need you to explain jobs to them."

I immediately said something everyone in my neighborhood says if a person asks whether you speak Italian. "No, we don't talk Italian, Mr. Williams. We talk the Sicilian dialect like our parents."

Mr. Wendell stared at me. "Actually that's great. Most of these prisoners are from Sicily."

I felt a surge of excitement, lifted myself up on the balls of my feet, clenched my fists together, and took a quick step toward Mr. Williams. "I can't wait to meet them! My gang is gonna wonder if any of these prisoners are cousins."

"Take a minute, go over to that shed, and introduce yourself.

Then when you have to tell them something, they'll know who you are. I'll tell Mr. Kelly he can take you later to the Riverway field where your gang will be working. I decided to assign the Middletown gangs to the same field."

I hopped out of the cabin, jogged up the road, and approached the shed where the prisoners were housed. The barbed-wire fence set around the shed immediately caught my attention. I stopped for a moment and mumbled, "Why the hell do they have them caged in?" and then answered myself. "Well I guess that's what the army has to do. But at least they have some space to walk around in." When I reached the fence, I spotted several prisoners standing outside.

"Hey! *Paisani!*" The prisoners stopped chatting, stared at me in disbelief, and smiled. *"Mi chiamu, Santo. Non pozzu parrari a lingua italiana. Sulu parru la lingua antica di Sicilia."* ("My name is Santo. I can't speak the Italian language. I only speak the ancient, Sicilian dialect.)

The prisoners laughed. One of them yelled back, *"E iu puru sugnu sicilianu! Mi chiamu Mario!"* ("And I also am Sicilian. My name is Mario.")

Prisoners rushed out of the shed and crowded around Mario as he asked me about my background. "Me and my brothers and sisters were born in the United States. Before the war, my parents, aunts and uncles came from a village near Syracuse, Sicily."

One of the prisoners screamed. *"Siracusa! Iu sugnu di Siracusa! Mi chiamu Nunzio."* ("I am from Syracuse! My name is Nunzio.").

Other prisoners immediately shouted the names of their villages, and emphasized whether their village was on the same side of the island as Syracuse or on the western side. I knew how much Sicilians were invested in defining, as special and better, the part of the island in which they lived. While the names of villages were being called out, one of the prisoners raised his arm. *"Basta!"* he exclaimed. *"Una razza, una faccia."* ("Enough! One race, one face.") Everyone burst out laughing.

I was familiar with that Sicilian metaphor. Although most of the families in my neighborhood came from a village located in the southeastern part of the island of Sicily, a few families came from villages located in the northwestern part of the island. On occasion, influenced by discussions their parents had, kids argued about which part of the island was the best and had achieved the most.

Just this past Sunday, one such debate had taken place which flashed through my mind as soon as that prisoner shouted, "One race, one face." My friends and I were arguing with a couple of boys from Rapello Avenue. To support why the southeast part of the island is the best, I argued, "How about Archimedes! Remember what he did when a Roman Army surrounded Syracuse for three years. But they couldn't capture the city because he invented these fantastic catapults that were really accurate and smashed the Roman ships in the harbor. You know he was born in Syracuse and lived there."

A boy from Rapello Avenue didn't give me a chance to finish. "Are you kidding? Do you realize how many artists and poets lived in Palermo?" At the close of the argument, all of us, as did our parents, burst out laughing and announced that ancient proverb, declaring all Sicilians shared one race and one face.

When another prisoner spoke up, I understood some of what he said, especially that he was not from Sicily. He shouted with pride, "I come from a village east of Naples. I do not carry a Sicilian face. So I am definitely not a member of that race." Everyone burst out laughing. Nunzio and several other prisoners playfully pushed him to the ground.

Another prisoner looked down at the prisoner on the ground and shouted, "Let's not forget there was a time when Naples and Sicily made up the Kingdom of the Two Sicilies! So my friend, you don't have a choice! You belong to the Sicilian race and wear its face." All of the prisoners burst out laughing again.

When the prisoners quieted down, I held up my hand. "Is any one from Melilli? That's where my parents are from and a lot of the other parents on my street." The prisoners turned and looked around at each other. No one responded. I was disappointed since I had hoped I could return to my neighborhood with the news that some of the prisoners were from our village, or nearby.

One of the prisoners must have noticed I was disappointment because he tried to cheer me up by stepping closer to the fence and asking me what my family had for dinner last night. I felt like showing off, pushed my chest out, raised one arm and grinned. "Since fresh basil is growing in everyone's garden along the River, we had pasta with pesto sauce made from ground up fresh basil leaves, parsley, garlic and olive oil. Of course we had homemade wine." I paused and scanned the faces of several prisoners who seemed to be drooling. "We also had fried calamari. And to nibble between courses we had homemade bread dipped in olive oil, provolone cheese, and anchovies."

"Magnificent!" One prisoner exclaimed, "How did you end the meal?"

"We had fruit, almonds and walnuts."

While I shared the items we had, the prisoners listened with intense interest and made clear the importance family meals held in the lives of southern Italians. So I wasn't surprised when, upon hearing each dinner item, one or another prisoner sighed and whispered "*mararigghiusa* (wonderful), *un sonnu* (a dream)."

Suddenly, a prisoner raised his arms high and shouted, "*Roba della mia mamma.*" ("The garment, the essence, of my mother"), a saying other prisoners immediately echoed.

Everyone was really turned on, as another prisoner wondered, "So who sat down to eat this meal?"

"The meal was shared as always by my parents, sisters, and brothers. And last night one of my aunts and uncles and their kids were there too."

Mario stepped forward, raised his right hand at eye level with his palm forward, and index finger pointing to the sky. Everyone immediately stood still and watched him. Several prisoners even nodded in his direction. I was certain that Mario held authority and special respect among the prisoners. He shared how impressed everyone was that, although my family and other families had been in the United States for only about twenty years, they continued to follow and benefit from old Sicilian customs. "Santo," he added, "*cu lassa la via vecchia pir la nuova sa chiddu ca perdi, ma non sapi chiddu ca trova.*" ("Whoever

265

completely leaves the old way for a new way knows what he is losing, but may not know what he will find.")

I had heard that before when my parents, aunts and uncles were engaged in discussions about whether and how to fit their early days in Sicily with their experiences in the United States. I stared at Mario and nodded. He understood how much I appreciated the opportunity to meet them. Suddenly I realized that I had to get back to my gang. I raised my arms, scanning the crowd. "*Mi dispiaci* (I'm sorry) I have to get back to work. I will see you whenever a job needs to be explained." As I jogged to the Central Lot, I glanced over my shoulder and spotted prisoners waving with enthusiasm, obviously pleased that persons were on the Farm who understood their needs and ways of thinking.

When I arrived at the Riverway Fields, I ran toward my gang and gave them the news. Everyone became excited and looked forward to meeting these prisoners.

At the end of that day, word quickly spread throughout the neighborhood that Italian prisoners were working at the farm and most of them were Sicilian. When Tony and I entered our apartment, I couldn't resist announcing the news immediately. "Wow! Everybody! You won't believe this! There's a bunch of Italian prisoners working on the farm and ..."

Anna was leaning over, setting plates on the table. Instead of responding to what I had just said, she stared at Tony, "How do you feel? You don't look good."

I couldn't understand why the news I just shared didn't grab her and got angry. "Did you hear what I just said?"

I was stunned when she snapped back. "We'll talk about that later." She turned and continued staring at Tony.

Tony stepped toward her and stood very still. "I don't know what it is. I had a hard time last night. I think I caught some kind of bug. I felt lousy all day at the farm. It was *na iurnata brutta* (a nasty day). I'm glad the week's over."

Mamma also did not react to what I just said about prisoners at the farm, which surprised me even more. She turned around from the stove, slowly lifted a spoon, carefully held it over the pan, and with a look of concern also engaged Tony. "*Dimmi na*

266

cosa, figghiu miu. Chi fa, sì malatu?" ("Tell me, my son. What, are you sick?")

I looked down at the floor. "Okay, I see no one cares what I just said about Italian prisoners at the farm." Tony was totally glued to the attention he was getting from Mamma and Anna. Since he mentioned he had a hard time last night, I couldn't resist reporting something. "Mamma, Tony had more than a hard night. He didn't sleep at all, and neither did Teodoro and me. Tony kept moving around and kicking my head."

Apparently Teodoro was in our bedroom listening to the conversation, because he jumped into the kitchen. "And he kicked me too. He was awake until *mezzanotte* (midnight)."

Tony, Teodoro and I shared a bedroom. We also shared a bed. To avoid having our shoulders and arms bumping into each other, two of us slept with our heads at one end of the bed. Between us slept the third brother with his head at the other end of the bed, and his feet between the shoulders of the other two. Each night we rotated the arrangement. Last night because Tony complained he felt sick, we decided he should sleep at the foot of the bed to try to prevent his illness from spreading to us.

After hearing what Teodoro and I had said, Mamma rubbed the palms of her hands on her apron, and gently pressed them on Tony's forehead, chest and stomach. "Where do you feel the most pain? You seem to have a high temperature."

Filomena who also had been listening to the conversation, while folding laundry in the girls' bedroom, stepped into the kitchen immediately after Momma made her comment, and placed the palm of her hand on his forehead. "Ma, you're right. Tony's got a temperature of at least a hundred degrees." I knew Filomena would once again show something else she learned at college. "We had this first aid class. The teacher had us put our hands in different bowls of water and guess the temperature, and then look at the thermometer. After a lot of practice we got pretty good at it."

I became submerged in everyone's concern, and thought it would help if I urged Tony to share what he dealt with since last night. He never liked admitting he didn't feel well, because he was sick nearly every winter when he was a little kid. "Tony, tell Mamma what's been going on today. It could help her figure it out."

Tony stared at Mamma and then at me. I nudged my head and shoulders toward Mamma, urging him to speak up. He lowered his head as if he had done something wrong. "*Mi veni di vumitari e haiu a nausia.* (I vomit and feel nauseous.) *Mi sentu assai mali.* (I feel really sick.)"

Mamma clenched her lips with concern. "Even though you don't have to work tomorrow, you should see Mrs. Carrado right away."

Mrs. Carrado was the neighborhood healer or *mavara*. When someone who was sick visited her, she quietly mumbled ancient chants, intended to drive away evil spirits contributing to the person's illness, carefully selected herbs, and gave the person instructions about how long to boil the herbs in water, and how often to drink a glass of the liquid.

Mamma turned to Gloria. "Go quick to Mrs. Carrado's apartment and ask her if she would please see Tony."

Filomena's eyes glared with anger. "Wait, Ma! I don't mean to be disrespectful, but don't you think Tony should see *u dutturi*?" (the doctor) I was amazed how much feeling Filomena had about Tony seeing Mrs. Carrado. Mamma felt the same, because her eyes widened, and her jaw sagged.

Anna immediately joined in with vigor. I wasn't surprised since she and Filomena had gotten into this issue with Mamma several times during the past couple of years. "Ma! I know everybody sees Mrs. Carrado when they get sick. I know she has helped a lot of people. But Filomena is right. Tony should see a doctor."

Filomena thrust her hand out with her fingers curved upward, making clear that she would not budge from her position. "Besides, Ma, I know you don't like the doctors at the Middlesex County Hospital because no one is Italian? But Ma, I heard Dr. Priore just started working there, and he's a *paisano*."

Mamma glared at Filomena and Anna and, in defense for her position, reached out with the palms of both hands turned upward.

"When I was growing up in Sicily, Mrs. Carrado's mother took care of everyone in the village for years. There were no doctors. There was only the *mavara* who helped anybody who was sick. And there was only the *colladro* who helped anyone who sprained or broke an arm or leg in an accident."

Filomena did not back up. She placed her hands on her hips, making clear Mamma's explanation did not make a difference. "Ma, I don't understand why you are getting so defensive. Doctors know what to do better than a *mavara*. When I told the kids in school about Mrs. Carrado, they laughed and called her a witchdoctor."

"Some things have to change from the old ways, Ma. Some things that we have now are better than the old ways," Anna growled. I was taken aback by how Filomena and Anna were ganging up on Mamma.

Papa arrived and must have noticed the angry expressions on the faces of Mamma, Anna and Filomena, their bodies leaning toward each other, and their clenched fists resting on their hips.

When Tony turned and saw Papa, he spoke out with a loud voice that was not at all like his usual tone, "Hey, I don't want us to get into some huge argument. I'm okay. Let's forget it."

Papa stared at Tony, and then at everyone, with a look of concern. "What's happening?" Mamma quickly summarized what had taken place. But Filomena and Anna immediately repeated their argument about why seeing Mrs. Carrado now, when someone is sick, doesn't make sense. From the expression on Papa's face, I wondered if he felt as if he was standing between two different worlds and agreed with both of them. He stepped toward Mamma and placed a hand on her shoulder. "*Giuseppina, tuttu canciatu. Tuttu a lu riversu. Ma sempri è la stissa musica da vita.*" ("Everything's changed. Things are all upside down. But it's always the same music about life.") With his hand still on Mamma's shoulder, he paused and scanned all of us several times, while we stood motionless staring at him.

Filomena took a step toward Papa and held her right hand out with her fingers curled back, as if she were involved in a debate. "Papa, remember when we were talking about the Old

Mafia and the New Mafia a few weeks ago, and how confusing it is when they're mixed together? Well the argument Anna and I are having with Mamma is the same, in one way."

"I agree," Anna interrupted with an edge of anger still in her voice. "Why can't we find a way to fit the old ways with the new ways so things are better?"

Papa's eyes opened wide with surprise as he looked back and forth at Anna and Filomena. "So, Anna, we have a chance right in front of us to try what you just asked. Who has an idea about how we can fit Mrs. Carrado and Dr. Priore together?"

Mamma took a quick step forward, wanting her way to stay in first place. She stared into the faces of Filomena and Anna, and slowly moved both of her hands forward with palms open. "What if Tony sees Mrs. Carrado right away, and takes the herbs she prescribes tonight and all day tomorrow. If he doesn't get better by Sunday, Tony could go to the hospital, and hopefully see Dr. Priore."

Papa smiled. "If the herbs do not help, I will arrange for Tony to see Dr. Priore. I know his father very well."

"Didn't Dr. Priore just graduate from medical school?" Anna asked.

"Yes," Filomena declared, still in a mood to debate. "So he's bound to know the latest stuff." But then she surprised me, and maybe everyone, when she slowly placed each of her hands on Mamma's shoulders. "But I guess Mamma's idea makes sense. I know certain herbs are good for you."

Papa smiled. "I will take Tony to see Mrs. Carrado ."

I immediately called out, "Papa, I want to go with him!"

Everyone looked surprised when Filomena jumped in. "Me, too!"

"*Bene, bene*," Papa responded.

Mamma turned to Anna, "Then you, Gloria and Teodoro can help me prepare dinner."

"Sure, Ma."

Papa walked slowly down Ferry Street. Tony ambled behind him with Filomena and I at his side, holding his hands. We turned into a narrow alleyway that led to Green Street. Clothes and bed sheets were flapping on clotheslines overhead, and a number of trash cans were pushed against the walls of the tenement houses. When we reached Green Street, we spotted Mrs. Carrado's husband sitting in a chair on the sidewalk among neighbors who had also brought out chairs for their early evening get together. One of the men in the group happened to look up, spotted Papa approaching, and immediately stood up. Others took notice, stopped their discussions and also jumped up.

"*Pi piaciri, sediti* (please, have a seat)." Papa waved. "We are here to see Signura Carrado." He stepped toward her husband and explained Tony's situation. Mr. Carrado raced into his apartment, returned after a few seconds, and waved to us to enter.

Mrs. Carrado stood at the entrance and gestured, asking us to go into the room next to the kitchen. We had been in this room before, and I noticed that nothing had changed. A rope was strung near the ceiling from one end of the room to the other, from which hung more than two dozen bunches of different herbs. On a long table set against one wall was a row of baskets in which were located branches of other herbs. A large crucifix hung on the center of that wall. To one side of the crucifix hung a large, framed print of St. Sebastian when he was executed, looking up at the sky with his hands tied behind his back to the trunk of a tree, and four or five arrows protruding from his chest and stomach. On the opposite wall hung a large, framed, black and white photograph of Mrs. Carrado and her parents and siblings taken a few years before she departed for the United States, and another of her and Mr. Carrado standing among immigrants at Ellis Island, each holding a bundle tied with a rope.

The aroma of herbs floated throughout the room. Filomena slowly raised her head and took a deep breath. I did the same while looking about the room. Papa reached up and gently touched the leaves of one of the branches hanging from the rope and pressed his fingertips against his lips.

As usual Mrs. Carrado was wearing a black dress that nearly touched the floor, but her chest and stomach were covered with a white apron. Her long dark hair, streaked with gray, was pulled to the back of her head and tied with a black ribbon. She nodded toward Papa, Filomena and me and gestured to chairs at one end of the room. Then she walked to the other end, asked Tony to make himself comfortable, and sat in a chair opposite him. She leaned forward, placed a hand on one of his hands, and asked him to share what was bothering him. Tony described the stomach pains, vomiting and fever he had been experiencing. She listened with interest and warmth, which was her usual way of relating, occasionally touching his forehead, the side of his face, and the top of his head.

When Tony finished with what he had to say, Mrs. Carrado brought up something from his past because, I thought, it would help him feel connected with her. *"Antonio, ti canuscivi quannu eri picciriddu."* ("Antonio, I came to know you when you were a little boy.") During the first six or seven years of his life, Tony had a very rough time. He frequently developed bronchitis during the winter months, and Mrs. Carrado helped him overcome these illnesses. *"Oggi tu sì malatu."* ("Today you are sick.")

Mrs. Carrado stood up and slowly walked about, chanting to ward off evil spirits, and scanning the herbs hanging from the rope and those stacked in baskets. She paused, took several herbs from one basket, walked around, took a few herbs from another basket, and then pulled down a small cluster from the rope. She stopped chanting, turned to Filomena and handed her the herbs. *"Chista è la chiù megghiu cura."* ("This is the best cure.") She asked Filomena to instruct Mamma to boil the herbs in water for two minutes. When the liquid cooled, Tony was to drink a glass before bedtime, and again around midnight. Tomorrow he was to drink another glass in the morning, again at midday, and again before bedtime. If he still felt sick, she would like Tony to return. Papa, Tony, Filomena and I stood up, thanked Mrs. Carrado, and returned to our apartment.

Minutes after we arrived, Mamma boiled the herbs in water. Tony drank a glass before bedtime, as instructed, and again in the middle of the night. The next morning Mamma prepared another glass of the herbal liquid, gave it to Tony, and encouraged him to try to relax in bed. At noontime, she repeated the treatment.

Later that afternoon Papa left to visit Uncle Gaetano and

several other men in the neighborhood. Mamma and the rest of us, except Tony, were preparing to stroll for an hour or two along the Connecticut River to gather dandelions. Each of us held a paper bag in one hand and a knife in the other, which we used to dig dandelions out of the soil. During the months of July and August, dandelions flourished, and hundreds of these flowers dotted the river bank, swaying in the breeze like miniature sunflowers. Families from the neighborhood routinely picked them for salads and other dishes. Just as everyone was about to leave, Tony walked into the kitchen from the bedroom. Mamma paused, and urged him to remain in bed so he could continue resting and get better.

Tony pushed his shoulders back. "But Ma, I feel okay. That sick feeling is gone."

Filomena took his hand. "That can't be, Tony. Please don't think you have to help us pick dandelions."

Gloria took Tony's other hand. "We'll be back in an hour or so. We're just going to get some for tonight and tomorrow, because Zia Maria and Zio Vincenzo are coming with the kids."

Tony pulled his hands away. "But, I'm telling you I feel okay."

Filomena placed her hand on Tony's forehead. "Wow! Your fever is gone."

I felt a surge of relief. "Those herbs worked."

Anna grinned. "We'll have to tell Papa that this time when we mixed the old with the new, the old way worked."

Mamma smiled and glanced at each of us with a sense of victory. "Yes, I'm pleased that this time the old way worked."

On Monday morning, the three gangs from Middletown continued Last Picking in the Riverway Fields. At lunchtime everyone sat at the far end of one of the fields that slopped to clusters of bushes bordering the Connecticut River which quietly rippled south. Boys from each gang sat close together, pulled out some item to eat and immediately began chatting, while scanning the vista before them.

Brian turned to me. "You know I've been thinking about what we got into last week when we were riding home. The more I think about it, the more I agree with you. Because the Irish have been around here since the early 1800's, they think they have completely melted into that American melting pot. The other day, I was talking about this with my dad who said we haven't melted in totally. He and a lot of guys he knows still feel like outsiders."

"Well how about us Blacks," Jimmy Lewis joined in. "We've been around way before you Irish, starting with the slave trade. But we sure as hell have not melted into that pot. Actually, we haven't even been allowed to get near the pot. Even though we aren't slaves anymore, we've got a fence around us. And a big sign on the outside of the fence says, 'KEEP THEM IN THEIR PLACE.' And another sign on the inside of the fence says, 'STAY WHERE YOU BELONG'."

Tom of Jimmy Lewis' gang, who rarely ever said anything, surprised me when he yelled, "Oh yeah, how about this. We just got a letter from my uncle. They live in Kentucky. His son got drafted. He's at Fort Knox getting trained. My uncle said they have separate barracks for colored guys. And most of the white guys won't even go near there."

"That says it all!" exclaimed Adam, another member of Jimmy's gang. "Nothing's changed. When they get killed in battle, do they get killed with different bullets and buried in a separate cemetery? Shit man!"

Billy Lynch suddenly spoke out with anger which was not usual for him. "Well I know the Irish in the army are not in separate barracks. But my father said the other day he went to this big store to see about a job. Even though there was no sign like there used to be that said, 'Irish need not apply,' from the way people talked to him, my father felt he shouldn't apply."

At this point Bart said something that really impressed me. "Never mind army barracks and stores. Look at us. We mostly get along, but we still feel we're different."

Dan O'Neil jumped up "You're right, Bart. Even though I love the pizza you Guineas make, some of that other stuff you

274

guys bring, like that eggplant, really stinks of garlic." Everyone laughed.

"It beats that peanut butter shit you guys eat," Filippo rebutted. The laughter grew louder.

A second later, Joe Harris did something that surprised and impressed me. He slowly passed his right hand over his left arm. "Never mind that peanut butter shit or the stink of garlic. Look at this skin, man. Because we're black, most people don't even want to know what we like to eat or don't like to eat."

Tony also surprised me when he reached into his pocket and took out two nails that were twisted together. "Look at this everybody!"

"What the hell is that?" Jimmy exclaimed. "Don't tell me Wops eat nails too." The crowd burst out laughing.

"Not quite. Instead of arguing about who eats better lunches, how about if we see if you Blacks and you Irish, are as smart as us Sicilians."

"Oh, I get it." Adam called out. "Do you hammer the nail in a guy's head, and if you have to hammer hard it means the guy's head is very thick?" Now everyone slapped someone on the back, while roaring with laughter.

Tony smiled. "No, Adam, I won't hammer the nails in your head. It's more complicated than that." He shared that a couple of months ago, one of our sisters brought this puzzle home and challenged our mother to see if she could figure out how to untangle them. And she did it in a couple of minutes. "I spotted them in the kitchen this morning," Tony added, "so I brought them to see if any of you thick-headed Blacks and Harps are as smart." Tony held the nails up high. "Okay, who's got the guts to step in?" Everyone looked about to see who would accept the challenge, but no one moved.

After a couple minutes Jimmy Lewis slowly stood up and took the nails from Tony's hand. With a touch of drama, he turned, faced the crowd, and carefully held the head of one nail with the thumb and forefinger of one hand, and the head of the other with his other hand. Then he slowly turned and twisted each nail, searching for a solution, with his lower lip sticking out.

275

"This is tougher than I thought." Jimmy glanced at me. "Since I can write now, I know I can do this." I smiled, pushing both of my thumbs up.

"Come on, Jimmy." Brian shouted. "You're a track star. Let your hands do what your feet can do."

Jimmy continued manipulating the nails. Suddenly his face glared with victory. "Hey guys! I think I figured it out!" With a dramatic gesture, he slowly twisted and turned each nail, obviously following a plan. When the nails separated, he raised his arms high and grinned in triumph, with each nail dangling from one of his hands. Everyone applauded.

"Nice going," Tony yelled. "You passed that test. Now, see if you can put them together again."

Jimmy brought his arms down, looked at each nail, and slowly retraced his movements. Gradually he returned the nails to their original positions. Again everyone cheered.

Tony was very pleased with what he started. He grinned and scanned the crowd. "I don't have a watch, but I'm guessing Jimmy took maybe four minutes to figure it out. So is there a four-leaf clover who wants to join the competition?" Everyone looked about wondering who would step in.

Brian Coleman stood up, jerked his head toward his gang, stepped toward Jimmy, and grabbed the nails. Jimmy remained next to Brian, watching him as he slowly twisted the nails. The crowd remained silent for several minutes. Suddenly, Brian held his arms high with one nail in each hand. The crowd screamed.

Jimmy shouted, "Brian, did you do it different?" He pointed to one of the nails. "I think I started here."

"I don't know, Jimmy. I think I untangled this twist first."

Smiling, Bart stepped toward them and said something that really impressed me. "Remember we were talking about how us Sicilians make a big deal about growing up in a *fasciu*, that tight bundle of sticks? Well, I guess a bundle of four-leaf clovers is different from a bundle of black sticks."

"Yeah!" Melo shouted. "And really different then the Sicilian bundle."

Joe Harris jumped up and began jitterbugging, gracefully shuffling his feet and twisting his hips. "The hell with those

276

twisted nails. Let's see if any of you guys can figure out how I'm twisting, and see if you can twist better than me."

Melo jumped next to Joe and slid his feet along the ground, dancing the steps of a tarantella. Jack Kane jumped up and began dancing the Irish Jig.

Bart pointed. "You see! Everybody has their own twist."

"You mean everybody's head is twisted in a different way," Joe Harris gasped while dancing, which triggered another roar of laughter.

Dan O'Neil called out with a tone that captured everyone's attention. "This nail thing, and dance thing, and *fasci* thing shows how hard it is for one guy with his twists to figure out another guy with his twists."

"That's it! You got it!" Tony yelled. "To figure out how you can fit into someone's bundle you have to learn how he's twisted."

I decided to join in and held up one arm to get some attention. "And that takes a long time."

Joe Harris began to jitterbug even faster and laughed. "Well, it's going to take a lot of lessons for anyone to learn these steps. So let me know when you want to start."

"Are you kidding," Jack Kane shouted, thrusting his arm. "I'm not going to give up the Irish Jig."

Melo exaggerated his Tarantella steps. "Well you don't have to give up your dance completely. Let's figure out how to fit that Irish Jig and the Jitterbug into the Tarantella."

"Like Hell!" Joe Harris shouted. "Figure out how to fit that Jig and Tarantella into the Jitterbug."

Dan was still gracefully tapping his feet, with his arms stretched out. "Forget it. The Jig is the only way, so fit your feet in here."

Bart jumped up, pointing at the dancers. "Good luck everybody! At least in this country we can try to weave different dances together." The laughter rolled on for minutes.

The next day in the Central Lot Mr. Kelly gathered the three groups from Middletown. "Mr. Williams decided that since all of you Middletown guys did a good job in the Riverway Fields, you're all assigned the Cromwell Meadows." Then he took me to one side. "I've had a chance to catch a little bit of what you guys have been into at lunch break. It's really great how you're working together."

At noontime, the three gangs again were clustered along one of the fields. Ever since Jimmy Lewis asked me a few weeks ago for help to finish Topping, the three gangs have slowly grown closer together. Like right at this moment, I noticed that a few members from my gang, and from the South End gang, and Brian Coleman's gang were sitting together.

Filippo and Vito, however, were standing side by side about ten yards away. They were playing a game my gang liked to play whenever they had a few minutes during lunch break. Each of them took turns flipping a stone into the distance.

Adam Smith of the South End gang walked over. "What are you guys doing?"

Filippo, who was leaning over, immediately stood up straight. "We're playing *scappeddu*." Several other boys had followed Adam and stood nearby.

Dan O'Neil, who had been eating lunch with Adam, also walked over. "Ska what? I mean some of your Sicilian words sound weird."

Vito inserted himself into the exchange. "Listen, jerk. Say 'sca' like in the beginning of the word scar."

"Sca!" Dan yelled, standing at attention and grinning.

"Very good little boy," Vito smiled. "Now say 'ppe' like in the beginning of the word peck."

"Ppe! Ppe! Ppe!" Dan sounded out, still standing at attention and grinning. By this time all three gangs surrounded Filippo, Vito and Dan, laughing and enjoying what was going on.

Vito patted Dan on the shoulder. "Very, very good, little boy. Now the last sound is spelled 'd' and 'u,' and is exactly like the word 'dew.' You know, like the morning dew."

Dan smiled. "Dew, dew, dew."

"Okay, Dan. You passed the lesson so far. Now you can play the game, if you put those three sounds together. Ready 'sca –

278

ppe – ddu.'" Vito ceremoniously and slowly enunciated the word.

"Sca – ppe – ddu," Dan called out. Everyone burst out laughing and cheered. "Now that I passed the exam, I'm asking you to answer Adam's question. What are you guys doing flinging rocks?"

Vito pointed up the road. "See way over there, we put a rock on the road. It's like home base, and the ground around it has to be kind of flat."

"What's that home base for?" Adam asked.

"That's like the target," Bart joined in. "The guys who are playing put a penny or a nickel on that stone. Whatever everybody decides you have to pay to play."

"Then what?"

"Let's say three or four guys are playing," Vito continued. "After they put their money on the home base stone, they stand about fifteen yards away, or the distance everybody agrees on."

Adam stepped forward with excitement. "And then you fling your rocks at it?"

"Not quite," Filippo responded. "You don't just fling your rocks at home base. First of all, you use a flat rock that you can throw so it hops and skips on the ground. And let's say each guy gets to throw three rocks. The guy who throws a rock that is closest to the home base rock gets the money that's on the rock. But if any one of your rocks hits or touches the home base rock, that rock doesn't count."

"There's one more thing that makes this game extra fun," Vito added. "If somebody's rock is close to home base, and it's your turn next, you can try to knock that rock away by hitting it with your rock."

Filippo grinned with his eyes gleaming. "That's what I really love about *scappeddu*. You get a chance to really whack a guy's rock. It takes a lot of skill to aim your rock and have it skip ahead, and knock a guy's rock away."

"What you guys just described is exactly like the game called *Bocci*. I've seen that game at the state park," Billy Lynch commented. "Except you guys don't roll balls toward a little ball to see who gets closest. You guys flip rocks."

Tony decided to introduce some education about the game. "I often wondered about that. Since the game *scappeddu* came from Sicily, my guess is that because they had a lot of rocks over there, they used rocks."

"They used rocks because they didn't have any balls," Billy Lynch laughed.

Jimmy Lewis screamed. "Are you kidding! If there's any place that had balls, it's Sicily." Everyone laughed. Lately I noticed that not only did guys from each gang sit together at lunch time, but also everyone joined together more easily when there was something to laugh about.

Tony raised his arm, still in the mood to be a teacher and add to everyone's education about this game. "My brothers and sisters and cousins have talked about the name of this game. It is like *Bocci*, but we think Sicilians call it *scappeddu* because that word comes from *scappari* which means 'to flee' or 'get away.' We think the game got its name because you're getting away from having your rock whacked, like Filippo said, and you're going close to the home base rock, where it's safe, and you win."

Adam stepped into the center of the crowd and waved his arms to quiet down everyone. "Hey! I'm the one who asked Vito and Filippo what they were doing. So show me how you skip a rock. I think I'll like this game."

I regretted that I had to stop the fun everyone was having. "Hold it Vito! Lunch time is almost over. But I have an idea. We play *scappeddu* right by the river at the end of William Street. There's a stretch of ground there that's flat."

Adam waved his arm. "I know where that spot is."

I scanned the crowd. "Okay, whoever wants to play, we could meet this Saturday around four o'clock for an hour or so."

"I'll be there," Dan O'Neil declared. "After all, I passed the language test, so I guess you guys will let me into Dago town."

"Very funny," Filippo retorted. "I hope you do show up. Then I can knock your rock off." Everyone kept laughing.

Louie raised the palms of his hands. "Well, I wish I could be there. But I gotta help my uncle get some woodwork finished."

Melo looked frustrated. "I'd love to be there too. But I'm

working Saturday afternoon helping Vecchitto sell *gelato* from his truck."

"Well, whoever can make it, let's meet there, and we'll have a *scappeddu* contest. Everybody who comes should bring three nickels."

That Saturday, in the late afternoon, Tony, Filippo, Bart, Vito, Angelo and I were chatting along the river at the base of Williams Street. "I wonder if any of those guys will show up." Angelo commented.

Bart sounded hopeful. "Even though some of them have never been in this part of town, I'll bet they'll show up."

Filippo pushed his arm out, pointing toward the South End. "Look! Here come Jimmy and Adam."

A minute later Tony pointed toward Main Street. "And look who's walking down William Street! Here come Brian and a couple of his buddies."

When everyone arrived, we greeted each other. Billy Lynch turned his head around and scanned the area. "Well, this is the first time I've been in Dago town. My grandfather lived over that way on William Street when he was a little kid. He said he liked it near the river."

"I've been along here a few times," Adam joined in. "I always like walking near the river."

We turned, faced the river and paused. The water glistened under the bright sun. Dan O'Neil pointed north. "Look! Here comes a barge!"

"My uncle works on one of those loading boxes from the textile mills," Angelo shared. "It's probably headed for Manhattan or Long Island."

Billy Lynch pointed south. "And those guys in that small boat over there must be having fun fishing. I wonder what they're catching."

"They catch a lot of eels this time of year," Vito commented. Each of us continued scanning the river .

Billy Lynch stretched his arm out, slowly moving it from his far left to his right. His blue eyes sparkled, and his expression looked like he was viewing a miracle. "Wow, the river is really beautiful here."

Filippo interrupted. "Okay. Never mind the river. Are you guys up to getting your rocks knocked off?"

I jumped in because I wanted this to be a happy experience for our visitors. "You know what? I've got an idea. Since you guys have never played *scappeddu*, what if each one of you is a partner with one of us Dagos. And my brother Tony can be the referee and measure how far rocks are from the home base rock, and decide who the winner is."

"Santo, it works out," Bart commented with excitement. "There are three Irish guys and two black guys. That means each of us five garlic balls gets either a four-leaf clover or a chocolate bar for a partner."

Adam laughed. "Santo, I know you're the straw boss of the Fast Gang, but I didn't know you were the boss in Dago town."

Bart stared at Adam with a look that said more than his words. "You gotta be kidding. Somebody's got to decide how things go, or we'll get nowhere. So as long as you're in Dago town, follow orders from Santo."

"Yes sir!" Adam stood at attention and gave Bart a military salute.

Tony realized that Adam's saluting could have bothered Bart because his older brother was in the army, which upsets his parents a lot. "Let's quit the joking. Since I'm the referee, did you guys bring your nickels?" They nodded and reached into their pockets. "Brian, we'll start with you. Flip one of your nickels to the ground. If it comes up tails you'll be Bart's partner. If it comes out heads you'll be Vito's partner."

Brian flipped his nickel. "Oh, Vito, I guess you're stuck with me."

"No," Vito grinned. "I think we can really kick ass now." The others took turns flipping a coin and forming partnerships.

Tony continued playing the part of a referee. "Okay guys, the teams are set. Let the tournament begin. We brought rocks for you guys since you never played before. Each guy throws two rocks." Then he announced that he will now flip a coin to see which team goes first. "Okay, here it goes. I'll start with Filippo and Dan. Heads you go first, tails you go last." Tony flipped the coin.

"Tails!" Filippo screamed with glee. "Dan, do you realize that you and I can now really kick the rocks off these guys so they don't make it to home base."

Tony turned to Bart and Billy Lynch. "If I flip heads you go first; tails you go fourth." Tony flipped the coin. "Heads it is."

Bart reassured Billy, reminding him that the aim of the game isn't to knock a guy's rock off, but it's to get your rock close to home base. "So with the first shot, we'll have a good chance to do that because no one will be in our way."

"We'll see," Filippo laughed. "I hope you're wearing protection where it counts." Everyone laughed.

Tony assigned each of the remaining partners a place in the lineup, and set the home base rock with its coins at the far end of the strip. "Let's get started."

Bart stepped to the line Tony had scratched in the dirt. "Look Billy, watch me."

Billy Lynch and the other visitors looked nervous. I rushed to Bart's side. "Wait! Let's make this first round practice. These guys never played before."

Bart nodded and continued demonstrating, flipping the rock, as if he were throwing a discus or Frisbee. It soared through the air, skipped across the ground, and flopped to a stop about twelve inches from the home base rock. He looked up at Filippo and grinned. "How about that?"

Filippo gasped. "Damn it! That's really good. Let's see if you stay there when it's my turn. I hope I can send your rock in the river."

Dan tried very hard to throw his rock the way Bart demonstrated, and each boy took a turn. Everyone watched with interest, as each rock slammed to the ground, sliding to a stop. When it came to Filippo's turn, there were two rocks close to home base. Bart's was still the closest. With much ceremony, he took a long look at the home base and threw his rock which flipped up and down a few inches above ground directly toward Bart's rock, obviously his target, then over Bart's rock, stopping about two feet from the home base rock. Disappointed, Filippo stood up and looked at Bart. "You won, man."

"Filippo, that was great!" Dan screamed. "My rock almost flipped in the river. I can say the word, *scappeddu*, but I need more practice with this game."

"And mine landed four feet in front of home base," Adam joined in. "I need more practice too." For the next hour, we continued playing, enjoying the competition, and harassing each other.

On Wednesday evening of that week, while my family was sharing dinner, Filomena tightened the grip on her fork and stared at Anna. It was obvious she was nervous and had something very important on her mind. She looked at Mamma, turned and took a long look at Papa. "Mamma, Papa, I have something to ask you."

Mamma also noticed that Filomena seemed nervous because she answered with a very reassuring tone. "*Chi è, figghia mia?*" ("What is it my daughter?")

"While I was walking on Main Street on my way home, I ran into a girl I go to college with."

Anna tapped the palm of her left hand on the table. "Who was that, Elizabeth, the one who lives up there on High Street?" With the word 'high,' she pushed the fork she was holding in her right hand toward the ceiling.

"No, it was Allison Pickett. I've mentioned her a few times to you."

"The one whose father teaches at Wesleyan University, up there?" Now Anna emphasized the words 'up there' with sarcasm, and again jabbed her fork toward the ceiling.

"Yes, that's the one."

Mamma quickly stepped in to prevent an argument from starting. Everyone in the family was familiar with the fact that, for some reason, Anna had some kind of prejudice about Filomena's friends who lived in the American district. "*Pir piaciri dimmi na cosa.*" ("Please tell me what you are wondering.")

Filomena glanced at Mamma and Papa, and then took a long look at Anna. "This girl, Allison, would like to visit here this Saturday before we go back to school in a few weeks. Maybe she would even like to stay overnight."

Anna glared at Filomena. "What! Why would she want to mix with us?"

Papa glanced at Anna, held the palm of his hand up. "*Basta* (Enough)." Then he nodded at Filomena.

"*Scusami, Mamma, mi vogghiu spiegari.*" ("Excuse me, Mom, I want to explain.") "I realize that Anna does not like people who live in the American district, up there on the hill, as she likes to say. But this Allison, *è brava e di cori sinceru*". ("is good and has an honest heart")

Gloria slapped the back of her hands on the table and turned, pushing her face within inches of Filomena's. "She even wants to stay overnight? Isn't that strange? She doesn't know us, and we don't know her."

"And she isn't even Italian, "Anna barked. "What is she anyway?"

Filomena took a deep breath. "I believe her background is British. But anyway, she's fifth or sixth generation. So she thinks of herself as American. I haven't noticed her bringing up her ancestors."

I was surprised when Gloria's tone became softer. "That's interesting that she wants to visit us. How did that happen?"

Filomena glanced at Gloria, stared at Anna and explained that she and Allison attended several of the same classes during the spring semester and became friends. Allison was intrigued that Filomena was from a Sicilian immigrant family, because she was very interested in Italian history and culture. "Actually," Filomena added with a broad smile, "she's also very interested in Italian food."

"Is she fat?" Tony asked. Everyone laughed, and Teodoro slapped his belly.

"No, Tony, she's tall and has a really nice figure. Anyway, when she learned that Mamma and Papa were from Sicily, she mentioned several times that she would like to visit us. Besides, she was on campus when you guys took me there two years ago, standing with that bunch of girls who watched us carry my stuff into the dorm. Remember?"

"I'll never forget," Tony mumbled. "I felt like I was in a different country." What Tony just said captured the way I felt when I went with everyone to help Filomena move into Teachers College.

Teodoro leaned over, pressing his chest on the table top and staring at his sisters across the table. "That's what Tony told me when all of you got back. Remember Ma? You said you felt like you were on Ellis Island again."

Gloria yelled, sweeping her hand over the table. "Everybody was staring at us, Teodoro! The looks on their faces made me feel like they were saying 'What the hell are you doing here?' And I heard some of them mumble nasty things!"

Filomena was now very upset. "If anyone did, Allison wasn't one of them. She continued at a very rapid pace trying to set Allison apart from other students who had looked at us with disgust and occasionally mumbled some ethnic slur. Filomena shared that Allison remembered us walking back and forth from the dorm to the truck Papa borrowed, carrying all those packages of food Mamma had wrapped up in that thick, brown paper, and other things wrapped in cloth and tied with a rope. She was especially fascinated because Filomena came with more food than clothes.

"Well, I was fascinated by how different all those girls smelled when we walked by them," Gloria joined in, grinning. "Remember, Filomena, when you came home for the Christmas vacation, you said everybody at school smelled different, and we couldn't stop laughing."

Tony pushed his arm across the table toward Gloria. "Wait a minute. I don't know why we're talking about how they smelled. What I'm wondering is, if this Allison stays overnight, where is she going to sleep."

Filomena clutched her hands together, glaring back and forth at Anna and Gloria. "She can sleep in my bed. Gloria can sleep with Anna." There were two beds in the girls' bedroom. Filomena and Gloria shared a bed, and Anna had a bed of her own.

"And what about you, Filomena?"

"I can sleep on that mattress we keep under Anna's bed for when our cousins stay over."

Anna's eyes now told everyone she was on fire. She slammed her fist against the table. "But if she stays overnight, there's another problem. Zio Gaetano and Zia Concetta are supposed to come over Sunday with their kids. Right, Mamma?" Mamma nodded, glanced at each of us, and I couldn't figure out what she felt about this stranger visiting.

All through this discussion, Papa had been watching with his arms folded. When Anna brought up that our cousins were visiting, he slowly raised the palms of his hands, staring straight ahead. We were familiar with this gesture and the expression on his face which declared, "Enough, stop bickering," and commented. "It's obvious all of you are nervous about Filomena's friend visiting." He continued, sharing a personal experience. When he enters the office of the police department, and finds himself in the middle of all those Irish policemen, sometimes he feels like he's in a different country, similar to what Tony said he felt when he was at Teachers College. He realizes that when he is working as a supernumerary police officer, he should find out how he can fit his old ways with new ways that are all around him. After taking a long look at Mamma, he grinned and waved his arms to include all the space around us. "If this Allison stays overnight, and Zio Gaetano and Zia Concetta arrive on Sunday with their kids, this whole kitchen will be the coliseum, and all of you gladiators can fight about how to fit old ways with new ways." We exploded with laughter.

That Saturday afternoon, Filomena and Allison walked into our apartment. Mamma and Gloria were folding clothes, and Anna was spreading out a tablecloth. "Hey everyone, this is Allison Pickett," Filomena called out. Tony, Teodoro and I were playing a card game, called *scopa*, in our bedroom. Without saying a word, we peered into the kitchen, wondering how things would turn out. Filomena seemed really nervous as she pointed to each person in the kitchen. "This is my mother, this is Anna, and this is Gloria."

Mamma and Gloria stopped folding clothes, looked at Allison and nodded. Anna continued carefully adjusting the tablecloth. "Hi." Then she stood up, stared at Allison, and slowly reached out to shake her hand.

I was surprised, and also pleased, that Allison seemed calm. She smiled, reached out and took Anna's hand. "Hi. I've heard so much about you."

Mamma's way of welcoming Allison was to focus immediately on the menu for the evening. She turned to Filomena, "*Vogghiu fari la spisa.*" (I would like to make dinner.")

"What did your mother say?" Allison asked.

Filomena anxiously grabbed Allison's hand. "She wants to make dinner. I'm sure she's nervous about whether you'll like what she might prepare."

Mamma glanced back and forth at Allison and Filomena, "*Per pranzo pozzu fari scungilli, pasta cu sugu, e stemperata di pollo.*"

Filomena turned to Allison, "She could make fresh conches for an appetizer, then pasta with fresh tomato sauce and..."

Allison pressed her hand on Filomena's arm. "That's wonderful your mom speaks in Italian. What's the last thing she mentioned? It sounded like stampede?"

"Well, Allison, my Mom is speaking the Sicilian dialect not Italian. The word is not stampede the word is *stemperata.*" Filomena pronounced the word very slowly and continued with a nervous grin. "We don't eat horses that are stampeding. *Stemperata di pollo* is made with pieces of chicken, eggplants, green peppers, olives, capers, chopped celery, garlic and olive oil. You can also make *stemperata di coniglio* which has rabbit instead of chicken."

Mamma stepped in again still anxious about how to make Allison feel welcomed. "*Filomena, posso fare anche la bruschetta, e cotolette di vitello con funghi.*"

"My mother just said she could also make bruschetta which is a slice of homemade bread rubbed with freshly ground green peppers, garlic and olive oil and grilled over a fire until it's crispy. And she could also make veal cutlets grilled with mushrooms."

"Wow! That's also great! I hope she's not doing that just for me. My mother usually makes a meatloaf and mashed potatoes."

Filomena jerked her head back and forth. "Oh no, we have something like that every night. You know how we Sicilians are. Actually, I think all Italians are really into having delicious meals. They're a big part of life."

Allison pressed her hand on Filomena's arm. "Please tell your mother any of what she mentioned would be great. "

Filomena conveyed to Mamma what Allison said, and urged her not to worry.

Anna and Gloria had been listening and watching with intense interest. Anna has always been very direct, so what she said at this moment didn't surprise me or my brothers. She pushed her shoulders back, turned toward Allison and declared. "I can tell you're not faking. I think you're being real about liking what our Mom just said."

With a shy grin Gloria decided to join in because she felt safe with Anna by her side. "Me too, Allison, I get the feeling you're not faking that you like to be here."

Allison's jaw sagged slightly as she looked back and forth at Anna and Gloria. "Well, uh, gee. I don't know why you were wondering if I was faking."

Now that everything was out in the open, Filomena decided that enough of Allison's introduction had taken place and grabbed her hand. "I'd like to show Allison the neighborhood. I hope that's okay, because I won't be able to help prepare dinner."

Anna pointed to the door. "Absolutely, be sure to take her to Joe-the-Jew's store. Allison, when you go there, you're going to see all these different cheeses and salamis hanging from the ceiling, and barrels of olives, and other stuff."

Allison quickly passed her fingers several times through her hair. "Thanks, Anna and Gloria." Then she reached out and gave Mamma a hug. "Thank you."

Anna stared at Filomena and Allison as they left the apartment. "Gloria, she isn't what I expected. She feels real."

"I agree. I don't feel her like some of those Waspy girls I run into in school who think they're everything, and we're nothing but garlic balls."

At this moment Tony, Teodoro and I stepped into the kitchen. Gloria quickly turned toward us. "You should have come in sooner. You missed meeting Filomena's friend."

"We wanted to finish our *scopa* game," Tony replied.

I did not want to let on that we had spied from our bedroom

and overheard the whole thing. "What was she like?"

Anna grinned. "Okay. I mean nice. She turned out to be better than I thought she'd be. Let's see what you guys think of her when you get a chance to be with her at dinner time."

A couple of hours later, Filomena and Allison returned. Mamma turned to Allison and gestured to Papa, Tony, Teodoro and me. "*Chistu è me maritu e chisti sunu i me figghi.*"

Filomena immediately translated. "This is my husband, and these are my sons." Each of us shook Allison's hand.

Mamma looked at everyone and announced, "*E' ura di mangiari.*" ("It's time to eat.")

Everyone took their usual seats. This evening Allison was tucked in between Anna and Filomena. Following another family ritual, Papa reached out and took Tony's left hand with his right hand and Anna's right hand with his left hand. At the same time, Mamma reached out taking Gloria's hand and Teodoro's hand. In the same way, all of us took the hands of the persons on our left and right. Allison looked around confused and glanced at her hands. Filomena coached her whispering, "We're holding hands to make a circle."

"Come on Allison, give me your hand." Anna's warm tone and smile confirmed that she really liked Allison. Allison smiled and took Anna's hand, giving it a warm squeeze. Still smiling, she turned and with her right hand took hold of Filomena's.

Now that everyone had joined hands, forming a circle around the table, Papa whispered, "*Famigghia*" (Sicilian dialect for family). All of us looked at Allison and smiled, showing how pleased we were that she had joined us..

Papa lined up glasses that had been set on the table to repeat his ritual of carefully measuring a certain amount of wine in each by placing his fingers against the side of the glass. When he reached Allison's, he asked if she would like a mouthful of homemade wine.

Allison quickly placed her clutched hand on her lips, coughing. "Well, uh, at home my parents don't drink wine during meals, but they do drink different cocktails before dinner and especially after."

Anna immediately tried to rescue her. "Allison, of course you don't have to have some wine. That won't bother us. It's just that we always have wine at dinner. And you see that kids, like Teodoro, just get a couple of mouthfuls."

Allison paused, scanned the glasses, and a smile swept across her face. "Thanks, Anna, I'm with you." She turned to Papa. "Yes, please, I would love to taste some of your wine."

With a dramatic gesture, Papa placed two fingers against the glass, slowly dripped wine into it, and slid the glass in front of Allison. "*Allora, mangiamu.*" (Okay then, let's eat.)

Everyone began eating and chatting. Anna turned to Allison with a grin, "*Ccà si mangia, ma non franco.*" Everyone burst out laughing.

Allison was about to place a piece of chicken in her mouth, but lowered her fork and turned to Filomena.. "What did your sister say?"

"She said here one eats, but not for free."

"I just want you to know your parents are going to get a bill for this delicious meal." Again everyone laughed.

Allison joined in. "My parents will be happy to pay the bill."

Mamma smiled at Allison, "*Mangia, mangia. Ti vogghiu vidiri mangiari.*" ("Eat, eat. I want to see you eat.")

When Filomena translated what Mamma just said, Allison picked up her fork, began feasting and exclaimed, "Delicious, delicious."

As everyone continued eating, several conversations were going on at the same time. At one point Anna whispered to Gloria, "I'm telling you for the last time, we can finish the rest of the laundry tomorrow."

At the same moment Tony turned and stared at me. "I'm certain I left my jack knife on top of the bureau. You gotta look in your drawer."

Teodoro grabbed Tony's hand. "Never mind the knife. I told you on our way home it was an accident. I didn't kick your shoe in the river on purpose. "

"Forget it, Teodoro," Tony barked. "If Papa says I have to pay for the shoe you're gonna pay."

When Tony, Teodoro and I were by the river earlier that day, we took our shoes off, as usual, and set them by some rocks. We always enjoyed walking bare foot while looking at birds flying overhead, and skidding rocks over the water. Today, Teodoro must have accidentally kicked one of Tony's shoes into the river.

Allison leaned over and whispered to Filomena, "What's everyone fighting about?"

"Allison, no one is fighting. They're just arguing. Maybe it looks like fighting to you."

Anna happened to overhear what Allison asked. "Allison, you've got a lot to learn about us. What's it like at dinner time at your house?"

"Well we pretty much sit quietly, and if my parents ask me about school or something, I'll answer them. Mostly, I listen to their conversation about the news or books they're reading."

"Sometimes we Sicilians look like we're fighting," Anna added, "but we're just having a discussion with all our feelings pouring out. It takes time to learn the difference between when we're fighting and when we're discussing."

Tony picked up a piece of grilled eggplant with his fingers and began nibbling on it, while holding another piece of eggplant with his fork.

Filomena immediately noticed. "Tony! Don't eat with your fingers! You know that's the old way and poor manners! That's what forks are for!"

Tony held his fork up high with one hand to dramatically display one piece of eggplant. At the same time, he chewed on the other piece with the fingers of his other hand. "Filomena, see, I'm just trying to fit in the old ways with new ways." We all burst out laughing, and Anna, Gloria, Teodoro and I immediately imitated Tony. I was thrilled when Allison did the same while she grinned, showing her beautiful smile.

Gloria reached up and touched Allison's hand which was holding a piece of chicken. "You're becoming one of us."

"And I love it. I just have to learn some of those Sicilian words and how to cook these delicious meals."

"Not quite, you're almost one of us," Anna chuckled. "I

haven't seen you take a sip of wine yet."

Grinning, Papa raised his glass toward Allison and everyone did the same. Allison glanced up and down at her glass, slowly moving her hand toward it. When she picked it up, everyone shouted "Salute!" Allison slowly moved her glass to her lips and took a sip.

Filomena placed her hand on Allison's shoulder and pointed across the table. "Look, even Teodoro is showing that he's beginning to fit new ways in with old ways, just like you are"

Teodoro stared at Filomena. "What do you mean? I'm eating with my fingers too, just like you guys."

Filomena grinned. "Teodoro you have a napkin on your lap. You did not tuck it around your neck like you usually do." Chuckling, she added, "When we sat down I saw you watching Allison, and when she stretched her napkin on her lap, you did the same. You've never done that before, so you're imitating her."

"*Maravigghia*! (wonderful) *Salute*!" Papa again raised his glass. Everyone raised a glass and echoed the salutation, smiling and glancing at Teodoro and Allison..

Later, while dessert was being served, Anna mumbled, "So Allison, have you decided to stay overnight?" Allison clutched her napkin with her left hand, holding the tip of a *cannolu* with her other hand inches from her mouth.

Filomena asked Allison with a very reassuring tone, "What did you decide?"

"Well, uh, I don't know. I did bring my bag but ..." Searching for clues, she looked across the table into the eyes of the boys, and then looked at Gloria's and Anna's expressions. "So I think it would be nice to stay over, but then I keep remembering things I have to get done at home and ..."

Anna placed her hand on Allison's, while her other hand was still holding a *cannolu* inches from her mouth. Anna and Allison turned toward each other so that their faces were only inches apart, and the tip of the *cannolu* Allison held was almost touching Anna's lips. Anna smiled, and a smile slowly crept across Allison's face. "You know, Filomena, I think the stuff I need to do can wait. I'd love to stay overnight."

Tony grinned. "Well, I better get the swords ready for all of us gladiators. Zio Gaetano and Zia Concetta are coming tomorrow with Alberto, Isabella and Olivia. So this place will definitely become a coliseum."

Teodoro sat up straight in his chair and raised his arm. "And if Zio Vito and Zia Felicia come by with Sofia, huge battles will definitely go on all day."

Confused, Allison turned to Filomena.

Filomena patted Allison's hand. "It's a family joke."

Anna took hold of Allison's shoulders, turned her around so they faced each other, and playfully jiggled her. "When our cousins arrive, you're going to get another big taste of who we are, and maybe some of them will place their napkins on their laps like Teodoro did.

After I had introduced myself to the Italian prisoners at the farm, during the weeks that followed, I discussed various jobs with them on several occasions. Whenever I interacted with them, they seemed like the young men in my neighborhood, a number of whom had already been drafted into the United States military. In my discussions with Nunzio and Mario, one of the things I learned is that they were very dissatisfied with the food they were being fed. The reason why became very clear when I walked over to the prisoners' compound at the end of one day to chat for a minute. Nunzio and Mario spotted me and walked over to the fence followed by other prisoners.

I raised my arm, "*Comu stai?*" ("How are things going?")

Nunzio stepped close to the barbed wired fence and showed me what he was holding in his hand. "Remember I told you we hate the food they give us? This is one of the things. I can't eat it."

I stared in disbelief. Nunzio was holding a peanut butter and jelly sandwich. What was even worse, the peanut butter and jelly were spread between two slices of thin, soft, very white bread, what everyone in my neighborhood called, "American bread."

"*E' comu mangiari merda!*" ("It's like eating shit!") added Nunzio.

The whole thing didn't make sense to me, and for a moment my head froze. "*Maronna*! Let's see what we can do for you guys."

I returned to the Central Lot and asked one of the foremen to learn whether Mr. Williams would see me for a minute. The foreman entered the Main Cabin and seconds later poked his head out from the doorway and waved to me. I entered and explained to Mr. Williams why the prisoners were very dissatisfied with the food they were being fed, like peanut butter sandwiches. I struggled to find a way of making a convincing case. "Mr. Williams, I think they would do a much better job in the fields and sheds if they are given some Italian food."

Mr. Williams immediately made clear to me he could not deal with the issue. "Sorry. It's none of our business. What they eat is being taken care of by the military. Our job is to give them work."

My jaw sagged, and suddenly I felt angry. "Mr. Williams, that doesn't make sense!" But then I clenched my teeth and said to myself, "*omertà, omertà*". I thanked Mr. Williams for seeing me and walked out of the cabin.

When Tony and I arrived home, we shared what the prisoners were eating for lunch. Everyone was shocked and wondered how those men could survive. After dinner, my parents talked to other parents in the neighborhood who had already learned from their sons the predicament the prisoners faced. The neighborhood was buzzing with the reminder that the food one eats was a critical part of life.

The next day when my gang and I arrived at the Central Lot, Mr. George happened to be standing on the road leading to the prisoners' compound. Even though I regretted the bad luck we were facing, I thought we should continue our mission. I approached him. "A few of my gang are going with me to the compound for a minute to see if the prisoners need any help with the jobs they got today."

Apparently from the looks on our faces, and that we were carrying boxes, Mr. George realized that we were covering up something. "What do you guys have in those boxes? They don't look like anything that has to do with their work here." In the cardboard boxes we carried were stuffed many items prepared by our mothers and other mothers of the neighborhood.

Bart tightened his grip on the cardboard boxes he was holding under each arm. "Oh, we're just bringing them a few things."

Tony also clutched his boxes. "Yeah, you know like pieces of soap and stuff."

I stepped toward the compound, hoping to continue our mission, but Mr. George growled. "Wait! Stand right there, Santo! All you're supposed to do is explain jobs to them, not bring them soap and stuff." While barking at us, he quickly flipped open the lid of a box Angelo was holding, and of a box Melo was holding. "What the hell! Are you guys nuts! You're bringing them food? These guys are prisoners. They're the enemy of the United States! Beat it!"

I glared at Mr. George. "For you they're the enemy. Not for us. And I don't know of any rule that says we can't give them some food, and ..."

"Santo!" Mr. George growled again. "Maybe Mr. Williams won't care, but I do. For me, those Wops are the enemy. I'm warning you, if you take that food to them, the rest of the summer is going to be hell for you and your gang."

What Mr. George just said, and how he said it, made me feel that he was the enemy, and we had to deal with this challenge. I tucked a box under my left arm, extended the index finger of each hand toward my friends, and placed them side by side, expressing a message in Italian body language they all knew very well. I slowly turned away from Mr. George and walked toward the Central Lot with my friends clustered around me.

"What a jerk," Bart whispered. "He talked about our paisani as if they were rotten, no good shit."

Tony mumbled with a troubled expression. "For God sake, those guys are not the enemy; they're just like our older brothers and cousins. And some of our cousins, like Lucky, gave up their lives for this country."

Angelo placed his hand on my shoulder. "We really have to figure out how we can outsmart that jerk."

Tony stepped in front of me. "Yeah, Santo. But we're all going to use *omertà*, right?" Everyone nodded.

As we entered the Central Lot, I stopped and stared into the distance for a moment. "I've got an idea."

Tony turned his head in the direction I was staring. "Are you looking at Mr. Kelly over there?"

"Yes. I'm going to ask him for help. I think we can trust him."

Tony pushed his fist forward. "I know we can trust him."

I walked toward Mr. Kelly with my friends close behind. Mr. Kelly must have noticed expressions on our faces. "What's the matter? Is one of your gang hurt?" I quickly described what just happened with Mr. George.

"My God!" Bart exclaimed. "Why would he want to give us a hard time the rest of the summer if we give them food? Those prisoners are like cousins. He's the enemy not them!"

Mr. Kelly placed his hand on Bart's shoulder. "I'm embarrassed. You know how some people in this country feel these days about the Italians, Germans and Japanese who live in this country. Even though they belong here, some people feel they're the enemy."

Bart sighed. "We got plenty of shit from a lot of kids at school this past year."

Mr. Kelly placed his hand on his chin and took a long look at us. "But like you said, Bart, the Italian prisoners we have here are like cousins for you guys. I don't blame you for wanting to give them food they'll enjoy. But I'm worried, because we all know Mr. George can find a lot of ways to make you miserable, if he catches you giving them food." He raised his head and stared in the direction of the prisoners' compound. The look on his face gave me a surge of hope. "I think there might be a way we can handle this."

We glanced at each other. Tony took a deep breath. "Thanks for the offer. What do you have in mind, Mr. Kelly?"

"Here's a plan." Mr. Kelly explained that a big section of one of the fields in the Riverway needs a lot of posts set back up, because the huge rainstorm that occurred last weekend loosened some of them. He added that since it involves a big project, he must ask Mr. George to check it out before anything is done. "Instead of driving him out there tomorrow, I'm going to ask him to come with me now. So while I take him to the Riverway

Fields, you guys can go to the prisoners' compound."

Melo spread out his arms as if he had just received a present. "Gee, that's great."I shook Mr. Kelly's hand and so did Tony, Bart and Angelo.

Suddenly, Mr. Kelly said, "There's only one catch."

Angelo spun around, confused. "Hey! What's the catch? I thought you wanted to help us."

I had no idea what Mr. Kelly had in mind, and I stood very still, as mixed up as Angelo.

Tony solved the problem. "Angelo, the eyes always tell the truth. Look, he's kidding."

What Tony just said helped me notice the sparkle in Mr. Kelly's eyes. "I'm guessing you want us to bring you some of this delicious Italian food. You mentioned how you and your family like to go to Listrino's restaurant in the North End."

Mr. Kelly chuckled,"Very good, Santo. You guys can pay me on another day." Then his tone became serious. "Stand over there behind that cabin and wait until you see me drive off with Mr. George."

We jogged over to the cabin and stood in a row with our backs along the wall. I peered around the corner a couple of times, and after several minutes, spotted Mr. Kelly and Mr. George in a pickup truck. "There they go."

We quickly ran toward the prisoners' compound, and I called for Mario and Nunzio. When they rushed out of the shed, I quietly explained in Sicilian, "Pretend you're asking me to explain something." While other prisoners milled about, and Mario and Nunzio asked me and my friends several questions, we passed the food to them.

Mario opened one box that was handed to him and whispered, "*Marone! Bruschette!*" (Slices of homemade bread grilled over a fire until crispy and rubbed with garlic, olive oil and freshly ground pepper.) At the same time Nunzio opened another box and exclaimed, "*Cotolette di vitello con funghi!*" (Veal cutlets with mushrooms).

The other prisoners had crowded around Mario and Nunzio, sighing with excitement as if they had just won a huge prize in a casino. Nunzio opened two boxes in which were containers and exclaimed in disbelief, "*Pasta con salsa di pomodoro!*" (Spaghetti with fresh tomato sauce). Gasping, Mario opened another box. "*Capunata!*" (an appetizer of pieces of eggplant grilled on bread). At the same time Nunzio opened another box and exclaimed "*Schiacciata con arugula!*" (Pizza stuffed with arugula and sun dried tomatoes). Other boxes contained fried calamari. While all of this was going on, prisoners quietly exclaimed, "*Roba della mia mamma!*" (My mother's nurture), "*E nu pastu beddu!*" (It's a wonderful meal), "*Ora iu' mangiu mangiu!*" (Now I eat, eat).

Later that day when Tony and I returned home from the farm and stepped into the kitchen, we froze at the entrance. Mamma was kneeling on the floor, sobbing in Papa's arms, surrounded by our sisters and Teodoro. More than that, our apartment was crowded with our aunts, uncles and cousins. Filomena turned and called out to Tony and me. "We got a letter. Mamma's mother got killed." Tony and I immediately flopped to the floor and joined everyone.

A letter had arrived from a relative in Sicily informing us that Mamma's mother, whom none of us children had ever seen but had heard a great deal about, was killed early in July about a week after the armies of the United States, Britain and Canada swept across Sicily, battling Nazi forces. The letter went on to say that when the invasion was underway, most of the peasants left the village and settled in caves located along nearby mountain slopes. One day, because it seemed as if allied forces had passed through on their way to Messina, Mamma's mother ventured toward the village to obtain some water. On her way, she was suddenly caught in crossfire.

Mamma gradually composed herself, turned and reached out to her sister, Maria, who was kneeling a few feet away, crying in the arms of her husband, Vincenzo, with her daughter Maria *Nica* (small Maria) at her side. Their two sons had also been drafted into the military. Still on their knees, Mamma and Aunt Maria moved toward each other and embraced. Then they slowly wobbled up on their feet and sat in nearby chairs. Relatives insisted that Mamma and Aunt Maria remain seated while they prepared food for everyone. In the meantime my sisters, brothers and I, and Maria *Nica*, gathered in the girl's bedroom. Minutes later Papa walked in reminding us that our grandmother will speak to us in a few months on the morning of November second.

He was referring to an ancient custom followed by Sicilian families. November second was the feast of all souls, *La Notte dei Morti*, when Sicilians celebrated the memories of family members who had passed away. On the evening before this feast day, viewed by many as the most joyous night of the year, children placed their shoes outside, near the entrance to where they lived. According to tradition, sometime after midnight deceased ancestors placed items in these shoes to communicate with the children. The items typically included trinkets, bracelets, or pieces of knitted cloth which contained particular designs, all associated in some way with ancestors. Items also included a piece of candy made with sesame seeds, or almonds, and other treats.

On the morning of November second, children rushed outside, examined what they found in their shoes, and engaged in discussions about what the deceased relatives were telling them with the items. Since family members frequently discussed deceased relatives, children interpreted the meanings of the items they found in their shoes in terms of these stories. Of course, the items were placed in the shoes by parents. Typically children younger than nine years believed that ancestors left the items. Although older children knew that their parents had placed the items in the shoes, they still used the event as an opportunity to share memories of experiences with the deceased, or what they had heard about them.

Mamma, Aunt Maria and Uncle Vincenzo walked into the bedroom. Mamma thanked us for the support and love and added that she was reassured by the fact that her other sister, who had remained in Sicily, and her sister's husband, would be able to take care of her father. Then, as Papa had already done, she reminded us that we will hear from our grandmother on the Feast of All Souls.

Anna placed her hands on each side of Mamma's face and leaned toward her. "Mamma, we don't have to wait until November. We're going to keep hearing from *Nanna* (grandmother, Sicilian dialect) Mariuzza. You know, us girls and you are always talking to her when we're cooking with you or cleaning the apartment."

Anna was referring to a custom my sisters and Mamma frequently followed. While they were engaged in some chore, and one of them asked Mamma a question, she shared her thoughts. Then, sometimes, she commented, "Let's see what your grandmother thinks about that?" Mamma would pause, look up, and express aloud her mother's opinion about the issue that had been raised.

"Yes, Mamma," Filomena added, "We learned a lot from your mother."

Maria *Nica* hugged her mother. "And I can't wait to hear what she has to say to us in November."

Staring at the floor, Teodoro whispered, "And we're going to hear from Lucky too."

Tony glanced at Papa. "And maybe Papa's mother and father will tell us what they think about all of this."

Mamma looked with devotion into the face of each of us. "Yes, all of this has to do with fitting old ways that are good with the new ways of America."

Aunt Maria wiped tears from her cheeks with the back of her hand. "Keeping dead relatives alive by talking about them, and trying to figure out their opinions, is a very good custom."

Uncle Vincenzo rarely said anything unless it had to do with growing vegetables, which he loved to do. I was surprised, therefore, when he added a comment immediately after his wife spoke. "And Sebastiano and I often talk about how that custom helps everyone keep the old ways alive and figure out how to fit them in with new ways."

I ran into the boys' bedroom, returned in seconds and turned to Papa. "It's definitely alive in all of us." I held out my hand with my palm spread open. "Here's that rock you brought from your village that was on the ground near the spot where your parents died. Sometimes when I hold it, I get ideas that really help with what I'm wondering."

Everyone spontaneously formed a circle, and engaged in a group hug.

Mamma whispered, "*è ura di mangiari a robba di me mamma*" ("it's time to eat the essence of my mother").

The next day when Tony and I arrived from the farm, I walked into the kitchen with my head hanging low and didn't acknowledge anyone. I realized I must have looked strange, but for some reason could not do anything about it. I mumbled, "I'm going to take a quick bath," and stepped into the bathroom. While I got ready to wash up, I stood near the door so I could hear them talking..

Gloria asked Tony, "What's the matter with Santo? He didn't say Hi to anyone."

Anna mumbled, "He seems really down. Or is he all wrapped up in his head again?"

Tony tried to explain. "All day at the farm he seemed to be somewhere else. Once Mr. George, the big field boss, had to yell a bunch of times before Santo walked over to see what he wanted. Even the guys in our gang noticed it."

Filomena stepped into the kitchen from the girl's bedroom because she must have overheard the conversation. "I wonder if it's the letter we got about our grandmother getting killed."

Now Tony was irritated. "Filomena, I already asked him a couple of times today. But I never got any answer."

Papa, who had arrived earlier than usual, was also sitting in the kitchen when I walked in, scanning the newspaper. "When he walked in I noticed he was really different. Let's wait to see if he gives us some idea about what's going on."

I began taking a bathtub and could not hear what else they were saying for several minutes. When I stepped out of the bathroom, and walked toward the boys' bedroom, I noticed Papa nodding to everyone in the kitchen, asking them to wait before saying anything.

After Tony took his bath, he came into our bedroom. While getting dressed, he tried to engage me a couple of times, but I ignored him. I still had too much on my mind, and felt disappointed in myself. Tony left the bedroom, and Mamma announced it was time for dinner. Everyone took their seats, but I remained in the bedroom.

I could hear them mumbling and wondering why I didn't join them. Tony decided to come to my rescue. "I'll get him," he announced with determination. I was sitting on the edge of the bed holding that large stone that Papa had given me. "Santo, it's time to eat, you know. And why are you holding your Sicilian stone?"

At first I felt very annoyed, but then realized he wanted to help me in some way, so I set the stone on the bedside table and whispered, "Okay, Tony." I stood up, slowly walked into the kitchen, and sat in my chair.

Mamma immediately turned to me. She was always eager to help anyone of us when it looked like we're in trouble. "*Ch'è successu*, Santo?" ("What's the matter Santo?")

I wanted to share some of what was on my mind but then, for some reason, I pulled back. "Ma, let's eat first. Okay?"

Mamma nodded, served the food, and everyone began eating and chatting. But I did not join any of the conversations. When fruit and nuts were served for dessert, Papa turned, stretched his right arm past Tony and placed his hand on mine, just as I was about to pick up a peach, "Do you feel ready now to share what's on you mind?"

I stared at Papa and saw that expression in his eyes urging me to let out whatever was troubling me. "Well today I feel extra sad. I've been thinking about Mamma's mother getting killed. What a lousy thing to happen."

"We're all very sad about that," Anna whispered.

I glanced at everyone, realized I was choking on the issue troubling me and decided to let it come tumbling out. "But there's something else. Today my gang was doing Last Picking in the Portland Hills. Mr. George called me over. You know, he's the senior boss. He said Vito, one of my haulers, bruised some leaves really bad because he found one of his baskets tipped over. He said the whole gang may have to get docked. He had that damn expression on his face I've seen before and can't stand. He enjoyed what he was telling me. I hate that bastard. He's bugged me all summer."

It must have been easy for Gloria to guess that there was much more to what had me so upset. She slid her hand across the table. "What happened?"

Tony reached out and touched Gloria's hand. "Wait. Mr. George's shit gets even more ridiculous. Me and Angelo, and Jack Kane from another gang, happened to be near the edge of the field pulling out our baskets. Each of us saw Mr. George push over one of Vito's baskets."

Anna slammed her fist against the table. "He is a bastard! It was a set up!"

"It sure was," Tony sighed. "But it didn't work." He added that after Angelo and our friend, Jack, told him what they saw, he suggested that they all tell Mr. Williams. But Angelo refused because he thought Mr. Williams wouldn't believe them. Tony added that he remembered what Papa said weeks ago, when we were talking about *omertà*. If we wait, the time will come when we'll have a chance to get back at Mr. George the right way. Tony took a deep breath. "I told Santo what Angelo and I saw, especially that a guy from another gang saw it too, gave us a chance to pay back that ass."

I was glad that Tony filled in what happened. I raised my head and took a deep breath. "We went to see Mr. Williams. Tony, Angelo and Jack Kane told him what they saw. Mr. Williams told us he would talk to Mr. George about it."

Filomena stretched her arm across the table and touched my hand. "So at least you and your friends spoke up and told Mr. Williams your side of the story."

"Yes, we did." I lowered my head again. "But there's something wrong with me, because I didn't feel we got the right revenge."

Tony jerked his head around and stared at me. "What do you mean? At least we had the guts to tell our story to Mr. Williams."

I tilted my head down even more. "I don't know what's wrong with me. Later, when we were getting ready to go home, I happened to see Mr. George talking with another foreman. While I stared at him, I began to feel he was like Mr. Alba. What's even worse, I began to imagine I was our grandfather's brother, who gave Mr. Alba what he deserved."

Anna slapped the table again. "Santo, for God sake! Are you saying you wanted to kill Mr. George?"

I felt pain crawl across my face. "Yes, all day I kept picturing myself doing that. The shit he gave me this summer just kept turning round and round in my head."

Filomena reached across the table again and touched my hands. "What did you think of doing?"

I dropped my head so low my chin almost touched my chest. "At least a hundred times today, I kept seeing the same thing over and over. I tell Mr. George I have something to ask him about. I take him to the far end of the field, away from everyone, and tell him, 'Remember last summer when you whacked Emilio with a hauler's hook?' Then I hit him on the head with a hook."

Tony stared at everyone, worried. "On the way home Santo told me about this. I didn't know what to say."

I glanced up at the ceiling and then lowered my head. "Isn't that sick?" I surprised myself when I immediately began sharing that all summer I've been thinking about these feelings I have in me from what I heard since I was little, about things that happened in Sicily. I added that I have been trying to think about which feelings work and which ones are bad. Then, with shame, I admitted that today I kept imagining myself whacking Mr. George to death over and over again. "There's definitely something wrong with me."

Because I wondered if Filomena was worried that I'd do something really bad, I was surprised by what she said. "No, Santo, there's nothing wrong with you. You imagined killing him, but you didn't do it. Okay, so you heard stories about what happened to people like Mr. Alba, but you must have heard a lot of other stories that scream, 'Don't do it!'" Now the tone of her voice became angry and loud. "And there's one more thing. Mr. Alba got what the old way said he should get." Then she whispered. "But you know, Santo, that doesn't fit with the way this world works now."

Papa raised his hands toward me. "Like Filomena just said, what happened to Mr. Alba is a part of the old way that most Sicilians have left behind. The new road gives us other ways to handle these problems."

I raised my head and took a long look at Papa. "I understand. But since the letter came about our grandmother getting killed, I keep thinking about what I heard happened to your mother and father." I surprised myself when I shared that whenever I hold that stone, I feel like I'm there, watching the whole thing. Now I felt very nervous and glanced at Mamma and Papa. "I've heard some talk about it. Could just us go over it now?"

Anna leaned back in her chair and held her hands together. "I think it could help all of us."

Mamma glanced at each of us. "Your father and I were babies when the tragedy happened. But when we grew up, we learned all about it from relatives and *paisani* in the village." She paused and nodded toward Papa.

Papa folded his hands on the table in a way that said we should all pay close attention. "To make some sense of what happened to my parents, you have to keep in mind some things we have talked about many times." He asked us to keep in mind that in the old days, Sicilians had to cope with many invaders from different countries who ruled them, and sometimes abused them. But when Italy finally became a unified country in 1870, after Garibaldi and his army of volunteers defeated the Bourbons in southern Italy, things got worse not better. Papa's voice became more raspy than usual. "But a lot of people don't realize that Sicilians began to hate this new government more than they hated the Bourbons."

Filomena interrupted Papa, which she rarely did, because she again could not resist the opportunity to give a lecture. "I know, Papa. The politicians of this new country of Italy were all from Piedmont in the North. They imposed their regulations and didn't care at all about the problems the peasants in the South were having, especially in Sicily." With anger she added, "Sicilians thought they would have some say in how their region should be run, especially since a lot of them joined Garibaldi's Army. But it soon became clear to them that northern politicians had no interest in sharing their power."

Papa raised the palm of his right hand in Filomena's direction. "That's a good point, Filomena." He added that one reason why Sicilians began to hate the new government was that the owners of large estates and sulfur mines in Sicily, who were from the north or other countries, worked closely with the government and arranged to have more power than they had when the Bourbons ruled.

Anna tapped her hand on the table to get everyone's attention. "Papa, I hear the old timers talk a lot about how the new tax laws favored the rich and discriminated against the peasants. They laugh about how mules were taxed, which peasants owned, but cows owned by the *latifundisti* (rich landowners), weren't taxed."

Tony couldn't resist joining the discussion. He pushed his arm straight up. "Wait everybody. I heard Zio Gaetano say that what upset Sicilians most of all was the new law which said all young men had to serve seven years in the military. Everyone knew that the sons of landowners were getting excused."

Gloria decided to mention something that had been discussed often. "We said many times that even though Garibaldi promised Sicilians they would get some land to farm, owners of those estates used political connections to keep possession of the land."

Papa raised the palm of his hands, interrupting the comments that were being shot out from both sides of the table. "Good. You understand the conditions that were going on when my parents were killed."

Because Mamma cleared her throat, which she rarely did, we turned and focused on her. Even though she usually didn't say very much when this kind of topic was being discussed, she reminded us that we have discussed many times how Sicilians in each village organized a *Fasciu* and joined the *Fasci* League, how that movement spread across the island to deal with what everybody was facing, and how each *Fasciu* chose a *Capo* they respected, who protected their rights, which the police refused to do. Mamma tapped the table with her fingers. "As the Capo of our village, one of the things your grandfather did to help had to do with the sulfur mine near Siracusa where a lot of the men and boys from the village worked."

Mamma nodded at Papa, but because I felt a surge of excitement, I couldn't stop myself from interrupting. "Our friends at the tobacco farm couldn't believe *i carusi* (the boys) pulled sacks of sulfur, each weighing almost seventy-five pounds, to the top of the shaft, sometimes for a half mile."

Papa grimaced. "Yes, and worse, they were not being paid fair wages, and the owners did nothing about the accidents that were happening in those shafts." A couple of times, he added, our grandfather organized the men and boys to strike.

Filomena nearly screamed. "Remember, once when the owner arrived, grandpa had the men and boys come out of the shaft, throw down their picks and sacks and yell at him, 'You dig the sulfur yourself!' The owner talked things over with our grandfather and made the wages and conditions better."

Anna raised her hands and smiled. "That's why his nickname was *Paraceddu* (He flies like a bird). He really got things done, didn't he."

Filomena stared across the table at Tony, Teodoro and me. "Always remember your grandfather flew from one thing to another and got a lot of things done."

Mamma cleared her throat again, so everyone turned toward her. "Things like that sulfur mine were happening all over the island. Some villages even revolted. So the Italian government sent more troops to Sicily and ..."

Again, Filomena could not hold back. "Ma, I read about that!"

Anna did not like that Filomena interrupted Mamma. She flipped her hand against Filomena's arm. "There goes the teacher again. Now what did you read?"

Filomena's dark eyes gleamed as she thrust out her index finger. "I think we need to know what Ma meant when she said the government sent more troops." Filomena explained that the new Prime Minister, Francesco Crispi, believed that the rioting going on was part of a conspiracy that was being paid for by France, because France wanted to separate Sicily from Italy. So Crispi sent forty thousand more troops to Sicily with the job of crushing the Fasci League. The troops were ordered to arrest the

Fasci Capo of each city, and even of small villages.

Mamma raised the palms of her hands toward Filomena. "All these soldiers searching around for members of the *Fasci* League were a constant reminder to Sicilians that they were nothing, and had to stay on their knees." Mamma was upset about what she was going to say next. "Remember what those soldiers did to the peasants in the village near Messina who refused to get off the land they were promised? They killed them."

When Mamma shouted the words 'they killed them,' Papa looked down and commented in a soft, raspy voice, "Maybe now your mother and I can go over what Santo asked for a little while ago." I nodded clutching my hands.

Mamma quickly spoke up. It wasn't usual for her to take over this kind of conversation, but we understood she wanted to help Papa because we were getting closer to very painful memories. She asked us to keep in mind that when Mr. Alba took the job of superintendent of the estate near the village, he had been jealous of our grandfather's success for years. And we should remember that when government troops arrived to try to capture Antonio, he was hiding in caves outside the village, and our grandmother, Anna, was taking care of their six children. Of course, she and villagers told the soldiers they did not know where Antonio was. At this moment Mamma lowered her head, paused and whispered, "Vincenzo was the last friend to visit Antonio in one of those caves. He was married to your grandfather's sister, Filomena." Mamma looked with affection at Anna and Filomena and reminded us that in keeping with Sicilian custom she and Papa gave our grandmother's name to their first daughter and the name of our grandfather's sister to their second daughter.

Mamma and Papa continued to share, each one stepping in when it looked like the other was becoming too emotional. My sisters, brothers and I listened carefully.

Papa sighed. "When Mamma said Vincenzo was the last friend to visit your grandfather in the cave, it reminded me that some details should be shared." What he summarized happened, I had heard before when relatives were having discussions, but it helped to see how all the pieces fit together. I felt as if I was there, watching the whole thing unfold.

Vincenzo arrived in the cave where Antonio was hiding not only to bring food and water but also to inform him that his brother, Gaetano, had been arrested by soldiers. Vincenzo also urged Antonio not to enter the village at this time because Mr. Alba seemed to be relating with the soldiers in a way that was too friendly. But Antonio shared the plan that, if he did decide to enter the village, Vincenzo must arrange for Antonio's family to stand in the village *piazza* among a lot of villagers and children. In this way the soldiers would not be able to identify him. So when Vincenzo left the cave, and saw that Antonio had made up his mind to enter the village, he ran ahead to make the arrangements.

Mamma raised her hand, "So Vincenzo was standing there by the well with your grandmother, who was holding your father in her arms, and her children by her side. We were told years later that every one of them struggled to hold themselves back, because, when they saw their father, they wanted to run toward him."

I don't know why I lost control of myself. I slammed the table. "But why did he go into the *piazza*? Didn't he know that it was dangerous to be in the wide, open space with soldiers around?"

Papa reached over and placed his hand on my arm. "Like we said, Vincenzo and your grandfather thought the safest thing for him to do was to meet his family in the middle of a lot of people instead of in a house. The soldiers didn't know what he looked like." Now it made sense to me.

Papa and Mamma continued sharing details they had learned. Antonio strolled toward the village well, returning greetings from villagers. Everyone could tell he was eager to touch his family. He stepped into the middle of the group of people, standing around the well, and paused near his wife. After he greeted and touched a few villagers, he placed his hand on his wife's shoulder, touched the forehead of each of the children standing around her, and kissed the forehead of the baby cuddled in her arms. After this brief pause, Antonio walked slowly to the other side of the well. Suddenly, Salvatore Alba called out, "*Antonio, ciao, benvenuto.*" ("Antonio, hello, you are welcomed.") He pushed his way through villagers, approached Antonio, placed his arms around him, kissed each of his cheeks, and slowly walked away.

Mamma shared the next detail with much feeling. "Vincenzo and your grandmother became very nervous. Vincenzo whispered to her something like, 'Now he's acting friendly! I don't believe it! Something is up!' "

Now Papa took over, griped with sadness because this was the tragic conclusion. He elaborated that Antonio also must have been suspicious. Instead of remaining by the well, he walked toward the edge of the piazza to enter the village. When he turned and gestured to his wife and Vincenzo, two soldiers, with rifles in hand, suddenly appeared from behind a small building. He paused, and the crowd stood motionless, but Anna quickly pushed her baby, our father, into Vincenzo's arms and dashed toward the soldiers in a desperate effort to help. At the same time, Antonio raced down the narrow road into the village. Although Anna managed to push one of the soldiers, disrupting his aim, the other was successful in shooting Antonio who tumbled to the ground. Suddenly, the solider Anna had pushed regained his balance and killed her. The crowd quickly disbursed, yelling, "*L'hannu ammazzatu!*" ("They killed them!"). Vincenzo disappeared into the village with our father in his arms and five nieces and nephews, sobbing as they ran by his side.

Mamma and Papa paused. Some of us were wringing our hands. "Every time I hear this part of the story," Anna mumbled with tears rolling down her cheeks, "it makes me furious."

"And every time I hear about this," Filomena whispered. "I can't believe it."

Gloria's eyes were also filled with tears. "My God, Papa. What a disaster for you and your brothers and sisters." Tony, Teodoro and I also had tears in our eyes.

Mamma continued summarizing what happened. All of the villagers quickly ran off to places of safety. Vincenzo, assisted by Antonio's *cugini* (cousins) invaded the building on the outskirts of the village where Gaetano was being held prisoner, killed the guards and freed him. Several hours later they caught Alba. At first he denied having any involvement with the government troops, and insisted it was a coincidence that Antonio was shot shortly after he embraced him. But Gaetano stressed that everyone in the piazza noticed that when Antonio strolled into the piazza, the troops did not take action. It was only seconds after Alba embraced and kissed him that the troops jumped out and opened fire.

Papa glanced at Mamma, indicating he wanted to tell us what came next. His voice again became much more raspy than usual, which typically occurred when he was griped with emotion. Gaetano told Alba his story was not accepted. Alba immediately pleaded for his life and begged Gaetano and his cousins to understand. When they held to their opinion, Alba changed his story. Now he said the government troops insisted that if he did not identify Antonio, he would lose his job as superintendent of the estate, and his family would be arrested. Gaetano refused to accept this explanation and told Alba he was Antonio's murderer because, if Alba had not thrown his arms around him and kissed his cheeks, the troops would never have known who he was in the crowd.

The next detail of what happened spread throughout the village, and was mentioned often in the following years, because of the message it expressed. Gaetano reminded Alba that his name meant "dawn" or "day break" in the Italian language. But as he knew, the word for dawn in Sicilian dialect is "arba." Accordingly, his name and behavior made clear he was not truly a Sicilian and did not carry the respect and honor of a Sicilian. Gaetano took a long look into Alba's eyes and told him, therefore unfortunately, he will not see another dawn, and stabbed him to death. Papa quickly added that four remaining government troops, including the two soldiers who had killed his father and mother, escaped into the hillside. Much to their misfortune, however, these soldiers from the north were not sufficiently acquainted with the rocky hillsides of Sicily. Two days later they were found and also executed. Mamma and Papa paused and looked at each of us in a way that said they had finished describing what happened.

Tony broke the silence. "My God, Papa, you were just a baby! How did you survive with no mother and no father, and how did your sisters and brothers survive?"

Mamma stretched her arms out, turned the palms of her hands upward and sighed. "For every culture, when the mother of young children dies, it's a disaster. But for Sicilians, because the mother is the center of the family, if she dies, when she has young children, it's like the world coming to an end." Mamma paused and whispered, "But the world did not come to an end for your father and his brothers and sisters because they were saved by the Sicilian custom of *comparaggio* (Godparents)."

Papa stared at Mamma with affection and added that his Godmother and Godfather, and the Godmothers and Godfathers of his brothers and sisters, as well as everyone in the village, took care of them. "But every day, we got together at someone's house."

Mamma added that the priests and nuns located in the city of Syracuse, which was not too far from where they lived in the mountains, asked the villagers to give them Papa when they heard what happened. Papa's relatives refused.

Tony shouted again, pushing his arm forward. "But Papa, like I just said, how did you make it? You were only weeks old."

Mamma reached toward Tony. "Your father's oldest sister was eleven years old. What she did also became a legend in the village. Two or three times a day she carried him in her arms, sometimes with her Godmother or an aunt, and took your father to women who were able to breastfeed him."

Gloria smiled. "Fantastic!"

Papa pointed out that Mamma gave one answer to Tony's wondering how he survived. Another answer is that he took every detail he had learned about his mother and father from siblings, relatives and neighbors, and kept them inside of himself. In this way, he added, his thoughts, memories, and feelings of what happened helped him grow and be all he could be. So when he came to the United States as a young man, he could be a good *Capo*, like his father, and try to help people whenever possible. And these same memories and feelings helped him become a police officer.

Anna interrupted, "So you kept your parents alive in you, and Mamma is keeping her mother alive in her. And we kids will keep both of you, and all our ancestors, alive in us."

Mamma looked at Papa with tears in her eyes. "I hope everyone keeps the good part of the past alive."

Papa agreed and asked everyone to recall why I wanted to review how our grandparents died. "Santo imagined himself killing Mr. George like Mr. Alba was killed. Now it's clear that what happened to Mr. Alba fitted with the road Sicilians had to follow years ago and does not fit with the road we follow today." But he also emphasized that there are other parts of that old Sicilian road all of us should continue to use because they are still useful today.

Filomena interrupted Papa again, almost screaming, which caused everyone to quickly turn and look at her. "And those parts we should keep using are the rules of the family!"

Papa flashed a glance at Filomena and raised his hand for everyone's attention. While he agreed with her, he wanted to be sure everyone got the point he had just made. "You're correct Filomena. But like I said, it's important for all of us to understand that the part of the road that did what it did to Mr. Alba is no longer useful or necessary. As a supernumerary police officer I know that police are now committed to helping and protecting people."

Mamma suddenly thrust her hand out and spoke with a very strong tone, which was not usual for her. "I have something I want to share." She admitted that, since coming to America, she has struggled against trying to see how some of the old Sicilian customs could mix with some of the American customs so that a new recipe of how to live could be made. She added what all of us knew, that most of the time, she refuses to speak English and go into an American store. To defend her position she asked us to remember what happened when she went in the A&P store. "*Mi dispiaci, ma' iu nun sentu l'America.*" ("I'm sorry, but I don't hear America – I'm deaf to America.") Placing her hand across her chest, she added, "*Ogni jornu sono scantata di caminari in America pirchì ccà c'è la vita mia*" ("Everyday I'm frightened to walk in America because here in me is my life.") She moved the palm of her hand over her heart. "*Chista è casa mia.*" ("This is my house.") She paused and shared with much feeling that even though she has sometimes been deaf to America, she has often asked herself, "*Comu a stu munnu' un ti pò abituari, e comu fazzu?*" ("Why can't you get accustomed to this world, and what can I do?")

We were all very impressed with what Mamma was sharing. When she paused, Filomena spoke up with vigor. "What you just said reminded me that it's not easy to go from the old ways to the new ways and figure out how to connect them."

Now Papa interrupted Filomena. "What you just said is very important." Then he stared at me. "Santo, do you see how what you told us you wanted to do to Mr. George shows how hard it is to figure out which old ways should be connected to new ways? Did our talk help you figure that out?"

When Papa asked his question, I realized that during the last ten minutes or so, while I listened to what happened, and how Papa survived, a huge weight was slowly lifted off of me. I collected my thoughts and looked up at everyone. "Yes, Papa, it helped a lot. But what I'm about to say might sound strange to all of you." I explained that as I listened to what Papa and Mamma shared, I was looking at one stage in my mind. On that stage Papa's brother is stabbing Mr. Alba. Then I found myself looking at another stage, where Mr. George is hitting Emilio with a hauler's hook, and I begin hitting Mr. George over the head with a hauler's hook. I paused and explained that a third stage appeared in my mind that has to do with tomorrow. I emphasized that I had no idea what will happen at the farm tomorrow about the mess that has to do with Mr. George saying Vito knocked over a basket. In my fantasy, on the stage of tomorrow, I'm standing in front of Mr. Williams and Mr. George, wondering whether or not Mr. Williams believes what Tony, Angelo and Jack Kane say happened. Mr. Williams slowly turns to Mr. George, aims his finger at him, almost stabbing the finger in his stomach, and says, 'You're guilty.'

I barely finished what I wanted to say when Filomena screamed again. "Santo, what you just shared is hooked up with what you showed me the other day."

"What is she talking about, Santo?" Gloria wondered.

I was surprised that Filomena mentioned, at this moment, what I had shown her a couple of days ago. I collected myself and answered Gloria's question. "Mrs. Smith, you know she's the ninth grade English teacher I'm going to have this fall, gave the whole class a little bit of homework for the summer. Instead of giving us things to read, like she did with Tony's class last summer, she asked us to write something."

"Write something about what?" Anna asked.

"She asked all of us to write something that had to do with what it's like to leave grade school and start high school, so we can get more experience saying in English what we're thinking. I decided to write about the ideas that came to me after all those talks we've been having these past weeks about taking the best part of the old ways and trying to fit them into new ways. I wanted to say something about how hard and scary that is."

Mamma and Papa knew that I liked to write. "*Trova sta cosa.*" (Find that thing) Mamma called out, smiling.

"Mamma, Papa, I'd be happy to, but it's in English. I don't think I'll be able to say it all in Sicilian."

Filomena jumped in. "After you read each line, Anna and I can translate it into Sicilian."

I got up, raced into my bedroom and returned with a piece of paper in my hands. I stood still at the end of the table next to Papa, and noticed that my hands quivered a little. "Um, the title is 'Being in Yesterday, Today and Tomorrow at the Same Time.'" I slowly read the first phrase and waited until Anna and Filomena translated its meaning for Mamma and Papa. Then I did the same with each of the other phrases.

"I'm standing…gripped in a moment of hesitation….I realize I'm afraid….I'm very afraid and nervous.

Yesterday is close behind me….I know it well….I feel its warm breath on the back of my neck….Yesterday feels really good….It has its arms around me.

Beneath my feet is the grass and gravel of today….In a strange way, the grass and gravel seem both good and not good…. They feel both soft and hard.

Directly in front of me is tomorrow….It's like a brilliant light glaring….It's so uncertain….It's almost blinding me….I can barely see.

I hesitate….I feel the familiar, warm breath of yesterday behind my neck, and its hand on my shoulder….I feel my feet shifting and shuffling around on the grass and gravel of today….

My eyes strain to see what's ahead…I am still very nervous and afraid.

But suddenly I step into tomorrow….I feel this sense that I can do it ….I know I will find a way to fit together the best of yesterday, with today and tomorrow ….I know I will find a way to make the most out of being inside of yesterday, today and tomorrow, all at the same time."

Everyone stared in silence for a long moment. Mamma and Papa glanced at each other several times, grinning.

Teodoro broke the silence. "You know what that made me think of? If you fix a machine that was made a long time ago, with new tools that will be invented tomorrow, then that machine can keep doing its job but in a new and better way."

Papa took a deep breath. "*Tu hai ragiuni*, Teodoro. (You are right Teodoro.)" He added whenever Sicilians try to take in some customs of the United States to fix ancient Sicilian customs they become afraid because, for hundreds of years, they had to cope with many different cultures that ruled the island. They coped by trying to block out, as much as possible, the influence of strangers, keeping these cultures at a distance, and forming tightly knit communities, like the one the villagers from Melilli established in Middletown on the streets along the Connecticut River.

Suddenly Filomena sat up straight, her face making clear, as usual, she had something to say that was very important. "Yes, Papa, when Sicilians set up these tight communities in Sicily and even here in Middletown, it had a very positive side. It helped them cope and keep their way of life growing. But there's a negative side. If they don't reach out, other people can't learn what Sicilians have to offer that's good."

Gloria slapped the table. "That's what happened when we had Allison visit us last weekend. Look at how much she learned about our ways and liked them."

Of course Anna had to join in. "Let's have her visit again, Filomena, before you head back to college."

Mamma spoke with a very strong tone. "I agree. When we came to the United States, we kept away from the customs of

RESISTURS

strangers surrounding us. *Tutti Americani* (all Americans) notice we Sicilians stay in our own community." She admitted she tried to pass on to us that way of thinking, like when she objected to Tony visiting an American doctor instead of Mrs. Carrado. Then she surprised everyone when she agreed with Filomena that we have to help other people learn about us while we learn how American ways can fix, and make better, some of the Sicilian customs.

Tony grinned. "Well Papa has mixed the two pretty good. Some people won't believe it. He's a supernumerary for an American police force, and at the same time, he's doing all kinds of things for *paisani* as their *Capo*."

"And how about the Sunday food bags Mamma and her friends put together," Anna shouted. "It really helps *paisani*. That's one thing this damn war has given us. Food is rationed, but some families can't get food stamps because they're not citizens yet."

Filomena raised her arm. "Ok, Papa is reaching out on both sides of the street, and Mamma is showing how to help families. But there's a bigger reason why we Sicilians have to reach out to other people so they can learn what we have to offer."

"What's that?" Anna and Tony yelled out in chorus.

"It has to do with the Old Mafia and New Mafia that we talked about. You watch! In the next years, they're going to make movies about the Mafia and Sicilian gangsters, and everyone is going to be fascinated. We need to help people see what this New Mafia is about, and we need to help people understand what the Old Mafia is about, and how it's still helping."

Anna raised her wine glass. " That's a really great point. Let's say *salute* to Filomena since there's no other girl in our neighborhood who's going to college yet."

We all raised our glasses and yelled, "*Salute*."

Tony shouted even louder. "We know why she's the only one. Sicilians are still against education."

Filomena stretched her arm across the table and pointed her finger inches from Tony's stomach. She couldn't resist making what Tony just said the topic of another lecture. "There's a reason for that. We said that to cope with many cultures that invaded Sicily, the peasants believed that learning from another culture could destroy their own customs. So they pushed away education." Now Filomena jabbed her fingertip up and down against the table. "For this reason, I think Sicilians who immigrated to the United States brought with them a strong bias against education. They believed if their children went to school they would take on "*i tradizioni amiricani*" (American customs). They noticed that schools even ignored the language children spoke at home." Filomena thrust her arm out and pointed to me. "How about Ms. Mutt who hit Santo with a stick, because he made a mistake when he said a Sicilian word, instead of the English word." I looked up at the ceiling, because I wanted to forget that incident.

Papa sat up, tapped his fist on the table, and spoke out with a tone louder than usual. He described how embarrassed he felt a few years ago when he learned that the lowest proportion of children of immigrant families who were enrolled in schools in the United States were children from Italian American families. Then he shared something that I think helped all of us understand what we had to do. "When I arrived in the United States, I felt that my job was to keep '*la via vecchia siciliana*' (the old Sicilian ways) in my lungs while learning how to breathe other kinds of customs." He learned that way of thinking from a monk when he was twelve years old, and lived with other children for a while at the monastery near Siracusa. This monk had been to several countries and talked to the children about why it was important to breathe in other customs.

Mamma raised her hands. "I'm sure all of you remember when Filomena was about to finish high school, a couple of years ago, your father and I argued a lot." Mamma elaborated how Papa tried to get her to accept the opinion he just shared, and that if Filomena kept Sicilian customs in her lungs, while learning to breathe the air of other customs, she would be better able to decide what parts of the old customs help and don't help a person, and what parts of the new customs should be taken or pushed away. Mamma stared at Filomena. "I was against you going to college. But your father went ahead and arranged a scholarship for you with the Garibaldi Society." Mamma glanced at Filomena with pride. "You're showing everyone that someone from a Sicilian family can go to college and not completely give up *la via vecchia.*"

Filomena reached out toward Mamma with both hands. "But you know, Ma, it was very hard for me when I first got to Teachers College. Remember the first year? I came home and told all of you I felt really strange there. The food seemed weird. I looked different, and the way they talked with each other seemed strange to me."

Tony grinned. "Yeah, Filomena, remember when you said that you even smelled different than the other girls." Everyone chuckled.

Anna laughed, raising her wine glass. "It must have been all the *agghiu* (garlic) we've eaten over the years. *Viva l'agghiu.*" Now everyone burst out laughing.

Still speaking with a strong tone, Mamma interrupted the laughter. "I want all of you to know that now I realize that there is a lot more work to be done by all of us. I'm sure the families of immigrants from other countries face the same job. And..."

Filomena slapped the table before Mamma finished. "Mamma, you're absolutely right. All of us kids have more work to do to fit old ways in with new ways. But you know what, that reminds me of something I learned about Garibaldi in my history class." Again she began teaching a very familiar topic, namely that for Sicilians Garibaldi was a hero because he freed them from the Bourbons, and helped Italy become a unified country. Then with a great deal of drama she declared, "I'll bet you don't know what I learned in my history class."

Anna growled. "You're acting like you have some big secret to tell."

Filomena grinned. "A lot of people don't know that because Giuseppe Garibaldi had a reputation of being a fantastic, military leader, President Abraham Lincoln offered him the position of being a major general for the Union Army during the Civil War that was going on here in the United States. You see, at the time, Garibaldi lived for a little while on Staten Island in New York."

"So what happened, teacher?" Anna barked.

Filomena continued grinning. "Well, Garibaldi told President Lincoln something like he was sorry he couldn't accept the offer because he had more work to do in Italy. So we should follow him, because all of us have more work to do with fitting old ways in with new ways."

Gloria threw her hand out. "Now I realize that I liked Allison when she visited us a couple of weeks ago. She loved our food so much; I thought she wanted to be a Sicilian. But the more I thought about it, the more I realized I want to be like her in some ways. So I've got more work to do, too." Gloria turned to Mamma. "Which parts of the old way do you think should stay, Ma? I'll bet everyone has a different opinion."

Smiling, Mamma looked at each of us. "I think, like Filomena said a few minutes ago, what should stay are, *l'ordine della famiglia* no matter what: honor, respect, loyalty, *omertà*, *serietà*. And the mother must stay as the center of the family, and the father as the head. And the family should follow the custom of *comparaggio*."

Anna pointed to Mamma. "So our job is how to keep being educated and becoming more American while holding on to all those Sicilian ways."

Mamma was pleased with what Anna just said and shared that Sicilian peasants believed that all children should be *ben educati* (well educated). But this education was not about reading and writing. It had to do with educating children about the habits and customs of *l'ordine della famiglia*.

Anna glanced at Filomena and Gloria and stretched her arms on the table toward Tony, Teodoro and me. "What we've been talking about makes me think of something else. It has to do with all that stuff I heard when I was in high school about becoming American and melting into that pot."

"They still talk a lot about that in some of the high school classes," Tony added.

"Yes," Gloria joined in. "I'm really curious about that melting pot we hear so much about."

Anna raised her wine glass. "Well, I'm beginning to think that each of us should not believe we have to be like an empty glass, so teachers and people, who think they are pure Americans, can pour into that glass what they think is pure American water."

Filomena looked at Anna with pride, "That's a really good picture. I think there's no such thing as a pure American. Maybe we need to keep some Sicilian water in that glass."

Teodoro raised his arm. "How about if we make sure that the glass is always made of Sicilian clay and shaped like those ancient vases they made over there. Maybe I should start a business and make Sicilian vases, and sell them to all the kids in the neighborhood."

Tony patted Teodoro on the back. "Very good. With your business of fixing cars and making clay vases, you're going to make a lot of money." Everyone laughed.

I was really turned on by what happened after I shared the pictures in my mind of different things happening on different stages and then read my poem. "And, Teodoro, if every kid in our neighborhood is shaped like a Sicilian vase, then every kid will do a better job with what that Sicilian philosopher, Socrates, said we should all keep trying to do."

Tony teased me. "Here we go again! Now, what's that Mr. History?"

I raised my arm as if making a declaration. "Know yourself."

Mamma pointed to Papa. "This is a good time to remind everyone of that ancient Sicilian saying."

Papa grinned and his dark eyes sparkled because he enjoyed ancient sayings and metaphors. He raised his hands and spoke in a tone as if he were giving a sermon. "*P'aviri a vita assicurata amu à truvari natra nova strata. Ma amu a teniri la via vecchia puru, pirchì cu lassa la via vecchia pir la nova sa chiddu ca perdi, ma non sapi chiddu ca trova.*" ("To have an ensured life, we must find another new road. But we must also hold onto the old way, because whoever completely leaves the old way for a new way, knows what he is losing but may not know what he will find.")

We stared at each other, appreciating the strong family attachment we felt. At this moment I wanted to make sure everyone realized that the tension and tangle I had felt in me before this discussion started had now gone away. "I'm glad we talked about all of this. I don't feel as sad and mixed up as I did before dinner."

"*Bene, basta, per ora,*" ("Good, this is enough for now.") Mamma glanced with affection at each of us. "*É fatta la giornata per ora,*" ("Our day is done for now.")

Everyone stood up. As usual, Mamma began removing food from the table that had not been eaten, sorting what needed to be placed in the icebox and what could be returned to the pantry. At the same time, Filomena and Gloria began to clear dishes and silverware from the table, and Anna walked to the sink and started washing dishes. In the meantime Papa had taken the straw broom from the closet and was carefully sweeping the kitchen floor, a ritual he performed every night. Tony, Teodoro and I went into our bedroom. Each of us stood on one side of the bed. Teodoro slowly passed his hand over the quilt, which our mother had made with needlepoint, and commented, "I always like the way this feels."

The next day at the Central Lot, Mr. Kelly approached the gangs from Middletown which, as usual, were engaged in discussions. He paused at the edge of the crowd, and snapped his hand over his shoulder several times. Tony also noticed his gesture. "Santo I think Mr. Kelly wants to see you."

"Yes, Mr. Kelly, what is it?"

"Mr. Williams wants to see you for a minute. He's got Mr. George in there with him. I don't know what it's about."

I paused, glanced at the ground and then looked into Mr. Kelly's face. "I think I know what this is about." I clutched my lunch pail under my left arm and walked quickly toward the Main Cabin.

When I entered, Mr. Williams stared at me, and I knew this had to be about that damn basket. I glanced at one corner of the room where Mr. George was standing. Another thought flashed through my mind. "That bastard is ready for combat. Look at how he's holding one hand in the other." A surge of tension swept through me as I looked back and forth at the two of them. But then all of what my family got into last night flashed into my mind which made me feel less nervous and more confident. "Yes, Mr. Williams, you asked for me."

Mr. Williams slowly tapped the top of his desk a couple of times with the pencil he was holding. "Santo, Mr. George and I were talking about what you and your friends told me yesterday. Please go over it again."

I quickly glanced at Mr. George and then stayed focused on Mr. Williams. "Like I told you, Mr. Williams, yesterday we were doing Last Picking in the Portland Hills. Mr. George called me over and showed me a basket that Vito, one of my haulers, had pulled out. It was tipped over. A lot of leaves were bruised. Mr. George said my whole gang might be docked."

Mr. Williams turned to Mr. George. "Is that correct?"

"Yeah, that's right."

I took a deep breath and imagined I was stepping into the ring for a boxing match. I also felt determined and decided that I was definitely going to stay in the ring and fight this jerk until one of us got knocked out. "But, like we told you yesterday, my brother Tony was pulling a basket out of the south end of the Portland Hills, and Angelo was doing the same. And it just happened that from the north end of the Hills, Jack Kane, a hauler for Brian Coleman's gang, was pulling out a basket too. All three of them saw Mr. George flip the basket over with his foot and then kick it." I tried to feel all of what my family talked about last night, and again glanced back and forth at Mr. George and Mr. Williams.

Because the expressions on the faces of Mr. Williams and Mr. George seemed blank to me, I became nervous again. I took another deep breath, glanced up at the ceiling, and continued with a tone that was more firm. "Mr. Williams, they wouldn't make up that kind of story. Besides, Tony and Angelo told me what they saw Mr. George do before he showed me the basket. And later, Jack Kane came over and told me what he saw. He didn't even know what Tony and Angelo had told me, or that Mr. George said we might be docked."

Mr. Williams remained seated, folded his hands together, and looked up at Mr. George. "Well."

Mr. George stiffened his posture, and still held one hand in the palm of the other. "Now that I think about it, maybe I turned to step into the next row and nudged the basket with my foot. It was an accident. I don't know why I told Santo his gang might be docked."

With his lips close together forming a slight grin, Mr. Williams stared into my eyes. "Santo, thanks for sharing and clearing things up. No one in your gang is getting docked. Mr. George and I will take over from here. You can go now."

I could not believe what had just taken place. I stood very still clutching my lunch pail under my left arm. My thoughts whirled back again to my family's discussion last night, and to comments Papa made weeks ago when the family was discussing why it was important for me to practice *omertà*, especially when dealing with Mr. George's abuse. Then my mind jumped to Papa saying that if I practiced *omertà*, someday the opportunity would come along when I could pay back Mr. George with what he deserved. Realizing this was that moment, I took a deep breath, raised my head high and exhaled. I relaxed my left arm and lifted the lid of my lunch pail. I rummaged around for a few seconds, lifted out a piece of Genoa salami and a piece of provolone cheese and held them with my fingertips. I waited for a brief moment, took a step forward and stretched out my arm. "Mr. Williams if my parents were here, they would say that you are no longer a *straniero* (stranger). You are now one of our *amici* (friends)."

Mr. Williams reached out and took the salami and cheese. "I heard those words before, Santo. This past spring Mr. Serra worked here. He's from your neighborhood and repaired a lot of the sheds. Every time I had a meeting with him to discuss what had to be done, he took out food and gave me some. He used to laugh and say you Italians don't discuss anything important unless you share food."

I managed a slight chuckle. "We don't. But, Mr. Williams, we Sicilians like to say we're not Italian, we're Sicilian."

Mr. Williams smiled. "I forgot. Mr. Serra used to say that all the time when I asked him how were things in Italy."

I grinned and pulled out another slice of Genoa salami from my lunch pail, stuffed it in my mouth, and chewed it with pleasure.

"I really like these things you Italians, I mean Sicilians, eat," Mr. Williams added, slowly chewing on his salami and cheese.

I reached into my lunch pail again and took out two figs.

"Here's your dessert, I hope you like *fichi* (figs)."

"I really do. Mr. Serra had them all the time." Mr. Williams looked up at Mr. George, who was still standing motionless, scowling and holding one hand in the palm of the other, and turned to me. "Again, thanks for clearing things up, and telling me straight out what happened. Mr. Kelly has plans for what your gang is doing next. He's out there in the Central Lot."

I think because we had shared food, like paisani do when they discuss something important, I thanked Mr. Williams in dialect without realizing it. "*Grazzii.*" I was surprised when he responded, "*Pregu.*" ("You're welcome.") I was really impressed that he used the Sicilian word, "*Pregu,*" instead of the Italian word, "*Prego,*" which proved that he learned a lot from Mr. Serra. I grinned, walked out and jogged toward Mr. Kelly. "I'll tell you later what went on in there. Mr. Williams said you have a plan for what my gang is going to do next."

"Okay, I need your guys over here, and Brian's and Jimmy's guys."

I quickly ran over to Jimmy and Brian who gathered their gangs, and we all stood before Mr. Kelly.

"Mr. Williams decided that the Middletown gangs will take on the fields of Four Corners. It's the last big bunch of fields ready for Last Picking."

"That's great," Pesci commented. "That's where all of us started First Picking."

Tom Murphy looked at Pesci, "Since then we've been fitting our sticks into the same bundle." His comment really grabbed me, because it made clear that everyone had gotten into the discussions we had during these past couple of weeks.

Joe Harris of the South End gang burst out laughing. "Well, man, I don't know if the black sticks got all the way in that bundle yet. Maybe one end of the sticks is in."

Mr. Kelly interrupted. "I've heard some of what you guys have been talking about. But we don't have time for that now." He thrust his arm out, pointing, "There's your trucks. Maybe before you guys are done with Four Corners, you'll have that bundle of sticks you've been talking about all tied up together."

Everyone ran and scrambled onto the trucks.

When the gangs arrived at Four Corners, we waited for our assignments. Some of us wondered if the gangs would be mixed together again, but it turned out not to be the case. Mr. Kelly climbed out of his pickup truck. "Santo, because we have a tight schedule this week, your fast gang will take on the Forty Bender, Brian Coleman's gang the Thirty Bender, and Jimmy Lewis' gang one of the Twenty Benders. Let's see how things go. If all of you guys finish on the same day, you can get together and take on the other Twenty Bender, and then Four Corners will be done." Each gang began walking toward the field assigned to it.

"Hey!" shouted Jack Kane. "Even though we got separate fields, the corners of those fields are connected, right?"

"Nice going, Jack," Tony yelled back. "You're right on. We're in separate fields but the roads to each of them are connected."

"Well don't be sad, guys," laughed Adam Smith. "Maybe we'll finally be on the same street when we come together to finish the last Twenty Bender."

I wasn't surprised when Joe Harris began to jitterbug toward the field assigned to the South End gang. "Until we come together in that Twenty Bender, if any of you guys want a dance lesson just come down my street. After all, what do you Dagos say? We're all *paisani* now!" Everyone laughed.

Since all members of the South End gang began to jitterbug toward the field assigned to them, the members of Brian Coleman's gang began to dance the Irish jig toward their field. At the same time the members of my gang danced the Tarantella toward our field, exaggerating their steps. Tony shouted, "When we get together in the last Twenty Bender, we can see if we can mix these dance steps in the same bundle. Then we can be *paisani*, and cousins who help cousins."

An idea, actually a picture, flashed through my mind, which happened often. The picture was so vivid I lost control of myself and yelled, "Wait!" Everyone must have recognized from the tone of my voice that I had something very important to say, because they suddenly stood still and remained quiet. "I've got an idea." Following the picture that had flashed into my mind, I ran to the center of the intersection of the two roads that formed the boundaries of the four fields. For a moment I stood still with my back toward the Forty Bender my gang was assigned, and yelled, "Me and my guys got the Forty Bender, so I stand here." I pointed to a section of the road a couple of yards in front of me and gestured to Jimmy Lewis. "Jimmy, stand here with your back toward the Twenty Bender you got assigned and face me." Jimmy looked confused. He had no idea what I was up to, nor did anyone else. As he walked over, he twirled his finger over his head, gesturing to everyone that I was going out of my mind. A number of the guys chuckled.

I pointed to the road on my right, "Brian, you stand here with your back toward the Thirty Bender your gang got assigned." Brian walked over and made the same gesture that Jimmy made, confirming I was out of my mind. "And Tony you stand here, facing Brian, with your back toward the Twenty Bender we'll all be picking together to finish this season." Tony shouted, "*è pazzu*." ("He's crazy.") I could hear the roar of laughter and remarks, but I remained lost in that picture in my mind. Jimmy, Brian and Tony assumed their positions. The four of us faced each other, forming four sections of a circle.

I lifted my right arm parallel to the ground toward Jimmy Lewis. "Put your right arm out like this, so we can grab our hands together to make a bundle." Jimmy, Brian and Tony each raised his right arm, and placed his hand on mine so that we formed a cross with our arms. "See, now we are connected, making that bundle of sticks and four corners. And what we don't finish this summer making that bundle, or that *fasciu*, we'll have next summer to keep going."

Tom Murphy yelled out from the crowd standing around us. "And we're going to keep stirring that tomato sauce in all those plates this Sunday!"

While still holding his arm out, Jimmy Lewis scanned the crowd, and yelled something that really grabbed me. "You know what? If we keep stirring that tomato sauce with you guys, then us Blacks will start melting in with you Four Leaf Clovers and Garlic Balls. That'll be the best tomato paste that was ever made."

Tony lifted his arm. "Never mind the *strattu*. How about when we get to the last Twenty Bender next week, we'll see if we can mix some of our dance steps together in the same bundle."

"Are you kidding," Joe Harris shouted, laughing. "Every one of us is going to argue about which moves and steps to keep and which ones to throw out. It'll never happen."

I felt great that what I had us do got everyone turned on. More than that, everyone seemed to get the point I was trying to make. I yelled as loud as I could. "If we don't get that new *strattu* and new dance done, we'll have next summer."

Everyone cheered, entered the fields assigned to them, and began picking.

I learned later the details of what happened in Middletown that same morning. Papa walked to the end of William Street where the garages of the city's water department were located. Crew members were bustling about, placing picks and shovels and other tools on the back of one truck, and lifting water pipes onto the platform of another truck. Papa spotted Mr. Misenti, quickly stepped over and placed a hand on his shoulder.

Mr. Misenti spun around. "Don Iano!" (the nickname for Sebastiano). "Thanks for coming by." Then he glanced to his left and right. "Remember Mr. Lewis that man whose son was having trouble in school, and you had Santo help him?"

"*Si, mi ricordu.*" (Yes, I remember)

"Yesterday our boss left him and two other *niuri* (Blacks) on Court Street, and Garafallo too. You know he came over to this country just when the war started. We dug a long ditch on Court Street and put in a pipe." Again Mr. Misenti twisted his head back and forth looking to see if any passerby noticed that he was talking to Papa. "Something happened that's making Mr. Lewis really nervous."

"*Ma ch'è successu?* (But what's the matter?) Why did you ask to see me?"

"Mr. Lewis wants to tell you about it."

"*Allora, chiama a iddu.*" (Well, then, call him.)

Mr. Misenti rushed off and returned with Mr. Lewis. The rest of the crew continued loading the trucks, but now they moved slowly and seemed concerned, as each of them occasionally

329

glanced at Mr. Lewis, Mr. Misenti and Papa.

Mr. Lewis stood still for a moment, ringing his hat and passing his hand across the top of his head. "Here's the story. Yesterday me and three other guys got the job of shoveling the dirt back in the ditch, after the Wilbur Sand and Gravel Company dumped gravel over the new pipe that we put in."

Papa noticed a worried look on Mr. Lewis' face. "I know that company."

"Well they came and dumped only two feet of gravel on the pipe. They're supposed to dump four feet." Mr. Lewis paused and pointed to two African American men standing still a few yards away. "Those guys over there and me decided to tell the Wilbur Company boss we won't shovel the dirt back unless they put the rest of the gravel in."

Mr. Misenti thrust his arm out. "*Era na minchiata!*" (It was a damn thing!) "They're cheating the city."

Mr. Lewis stared at the ground. "They are. They did the same thing a few weeks ago on Rapello Avenue." Now the rest of the crew was standing motionless, staring at them. "The Wilbur Company boss said it's none of our business, but he'll give each of us ten bucks if we keep our mouths shut."

His eyes glaring with anger, Mr. Misenti turned to Papa. "*Hanno fatto na proposta di naso.*" (They made a proposition from the nose – a proposition you can't trust.) Papa nodded in agreement.

Mr. Lewis clenched his fist. "We told this guy what if some day there's a leak? Then when they dig, they'll see there's not the right gravel. That Wilbur boss got pissed off and told us if we say anything, he'll make sure we lose our jobs. He's connected with some guy from the city."

Papa placed his hand on Mr. Lewis' shoulder. "Don't worry. I will talk to the director of the water department and street commissioner. There won't be a problem for you or your friends." Then he turned to Mr. Misenti. "That Wilbur Company boss *è veramenti nu svergognatu e sfacciatu.*" (is truly shameless and rotten)

Mr. Lewis turned to Mr. Misenti. "This is one time us blacks and you spaghetti benders joined forces so we don't get screwed."

A few days later, the trucks crammed with the Middletown gangs from the farm rumbled off the bridge into the open area by the river. Unlike the end of each day during the summer, this time boys slowly hopped off and looked about. Several of them raised their arms and yawned. Others stood still and gazed at the sun which was just beginning to slip down behind the trees on the other side of the river.

Bart pointed at the sun and yelled. "Hey, Dan look!"

Dan O'Neil was already walking up the ramp with friends toward his neighborhood. He quickly turned around. "What? It's all over, Bart. See you soon when school starts."

Bart continued shouting. "Dan! It's not over! Guess what? When the pizza hits the floor, it doesn't go 'wop!' It bounces up into the sky! And there it is!" Bart thrust his arm back and forth, pointing at the setting sun. The boys who heard Bart shouting stopped walking, turned to look at the sun, and laughed.

Brian Coleman yelled, "I'll take a slice!"

Dan O'Neil took a few steps back down the ramp toward Bart and my gang. He lifted his arm. "The next time you have one of those salads filled with those tomatoes, cucumbers, lettuce and garlic, everything swimming in olive oil, make sure you put a bunch of four leaf clovers in there."

"Are you kidding!" Melo screamed. "No thanks!" We all laughed.

My gang turned and continued walking along the river toward Rapello Avenue, Green Street and Ferry Street.

"It's been an okay summer," Vito mumbled, looking down at the ground.

I noticed that Baggi seemed uneasy. But as it turned out, it had nothing to do with this being our last day at the farm. Because his pants were sagging, he held onto the rope wrapped around his fat waist with his left hand, and reached around to tug his pants up with his right hand. I spotted what he was about to discover. "What the hell!" He flipped his fingers up and down and felt a small cluster off straw fibers tucked under the rope and hanging over his behind. He yanked his arm back and held the straw at eye level. "Where did this come from?" The gang continued walking and chatting. Baggi stopped, glared at everyone and raised his arm. "One of you must have but that straw there!"

Everyone turned around. Pesci grinned. "I don't think so. I thought you put it there to remind everyone your name is '*Pagghia nculu*' (straw in the ass)."

Baggi leaped toward Pesci, flinging wild punches, and knocked him to the ground. "You bastard! You did it!"

Tony, Bart and Melo immediately pulled Baggi off of Pesci. Tony wrapped a hand on each of Baggi's shoulders, and shook him. "Come on! It's a joke!"

Baggi struggled to free himself, yelling at Pesci. "And since your name is fish, when you start seventh grade next week, you're gonna find a dead fish on your desk at school."

I did not want to end our summer with these collisions, so I quickly held my hands up. "Hey, everybody, let's not ruin the great summer we had." I turned to face the river. "Look at that beautiful sky. More than half of the sun is already behind the trees."

Tony got my message. He spread his arms out and also turned toward the river. "Let's all sit down for a minute." Everyone flopped on the ground facing the river, realizing that we should find a good way to close this summer.

Vito leaned over, turning his head toward Melo. "Hey, I'll bet you can't wait for the fall. Then we can sneak into the Baldwin Apple Orchards again and climb up those trees."

Melo took his cap off and spun his head toward Vito. His thick, dark brown hair at the back of his head was glued together with sticky tobacco juice, because his cap had only protected the hair at the top. "You bet I can't wait! When I'm sitting high up in those trees, chewing on an apple, I think I'm in heaven."

Filippo pointed across the river. "Look, now the sun is almost all the way down. There's just a sliver left."

"Well that's it," Vito mumbled. Now his tone was very serious. "There's just a sliver left of the summer. We're back to school in a few days."

"So this is the end," Angelo whispered.

Tony turned and pushed his hand toward Angelo. "No it isn't. The end always marks a new beginning."

"What the hell are you talking about?"

I continued staring across the river. "I think my brother is right, Angelo. After every end, there's always another beginning."

Ancio looked at Sal. "I don't know either what these guys

332

are talking about when they say it's not the end."

Louie, who was sitting next to Ancio, placed a hand on his shoulder. "When you get a little older, you'll get it, Mr. Anchovy. After you gobble up the last anchovy from one of those big, tin cans, your mother or father opens another can, right?"

Tony stood up and stepped toward Ancio. "That says it. Because we just finished Last Picking, it's not the end. Next year, if we get hired, we'll go back and start First Picking all over again."

"But what if I don't get hired next year?" Suggi exclaimed. "It'll be the end for me."

Musca grinned. "You can suck your fingers, Suggi."

Suggi turned and glared at Musca. "Shut up or you're gonna be a dead fly! That's if you make it to next summer."

I stood up and spread my arms apart. I was really caught up with what Tony got us into. The idea that Last Picking didn't mean the end for us really grabbed me. "We'll all be together again for First Picking next year. Like Tony just said, the end always marks another beginning."

Bart jumped up and thrust his arm out which had little hair left because most of it had been plucked away throughout the summer by the sticky tobacco juice. " Every Sunday, when we're at those boxing matches, we know that the end of one round marks the beginning of the next round. But you know what Santo that makes me remember something that my grandfather said when he left for Sicily just before the war started."

Vito looked up at Bart. "When we pulled our last basket out today, you told me what happened."

His dark eyes gleaming, Bart looked at everyone. "My grandfather was talking to my father in the cellar, telling him why he had decided to go back to Sicily. Me and my brother happened to be there. My father got upset. He told my grandfather things like 'whose gonna make the wine the way you make it? The barrel is almost empty.' Then he said something like 'This means it's the end for all of us.'"

Louie pushed his arm toward Bart. "My father always said that your grandfather made fantastic wine."

"He sure did!" Bart shouted as he spun around and stared at Louie. "My grandfather pointed to the press where he crushed the grapes and told my father it isn't the end for you. He said,

'*La vita è come una ruota. C'è chi scende ma c'è chi sale.*' (Life is like a wheel. Things go down, but things go up.) He told my father that he can take over and make the wine and said something like, because I'm gone, your journey is not finished. Then he came up with another one of those Sicilian sayings our parents like to tell us about. He said, '*Quannu l'arba nova spunta, chista è la vita.*' (When a new dawn is breaking, this is life.)

Louie turned to Bart again. "Some of my relatives say your father is now making really good wine, too. So it wasn't the end, was it?"

Tony stood up, stared at the river almost whispering, "Well, how about my father. His parents died when he was a baby, and it didn't turn out to be the end for him. He kept going on that road and tried to do the best he can." Tony turned his head to one side, staring in silence for a long moment, while most of us continued to look at him.

I thought he was upset because of what he just said. "Tony, what's the matter? What are you looking at?"

"That tree over there. When Louie told us his grandfather said that when things go down, things go up, and Melo said he feels he's in heaven when he's sitting way up in an apple tree, it made me think of something." Everyone was staring at Tony.

"Made you think of what?"

"Santo, I think that tree is saying what we're trying to say about the beginning and the end. There's no end. It keeps branching out and getting taller."

Suddenly Bart became very excited, pointing to the younger members of our gang. "Tony is right. That tree will help you seventh graders get what we're saying and ..."

Tony interrupted. "See, Ancio, that trunk is the beginning. Each of those big limbs coming out of the trunk is like ancestors or grandparents. And the branches that reach out from those limbs are different parents, and all of the smaller branches sticking out of the bigger ones are their kids."

Given that he loves to climb trees, Melo couldn't resist jumping in. "Right, Tony! And next year, and the years after, those little branches will get bigger and other little branches will get bigger, and more little branches will grow out of them and..."

Bart interrupted Melo. "And next year new leaves will be

born on those little branches."

Tony stared at Bart. "What you just said has to do with the point I wanted to make before you and Melo got into the act. All those leaves that will fall off when summer is over, doesn't mean it's the end. Next spring new leaves will come out for a new beginning." Tony continued staring at Bart whose head was now hanging very low. More than that, his hands were clutched together. I think everyone noticed this. "Bart, what's the matter. A minute ago you were turned on by what I said about the tree. Why is that upsetting you now?"

Bart did not look up or respond. I walked over and placed my hand on his shoulder which helped him share what was on his mind. "When you were talking about that tree, and I said next year new leaves pop out, I was thinking about something else that I've kept underground for the past few days."

Tony also put a hand on Bart's shoulder. "What? "

"Tony, you know that my Aunt Rosa has cancer and has been dying for the past couple of days."

Tony sat next to Bart and put his arm around his shoulders. "We know that Bart. We know you must feel like Santo and I felt when we learned that Lucky was killed, and our grandmother too. Bart, how does your Aunt connect with the tree thing we were talking about?"

Bart raised his head and glanced at all of us. "Well this is going to sound really weird. My aunt's daughter, my cousin, Carmela, who lives on the next floor up from her mother, is going to have a baby in a few days. My mother told me yesterday that when she was sitting by her sister crying, her sister said something like, 'Yes, I am dying, I am going away, but upstairs there will soon be a new member of the family'."

Tony took a deep breath. "That's really connected with what we were saying."

Bart coughed a little because of all the feelings that were tangled inside of him. "That's why I jumped on what Melo said about new leaves will be born on those branches."

By now the whole gang was gathered around Bart. I turned and stared at him with a lot of feeling. "Bart, I know you know what you just shared is a powerful example of what we're trying to say, that every end has a new beginning. Because we just finished last picking does not mean it's over, it's the end."

I turned and pointed to the bridge spanning the river. "In all of the tomorrows every one of us will have more chances to cross that bridge again. It's always hard to know what we'll find on the other side. But we gotta keep going." Everyone stared at the bridge. "We better head home. See, the sun has gone to bed."

Tony slowly waved his arm from left to right. "And look at the beautiful red and orange blanket the sun spread across the sky again."

At that moment, one more thing crossed my mind that was triggered when Bart reminded us of the old Sicilian saying that when a new dawn is breaking, this is life. I stood next to Tony. "You're right. The sun will soon go to bed and end the day by wrapping it in that beautiful blanket. But we all know that the sun is going to wake up again in the morning and give us a new tomorrow."

Everyone stood up, gazed at the sky, and slowly walked toward Green Street and Ferry Street.

In September, after a couple of weeks of school were over, several of us decided to meet after dinner at the foot of Ferry Street by the river. Tony, Filippo and Angelo were now sophomores in high school and Melo, Bart and I were beginning our freshmen year.

Tony stared at the river. "Have you guys noticed how much more we're connected with guys from Jimmy Lewis' gang and Brian Coleman's?"

Filippo grinned. "Yes, even Joe Harris. Last year he spent only a minute with me when I asked him about something. This past week, he's come over to rap with me nearly every day, when I'm standing by my locker."

"He keeps joking with me about why we have to learn his way of jitterbugging," Angelo laughed.

Melo blurted out what I was about to say. "How about Dan O'Neil? Remember when we were in eighth grade last year, he always bugged us about the sound pizza makes when it hits the floor. We knew he was pretending to use a joke as a way to tell us off. But these past days, he's been like a buddy."

What Melo just said reminded me of the same thing. "Every time Dan asked that question, Jack Kane always loved to yell out the answer, wop. It was obvious that at least half of what he was saying was not a joke. But you're right, Melo, now these past days in school both of them feel to me like their *paisani*, and ..."

Bart interrupted. "It's great that we're connected more with these chocolate bars and four leaf clovers, but I'm still wrapped up in those talks we had on the way home, after the last day at the farm, about there's always a new beginning after every end." Bart slowly lowered his head.

Tony put an arm around his shoulders. "I think I know what you're into Bart."

"Yes, Tony, those talks helped me deal with my Aunt Rosa dying last Wednesday. It seems really magical that the next day her daughter gave birth to Salvatore. Remember my Aunt told my mother even though it's the end for her, the family has a new beginning with the baby?"

Tony whispered, "Bart, it's all over the neighborhood. It's a fantastic example of what we've been saying that there's a new beginning to every end." Tony looked at me with excitement sparkling in his eyes. "Santo, tell Bart and the guys about the other example we were talking about at dinner last night."

"You're right Tony. That fits in really good. Listen. All of us know that a few weeks ago King Vittorio Emanuele threw out the governing power of Mussolini and put General Badoglio in charge of the government. Now it's all over the news that yesterday the Italian government asked for and signed an armistice with the United States. So for Italy, and for us Italian Americans, the war is over, and we have a new beginning even though the Germans are still fighting the British and United States."

Filippo yelled. "You're right! For us Italians we can start a new beginning!"

Angelo jumped up and raised his arms. "And we Italians, especially us Sicilians, are going to show this country what we are and what we have to offer."

Bart also jumped up. This time his mood was happy. "I saw in the Italian newspaper my father gets that more than one million Italian Americans are part of the sixteen million guys serving in the United States military. Maybe when that word gets around, people won't think of us as enemy aliens."

Tony yelled. "Santo and me, and especially our sisters, have been all about showing the United States that we Sicilians have more to offer than all that Mafia stuff this country is caught up in!"

I looked at Tony and grinned. "But don't forget, like Filomena and Anna keep saying, what we will show this country we have to offer has to do with the Old Mafia, and the family rules, not the New Mafia."

Angelo who was always into baseball screamed, "We're already showing this country we have more to offer than the New Mafia. How about, Joe DeMaggio? Just two years ago, he hit 29 home runs and got one or more hits in fifty-six consecutive games that set a new record!"

Filippo tapped his chest as if he were Tarzan. "I'll bet no one will beat that record for a long time."

Bart shook his head. "We have another example right here in Middletown when Santo helped Jimmy Lewis finish his paper and move on to high school. Now Jimmy is already showing that he's going to be a track star and set new records."

"Well, you guys know I'm more into music than baseball and track." Melo announced. "We already have a Sicilian American showing that we have a lot to offer. Frank Sinatra is now singing with the Tommy Dorsey band and his first record is sweeping across the country."

We stood up with pride as Tony announced, "So let's keep going and see what we and our families and relatives can keep doing tomorrow and show what Sicilian Americans have to offer."

A few years later Santo's family moved from Ferry Street into the "American District" breaking one of the blocks on High Street, since they were the first family to reside in this area that was not of British or Irish decent. They settled in a two story, four bed room home located next to the residence of a municipal judge and his family. Gradually they negotiated friendly relationships with their neighbors and other families in the neighborhood. Actually three, third generation Irish brothers, in their late twenties and early thirties, who maintained a farm outside of town, kept cows in a barn that abutted one side of Santo's family's backyard. They became friends and often dropped by for brief visits, especially because they loved the Italian food Santo's mother prepared for them.

And during the years that followed, Santo's family and relatives showed that Sicilian Americans had much to offer as they took in customs of the United States, while continuing to breathe with Sicilian lungs, and found ways to mix together American and Sicilian customs. For example, in addition to being promoted by the Middletown Police Department to the rank of sergeant, then lieutenant, and then captain, Santo's father was instrumental in establishing the Police Local Union, serving as its president for ten years. He also became active in the community outside of the police department. For example, he served on a committee that had been organized to expand the local county hospital and was instrumental in having each member of the police department contribute two days wages to the building fund. In addition, he was one of five original signers of the first labor contract negotiated with the Russell Manufacturing Company, where he had worked operating weaving looms after arriving in the United States. He also served on a committee to establish a credit union that made low cost loans available to all employees of the city of Middletown and their families, whether they were digging ditches or serving as the Director of Parks and Recreation, a position held years later by Santo's brother who organized activity programs for children of low income families.

As other examples of what Sicilian Americans offered, Filomena taught in a local public school for 20 years, Anna served as an administrative assistant at Wesleyan University, and Santo served on the faculties of several universities, eventually establishing a nonprofit agency to provide pro bono mental health services to children of low income, minority families who had been traumatized by various tragedies. Teodoro set up an automotive repair shop and trained immigrants to become skillful, automotive mechanics. The services they provided became very popular with auto owners of all ethnic backgrounds, not only because Teodoro invited customers to enjoy a wide range of Sicilian and Italian snacks while waiting for their automobile to be serviced, but also because of his excellent ability to diagnose automotive problems, and prescribe solutions.

In addition, one of the grandsons of Santo's uncle, Gaetano, became Fire Marshall of the City of Middletown. Along with performing these duties, he volunteered each year to participate in one event that bore special significance. Every Christmas he dressed up as Santa Claus, playing this role for one activity organized by his cousin, Raymond, the Director of Parks and Recreation, for children of low income families, especially African-Americans. He sat near a huge basket of gifts. A long line of children, escorted by adults, waited for a turn to visit Santa. Each child, stepped forward, sat on his lap, and expressed Christmas wishes, while another volunteer took a photograph that was handed to the child along with one of the gifts. Because many of the children who attended this event were African Americans, the Director of Parks and Recreation felt that this annual event was one way to mix black sticks and white sticks in the same *fasciu*.

Two other examples illustrate what Sicilian Americans from the Ferry Street area of Middletown contributed inside and outside of politics, and also illustrate what Sicilian Americans across the United States have contributed, and will continue to contribute, to American culture. Anthony Sbona, a friend of Santo throughout grade school and high school was elected Mayor of Middletown and was admired because of the programs he initiated that benefitted all citizens. Joe Vecchitto's unique contribution took place outside of politics. It represented the value of integrating the food you prepared and served to customers with expressing friendship, a combination celebrated on a daily basis in the Ferry Street neighborhood, and that emerged over the years in restaurants operated by southern Italian Americans in cities such as Hartford, Boston and New York.

The following information about Joe Vecchitto, who was known as "Joe Slush," was included in an article that appeared in the Hartford Current on June 23, 2007. The article announced his death at the age of 94 and described how he had become a legend that lives on. His parents started making and selling Italian ice in the 1930's in the Ferry street area. Every day the line at the Vecchitto Italian Ice store stretched out the door, with young and old locals and out-of-towners waiting for their lemon ice. When he was a kid, Joe worked with his father making and selling small and large cups of Italian ice for 3 cents and 5 cents, while joking and chatting with everyone. And everyone had fantastic memories of Joe and his father going up and down Ferry Street selling lemon ice from a push cart.

When World War II broke out, Joe was drafted into the army and went to California for basic training. He happened to meet Humphrey Bogart there at a watering hole, and they joked around. Bogart challenged Joe to a foot race, announcing that if he won, he would get the prize of appearing in Bogart's movie "Sahara," which he was filming at the time. Joe won and appeared in a scene near the end of the movie.

After completing basic training, Joe fought in Normandy and received a Bronze Star because he saved a fellow soldier in the face of enemy fire. His family did not learn about his heroic efforts until years later, and Joe never showed off his medal because he didn't want to be a hero or famous. Yet years later, Middletown city officials gave him his own day, declaring August 6, 2003 Joe Vecchitto day.

After the war, Joe was trained in plumbing and worked at a factory. At the same time, however, during late afternoon and early evening, he continued to help his father make and sell Italian ice cream. When his father died in 1961, Joe took over the shop and locals and out-of-towners continued to flock there for delicious Italian ice. But as one customer from North Carolina noted, it was not only the lemon ice that drew everyone to the store, it was Joe himself. Before moving to North Carolina this customer had been a regular at Joe's shop, and now it's the first place she goes to when she visits Connecticut. She emphasized that when she and her friends came for Italian ice, they lingered for a while just to visit with Joe Slush. "He's always smiling and chatting. Everybody loved him. Everybody knew him."

Joe Jr., who worked with his father, has continued the business since his father's death, providing an excellent example of the Sicilian view that with every ending there's a new beginning. Joe Jr. said that for his father, it wasn't just a job having to do with making and selling Italian ice. His father found pleasure in watching a child smile, and knowing that, as he served Italian ice to that child, he also had served it to the child's parents and grandparents. After the shop was closed for a couple of days for Joe Slush's funeral services, Joe Jr. opened the shop again and declared, "It's never going away."

Although Sicilians endured discrimination and abuse in ancient and modern Sicily, and also in the United States during many yesterdays, Santo's family and relatives, and those of Joe Vecchitto and the Sicilian American neighborhood of Middletown, are examples of contributions Sicilians have made in the United States today and will continue to make during each tomorrow. Santo's family and relatives, and Joe Slush's, also illustrate the Sicilian proverb, "*Cu lassa la via vecchia pir la nova, sa chiddu ca perdi, ma non sapi chiddu ca trova.*" (Whoever completely leaves the old way for a new way knows what he is losing, but does not know what he will find.) These families, and other Sicilian families, also provide examples of how Sicilians in the United States have woven Sicilian customs and the family rules of loyalty, honor, respect, commitment and self-control into their American activities, and illustrate what results from keeping these family rules in your lungs as you breathe in customs from other cultures of the United States. Of course, what Sicilians in America contributed yesterday, what they contribute today, and will contribute tomorrow is not perfect, or free of mistakes, because according to another Sicilian proverb, "*Cu mancia, fa muddichi.*" (Literally: He who eats makes crumbs; idiomatic: You have to break a few eggs to make an omelet).